THE YEAR'S BEST MILITARY & ADVENTURE SF
VOLUME 3

THE YEAR'S BEST MILITARY & ADVENTURE SF

VOLUME 3

Edited By
DAVID AFSHARIRAD

The Year's Best Military and Adventure SF, Vol. 3

A Baen Books Original

Baen Publishing Enterprises
P.O. Box 1403
Riverdale, NY 10471
www.baen.com

ISBN: 978-1-4814-8268-4

Cover art by Greg Bobrowski

First Baen printing, June 2017

Distributed by Simon & Schuster
1230 Avenue of the Americas
New York, NY 10020

Printed in the United States of America

10 9 8 7 6 5 4 3 2 1

TABLE OF CONTENTS

★

THE YEAR'S BEST MILITARY & ADVENTURE SF
VOLUME 3

You Decide Who Wins!

Other anthologies tell you which stories were best—we want you to decide! Baen Books is pleased to announce the third annual Year's Best Military and Adventure SF Readers' Choice Award. The award honors the best of the best in the grand storytelling tradition. The winner will receive a plaque and a $500 cash prize.

To vote, go to:
http://www.baen.com/yearsbestaward

You may also send a postcard or letter with the name of your favorite story from this year's volume to Baen Books Year's Best Award, P.O. Box 1188, Wake Forest, NC 27587. Voting closes August 31, 2017. Entries received after voting closes will not be counted.

So hurry, hurry, hurry!
The winner will be announced at
Dragoncon in Atlanta.

THE YEAR'S BEST MILITARY & ADVENTURE SF

VOLUME 3

PREFACE

★

by David Afsharirad

A YEAR HAS PASSED since last we talked, and that means it's time for another installment of *The Year's Best Military and Adventure SF*. Whether you've read the first two volumes in the series or are trying it out for the first time, within these pages you will find high quality, edge-of-your-seat science fiction stories with a military and adventure theme. Stories that challenge, provoke, thrill, and entertain. Stories like . . .

But I'm getting ahead of myself. First, let's talk about The Year's Best Military and Adventure SF Readers' Choice Award. Handed out each year at the Baen Traveling Roadshow at DragonCon, the Readers' Choice Award is decided by an online poll. The table of contents of *The Year's Best Military and Adventure SF* serves as the ballot, and readers are encouraged to vote for their favorite story. That's right, Baen asks you to pick the Year's Best Military and Adventure Science Fiction story! The winner receives a handsome plaque and a $500 cash prize. To find out how to vote for in this year's poll visit http://baen.com/yearsbestaward. But don't hesitate—voting closes August 31, 2017.

So, who won last year? When making the announcement I said, "If you give out an award for military science fiction, you really shouldn't be surprised when David Drake wins it." The line drew thunderous applause, more for Drake than for my clever phrasing, I imagine.

1

And speaking of David Drake . . .

. . . his short story "Cadet Cruise" kicks off this year's volume. This marks Drake's third appearance in *The Year's Best Military and Adventure SF*. He was kind enough to write the introduction for our inaugural volume, and if you've read the paragraph above, you've no doubt deduced that his short story "Save What You Can" was included in last year's book. That story took place in Drake's genre-defining Hammer's Slammers universe; "Cadet Cruise" is set in another of his long-running series. Readers of Drake's popular RCN (Royal Cinnabar Navy) novels will recognize the intrepid Daniel Leary as the hero of our story, although this tale is set long before Leary rises through the ranks of the Royal Cinnabar Navy. As the title suggest, "Cadet Cruise" takes place at the beginning of Leary's military career. Fans of the RCN novels will find much to enjoy in this prequel story, but I have no doubt that newcomers will find it every bit as engaging. When it comes to military SF stories, Drake knows how to write 'em!

And while we're on the subject of past Year's Best Military and Adventure SF Readers' Choice Award winners, let's discuss Michael Z. Williamson. Williamson was the winner of the award the very first time we handed it out all those years ago—way back in 2015. The story that won was called "Soft Casualty" and was set in his Freehold series, as is "Starhome," which you will find here. In it, Jackson Burke is the leader of the smallest nation in space, a tiny asteroid known as Starhome. But when a war breaks out between Earth and the Freehold of Grainne, he'll find that maintaining neutrality is easier said than done.

Also returning to the series this year is William Ledbetter with his short story "Tethers," a white-knuckle disaster set in orbit around Earth. Ledbetter administers the Jim Baen Memorial Short Story Award contest; he's also a Nebula Award nominee this year. (We're pulling for you, Bill!) All that to say that he knows what makes a good short story and he sure as H-E-Double-Hockey-Sticks knows how to write one.

And that's all from the repeat offenders—er, alumni of past years. But not to worry, we've got a great crop of new recruits this year. Now, some of these "new recruits" have been writing top-notch SF for decades, but Volume 3 marks the first time any of them have appeared in *Year's Best Military and Adventure SF*. They are:

Paul Di Filippo, who serves up a heaping helping of bio-punk in his short story "Backup Man." It's a hardboiled tale of a genetically engineered plague, a golden calf, and a land rush unlike any seen since the late 19th century. There's also a sentient mushroom man in there, but I don't want to spoil the fun.

Eric Del Carlo's story also features bio-engineered humans, this time in a military setting. In "Unlinkage," handlers are mentally linked to their Brutes—super-strong soldiers with limited intelligence—through a miracle of modern military science known as biomoss. Etta Pryor was a handler, her Brute a soldier named Conroy. But that was over a decade ago, and Conroy is dead. So why is she once again receiving signals from her biomoss?

From the Liaden Universe® comes "Wise Child" by Sharon Lee and Steve Miller. Here you will find a tale of the corrupt Lyre Institute that enslaves humans and artificial intelligences alike; a man no longer willing to live in bondage, denied even the dignity of a name; and a starship with a heart of gold—and nerves of steel.

In "Sephine and the Leviathan" by Jack Schouten, a teenage girl must risk everything to save her twin brother. Set against the backdrop of an interstellar war between humanity and the alien Fractured, this harrowing tale of courage and determination will keep you in suspense until the very end.

With "The Last Tank Commander," Allen Stroud brings us a story of a retired soldier who thought he had left the battlefield behind when he took to the stars. But when the colony ship on which he is a passenger touches down on an alien planet, he finds that war is universal.

David Adams' "The Immortals: Anchorage" is intense military SF at its finest. When a band of mercenaries gets a job investigating the wreckage of a passenger liner, what they hope to find is Earthborn technology they can sell as salvage. What they *do* find is . . . something else entirely.

In "The Art of Failure" by Robert Dawson, a young xenolinguist with some serious debts to pay gets more than he bargained for when his ship makes first contact with an alien species.

Submitted for your approval: Michael Ezell's story "The Good Food," which takes us to a far-flung planet that two centuries of terraforming has transformed into a lush jungle world. But something is amiss, and it's up to a former soldier, his K9 companion, and a smart-aleck AI to figure out what.

In a mind-bending tale of future warfare, Adam Roberts explores how weaponry might be much more unusual than the standard-issue raygun. The story is called "Between Nine and Eleven" and scores a perfect 10 in my book.

People love zombies—and zombies love people, but unfortunately not in the same way—and your faithful editor is no exception. Normally, I have to leave the zombies at the door when reading for *Year's Best*, but not this time. In his Black Tide Rising series, John Ringo has created perhaps the most scientifically plausible explanation for zombies yet, situating the books firmly in the science fiction genre. Ringo has written four novels in the series to date, but readers wanted more, so Ringo and co-editor Gary Poole invited authors to play in John Ringo's zombie sandbox (if that's not a band name, it should be). The result was the anthology *Black Tide Rising*. From that collection of zombie tales comes Kacey Ezell's "Not in Vain," a story of a retired military helicopter pilot who now spends her days as a high school cheerleading coach—that is, until the zombie apocalypse breaks out. *Give me a Z! Give me an O! Give me an M! Give me a B-I-E! What's that spell?!?!?!?!*

For a more personal apocalypse, we turn to "One Giant Leap" by Jay Werkheiser. The world may not be ending in this gripping tale, but it may well be "lights out" for our protagonist. A freak accident hurls Kent down through the poisonous atmosphere of Venus. As he descends toward the planet's surface, his time is running out.

Finally, Baen publisher Toni Weisskopf has said that science fiction should be fun, and I couldn't agree more. But I also think that science fiction can—nay, *must!*—serve a greater good. Here then we have a short story with a *very serious* warning about the dangers of temporal displacement. It's called "If I Could Give this Time Machine Zero Stars, I Would," coming courtesy of James Wesley Rogers by way of Alex Shvartsman's *Unidentified Funny Objects 5*.

Earlier I said that there were no other returning writers from past years. That wasn't entirely true. *New York Times* best-selling author of the Honor Harrington series David Weber has once again provided a stellar introduction. Normally I'd say that introductions to short story anthologies are skippable. Now, I can't stop you from skipping over

Mr. Weber's intro, but I will say that I think this one is required reading for SF fans.

But enough from your humble editor.

Turn the page and discover the new Golden Age of science fiction. Excelsior!

—David Afsharirad
Austin, TX
February, 2017

INTRODUCTION
★
by David Weber

WHAT *IS* "MILITARY SCIENCE FICTION"?

Human beings are toolmakers. We are also list-makers. We like to be able to label things, group them together for easy conceptual handling. Marketing people are especially fond of that tendency on our part, because sticking a label on something is a form of shorthand that makes it easier to reach a specific readership, and the marketing classifications assigned to some stories probably end up with a lot of readers scratching their heads and wondering what the heck marketing was thinking.

"Military science fiction" is all too often a case in point.

I've been writing it for about thirty years now, and the one thing that I can tell you for certain about the genre's definition is that it means different things to different people. It comes in all sorts of flavors and, like all storytelling, it can be well told or badly. It can range from what I think of as "splatter porn," stories in which the gore runs as deep as a slasher movie, to stories in which there are no casualties at all. It can be "space opera," written on the macro scale about entire nations, armies, and fleets, or about just two opponents . . . or even about only a single character. It can come from any political or ideological perspective, it can worry about the "why" of a war or concentrate solely on the "what" of the human beings caught up in it. The one thing "military science fiction" isn't is a neatly defined, no-problem-to-label genre.

The stories in this year's anthology illustrate many of the previous paragraph's points, especially the last sentence's, and add a few wrinkles of their own.

Personally (and not just because they publish so many of *my* stories, honest!), I think Baen Books may have the best feel for what constitutes military science fiction, and the inclusion of the stories I just listed above in this anthology is one reason that I do. Baen understands that the central aspect of military science fiction—like any form of fiction, when you come down to it—resides in the characters' struggles to overcome adversity. In this particular genre, struggles are more likely to be ones of life or death, but that isn't always the case, any more than that sort of mortal conflict is unique to military science fiction or military fiction generally.

I think part of the problem with nailing the genre down is that list-making tendency of ours itself. We want neat boundaries, clearly discernible delimitations. That's why we make lists in the first place, for goodness sake! And, like most things which concern human beings, the boundaries for "military" fiction are usually pretty sloppy. Put another way, there's a lot of "bleed" in the borderlands between stories which belong unmistakably to any one genre and those that belong equally unmistakably to another. Like war itself, stories about it don't admit of ease of labeling.

Science fiction is a very broad field, with plenty of room for all sorts of stories, all manner of genres and subgenres. As I have a tendency to point out on panels at science fiction conventions, science fiction is the fairytales of a technological society. Instead of wizards, golems, and deadly curses, we have scientists and engineers, AIs and androids, nanotech and genetic engineering. We use different tools, different exemplars, because we have fundamentally different concepts and understandings of how the universe works, but we are telling the same *stories*. And we are telling them for the same purposes: to inspire, to explain, to caution and warn, and—always—to engage the people in our audience, whether they are sitting around a Neanderthal campfire knapping flint while they listen or kicked back with an e-book reader in their laps while Lady Gaga plays in the background. Military fiction, whether it be the tale of Arthur at Camlann, of Roland at Roncevaux, of Aragorn leading Gondor and Rohan to the Black Gates, or of Lieutenant Colonel Bill Cage and Rita Vrataski dying again and again in alien-occupied France, is still about the same challenges, the same sacrifices, and the same costs. It still tells us the same things about ourselves.

Writers are entertainers. Now, "entertain" can have more than one meaning. For example, my ancient and beloved, genuine hardcopy, *American Heritage Dictionary*, defines entertain as:

1. To hold the attention of with something amusing or diverting;
2. To extend hospitality toward: *entertain friends at dinner*;
3a To consider, contemplate: *entertain an idea*;
3b To hold in mind; harbor: *entertained few illusions*.

As craftsmen, we take that first point seriously, if we are going to practice our craft well. And, of course, if we hope to be able to actually pay the bills at the end of the day. If we don't accomplish that aspect of our job, our readers aren't going to reward us by actually, you know, *buying* our stuff. But we also need to be "entertainers" in the sense of the third point of that definition. And for purveyors of military fiction, that means we need to examine—"contemplate"—what it is to be a human being in the crucible. We need to share with the reader what it means to face and survive—or *not* survive—in the midst of carnage, confusion, and conflict. We need to caution, to warn, and, yes, to inspire.

Today, in the Western World, personal experience of military conflict is actually quite rare and concentrated in hugely disproportionate fashion among those who volunteer for military service. Civilians take it for granted that they will be protected from conflict by those who serve in the military, and those who do *not* serve in the military have little or no first-hand familiarity with what our military guardians experience in our place. Most professional Soldiers, Sailors, Airmen, and Marines of my acquaintance think that's the way it's supposed to be. That if it *isn't* that way, they aren't doing their jobs. But because they are, those of us standing behind them have no personal, experiential guide to what it is we truly ask of them.

One of the responsibilities of those of us who write military fiction is to provide a window into what we ask of them. Into the consequences of what is demanded of them. Not simply to venerate them, or to celebrate the "thin line of heroes," although that *is* one of our responsibilities, because the men and women who have died for us deserve to be venerated and celebrated, but also to help us understand. To recognize not just what they have given and are giving for us, but the fact that they stand where they stand, face what they face, *because we put them there.*

And we need to understand the price they pay for *being* there because if we don't—if we trivialize it or romanticize it into something one bit less horrible than it is—we forget that the reason we put them there had *damned* well better be worth that price.

And we also need to understand that war isn't going away.

Ever.

War is an obscene thing, but it is also a very human thing. We can—and over the millennia, philosophers have written millions of words to—deplore that second truth, but we cannot *deny* it with any degree of intellectual honesty. War, conflict, violence, the solution of irreconcilable differences by violence, is one face of who and what we are. Understanding it is a part of understanding – or at least facing— our own inner nature. And, like our inner nature, war is so complex, so ambiguous, so dependent upon the observer's perspective, that it simply will not admit of the neat definitions and limitations so dear to our list-makers' heart.

Which is why writers of military fiction portray it in so very many different ways. If we're honest with ourselves and our readers, it's not the story of how one side is universally heroic and noble and the other side is universally vile and depraved. It's also not the story of how only "bad guys" get killed, of how the characters we love get free passes, of how civilians don't get ground to pulp in the gears, or of how those maimed and crippled physically or mentally always triumph over the lingering consequences of what's happened to them. "Honest" military fiction doesn't all have to be dark and savagely brooding, as some of the stories in this very anthology demonstrate, and it doesn't all have to argue that all war is automatically evil any more than it needs to simplistically celebrate the fact that "our war" was just and noble. (It was, of course, because we are such inherently just and noble people, right? *Riiiiight!*) But it does need to play fair with its subject matter and its readership.

At bottom, military fiction, like war itself, is about both yin and yang, about both war's destructiveness and what it preserves. About the carnage and about the war-fighters—not all of them soldiers—who protect the civilians behind them. I think we read military fiction for the same reasons we read most kinds of fiction: to see inside ourselves. Oh, we read it for the heroes and heroines we admire and love, for the villains we despise and hate, for the excitement and the conflict. But all of those things—heroes, villains, excitement, conflict—are vehicles for understanding who *we* are, both as a species and as individuals.

Humanity didn't claw its way to the top of the evolutionary ladder of an entire planet by being shy, retiring, and timid. We got there by being the meanest bastards in the valley. That doesn't mean we can't be perfectly nice people, doesn't mean we can't care deeply for those we love and cherish, doesn't mean we can't build societies designed to limit the consequences of our inner bastards. It doesn't mean we can't recognize the consequences of our actions and seek to ameliorate them, and it sure as hell doesn't mean we can't at least try really, really hard to resist the darker side of our nature. It does mean that we are who we are, though, and that's the side of us that military fiction, specifically, examines.

Military *science* fiction simply examines those same aspects of who and what we are in a science fiction format. Projected into the futures, the alternate possibilities, science fiction plays with every day. Those of us who write it write it because examining those aspects is important to us, for whatever reason, and those of us who read it, *read* it because examining them is important to us. It's really that simple . . . and that incredibly complex.

Baen Books has brought you a collection of short stories that come at "military science fiction" from a vast number of perspectives. I almost said "from every conceivable perspective," but that particular bit of hyperbole would be especially ill chosen talking about something like, oh, conflict, human nature, and the vast complexity of why human beings make war.

But one thing we do know. As long as human beings are human beings, there *will* be war. And as long as there are wars, storytellers will tell stories about the men and women who fight them, who die in them, and who survive them.

That's what this anthology does, and I think it does it well.

Now go read it.

Readers know Daniel Leary as the protagonist (along with his friend the cyber-librarian Adele Mundy) of David Drake's popular RCN series. But before he was a lieutenant in the Royal Cinnabar Navy, Leary was a cadet with a well-earned reputation for finding trouble. So when he invites Cadet Pennyroyal to accompany him on leave to a high-end gambling establishment, she knows that things are likely to get . . . interesting. Just how interesting—and dangerous—she'll have to wait to find out.

CADET CRUISE

★

by David Drake

PENNYROYAL KNEW that Cadet Leary was supposed to have remained aboard the *Swiftsure* until 1700 hours with the rest of the Starboard Watch. That said, she'd gotten to know Daniel Leary pretty well during their three years at the Academy. When she couldn't locate him in their accommodation block or the cable tier where he was supposed to be on duty until 1630, she suspected that Leary had managed to slip ashore with the Port Watch.

It was more out of whim than from any real expectation of finding the other cadet that Pennyroyal went out on the hull through a forward airlock. The Dorsal A antenna was raised while the *Swiftsure* was docked in Broceliande Harbor. Daniel was sliding down a forestay, his rigging gauntlets sparking against the steel wire. A bosun's mate named Janofsky was following him down.

"You're supposed to be inspecting cable, Leary," Pennyroyal called, amazed and a little exasperated at what her friend had gotten up to. "If an officer catches you fooling around in the sunshine, you'll lose your liberty. At *least* your liberty."

Daniel Leary wasn't any more interested in astrogation theory than Pennyroyal herself was, but he had an obvious gift for astrogation. He could be a valuable officer of the Republic of Cinnabar Navy—if he weren't booted out of the Academy before he graduated. Leary treated discipline the way he did religion: it was all very well for others, if they really wanted to go in for it.

"Pardon, ma'am, but that's just what we're doing," said Janofsky, touching his cap. "I directed Cadet Leary to inspect the standing rigging of Dorsal A under my supervision."

In theory the cadets were classed as landsmen: they were junior to able spacers, let alone to a warrant officer like Janofsky. In practice, outside of actual training many of the *Swiftsure*'s cadre treated cadets like the officers they would become when they graduated.

Now, with the Republic of Cinnabar and the Alliance of Free Stars in an all-out war, spacers were valuable commodities. It was necessary to provide cadets with practical experience before they were commissioned, but a training ship's complement tended to be made up of personnel who for one reason or another could be spared from front-line combat vessels.

Some of the *Swiftsure*'s cadre had persistent coughs, stiff limbs, or were simply old. Janofsky probably wouldn't see seventy again. Others drank or drugged or were a little funny in the head.

But no few were ring-tailed bastards who were doubly hard on cadets. Cadets had the chance of bright futures, which none of those in a training ship's cadre could imagine would dawn for them.

"Ah," said Pennyroyal. She didn't believe the story, but it couldn't be disproved if Janofsky was willing to swear to it. Captain Landrieu herself couldn't punish Cadet Leary, and a veteran spacer like Janofsky knew that he was effectively beyond discipline. Old though he was, the bosun's mate carried out his duties—both working ship and training—with a skill that set him above most of the cadre.

"Come to that, Penny," Leary said, "you knocked off early yourself, not so?"

"I was on galley duty," Pennyroyal said. "With three quarters of the crew ashore, there was bugger all to do by mid shift. Cookie excused me and the other cadets. I wanted to find you."

Janofsky had gone below, leaving the two of them alone on the ship's spine. Though the *Swiftsure* was nearly sixty years old, she was still a battleship. She loomed over not only the rest of the harbor traffic but the buildings of Broceliande, none of which were over six stories high.

Foret was subject to the Cinnabar Empire—a Friend of Cinnabar if you wanted to be mealy-mouthed. It was a pleasant enough planet but of no real importance in galactic politics, making it a natural port call for an RCN training vessel. Part of what an RCN officer needed to know was how to behave on worlds which had their own cultures. Foret provided that, and the trouble you could get into on Broceliande stopped short of being eaten by the locals. There were ports where that wasn't true.

"I didn't mean to seem mysterious, Penny," Daniel said after glancing around. "Janofsky was doing a favor for me and I didn't want to embarrass him in front of a stranger. Which you pretty much are to him."

"And you're not?" said Pennyroyal. The sun, setting beyond the harbor mouth, stained pink the white-washed facades of buildings. The landscape beyond the city was heavily wooded. The ordinarily dark-green native foliage had a purplish cast in the slanting light.

"I met Janofsky when I was six, in my Uncle Stacey's shipyard," Daniel said. "I didn't remember that—remember Janofsky, I mean. There must've been hundreds of spacers dropping by to give their regards to their old captain. Janofsky had been a young rigger on the *Granite*, the dedicated exploration vessel that Uncle Stacey made his Long Voyage in."

"When they discovered twenty-seven worlds that'd been lost to civilization for two thousand years?" Pennyroyal said. She had known that Daniel's "Uncle Stacey" had been in the RCN, but until now she hadn't connected the name with Commander Stacey Bergen, the most famous explorer in Cinnabar history. "No wonder you're such an astrogator!"

"I had a leg up," Daniel agreed with a slight smile. "Uncle Stacey never got rich, but the spacers who served under him say he was the greatest man who ever lived. The greatest captain, anyway. Janofsky asked about Uncle Stacey when I came aboard the *Swiftsure*, and I asked him to make some contacts for me in the shore establishment here when he went on liberty yesterday."

"Well, as a matter of fact," Pennyroyal said, "it was about liberty that I wanted to talk to you. You remember that story Vondrian and Ames told, about going on liberty on Broceliande with a ship's corporal?"

"Yes, I certainly do," Daniel said, his expression suddenly guarded. The corporals were the assistants to the Master at Arms, the ship's policemen. "They went to a gambling house that was raided by the police. One of the guards started shooting. If Vondrian hadn't been able to bribe the police to release him and the other cadets, they'd have been jailed for conspiracy to murder."

"Well, I always suspected that was a set-up," Pennyroyal said. "Today I heard that one of the ship's corporals, Platt, had offered to guide a group of cadets to a place at a distance from the harbor where the drinks were higher class. I remembered Vondrian's story and thought we ought to warn the others."

Pennyroyal could have done that herself, but she knew that if the story came from Leary it would be believed. If *she* told people what she'd heard during a night of drinking with two friends from an earlier class at the Academy, she'd be mocked as faint-hearted. An RCN officer with a reputation for cowardice wouldn't stay an RCN officer long.

There were plenty of people, instructors as well as cadets, who thought Daniel Leary was bumptious, a fool, and even certifiably mad. The rumor about him pleasuring the commandant's daughter in the Academy chapel justified any of those descriptions—and Pennyroyal, who had been on watch in the choir loft, knew the story was true.

Nobody thought Leary was a coward.

"Well, as it chances . . . ," Daniel said carefully, "I *had* heard about the expedition and thought I'd join it. I'm not fancy about what I drink, but Platt says the women are higher class too. They *do* interest me."

"Are you joking?" said Pennyroyal, though he clearly wasn't. There had to be something behind Leary's bland smile, though.

Another thought struck her. "Say!" she said. "Is your man Hogg going along? I don't doubt he's a real bruiser even if he does look like a hayseed with maybe two brain cells to rub together, but you can't muscle your way through a dozen cops!"

"Umm, Steward's Mate Hogg has business of his own to attend to tonight, he told me," Daniel said. "He's not really my man, you know. He insisted on following me from the Bantry Estate when I broke with my father and entered the Academy, but I can't afford to keep him.

He's living on his pay and whatever he might add to that by playing cards."

Hogg's winnings were greater than his RCN pay, from what Pennyroyal had seen in the galley; but however the former Leary tenant made his living, he continued to refer to Daniel as "the young master." Still, Hogg doubtless had a life beyond service to Cadet Leary.

Pennyroyal stared at her friend. "What are you planning, Leary? You've got *something* on."

Daniel shrugged. "I plan to go to a high-class entertainment establishment . . . ," he said. "And have a good time. That's all."

"If you're going, then I'm going along," Pennyroyal said. "That's flat. Understood?"

This time Daniel grinned. "You know I'm always glad to have you beside me, Penny," he said. "But don't act surprised at anything you may hear, all right?"

"All right," said Pennyroyal, grinning back. "It's about time we change to go on liberty, then."

She wasn't sure it would be a night she'd remember as "a good time," but she knew it would be interesting.

Pennyroyal and Leary had bunks near each another in the stern. The accommodations block already swarmed with cadets changing into the clothes they would wear on liberty. A few cadets had sprung for gray 2nd class dress uniforms. Though only commissioned or warrant officers had a right to wear Grays, senior cadets were customarily allowed the privilege.

That wasn't an issue with Pennyroyal: she couldn't afford to buy *anything* unnecessary until she graduated and was commissioned as a midshipman. Midshipman's pay wasn't much, but it was something.

"Leary, where did you get those!" Pennyroyal said as she finished pulling on the clean utilities she would be wearing and got a good look at her friend—wearing Grays.

"Umm, they're from a hock shop on the Strip," Daniel said, touching his left lapel with two fingers. There was barely visible fading where rank tabs had been removed. "A mate of Janofsky's tailored them for me. Some of these senior spacers do better work than you could get on the ground."

"Right, but you were broke!" Pennyroyal said. "Where did you find the money?"

"I *was* broke," Daniel said. "But I found the money. I'll explain it later, but for now I want to catch Platt before he leaves his cabin."

Pennyroyal fell in beside Leary, though he was walking toward the pair of aft companionways instead of the set amidships with the rest of the cadets. She said, "But we're supposed to gather in the main boarding hold at 1730. At least that's what I heard."

"I had a different idea," Daniel said. "Don't worry, we'll get there."

They skipped up the companionway in a shuffle of echoes. Even with only the two of them in the steel tube, their boot soles on the nonskid treads were multiplied into a whispering chorus as overwhelming as surf in a storm.

Most warrant officers bunked in curtained cabins ahead of the racks of the common spacers. The master at arms and his—her, on the *Swiftsure*—four corporals were a deck above for their own safety and comfort.

The ship's police were responsible for enforcing the ship's discipline. Even the best masters at arms were corrupt to a degree: there *would* be gambling during a long voyage despite regulations; limiting it to a few rings which paid for the privilege was better for discipline than a rigid ban.

The *Swiftsure*'s police were at the far wrong end of the corruption scale, however. What Pennyroyal had seen since she and the rest of the cadets boarded made her even more sure that Vondrian, known to be wealthy, had been set up by the ship's corporals in collusion with locals.

She and Leary left the companionway and almost collided with a lieutenant whom Pennyroyal didn't know by name. She jumped to the side of the narrow corridor and snapped a rather better salute than Leary, ahead of her, managed.

"What in blazes are you two doing on this level?" the lieutenant demanded. His words weren't slurred, but the odor of gin enveloped them.

"Sir!" said Daniel, holding his salute. "Corporal Platt ordered us to attend him in his quarters, sir!"

"Platt?" the lieutenant said with a grimace. "Bloody hell."

He pushed past and into the companionway. He had not returned the salutes.

Leary apparently knew exactly where he was going. They were nearly at the sternward end of the corridor when he stopped at a door, not a curtain, and knocked on the panel.

"Cadets Leary and Pennyroyal reporting, Corporal," he called toward the ventilator.

For a moment there was no response; then Platt jerked the light steel panel open. He held a communicator attached by flex to the flat-plate display against the outer bulkhead. There was a scrambler box in the line.

Platt's scowl turned into a false smile. He took off his headphones and said, "I was on my way down in a few minutes, Leary. I just needed to take care of a few things for tonight."

"We came about tonight, Corporal," Daniel said. "Pennyroyal and I had the notion of just the two of us going with you. Instead of thirty or forty cadets chipping in for a cattle car or whatever you've got laid on, I thought I could spring for a taxi. All right?"

"Umm . . . ," said Platt. He hung the handset and earphones back beneath the display. He was a middle-aged man, balding from the forehead, not fat but soft looking. "Well, if you're willing to pay . . ."

"I don't mind spending my father's money on giving myself a good time," Daniel said. "There was no bloody point in sucking up to the Speaker if I wasn't going to get something out of it."

Pennyroyal felt her face stiffen. In the past Leary had spoken of his politically powerful father only when he was drunk and someone asked him a direct question. His answers then had been uniformly curt and hostile; she would have said that Daniel was more likely to become a priest than ever to make up with his father.

As for money, Daniel had seemed interested in it only when he wanted to buy a round of drinks for the table but didn't have it to spend. The notion that Daniel Leary would patch up a bitter quarrel in order to afford taxi fare was ludicrous—except that was clearly what he had just implied.

"All right, Leary," Platt said. He stepped into the corridor and latched the door behind him. "I'd heard your Hogg saying something like that. Your old man's pretty well heeled, ain't he?"

"I'll say he's well heeled," Daniel muttered as Platt led them along the corridor toward the down companionway. "Anyway, it's just too much money to walk away from."

Platt glanced at the cadets—glanced at Leary, anyway. "I'll tell you what we'll do then," the corporal said. "We'll go out through the forward hatch. That's for officers' use, but I can square it. That way we won't run into the rest of your cadets in the main hold, and there's a better class of hire cars waiting."

"Sounds great!" said Daniel. He pulled a hundred-florin coin out of his belt purse. That was even more of a surprise to Pennyroyal than seeing her friend in Grays. "Say, are they all right with Cinnabar money at this club you're taking us to?"

"They're all right with any kind of money at the Café Claudel," said Platt. "And the more, the merrier."

From the purr in the corporal's voice, the same was true of him.

"What's the fare in Cinnabar florins, my good man?" Leary asked in an upper class drawl as they pulled up under the porte-cochére.

The hire car was a limousine with room for eight in the cabin, though there were signs of age and wear. The leather upholstery was cracked, much of the gilt was gone from the brightwork, and the soft interior lighting was further dimmed by burned-out glowstrips.

Even so, it was the most impressive private vehicle Pennyroyal had ever ridden in. She wasn't sure that she could have found its equal on her homeworld of Touraine. If she had, it still wouldn't have been carrying the orphan daughter of a parish priest.

"Thirty Cinnabar florins, master!" chirped the driver through the sliding window into the cab.

"Bloody hell, Leary!" Pennyroyal said. "Ten'd be high! It's not but three miles from the harborfront!"

A pair of husky servants in white tunics and gold braid opened the car's double doors. They weren't carrying weapons.

"Here you go," Daniel said, handing a fifty-florin coin through the window. "If you're still around when I'm ready to leave, there may be another one for you—but I'm on a twenty-four hour liberty and I don't expect to end it early."

Platt had gotten out of the vehicle and was waiting beside the house attendants. Pennyroyal got out with Daniel following her. The driver called, "I'll be right here in the VIP lot, master. You can count on me!"

"I dare say we can, for that kind of money," Pennyroyal muttered.

"My father always said 'Spend money to make money,'" Daniel said cheerfully. "Well, that was one of the things he said. Regardless, Corder Leary certainly made money."

Café Claudel must have originally been a country house, though Pennyroyal had gotten only a glimpse of the building as the limousine approached by a curving drive. The gardens facing the house seemed overgrown, though the late evening light wasn't good enough for certainty.

Platt led the cadets up steps to the doorway where an attractive blond woman wearing a morning coat and striped trousers waited. "Say, Dolly?" Platt said as they approached. "These two are with me. See that they're treated right, okay?"

"The Claudel treats all of its guests properly, Master Platt," the woman said with a professional smile. She was older than Pennyroyal had thought from a distance.

"I need to talk to Kravitz," Platt said. "Is he—there he is."

He turned and said, "I need to chat with the manager, Leary. You two come in and have a good time, okay?"

A trim little man with a goatee had just entered the anteroom from the lobby. The corporal went off with him. The doorkeeper's eyes followed them, then returned to Pennyroyal and Leary.

"You'll find a bar to the left within," the blond said. "There's gaming off the lobby to the right. Upstairs, if you're interested in no limit games . . . ?"

She raised an eyebrow.

"No!" said Pennyroyal, more fiercely than she had intended.

"I might be later," Daniel said, "but just for now I'm hoping to find a drink."

"The Claudel's cellar is famous," the doorkeeper said, "and we have a wide range of off-planet spirits also. If your particular preference isn't available, our bartenders can suggest a near approximation, I'm sure."

Pennyroyal wondered what the staff would suggest if she asked for industrial ethanol, the working fluid used in the Power Room, cut with fruit juice. They could probably find a high-proof vodka with a similar kick—though at a much higher price. But that was another matter . . .

"And perhaps . . ." Daniel added, "a friend or two to show me the establishment's sights. Eh?"

The doorkeeper's smile was minuscule but real. "I think you'll be able to meet someone congenial in the lobby, sir," she said. "If not, a word to any staff member will bring a further selection. And there are rooms upstairs for whatever sort of discussions you'd like to have."

A group—two older men and a woman of their age, accompanied by three much younger women—arrived. Daniel and Pennyroyal stepped into the lobby to clear the anteroom.

Pennyroyal whispered to Daniel, "This place is *way* beyond my budget, Leary. Even if the drinks are cheap. Look at the clothes these people are wearing!"

"Give me your hand, Penny," Daniel said. "I'm pretty sure they aren't going to throw you out for hunching over a beer and looking miserable, but right now you're part of my protective coloration."

"Pardon?" said Pennyroyal. When she didn't move, Daniel took her right wrist in his left hand and pulled it toward him, then gripped her right hand with his own. There were two large coins in his palm.

"Leary, I can't take this!" she whispered, closing her fingers over the coins. They were hundreds from the size.

"I'll get it back, Penny," Daniel said cheerfully. "Trust me on that."

Grimacing, Pennyroyal transferred the money—two gold-rimmed hundred-florin pieces, all right—to her purse. *What in blazes is going on?*

The lobby was a high room with a railed mezzanine; the three tall windows at the back were capped with arched fanlights. The zebra-striped bar, running the full depth of the room, was staffed by three female bartenders. Daniel walked up to the youngest-looking and took out another hundred-florin coin.

"Can you break this for me, my dear?" he said, holding it up between thumb and forefinger.

"Certainly sir," the woman—close up, she was over thirty—said. "Do you care what form the change is in?"

"So long as I can spend it here, it doesn't matter," Daniel said with a laugh. "I don't expect to have any left when I leave."

Pennyroyal assumed the bar was made of extruded material. Daniel rapped it with his knuckles and said, "Natural wood, by the gods! Is it native to Foret, my dear?"

"I believe it is, sir," the bartender said, her eyes on the small stacks of coins and scrip she was arraying on the bar in front of herself. "But from the southern continent. Master Kravitz may have more details."

"Ale for my friend and myself just now," Daniel said, who had been sweeping his eyes around the room. There were forty-odd people in the lobby, half of them at the bar. He glanced at the price list on the back wall between a pair of paintings—mythological, presumably, since the men and women had feathered wings. He slid a local note back to the bartender. As she turned to draw the beers, Daniel stuffed a similar note into the brandy snifter of tips for her station.

"Let's circulate, shall we, Penny?" Daniel satd as they turned away. On the couches between the windows and to either side of the anteroom sat attractive women and men, not couples though mostly in pairs. He sipped his beer and added, "Not bad at all."

Without changing his mild expression, Daniel said, "I'm not one to preach, Penny, but we might decide to leave here rather suddenly. I'll probably be nursing this—"

He tapped the rim of his earthenware stein with a fingernail; it rang softly.

"—a lot longer than you're used to seeing me do."

Pennyroyal grinned. "Well, don't do anything I wouldn't do, Leary," she said. "Unless it involves those women, in which case feel free."

Pennyroyal walked toward the gaming room. She didn't like beer well enough to have an opinion as to whether this was a good brew, but she hadn't needed Leary's warning to decide that she wasn't going to get drunk tonight.

She didn't have any idea what Leary was planning, but she was rather looking forward to it. And that meant being fully ready for action when the time came.

RCN forever!

The gaming room was large enough not to be crowded by what Pennyroyal estimated as over two hundred people. The roulette table near the door was getting the most attention, but it held no interest for her. She kept moving toward the windows at the back, checking each table as she passed.

Everyone, even those among the attendants, was better dressed than Pennyroyal. Nobody seemed to care, though. And at least her utilities were brand new, though after tonight they would be going into the regular rotation with her other two sets.

On a two-step dais in a back corner, a young man with a faraway expression plucked a harp. In the corner across from him was a 21 table with modest amounts showing and two empty chairs. The pair of windows reached down to the floor; they could be swung open.

Pennyroyal took a chair and turned one of Leary's hundreds into chips. The table limit turned out to be the equivalent of seven florins. She stayed at five, playing carefully but not cautiously. She was a moderately skillful player—astrogation was a great deal more complex than keeping track of the cards already showing on the table—and she was perfectly willing to lose the whole two hundred florins plus her own eighty-five while she waited for something to happen.

The others around the arc of the table were locals; their garments, viewed closely, showed signs of wear. Their haunted expressions were an even clearer hint that they were on the downslope of life. The dealer was young and sometimes fumbled when she took a card from the shoe; occasionally Pennyroyal caught a flash of contempt on her face.

At least in part because Pennyroyal was alert but unconcerned about the results, she began to win. She stuck to her limit so that the results came in five-florin increments, but by the time she'd taken her third beer from a server she had more than doubled her stacks of chips.

The only other thing of interest that happened was that the harpist picked out a song Pennyroyal recognized as "Sergeant Flynn," about an ancient military disaster. Her father had been a trooper with the Land Forces of the Republic before he returned home and joined the Church.

Parson Pennyroyal didn't drink often, but when he did he was apt to sing that one: "*Your head is scalped and battered, and your men are dead and scattered, Sergeant Flynn. . . .*"

Pennyroyal didn't touch her beer after that played. She'd known from earliest childhood what it meant to go into action. Tonight she was going into action.

She kept an eye open for anything of interest in the room. Daniel passed through once with a pair of redheads: one plump, the other willowy. Pennyroyal nodded to her fellow cadet, then smiled faintly and returned to her cards. Daniel was a bright, personable fellow, but the women he chose were as dim as they were lovely.

She didn't see Platt until shortly after she'd taken her third beer. The ship's corporal came from behind the dais where a wall concealed a passageway. Pennyroyal had noticed members of the house staff passing to and fro that way during the evening, so presumably it was the office.

The rest rooms were on either side of the doorway to the lobby and bar. That had surprised Pennyroyal initially; then she realized that the location encouraged those who had entered the gaming room to remain here rather than to leave for any reason.

There was even a small bar between the back windows. Servers shuttled between it and the players, sometimes without being summoned. Regardless of its other virtues, the Café Claudel appeared to be skillfully run.

Daniel returned with a different pair of women—girls, rather; this time they were brunette and both petite. Platt was standing near a poker table, but he showed no sign of wanting to sit at one of the empty chairs.

A man came in from the lobby, heading straight for Platt. Though he was in a business suit, Pennyroyal recognized Riddle, another ship's corporal from the *Swiftsure*. He rushed past Daniel as though he hadn't noticed the cadet. Pennyroyal had seen that when Riddle had scanned the room on entry, his eyes had paused briefly on Daniel.

The two corporals spoke. Riddle waved his arms in apparent agitation. Pennyroyal scooped her chips together and dumped them into the right bellows pocket of her trousers. That was a big advantage of wearing utilities instead of more stylish clothing.

The other players looked at her in various mixtures of concern and puzzlement. The dealer paused with a faint frown and said, "Mistress?"

Platt and Riddle were heading for Leary. Pennyroyal rose from her seat and reached her fellow cadet just as the corporals did.

"Tim says there's about to be a raid!" Platt said. "We've gotta get you two out of here through the manager's office. It turns out the place is over the line and your liberty is only good for Broceliande!"

"Hell and damnation!" Leary said. "If my father hears I've been arrested, I'll be back out in the wilderness!"

That didn't match with what Pennyroyal had heard of Corder Leary's hard-charging personality, but a great deal of what she had seen this night was contrary to what she had thought she knew. She didn't speak.

"This way," said Platt, leading them toward the passage concealed behind the harpist. "There's a tunnel from the office over to the next street."

The floor-length windows on either side of the bar swung inward. People in rust-red uniforms stepped in, carrying batons or, in a few cases, carbines. Their shoulder flashes read Broceliande Police. More police appeared in the doorway to the lobby and on the mezzanine railing above the gaming room.

"Too late!" said Platt. "I'm afraid you cadets are in for it now. Riddle and me are okay because we've got jurisdiction anywhere on the planet, but you two have broken bounds for liberty."

"But you brought us here, Corporal!" Leary said. He sounded desperate. "Surely there's *something* you can do?"

Pennyroyal felt her lips tighten. Listening to Leary beg disgusted as well as surprised her. Leary had broken more than his share of rules—and had several times been caught. In the past he'd always taken his punishment like an RCN officer.

"Riddle, you know the local cops," Platt said. "Can you do something for the kids?"

"Well, that's Commissioner Milhaud," Riddle said, nodding to the man who had just waddled in from the lobby. The police official's uniform showed almost more gold braid than there was russet fabric visible. "But a quick warning, that's one thing. To get them—" he looked at Daniel "—out now is going to cost a bundle. Five grand in florins, at least."

"Can either of you raise that kind of money?" Platt said. Despite his "either of you," he was looking straight at Daniel when he spoke.

"Well, I can," said Daniel. He reached into his purse and brought out a credit chip. Holding it between his left thumb and forefinger, he said, "This is a letter of credit good for up to twenty, if I can get to a real banking terminal."

This is a scam! Pennyroyal thought. *What are you doing, Leary?*

The words didn't come out of her mouth. Leary had warned her not to show surprise.

"All right, we're in business!" Platt said. "Riddle, you go talk to your buddy. I know Kravitz has a terminal in his office. I'll be out with the money in no time at all, and the cadets'll just leave through the tunnel like they was never here."

The *crack* from outside could have been lightning rather than an electromotive carbine. The lighter *crackcrackcrack* an instant later was certainly from a sub-machine gun. A slug ricocheted from stone with a high-pitched howl.

Pennyroyal remembered that when Vondrian had been shaken down two years earlier, a guard was supposed to have shot a policeman. There wasn't any need for that charade tonight, though.

The nearest police turned toward the windows they'd just entered by. Dozens of helmeted figures approached across the grounds beyond; they wore dark blue and carried sub-machine guns.

The initial raid had caused only grumbling reaction among the players; Pennyroyal was pretty sure that she'd heard the raddled blond at her table mutter, "Oh, not again!" as police clambered in through the windows.

This was different, and the loudest reactions were from the municipal police. One whispered a prayer and flung down his carbine as though it had been burning his hands.

Riddle had almost reached the gilded Commissioner Milhaud. A squad in blue entered the gaming room and surrounded them. The newcomers' helmets were stencilled "Federal Police" in black, and their shoulder patches were low visibility.

One spoke, his voice booming through the public address system: "I'm Major Picard of the Federal Police. Those of you who are here for recreation have nothing to fear. We're arresting corrupt members of the Broceliande police force and their civilian accomplices."

Platt snarled a curse and sidled into the passage to the manager's office. Daniel was with him. Pennyroyal followed only a half-step beyond, though she wondered if the Federals now entering the room would have something to say about it. They didn't, but Pennyroyal sneezed from the ozone still clinging to the muzzle of a recently fired weapon.

The door to the right at the end of the short passage was marked Manager/Private. Platt pushed it open and stepped in.

"Why's the lights out?" he shouted. He found the switch plate; his hand was at it when the lights came on an instant later.

A small door in the room's back wall was open. Pennyroyal recognized the man on his back as Kravitz, the manager. The other man was sprawled face-down; his right hand had brought a gun halfway out of his pocket before he dropped. Two more men wearing distorting masks hunched before a banking terminal.

Platt turned to run. Leary grabbed him by the left arm. Platt's sleeve broke away and his right hand came up wearing a knuckleduster.

Pennyroyal caught the corporal's right wrist and was twisting it backward when Leary slammed Platt's head into the doorjamb. Platt slumped limply. The weapon clanged when Pennyroyal let go of his arm.

The kneeling men pulled off their masks. "I think that's got it," said Janofsky, the bosun's mate.

"Lock the door, will you, ma'am?" said Hogg, the other burglar. "Nobody's supposed to be coming in after you lot, but there's no point in taking chances."

Pennyroyal was trembling as she shot the two heavy bolts. The action had been too brief to burn up the adrenaline which was flooding her system.

Platt sounded as though he were snoring. He'd need medical help, and soon. Pennyroyal felt a twinge of concern, but not serious enough to say something on the subject.

Hogg drew his mask, a stocking of some shiny fabric, over Platt's head. "Thieves fall out, don't you think?" he said. "Pop it, Janofsky, and see how well we planned this."

"It'll work," said the bosun's mate. He touched a small control device. Six puffs of smoke spurted, three each from left and right of the terminal. The explosions sounded like a single sharp crackle.

There were tools on the floor. Janofsky put a drill stencilled "Swiftsure/RCN" in a bellows pocket of his tunic. He and Hogg wore ordinary spacer's slops.

"What—" said Pennyroyal.

The terminal's faceplate dropped two inches with a clang, then toppled forward. The manager's outflung hand muffled the second impact. Coins of many kinds spilled from broken chutes.

Hogg tossed an empty sack to Pennyroyal and handed another to Daniel. "You two pick up the spillage," he said, "and I'll open the storage cans."

The cadets began scooping handfuls of coins into their sacks. Janofsky was putting another tool in his left pocket, an imaging sensor like those Pennyroyal had seen being used to check welds.

Hogg had filled a bag from the containers at the back of the terminal. It was mostly scrip, but there were also rolls of coins. Pennyroyal had seen at least one bundle of Cinnabar hundreds.

"Time to go," Hogg said as he rose. Janofsky had already started out the door in the back.

Daniel waved Pennyroyal ahead with a grin. She wondered what happened next, but simply doing as directed had worked fine so far tonight.

Why change a winning plan?

The tunnel was lighted by glowstrips in the ceiling at long intervals. All they did was show direction: the tunnel kinked twice in what Pennyroyal estimated at 200 yards. There was nothing in the passage except for a central drain, and even that was superfluous at present: the concrete walls were dry to a finger's touch.

There was suction as the door at the far end opened. A pair of Federal Police waited outside the exit.

Janofsky passed through. Hogg stopped and set down his bag of loot; Pennyroyal jerked to a halt to keep from running into Daniel's servant.

Hogg fished scrip out of a tunic pocket. "I know you boys'll be taken care of in the share-out," he said, "but this is a little something from me personally. I appreciate it, right?"

He handed money to each policeman, then picked up his bag and strode on. "Come back any time," a cop called after him. They grinned at Pennyroyal as she passed.

Janofsky was climbing into the back of a high-roofed blue van stencilled "Federal Police" in the same style of black lettering as the police helmets. *It's a riot wagon!* Pennyroyal thought.

And so it was; but on the bench to the right sat a man whose blue uniform was of higher quality than those of the Federal assault force. Pennyroyal wasn't up on Foret's police insignia, but she was pretty sure that the horsehead on his lapel made him a colonel. The woman beside him wore RCN utilities with Shore Police brassards. Her subdued commander's pips implied that she was in charge of the whole contingent on Foret.

Two clerks sat on the opposite bench, each with a thick tray on his lap. One was dumping the contents of Hogg's bag carefully onto his tray.

"I'll take that," the other clerk said to Pennyroyal—and did so. The trays made small sounds as they sucked in coins and bills, counted them, and dropped them into storage compartments.

Leary closed the door behind him and passed his bag to the nearer clerk. His fellow said, "We may need those extra bins after all." He was breaking rolls and bundles of money so that they could feed individually.

The clerks didn't pay any attention to the cadets except to take their bags. The sorting trays whirred, clicked and occasionally pinged.

The van drove off sedately. Hogg and Janofsky seated themselves below the clerks, so Pennyroyal took the place beside the RCN commander. That officer grinned at her and said, "Impressive work, Cadet."

Pennyroyal swallowed. "Thank you, ma'am," she said. "Ah, ma'am? If I can ask . . . What's going to happen to us now?"

The commander smiled more broadly. "I suppose you'll report back aboard the *Swiftsure* at the end of your liberty," she said. "We'll let you out at the edge of the Strip; then you're on your own."

Pennyroyal swallowed. She said, "Thank you, ma'am."

The commander leaned forward to look past Pennyroyal. "You're Leary?" she said. "You planned this?"

"Ma'am, it was my idea," Daniel said, "but the details and the grunt work was all handled by other people. Including yourself, ma'am, and Colonel Lebel."

The commander chuckled and said, "You'll go far, Leary. If you're not hanged first."

The Federal colonel said something from her other side. The officers talked between themselves too quietly for Pennyroyal to overhear without making it obvious.

Turning to Leary on her other side, Pennyroyal said, "Daniel, how long have you been planning this?"

"Since Vondrian told us how he'd been robbed," Leary said. He grinned at the memory. "I didn't know quite how we were going to work it till I met Janofsky when we reported aboard. There's a lot of the *Swiftsure*'s cadre who've been spoiling for a chance to get back at Platt and Riddle. Hogg—"

He nodded toward his servant, who was talking with Janofsky.

"—was talking to people in Harbor Three and elsewhere on

Cinnabar. He got names and introductions to members of the Shore Establishment here on Foret. They've been pissed about the games the ship's police have been playing, but they couldn't touch the crooks without help. I said we'd give them help."

Pennyroyal felt herself grinning. "Now I see why you made up with your father, Leary," she said. "That was, well, a surprise."

Daniel's answering smile was hard. "This chip was blank," he said, holding up what he'd claimed was a twenty-thousand florin credit. "I haven't had any contact with Corder Leary since the afternoon I enrolled in the RCN Academy. Saying that I did was just to explain why I suddenly had money. The ship's warrant officers, the good ones, clubbed together and came up with enough florins to make a splash. They'll get a third of the take."

"A third," Pennyroyal repeated.

She hadn't added a follow-up question, but Leary answered without it. "The Federal Police get a third. They've been looking for a way to clean up the Broceliande force anyway. And the rest goes to Commander Kilmartin there for her people."

"But you?" Pennyroyal said.

Leary laughed. "I did it for Vondrian and for the RCN," he said. "Getting scum like Platt and Riddle out is worth more than money. I suspect they'll both go down for the burglary—somebody's got to be blamed. At any rate, Kilmartin'll make sure they're off the *Swiftsure* and out of the RCN."

Pennyroyal brought the remaining hundred out of her purse. "I've still got this," she said. "And a pocket full of chips that probably aren't worth anything. I don't guess the Café Claudel will reopen any time soon."

"Keep it," said Daniel. "Or better, the four of us can tie one on properly on the Strip before our liberty's over!"

Hogg, from the other side of the van, must have been listening. "*Bloody* good idea!" he said.

"I couldn't agree more," Pennyroyal said. She stretched, feeling relaxed for the first time since the evening had begun.

When working in the vacuum of space, following regulations can mean the difference between life and death. Sure, maybe doing things "by the book" takes more time and isn't as flashy, but when an orbiting fuel station malfunctions, mission engineer Hartman has every intention of making repairs in as boring and safe a fashion as possible. But soon the cold equations of space and the folly—and malice—of his all-too-human crewmate make a routine repair a desperate bid for survival. If he's to make it home alive, Hartman will have to think outside of the rules and regulations.

TETHERS

★

by William Ledbetter

SIEVERT WAS A JERK at the best of times, but he was mad at me and that made him much worse. He was tied with Alyona Gusarov at being four hours away from breaking the long standing one thousand hour EVA record. He'd wanted to tell the ground station I was sick so he could go EVA and make the repairs, but I was the mission engineer and had refused. To pay back my insolence, he opened an intra-suit connection the minute I left the ship and hadn't stopped harassing me since.

"You techies make bad astronauts," Sievert said, then gave me a long peal of barking, hiccupping laughter. His French accent grew more pronounced when he was angry and it made him sound even more condescending.

"You're too cautious and too timid, Hartman," he said. "By-the-book takes twice as long!"

I gritted my teeth and made another tiny adjustment to my slow, but steady, course toward the malfunctioning orbital fuel depot. Sievert could probably have made the repairs, just as I could fly the *Stolid*, but it was my *ass* on the line. Tyco Space Services Corporation had a ninety-eight percent quality rating for its orbital equipment and this was the first time one of these refueling depots went offline. I couldn't screw this up.

I ignored Sievert's ongoing abuse and watched the sun rise slowly over the Pacific below. Like every human who left the Earth before me, I never stopped being stunned by its beauty. Since this depot was in geosynchronous orbit, I wouldn't get to see the jewel encrusted night side during this EVA, but that also meant I didn't have to work in the dark.

My focus returned to the task at hand as the depot slowly dominated my field of vision. It was a cluster of round tanks surrounded by steel struts, all interconnected by armored piping, and roughly the size of a two-bedroom house. Fueling probes jutted outward in four directions, easily accessible by either crewed or automated spacecraft, and solar arrays sprouted from the top and bottom. Printed in huge letters next to the Tyco Space Services logo on the wide equatorial band was the identifier TRD27—or officially Tyco Refueling Depot number 27.

"Are you too nervous to talk, techie? Do you clench your teeth tight to keep them from chattering?"

"Twelve meters," I answered over the open company channel, but he was right about my being afraid. I just wasn't afraid for me. I had to stay alive for Dad.

My dad stood on the back porch, looking out at the dust cloud above the seventy acres of corn behind our house. Like him, the neighbors driving the combine and pulling the wagons were still wearing their dress clothes from the funeral. When the condolences were given, the food consumed and most people had left, these men had stayed to help with the already late harvest.

He turned to look at me and tears streaked his cheeks.

"Please don't hate me for this, son. I couldn't bear to lose you too."

The statement pulled me up short. "Lose me? I don't . . ."

"Because this is my fault," he said. "You were in space when the goddamned leukemia finally took your sister, but *I* was here. I was here and didn't support your mother. I went into the fields and the barns. I just . . . I didn't know how else to deal with it."

I swallowed hard.

"It was a cruel thing I did to your mother. She begged me to stay in the house with her in those days after Dana died. She was in so much pain and so very lonely, but I shrugged it off and went out to work."

Suicides only hurt the living. My mom's pain was ended, but it was the first time in my twenty-seven years that I'd seen my dad cry.

TRD27 loomed larger as the seconds ticked off and Sievert still hadn't shut up.

"It would be sad if you had a problem out there and wished you hadn't wasted that precious oxygen," Sievert said, then made gasping sounds and laughed at his own humor. The gas for my suit's maneuvering jets came from my breathing stock. The minuscule puffs I'd used so far might give me another couple minutes of air in an emergency, but Sievert had ranted on what he considered wasted oxygen many times before.

As the proximity counter dropped to zero, I readied myself. When close enough, I grabbed the nearest ring handle and held tight as I thumped down to the primary service platform, then rebounded slightly.

Per the regulations, I pulled the short safety tether from its pouch on my tool harness and connected one end to me and the other to the TRD. Then I detached the line tying me to *Stolid* and reconnected it to the depot structure. Only then did I allow myself to relax and report that I'd made contact.

Sievert laughed again. "If you get scared or see any alien monsters lurking around Turd27, just call and I'll come rescue you."

He was stupid to use that word to describe a TRD. More than one Tyco employee had been fired for that joke. Agatha Winston-Nguyen took the company's image very seriously. In her mind, the TRDs were a symbol of reliability and quality, but thanks to the acronym she selected, these depots would instead forever be associated with smelly brown lumps.

I pushed my boots into the spring-loaded cleats that locked me down to the platform. Having my feet anchored gave me the physical leverage I needed to use my hands and arms during the repair. Then, for the first time, I turned my attention to the real problem.

The insulation blanket had peeled away from one of the hydrogen storage tanks. Remote instrumentation indicated the tank's naked skin had heated in the direct sunlight, causing a pressure increase that triggered an automatic shutdown of the fueling nozzles. This was an "out of service" condition that greatly upset Agatha Winston-Nguyen.

I pulled the loose blanket farther away from the tank and moved my helmet lights slowly over the surface. Nearly the entire blanket had detached. From time to time, fasteners would fail, allowing a small gap or a corner to fly loose—but this was very odd. When I examined the blanket's attachment points, the failure was obvious. The blanket hadn't torn loose from the fasteners because there were no fasteners.

"Come in, *Stolid*. This is Hartman."

"Reading you, Hartman. What did you find?" Even over the open connection, I could still hear a hint of condescension in Sievert's voice.

What I found would get several employees and probably a few managers fired, so I decided to be careful with my wording.

"Can you check the TRD parts list and find out what fastener we use for blanket attachment? I'm going to need twelve of them."

I hoped he would understand and keep chatter about the failure to a minimum. Accusations and blame should be taken up by the Engineering Review Board, not orbital repair techs.

"Why twelve? Did they all break?"

I took a deep breath and mentally cursed. "No, they're all missing."

The connection was quiet for several minutes, presumably while Sievert discussed it with the ground.

"You're mistaken, Hartman. There is no way this TRD could have been launched with that much missing hardware."

I was shocked and simultaneously pissed off.

"I'm not mistaken. The grommets aren't torn. There is no hardware in the holes. My guess is that the flap's velcro was sealed for some reason before the bolts were installed. That would have held it in place through the launch, but once . . ."

"You're wrong, Hartman."

I gritted my teeth. I didn't want to argue with him over the radio, but I had to get this damned thing fixed.

"Just look at my video feed, Sievert," I snapped.

"No need to get angry, Hartman. Light plays tricks out there. The video doesn't clearly show the attachment condition, so I'm coming out."

I cursed under my breath. There was nothing wrong with that video feed. Sievert was just being an ass and seizing an opportunity for an unscheduled EVA. Under normal operating circumstances one of us was required to stay in the ship. I wondered if he made the decision on his own or if someone on the ground had classified the situation as an emergency. Both explanations made me grind my teeth.

Since he was already wearing his excursion suit—also standard procedure when one of us was out of the ship—it took him less than ten minutes to don his helmet and cycle through the airlock. I spent that time getting extremely close video of the insulation situation and making sure it was relayed to the ground station.

Sievert made the leap between *Stolid* and the TRD without tether or gas jets. It was of course against company safety policy, but he was a macho, hot-shot space pilot and exempt from those silly rules. I could already see that he hadn't even worn his tool harness. He was going to be no help at all.

There were no women or news reporters around to see it, but he couldn't resist showing off. As he neared the TRD, he extended an arm and, at the last second, grabbed a strut and let momentum swing him around in a tight arc toward my position.

When I saw his speed and where he would land I panicked. "Sievert, no!"

His armored boots impacted the already stressed hydrogen tank's bare skin about ten feet above me, hard enough that I felt vibrations through the service platform.

The carbon-composite tank deformed in an almost fluid-like undulation, then exploded.

A bright flash flung me backwards. My boots—still locked into the service cleats—acted as an anchor point about which I swung a full hundred and eighty degrees, slamming back-first into one of the lower LOX tanks. Fiery pain erupted in my lower back and I screamed as something snapped in both knees.

I must have blacked out, but the cacophony of pain, beeping warnings and incessant radio calls gradually dragged me back to consciousness. At first I was confused, trying to make sense of the sounds and strange pains, then the fog in my head started to clear and alarm took over.

My eyes were blurry with tears or sweat and I had to clench my teeth to keep from crying out from the pain in my knees, but I had to focus. First priority was my suit integrity. I scanned the lights on my helmet display. Several yellows, but only one red. My suit exterior had been punctured in several places, but not with enough force to penetrate all three layers. The oily second layer, when exposed to vacuum, immediately hardened and, if the holes were small enough, sealed them like a high tech scab. I hoped it would hold.

Beneath the litany of status requests from the ground station, I heard an underlying chaotic string of grunts and cursing. It must have been from Sievert. Was he hurt? For the first time since the explosion I looked past my helmet display and saw the carnage surrounding me. Bits of carbon composite and insulation floated in a hydrogen haze on the lower edge of my vision. When I looked up I saw Sievert's partially shredded boots wrapped in hastily applied leak tape floating above me.

Why hadn't the explosion sent him tumbling into space? Maybe it had and he used his jets to fly back and help me. My blackout must have lasted longer than I thought.

I was about to call out to him when I realized he was tugging on me. With each of his grunts, the top of my utility backpack pulled upward. It took several seconds for his movements to register in my still addled brain. The bastard hadn't come back to help me; he was trying to get my oxygen reserves.

"Stop it, Sievert!" I shoved at him until the tugging stopped. At first there was no reply, then he uttered a low string of curses followed by a quick apology. "Sorry, I thought you were dead."

He was lying. The ground station received a constant feed from my suit's health monitoring system. He knew I was still alive. I kept my eye on him and took a deep breath to help me focus before finally responding to ground control.

"This is Hartman," I said, trying not to pant or groan. "I'm hurt, but my suit's intact. Both of my legs are hurt. Severe ligament damage for sure and possibly broken."

The woman's voice was reassuring and calm. "Good to hear from you, Hartman. We were worried for a while, but your vitals look good. No indicators of severe blood loss. Do you have pain other than in your legs?"

"Some in my lower back, but nothing compared to my legs."

"Any difficulty inhaling?"

"No," I said, and started to wonder just how long I'd been out.

"Good. You're going to have to hang on for a while, Hartman. We have a rescue team prepping to leave Tyco Orbital, but it'll be a long wait."

My brain was still a bit foggy, but something didn't add up. Why were they sending a rescue team? It would take them at least nine hours from Tyco Orbital. And why was Sievert trying to steal my air instead of helping me return to *Stolid*?

Then I understood.

I saw only a frayed stub of the cable I had used to attach the ship to the TRD, but *Stolid* was gone. At first I thought the spacecraft had vaporized in the explosion, but that didn't make sense. Sievert and I were both right next to the tank when it blew and were still alive. Then I saw her. The slowly tumbling object just hadn't registered as a ship. It was much too small. Made small by distance.

The explosion shouldn't have been strong enough to push a ship that size. I made myself focus on the *Stolid* and finally noticed a small plume of gas spewing into the void. Shrapnel from the explosion must have ruptured one of the small attitude thrusters, causing the spin and pushing the ship away.

Was that why Sievert was after my tanks? I did a quick calculation and determined that if I could push off hard enough with my legs, then use my jets to adjust my trajectory, then I should have enough air to reach the ship. My legs were still locked into cleats. I had to act fast.

Sievert chose that instant to strike again. This time he was ready for my resistance. He shoved me backwards, again slamming my back into the tank, then wrapped an arm around my helmet ring, grabbed the TRD structure behind my head and levered me tight against the metal. I screamed as bones and torn cartilage ground together, sending a tsunami of red hot agony through my entire body and swirling spots to cloud my vision.

The radio squawked in my ear: "Hartman? Give us a status!"

But I couldn't breathe or talk, only yank ineffectively at Sievert's pinning arm. He didn't tug on my pack this time, but instead started pounding hard against the side of my helmet.

"Sievert! Get off!"

"Say again, Hartm . . . ," came a partial response from ground control.

"Sievert's crazy," I yelled as I tugged against his arm. ". . . trying to kill me!"

My boots were not only still locked down, but my legs were too badly injured to give me leverage anyway. I was pinned tight. Through my watering eyes, I saw something white, about the size of a tennis ball, float past trailing wires and bits of plastic. It was the transmitter node from my helmet. Sievert had broken it off. Aside from my ragged breathing and thundering heartbeat, my world had grown very quiet.

I started hyperventilating, wasting more of my precious air. If I couldn't talk to the ground, Sievert would tell them anything he wanted. His arm still held me pinned to the TRD and I knew what would come next. He would try to kill me in some way that wouldn't breach my suit and waste my precious gas supply.

I didn't want to die, especially to help keep someone like Sievert alive. I groped at my tool harness until I found the screwdriver, then pressed its point against Sievert's arm and pushed as hard as I could with both hands. I was rewarded by a mist of venting gas. His arm jerked away, nearly tearing the screwdriver from my grip, and momentum carried him out to the end of his tether. He floated there— knowing he was out of my reach—while applying repair tape to his damaged suit. I couldn't see his face, but I knew he was glaring at me and I suddenly knew why.

His suit was patched in various places, even the hard to reach legs. He must have lost a lot of gas right after the explosion and didn't have enough to get to *Stolid*.

Screw him. Just let him try for my air again.

He pulled himself along the tether until he reached the TRD structure, then moved farther away around the curve of the depot.

Tether? He hadn't used a tether when he came across.

I looked down and saw that mine was gone. He must have planned my demise in great detail and now I would have to be very careful when freeing myself from the cleats. And I had to get loose quickly. Sievert wouldn't give up, so that meant his retreat around the TRD was only a means to reposition himself and come up behind me. It would be easy enough to do with me locked in place.

Normally a quick push from my heel would have released the cleat's spring lock, but I was already having a hard enough time thinking through the pain and suspected forcing my damaged legs down that hard might make me black out. I couldn't allow that. If Sievert didn't pounce on me I would still lose too much precious time.

I stretched my arm downward as far as I could, but my fingers were at least two feet from touching my heels, so I took stock of the tools in my harness. None of them were long enough to reach on their own, but I also had every astronaut's best tool: suit repair tape. I taped my long screwdriver to the end of my torque wrench, then placed two smaller wrenches and another screwdriver around the first joint and wrapped it as tight as I could. I paused for a second to groan at the nice splint I'd just made for a pair of tools. Maybe I should have splinted my legs instead?

"Probably not enough tape anyway," I mumbled into my quiet helmet. I glanced at my air gauge, noted that I had four hours and twenty-seven minutes left, then looked around for Sievert. I couldn't see him, but I didn't have a good view below me or behind me, so he might still have been nearby.

I positioned my makeshift spear against the back of the cleat and shoved hard. The tape held and the spring opened easily, but the downward motion made me curse and add a little more to my liquid waste bag.

My perch was now even more precarious. With the freed leg floating about, but of little use, it played hell with my balance and coordination. I quickly checked the taped joint; it had loosened some but was tight enough. I touched the screwdriver's tip to the cleat and pushed. It didn't open and I felt the taped tools starting to fold in the middle. In a fit of desperation or panic or just plain impatience, I shoved the tools again and shoved down with my hurt leg at the same time.

It felt like super-heated barbed wire had wrapped around the nerves in my leg, and then been yanked out, pulling the bones and nerves with it. I swooned, cried out and clenched my teeth against the blackness that threatened to drag me down.

The day after my mom's funeral I woke to the rhythmic clang of a hammer landing on metal. The sun wasn't up high enough to burn off the mist yet and the air carried the sweet musty smell of autumn as I walked down to the equipment barn. My dad stood next to his harvester's disassembled corn head with a cutter blade laid out on an anvil. I could see the blade's edge was bent and chipped.

"Let me guess. Albert Whittle turned wide and got into the fence."

Dad looked up and a faint grin flickered across his already dirty face. "He means well. But it sure would have been nice if he'd told me."

"Need me to run into town and get some new blades?"

"Nah, if I can beat a couple of these flat and resharpen them, it'll get me through these next few days."

He laid the hammer down, leaned on the anvil and pushed his hat back on his head. "When are you leaving?"

I looked down at the ground and focused on a rusty washer near the toe of my shoe. "I've decided I'm going to quit. I'd really like to stay here with you. And help out."

My mom had run the business part of the farm and I suspected that my dad would be lost in the books for a long time, if he ever figured it out at all.

"Like hell you are. You've always loved the idea of going into space and you busted your ass to get this job."

"Yeah, but it's really not all I thought . . ."

"Bullshit. If you want to pile hurt on top of your mom's death, then quit that job and move back here. Make me feel totally worthless. I couldn't save your sister and I failed your mother. I sure—"

"Dad . . ."

"No, you listen to me. You're the only person I haven't fucked up yet. If you quit on your dream because of me then I'll be a total failure."

I swallowed and nodded, but couldn't look at him.

He stood up and crossed to stand next to me. "But if you're going to be here for a while, I'll let you help me fix breakfast. I can rebuild a tractor engine, but cooking anything beyond frozen pizza is going to take some practice."

I floated in a groggy haze for several minutes, never really blacking out, but not quite conscious either, before I finally realized it had worked. Both of my legs were floating free and so was the rest of me. I had forgotten that I wasn't tethered.

I slowly extended a hand but was a foot from reaching the closest handle or strut and was still slowly drifting farther away. I fought down the panic and found my makeshift tool still attached to me via several lanyards. I turned it around slowly and extended it far enough to hook the torque wrench's driver post behind one strut and gently pulled myself in until I could grab the safety ring.

"Dumbass," I growled, and took a deep shuddering breath. Now that I was able to move around, I had options. I stared at the depot's dark, hulking form and felt a glimmer of hope. If I could keep Sievert off my back and had enough time, I might be able to fire the TRD's station keeping rockets to take us over to *Stolid*.

I rotated slowly to the left and then the right, but saw nothing. When I looked down I caught a glimpse of a space suit. Sievert watched from the other side of a LOX tank. That worried me, but at least I knew where he was.

I untaped my tools and put them away, checked my air—it was down to three hours and forty-nine minutes—then opened the TRD's control panel. Everything inside was dead and dark. The explosion had evidently severed a power line. Which meant I had to be even more careful. Chances of me getting into a grounded situation were much less likely in space than on Earth, but I wasn't thinking clearly so I decided to be extra careful. I closed the control panel and looked around.

From my location, I saw that all six liquid oxygen tanks were all still intact. The irony was almost painful. Like shipwreck survivors who die of thirst while floating in the salty ocean, I had a very good chance of dying from the lack of oxygen while surrounded by tons of the stuff. I briefly toyed with the idea of trying to rig a converter, but it would require more equipment and time than I had. So I looked around again, hoping for inspiration. Ahead of me, amid a tangle of piping lay two large manifolds, one for oxygen and one for hydrogen. Each tank feed pipe had a lever valve in the line just above where it attached to the manifold. And I finally had my idea.

I kept my voltage meter on and the probes at hand to test each metal object before I touched it, then slowly crawled deeper into the pipe maze using only arms. I braced myself and pulled the valve handle. At first it didn't move and I assumed it was frozen open. I immediately cursed the designers, then gave another hard tug and the handle moved. Once I was able to close it completely, I retracted my nasty comments about the engineering staff.

With the valve closed, I pulled a wrench from my tool harness and detached the flange from the manifold, leaving the twelve tethered bolts floating around the flange like Medusa's snakes. I checked my air supply and groaned. Three hours and nine minutes. I also remembered to look for Sievert. At first I didn't see any trace, then saw him watching me from between two struts. A chill trickled down my back. A lot of structure and piping lay between us, but I couldn't forget about him again. He wouldn't hesitate to kill me if he had the chance.

I scrambled up the pipe to the LOX tank, but that wasn't my goal. I needed to get to each of the five points around the tank's equator where it attached to the TRD structure. The only way to reach them without free flying would be to hold onto the cable race on the tank's exterior.

Dragging myself along the three-inch cable box proved easier than I thought, and with only one bolt at each connection, the work was quick, but moving between attachments—free flying along the tank with no handholds or tether—was nerve-wracking. And I realized at some point that I probably hadn't picked the best tank for my improvised rocket. It not only had the ten-foot-long manifold connection pipe sticking out one side but also the spacecraft fueling probe protruding fifteen feet out the other. That meant if I managed to get it pointed straight at the *Stolid*, I ran the risk of spearing my only ride home.

I looked back along the length of the TRD at one of the tanks without a fueling probe. If I used that one, and accidentally hit the *Stolid*, it would be a mostly depressurized composite ball hitting the titanium ship's hull. A much better risk, but did I have the time?

It was two in the morning and I was fifteen, standing in the equipment barn, trying to stay awake and waiting for my dad to finish repairs on the tractor. I would never have volunteered to help had I known I'd be up so late.

"Shit!" my dad said. "Hand me the vise grips. The big ones."

I pulled them from the tool box and pressed them against his leg where he could reach them easily, the way I'd been doing since I was five.

"C'mon Dad, let's save this 'til morning and go to bed."

He pulled his head out of the engine compartment and spun around, pointing the vise grips at me. I knew I was going to get blasted and braced myself, but instead he just stared at me for second, then shook his head.

"Because sometimes timing is everything, Son. Tomorrow is Sunday. I can't go to town and buy the part I need because they'll be closed."

"But you don't work on Sunday anyway," I said, not really caring about the stupid part.

"That's usually true, but they have forecasted showers all day Monday and Tuesday. If I can plant that corn tomorrow, it will get a good soaking. If I don't, then I may have to wait until Thursday or Friday for the fields to be dry enough to not bog down the equipment."

He turned around and dove back into the tractor. "Go on to bed," he said. "I'm not making you stay out here."

I stood there for a minute, my fifteen-year-old brain being slow to process what I'd just heard, then I stepped up close to him.

"I want to help. Is there anything I can do?"

"There sure is," he said. "Hold those hoses out of my way."

About twenty minutes later, while we were wiping down and putting away the tools, he paused.

"Thanks," he said. "You're a pretty sharp kid. You must have got that from your mother."

I decided to use the first tank and not waste more time. After removing the last mounting bolt, I worked my way back down to the closed valve, looked around for Sievert, but didn't see him. I had two hours and forty minutes of air left. I couldn't wait any longer.

I held tight to the valve housing with one hand and twisted the lever about a quarter turn with the other and was rewarded as finely crystallized oxygen jetted from the pipe and I started moving. Looking down, I saw the exhaust dangerously close to my feet, but when I tried to move them pain bloomed in my knees like twin supernovas.

Using only arms, I twisted my upper body to pull the useless legs away from the flow. It worked for a couple seconds, then just as I was about to clear the TRD truss structure, I was yanked downward and to one side. I glanced behind me and saw that Sievert had looped his tether around the top of my utility pack and was pulling his way up to me.

I immediately shut off the valve. Even though the thrust wasn't powerful enough to pull it from of my grip, I needed both hands to free myself from the line. As I struggled with the tether he kept waving at me. Was he making a truce? I didn't trust him and was unsure of his intentions, but there was no reason why the tank couldn't take both of us to the *Stolid*. The process would actually be much easier if we had one to control the valve and one to see over the globe of the tank.

Sievert gave me a small wave of reassurance when he came into view, then unlooped the tether from my back and attached the clip to a ring on the tank. I motioned for him to mount the tank at its equator, but instead he launched himself at me with a mighty push and squeegeed me off of the pipe.

My arms wheeled, seeking purchase, and finally snagged a hook on Sievert's utility pack. I held tight and the sudden anchor point swung me back, bringing the pipe up between my legs. I screamed as it bounced off of one busted knee, but I clamped my thighs together despite the pain. I knew this was my last chance. If I let go I'd die.

Using my leverage advantage, I pulled Sievert over my head as hard as I could and let go. He grabbed at me but missed and flew away from the tank and the TRD. I moved quickly up the pipe to the valve, expecting to have very little time before Sievert halted his departure, but when I glanced that direction I saw he wasn't using his thrusters to bring him back. He saved his gas, intending to let the tether halt his progress and had already starting pulling in the slack line.

I couldn't let him do that. Hand over hand, I dragged myself up to the tank, detached the tether and tossed the end out into the black. By the time I scrambled back to the valve he had realized his predicament and fired his thrusters to return, but I didn't hesitate. I held tight and twisted the valve fully open.

With a sudden lurch my rocket steed started moving, opening the distance between me and Sievert, but it had continued drifting while we struggled until the pipe nozzle no longer aligned with the direction of forward momentum. The added thrust created a slow conical spin.

As the tank spun, I saw that I had indeed cleared the TRD, but was having a hard time getting my bearings and couldn't see the *Stolid*. I had no choice but to act fast and get the tank under some semblance of control. With arms wrapped tightly around the pipe, I double-checked the direction of my nozzles, then triggered long bursts of my suit thrusters. The spin slowed, but not enough. I gave another couple bursts, shorter this time, and watched in near panic as my air supply dropped below the two-hour mark. With no other options, I didn't stop thrusting until the tank spin rate dropped to almost nothing.

Only then did I release one hand from the valve housing long enough to turn my body and look around. This time I was able to get a better understanding of my position. I saw the TRD amid a small cloud of debris behind me, but still couldn't see the ship. I used the cable race to crawl to the tank equator and look over. The ship was roughly ahead but about twenty degrees above me. Then I saw Sievert.

He was on a course that could intercept mine, but he floated like a man face down in a swimming pool, with arms and legs limp and a slight spin that kept turning his back to me. Had he set his course then went unconscious? He probably wasn't dead yet; his suit would have gone into automatic minimum life support mode in order to maximize his chances. It would provide enough air to keep him alive, but not conscious, for about thirty minutes. Of course he could also be faking.

Could I take the risk of trying to save him? And what the hell had he been thinking? He'd been safe. The two of us could have ridden the tank all the way to *Stolid* and both been saved. Of course then he would have had to explain his actions when I made my report. He would have been fired and probably jailed. Had he actually made getting rid of me a higher priority than even his own survival? Perhaps he expected to die and wanted to be remembered a hero, not a cowardly villain. Jerk.

After tracking him for a few seconds, I could tell we were going to miss each other. He would pass behind me if I kept accelerating. I shut off the valve and estimated the new intercept. We were still going to miss; he was coming in too high. If he were faking he'd have to act soon, but I worried about what I would do if he didn't act.

I counted down, carefully timing his approach, when an alarm sounded in my helmet. I hadn't checked my air in a while and it had just dropped below the forty-minute mark. The realization made bile rise in my throat and I had to fight a sudden panic. Then Sievert was upon me, not attacking this time, but about to speed past overhead.

If I stretched my arm I might be able to grab him. Did I dare? Would he try to kill me again? Worse yet, would his momentum break my tenuous grip on the tank and pull us both away from the tank to our deaths?

★ ★ ★

During my junior year of high school, Dad and our neighbor, Ted, had a dispute over land they both wanted to buy. Greed turned Ted mean. He told lies and jokes about my dad to folks at the co-op, but Dad just pretended nothing happened. It made me furious and embarrassed that he didn't kick the shit out of the loudmouth.

Knowing how much both men wanted the land, the retiring farm owner, Cecil Winn, decided to have an auction and see how much he could get. It poured rain the night before and by the time my dad and I arrived, the trucks and boots had churned Cecil's driveway into ankle-deep mud.

We stood beside Ted and he nodded to us and then turned to give a sly wink to rest of the crowd. When the auctioneer began to talk, Ted spun around too quickly, lost his balance and was falling toward the mud when Dad reached and grabbed one of his flailing hands and pulled the man upright with one powerful yank. He could have watched Ted make a fool of himself without lifting a finger, but instead he made a huge effort to keep the loudmouth from hitting the mud. Then he let the man beat him bidding for the land.

I crawled back in the truck and sulked. I couldn't believe he'd had the chance to pay Ted back—*twice*—and had let it go. I would have loved to laugh at Ted lying in the mud.

Dad raised an eyebrow and asked what was wrong.

"Why'd you do that?" I said, barely keeping my voice under control.

"What? Let Ted outbid me?"

I had meant saving him from the mud, but before I could answer, he laughed and turned on the truck.

"Hell, I didn't want Cecil's three hundred acres, but I knew Ted did and he had the money to pay top dollar. Of course he wouldn't if he could get it cheap. Cecil needed the money, so I thought I'd just drive Ted's bids a little higher."

I learned things that day. Dad didn't really care what others thought of him. And those men who were standing around smiling weren't making fun of my dad, they were laughing at what my dad had done to Ted. Finally I smiled and settled back in my seat. Dad gave me a conspiratorial wink and at that moment I even understood why he didn't let Ted land in the mud.

I stretched high and tried to grab Sievert's hand, but was too late and just brushed his glove as he slid by. I was about to use my suit thrusters to jet after him and saw the tether, my tether, one end still attached to Sievert, the other sliding along the tank ahead of me.

With a hard pull, I launched toward the rapidly departing line, snatched it with one hand and wrapped it around my wrist. I grabbed a clip ring on the tank with my left hand and gritted my teeth. The yank was more violent than I'd anticipated and a hard pop sent hot pain through my shoulder. I cursed and gritted my teeth, wondering how the hell I was going to handle it. I recognized this injury. I'd pulled my shoulder from its socket before.

The recoil brought Sievert back toward me, but at a more manageable speed. I latched the tether's free end to the tank ring, held on with my injured arm, and slowly reeled him in using my good arm. I clipped him to the ring, then transferred the tether to me.

I checked my air. Twenty-nine minutes for me and I had no idea if Sievert was even still alive. I needed to come up with some ingenious way to pop my shoulder back in place, but sweat stung my eyes and everything hurt. We didn't have much time and I just couldn't think. I drew deep of my precious air and crawled up to the tank equator to get my bearings.

Halting Sievert's momentum had pulled the makeshift spacecraft out of alignment with the *Stolid*. I mumbled curses and used more of my precious oxygen to turn the tank once again. When close enough, I turned the valve and a stream of oxygen jetted from the nozzle and I began moving in what I hoped was the right direction.

I left the valve open, then deposited myself on the tank's equator so I could make minor course adjustments as needed. I also had to come up with a plan to get me and Sievert from the tank to *Stolid*.

With Sievert on one end of the line and me on the other, we made quite a nice bolo. Using a couple more puffs of air, I lined us up properly on the narrow service "neck" behind the command module. When we lassoed the *Stolid*, I had dropped to ten minutes of air. Using only my good arm and a dose of panic, I pulled me and Sievert into the one-person airlock and cycled it. I took time while air filled the small chamber to tie Sievert's hands behind his back using the tether. I wasn't taking any chances.

Once inside, I yanked off my helmet, then Sievert's. He wasn't breathing and was grayish in color. I started mouth-to-mouth and pulled the medical box from beneath my couch, then rummaged through it until I found the mask. I attached the hose to the interior oxygen panel, pushed it over his face and started defibrillation.

He didn't wake up but started breathing on his own and I finally relaxed. My face was covered with tears and my only useful hand shook as I fumbled painkillers into my mouth. Only then did I notice the radio squawking in the background and replied.

"Good God, Hartman. Sievert told us you were dead. What's going on up there?"

I considered a white lie, telling them he panicked or had space sickness, but then he might go out with someone else and kill them one day.

"Sievert tried to kill me," I said as clearly and carefully as I could. "He destroyed my transmitter, then pinned me down and tried to steal my oxygen. He's in bad shape now. Unconscious. I barely got him inside, but I *did* bring him back."

There was a long pause on the other side. Who knew what he told them and what they believed. I was just too hurt and exhausted to give a damn.

"Roger that, *Stolid*. We are inbound. ETA three hours and fifty minutes."

I was starting to feel a bit dizzy from the pain killers and didn't reply.

"*Stolid*? Do you copy?"

"Yeah," I finally said. "Hey, do any of you know if Sievert's dad is alive?"

When I mentioned his name, Sievert woke up. He turned his head and focused on me, but his eyes held no emotion. I couldn't tell if the old Sievert was still in there or not.

The crew from the rescue ship finally replied. "Tyco Orbital says yes. His father is still alive. Why?"

"Hartman out," I said and signed off.

We stared at each other for several seconds, then I said, "I guess you broke the record. Congratulations."

He turned his head away. I checked his bonds, then settled into my seat to sleep while I waited for pickup. Before I closed my eyes, I buckled my harness, per the safety regulations.

Ten years ago, Etta Pryor was part of a clandestine military program. Her brain implanted with a top secret technology called biomoss, she and the other handlers remotely controlled Brutes—genetically altered super-soldiers with limited mental capacity. But all that was in the past. Now, all of the Brutes are dead, and Etta has moved on with her life. Why then, has her long dormant biomoss reactivated?

UNLINKAGE
★
by Eric Del Carlo

THE FIRST STAGGERED Etta Pryor. Literally—she was crossing the kitchen, then felt the impactful sensation, located just below her right collarbone, and her footing lost all rhythm as she lurched across the gleaming floor tiles.

The second blow hit just above the heart, and that sent her careening into the chromed refrigerator. Her feet went out from under her as she yelped her surprise.

She was on hands and knees, and Bethany was watching her with goggled eyes from the table, when the third invisible strike caught her jaw and turned her head halfway around on her neck.

Bethany screamed a perfect four-year-old alto scream.

Etta panted her way toward speech, toward instinctive reassurance for her daughter. Bethany had been colorsplashing on her tablet at the table while Etta was about to get breakfast started. It was a lovely morning, in a series of lovely mornings.

"Mommy! Mommy!" Bethany found her words first. She bound out of her chair toward where her mother had fallen.

Etta tried to wave her back, like there really might be an invisible assailant loose in their posh kitchen. But Bethany was on her and stroking her mommy's hair, a reflexive move to comfort her somehow, to do *some*thing. Amidst all the shock, Etta swelled with love and pride. Her little girl was just so perfect.

"It's okay, sweetheart." Etta pushed up into a kneeling position and took Bethany's small hands in hers. "Mommy just fell." A lie. And she'd also just referred to herself in the third person, a habit Bethany had lately pointed out was "sillybones." Etta amended, "I tripped on something. I'm sorry I scared you."

"Are you all right, Mommy?" Eyes still big, but no tears in them. She'd been frightened but wouldn't let herself cry until she knew what had happened.

Etta didn't know what to tell her. This was . . . impossible?

But the sensations, the impacts—she recognized them. She took a quick physical inventory. She touched her chest, her jaw. Already she knew there would be no swelling. The echoes of the blows still rang in her bones. Yet the hurt was a phantom hurt. She felt no real pain from the strikes. These had just been approximations of the impacts, to let her know they had occurred.

Right now she should be advising her Brute, passing strategy through the link, outthinking the enemy.

Etta shook herself and took her daughter into her arms. The blows had been ethereal, empty recordings of sensations, but she'd hit the refrigerator hard and dropped gracelessly to the tiles. Her shoulder throbbed, and she had banged her knee but good.

Bethany didn't let loose with her tears, but she made snuffling sounds, and Etta held her and rocked her, and these contacts felt utterly right and true. She loved her child with absolute conviction. And Bethany loved her right back. All was paradisiacal.

Except that at age thirty-six Etta Pryor's military career was over a decade behind her. She was no longer linked to her Brute. None of this should have happened here in her kitchen this morning.

Dr. Keita was a "not" doctor, and Etta liked that. It meant he led off assuaging her worst fears. It was not cancer, not a brain tumor, not Switcher's.

Etta sagged with relief in the humming white room. Dr. Keita had made time for her. She could afford a doctor who did that. Just like she could afford her home and, of immeasurably greater importance, could afford to give Bethany a stable and pleasurable life.

She had handled her post-military finances brilliantly. Everyone had tried to write a memoir, but her war account had been the best, just the right mix of the personal and combat gamesmanship. The money had paid for the in vitro, and by now her capital had taken on self-perpetuating life. She would never know want again. Bethany would *never* have to know it.

But she still didn't know what had happened this morning. And, it emerged, neither did Dr. Keita once his warmly related "nots" had run their course. Her financial stature couldn't alter these circumstances. It was no one's fault.

Still, she was the one who had to bring up the unmentionable subject.

Softly, barely above the efficient hum of the room's diagnostic equipment, she asked, "Is it . . . my biomoss?"

Dr. Keita moved around on his stool, evidently unable to find any comfortable position. "I don't have the instruments to make readings." He kept a mellow tone, but Etta heard both shame and outright rage beneath the words. "Biomoss is *proprietary*"—he pronounced every syllable with crisp precision—"and the military won't let us look."

Etta knew this. While she had vividly described the particulars of linkage, her book gave away no clues about the nuts and bolts workings of biomoss. She explained *that* it worked, not how it worked. She had never been provided with those details. But as soldiers in the program, she and her fellows had learned a thing or two about biomoss.

"But . . ." The doctor made a humming sound of his own, musing and confused. "Your counterpart is dead. Correct?" It was a question he didn't need to ask.

The biomoss in her head was linked to nothing. Its removal was an elaborate procedure, one with a tiny but appreciable fatality percentage. At best, the operation would lay her out for six months. That was half a year of Bethany's life, half a year of Mommy being a limp semi-vegetable—if all went optimally.

Etta fidgeted inside her medical gown. She answered the question with an answer she didn't need to give. "Yes. My Brute was killed."

She was mostly okay with thinking back on the war, on her special slice of it. But just as often she remembered the good times, the camaraderie, as well as squirming across the jungle floor, keeping within range of her Brute.

The comradeship had been intense. They were a lone unit, culled from the ranks. Nobody could figure out the criteria, what traits got them picked. Maybe it was just their willingness to undergo the procedures. Reger had speculated about "invincibility syndrome" or wholesale self-destructive tendencies.

Still, the ones who volunteered to be the Brutes—Etta still couldn't grasp how a person could do that. She wondered about it in her memoir, poetical passages questioning the nature of self and other easily digestible existential dilemmas. Some critics had called her the Thomas Kinkade of war memoirists. The public gobbled up her words.

Reger, Hollen, Maalouf, Barber, Stills . . . Twenty-eight in all. Soldiers. Kids, it seemed now. Full of juice. Burning with war fever, or at least the primal urge to do *some*thing. Maybe if terror hadn't turned the whole world into a battlefield, Etta and her fellows, in an alternate timeline, might have become criminals. Or terrorists themselves. This was not something she had pondered in her book.

She had accepted the offer to enter the program, and they'd pulled her out of Brighton and told her what they were going to do to her. The insertion procedure was apparently vastly more simple than extraction, practically outpatient. The group was to train in Florida, or what unsubmerged remainder of the state people had no choice but to call Florida. These were some of the good times she let herself recall. There had been a certain frat house wildness to their training. They quartered together. Drills consisted of weapons training—nonsmart weaponry. Etta described her first time handling such an instrument as "putting a musket's butt to one's shoulder, physically squeezing a trigger, and dreading the explosion and randomly vectored shot."

Otherwise, there wasn't much discipline within the program. The officers seemed more like observers.

Fourteen of the group had undergone biomoss insertion. The other fourteen were still receiving treatments of a wholly different order. The vats were on the base, and half the group went to them about every third day. And every time, they came back bigger. Bulkier. Roped with more muscle. It soon surpassed anything Etta had ever seen, bodies of such mass and strength they were grotesque . . . and beautiful. These were Conans, Hulks, Hydes.

But eventually they settled on a term: Brutes.

Another thing about the Brutes—they got less mentally sophisticated each time. That was the aspect Etta always had the hardest time grasping. Those fourteen were told their faculties would be impaired, but they had volunteered anyway.

As the vat treatments continued, the biomoss started to function. The links began, just as their half of the group had been told would happen.

Etta had illustrated that process in her book. Her biomoss—that mysterious gooey bioweapon-level substance—had somehow been directed to fix upon a particular Brute. Each of the handlers had a pre-selected partner. Hers was, or had been, a man named Conroy. She had interacted with him, talked at length in their barracks. They shared backgrounds and war stories and fraternized in the casual atmosphere. But those conversations ebbed and then stopped altogether after about six visits to the vat. Conroy's body swelled, and his mind shrank. He had difficulty forming complete sentences. His expression became dull, his responses simplistic, then simpleminded.

Etta's fellow insertees never received official advisement as to the biomoss' origins. But the medtechs weren't uniformly close-lipped, and it became a midnight-around-the-campfire ritual among the soldiers to share what scraps of information they'd gleaned.

The smart money, their modest gestalt eventually decided, was on permaculture. Specifically, plant guilds. More specifically—and about as far as they could conjecture before it all collapsed into layman guesswork—nanomechanical oscillations. That was: seeds talking to each other. Someone had broken open the suspect but apparently long-held secrets of plant "telepathy," and biomoss was the ultimate result.

The human application of that breakthrough was, of course, the much more astounding accomplishment. But none of them on the base ever figured that conundrum out. Etta tried to research it privately long after the fact, but adapting the human brain to communicate through vibrations seemed hopeless. Fine-tuning that process so one mind linked only to one specific other seemed like wizardry. Yet, evidently, the military had had just the right wizards in their bioscience division.

There was a sense among the group that they were operating outside military ethics. Young Etta Pryor had thought the whole thing vaguely unreal.

Buck Reger emerged as the resident philosopher/cynic. He called them all experiments in a mad scientist's lab, experiments who *knew* they were experiments, ones who'd entered into the exercise willingly. He was handsome, smirking, intelligent, the kind of guy Etta had slept with in college; and with the roughhouse ambiance on the base, Etta followed that same pattern. She hopped into bed with Reger, and no officer tried to stop her. Like most of her college lovers, Reger was selfish. And as with past bedmates, Etta didn't go back for a third time. Buck Reger met her refusals with a vast indifference.

It was Reger, however, who made a major deduction. Between weapons drills, the non-Brutes played a lot of basketball. It got competitive. Everybody played six moves ahead. Reger halted one afternoon mid-court, the orange ball balanced on ten fingers. He looked around and offered one of his self-satisfied smiles.

"We're all exceptional strategists," he said.

Etta saw right away that he was correct. All fourteen with the biomoss insertions thought quickly and clearly. They had also already proven themselves in combat situations.

They could do the thinking, as their Brutes could not. By now Etta was receiving sense-impressions from Conroy. All of them were linked to their respective counterparts. The base's officers interviewed the handlers, asked them how it felt.

"They've never done this before," Reger said. He grinned at this further deduction. "We're the first."

The Brutes by now were gargantuan. They too finally ran drills, strength tests. Etta watched the man who'd been Conroy pick up the front end of a truck. She felt it too, in that strange remote way, feeling without feeling. The next day she was told to direct the Brute's actions. It was like mental experiments you did as a kid, seeing if any of your friends had ESP or could light a candle just by thinking it. Etta stared at the great mound of warrior muscle that was Conroy, screwed up her face in concentration, and *thought* the orders she'd been given at him.

Immediately, he went into the exercise routine. Etta watched amazed, also following his movements through the link. He obeyed each step. It was incredible. The linkage was strongest when he was physically active.

Theo Hollen was another of the handlers. After all fourteen of them had put their Brutes successfully through their paces, he approached Etta. He seemed the shiest of the group, a lanky, unpretentious male. Etta, for no good reason, had thought he was gay.

"We will be sent into combat," he said to her privately in the barracks one night. He didn't make announcements the way Reger did. "All of us linked, armed with nonsmart weapons. We will be going somewhere where tech is useless."

"Useless?" Etta was half undressed. Hollen sat on the foot of her bunk.

He had soft gray eyes, the lashes long. He blinked at the wall beside her head. If he was good-looking, he had no idea he was, and self-confidence was what Etta had always keyed on. So Theo Hollen was something of a blank to her.

"Yes," he said with some urgency. "Our biomoss is organic. We know that much about it. The Brutes are merely enhanced humans. We've trained with purely mechanical weapons, no chips, no correcting tech."

Etta thought it a neat bit of analysis, though she didn't know why he'd come to her with it. The group speculated constantly about the purpose of the program. The officers answered no questions.

She was about to say something when Hollen looked directly at her and blurted, "Can I get into bed with you?"

It actually wasn't far off the beam from sexual negotiations on the base. Things were frank and playful. But Hollen at that moment had an intensity about him that gave Etta pause. And that hesitation apparently was enough to deflate his courage. He muttered something about just joking and slunk off to his bunk.

Summer camp behavior was disturbing in an adult. Worse in a soldier. But Theo Hollen's prediction about where they were going had turned out to be absolutely accurate.

If Bethany wasn't sensing that her mother was worried, Etta feared her daughter would sense that she was worried about making her child worried. It was one of those Möbius strips of motherhood—a fear you couldn't get on the other side of.

Then again, Etta had never had to face something like this since Bethany had been born. Of course, she'd had no reason to ever expect her biomoss to reactivate, if that was what was happening, even though it *couldn't* be happening. But Etta had so carefully arranged her life, made her world meticulously secure for her daughter's well-planned arrival. Etta had survived a problematic childhood populated with deficient parents. She had every confidence she could do better on her own. And these first four years of Bethany's glorious life had proven her right.

She told herself the car would smart itself out of any trouble if something happened to her behind the wheel. She'd promised Bethany this outing. Weather forecasting had in Etta's lifetime become an oracular science, but a day of local safezone climate had been predicted. Etta had promised her darling daughter the river, and by gum she was going to have it.

They sang on the way. Between pop tunes and cornball folk songs Bethany asked precocious mind-bending questions about random subjects.

"Where does light go when it's turned off?"

"How heavy is purple?"

"If I was a mermaid, would you still love me, Mommy?"

They were lovable questions. Etta did her best to answer and turned her answers into jokes when appropriate. She erred on the side of honesty with her child, aware that the lies piled up on her in her own girlhood had led, not indirectly, to her hell-raising teen years, and those years into military service. She didn't regret her military career, nor her participation in the handler/Brute program. But she wanted Bethany equipped to face every major decision of her life on her own terms.

The park along the river was full of other families. That was how Etta thought of Bethany and herself: as a *family*. No caveats, no disclaimers.

They spread a blanket and unloaded food, and Bethany went tearing across the grass. The sky was an almost unnerving blue, and there was birdsong and a gentle breeze. The river gurgled. Children frolicked, and Bethany fell in with temporary confederates who might as well have been lifelong friends. Etta sipped tea and nibbled a sandwich and watched her daughter. She chatted with other grownups enjoying the anomalous beautiful day. She had an ease with people which somehow had never translated into a close circle of friends.

And the whole time she feared that phantom contact. They had been blows, physical strikes to the body. If her long dormant biomoss was indeed active, then whatever it was reading had suffered those hits. But her 'moss could link to one thing and one thing only: her Brute. Yet that linkage had ended with Conroy's life over ten years ago.

The day of riparian splendor came to an end, and Etta drove her sated and exhausted daughter home. They lived on a gentrified street. The tension had eased in Etta somewhat. Dr. Keita yesterday had suggested, without actually suggesting it, that PTSD might account for her episode. Long-delayed combat stress. Etta could think of a thousand reasons why this would not be. But she did not—could not—rule out the possibility.

She pulled into the drive, unbuckled the sleeping Bethany, and lifted her out of the car.

Which was when she was struck in the stomach, a dead-on full-strength gut shot. No hurt accompanied the blow, but the painless translation was startling and traumatic enough that she doubled halfway over. Bethany slipped alarmingly in her arms and woke with gasp. Etta backpedaled two fast unsure steps, then fell.

She landed on her pert backside, putting all her effort into keeping any part of her child from colliding with the ground. As she sat on the cement, winded and frightened, she was struck again, in the ribs just below her left breast. Despite herself, she flinched. Bethany, big-eyed, was almost nose-to-nose with her.

"Mommy, why did you fall again?" There was still some sleepiness in her voice, but Etta heard the deep disquiet beneath.

Two more invisible blows landed, but she didn't wince at either one. She worked a knee, then a foot underneath herself and stood, holding her daughter tenaciously in her arms.

"I'm just a little clumsy lately, sweetheart." Maybe that wasn't untrue. Maybe her clumsiness was simply mental. Post-traumatic stress disorder, finally come a-calling.

She carried Bethany into the house.

"Etta?" said the male voice, because nobody answered "hello" anymore.

In another century she could have hung up. But by setting her personal netter to search and contact Theo Hollen she had revealed her identity and committed to this action. Still, it felt like she was calling someone from grade school who'd had a terrible unreciprocated crush on her. Actually, that wasn't too far from the truth.

"Theo, I know it's been a long time . . ." she began, since there was absolutely no other way to begin.

"I feel like it hasn't been that long. Every time I read your book, it's like I'm interacting with you."

Every time? Why did that sound creepy to her? But the social niceties beckoned. "How are you, Theo?"

He had an answer for her, a long one. The facts were simple: never married; became a financial advisor. Etta let him go on until he started to double back over the past decade.

"I have a problem, Theo." She couldn't have gone to anyone else from the program who had survived. In her memoir she hadn't named her fellows by name, using clever monikers instead, but several former handlers had tried to sue her anyway, once her book started raking in the money and making redundant everyone else's war accounts.

She was surprised at her own gall in contacting Theo. Her name for him in the book was Howdy Dowdy.

"How can I help, Etta?" he asked as eagerly as she'd expected him to.

She hesitated one last time, then unloaded. It was mortifying, but the mortification had an element of comfort to it. She was revealing this bizarre embarrassing thing, but revealing it to someone who could at least understand the basics. Biomoss, so far as anyone knew, had never been used again once the terror heads and the blankzone were destroyed.

But when she had finished her account of the two incidents, it was Theo's turn to pause, and that silence made her cringe. Perhaps she had made a serious error getting in touch with him.

In a subdued tone he finally said, "I dream about Farmer sometimes. In the dreams he's still a Brute, but he can speak. It's ordinary domestic scenes. Eating breakfast together, walking the dogs."

Etta swallowed. "What does he say?" Her voice trembled slightly.

"He talks about how successful our mission was into the blankzone.

And he wants to go on another one. He's trying to convince me to come along."

Etta had made an audio-only contact, but in that moment she wondered what Theo Hollen looked like. Others from their unit had crashed and burned, both financially and mentally. She'd seen Ching interviewed last year. She had contracted Switcher's Disease and was a frail doddering old woman at thirty-five. Theo was dreaming of Farmer, his dead Brute. Farmer had died just like she'd been told Conroy had, but Etta didn't dream about Conroy.

"Theo . . . I think Conroy is still alive." This was more than mortifying. This was a delicate momentous admission. Here she revealed her state of mind. But she had been driven to this conclusion. She still felt herself falling, felt Bethany slipping from her arms. Imagination cracked her daughter's skull on the concrete of the drive.

Theo said, "All the Brutes are dead."

"So we were told. I had two bullets in me. The shock had me delirious. I didn't know the mission was over until I was carried out on a litter."

"But . . ." Theo had a tremble of his own now. He took a breath, and it disappeared from his voice. "You felt the linkage break. You say so in your book. That could only happen if Conroy died."

She had written that. She'd *had* to. It was the memoir's denouement. Her editor had told her that moment needed to be in there. And it wasn't a lie, not quite. After she had been wounded, bleeding on the jungle floor, she had felt a wrenching, a disconnection. When the other surviving handlers described the same sensation, she understood what had happened. But some part of her always wondered if she had simply settled on the interpretation, finding it convenient, needing that finalization. Certainly it had boosted the quality of her book.

"I believe my Brute is still alive," she said, and saying it made her stubborn, confident or crazy.

Theo didn't hesitate this time. "Then we better try to find him."

Etta Pryor felt relief, then: "Sorry. *We?*"

Now she knew what Theo Hollen looked like these days. He was a bit chunkier, with wiry gray in his spiky hair. He moved slower but still as if he were nervously negotiating his way through a crowded room. His socially awkward tics were all intact.

Etta had been unable to stop him from coming. It was a ridiculous distance to travel, and she had no right calling in such a favor from him. All he had said was, "Nonsense. Nonsense."

Perhaps he had been hoping all these years for some way back into her life. Despite her unease, Etta brought him to her house. He complimented her at every turn. She looked beautiful. Her home was elegant. The cup of coffee she made for him was amazing.

But when they sat together in the kitchen and she described in detail the two incidents, Theo's unremarkable features lost their goofy cast. His face hardened. His long-lashed gray eyes glinted with militarily acute concentration.

Once again she experienced a sense of unburdening. Theo didn't coo and coax her. He just listened and made notes on his handheld netter.

When she'd finished, he took a long swallow of coffee, set aside the imported mug, and opened a map. It popped up from his device and hovered over the table. Etta saw with a start that it was her street and her neighborhood. A portion of the map changed color.

"That's the radius," Theo said. "Beyond that we couldn't read our Brutes." The map suddenly animated, traffic moving on the holographic streets, public access data pouring from every structure. "This is the time of your first event. And this"—the scene's details shifted—"is the second. Conroy was within this area at those times. We just need to find out where he was and what he was doing."

Etta couldn't help the gratitude she felt. Someone believed her. Yet she couldn't completely shake the disquiet. Theo's job as a financial advisor made him a productive member of society. He didn't act like a stalker or an obsessive. But maybe his relative normality was a cover, a shuck. Maybe he was "believing" her for his own ends.

She hated her distrust. Not one other person from the old program would have made this effort for her.

They studied his map awhile, discussing the possibilities. The afternoon was waning. Bethany was away on an extended playdate. It was amusing that she had more friends than Etta did. Or it should have been amusing.

Eventually Etta rubbed her eyes and leaned back in her chair. She hadn't even taken Theo into her expansive living room, rather consigning him to the kitchen, like he was the help.

"Etta, there's something you need to do."

In a suddenly cautious voice she asked, "What's that?"

"Try to read Conroy. See if he's within the radius right now."

It was something she should have done already, before even contacting Theo. She knew this, yet had hidden it from herself.

"Of course . . ." she murmured. She closed her eyes and reached out. On a deep level she listened for those supposed nanomechanical oscillations, like a seed conspiring with a friendly neighbor plant to produce weed-killing volatiles. The linkage was empty. She felt she had just tried to exercise an atrophied muscle. She opened her eyes. "Nothing."

He nodded, features still a hard mask.

She had a sip of cold coffee. "You ever hear from any of the others?"

That snapped him out of his fugue of concentration. He blinked long lashes at her. "Not for a long time. At first I tried to stay in touch, but after a few pretty nasty rebuffs I learned my lesson. Unless someone from the unit contacts me first, I just leave it alone."

Etta nodded. "Can I ask you something more personal?"

"Yes." He squirmed slightly on the other side of the table with a puppy dog eagerness.

She asked, "Did you have your biomoss removed?"

"I did. Farmer was shot forty-one times. Or at least he lived through the first forty-one shots. I felt every one, in the way we always felt things. Remotely. Ghost sensations. After the war I kept thinking about those last inputs and how my 'moss might still have them stored up somehow. I was very close to Farmer in a way. I didn't want to experience his death again. So I underwent the extraction procedure. I'm glad I did it."

Etta nodded again.

They made plans for tomorrow. Then Theo went off to his hotel.

It wasn't a matter for the police, obviously, so this investigating had an amateur sleuth vibe to it. The streets nearby Etta's home had been gentrified in recent years, which suggested that the neighborhood hadn't always been this well off. It hadn't. Parts were still somewhat sketchy. Some of those stretches lay within the biomoss' readable field.

She and Theo split up. Today she had arranged for a daycarer, one Bethany liked a lot, to come to the house.

A row of partially abandoned commercial buildings looked promising, but they would be the hardest to gain access to. She and Theo would investigate them together toward the end of the day. She went about her inquiries dutifully. She would have thought that not having Bethany around would leave her less leery of another barrage of phantom impacts, but she was still anxious. What was Conroy doing? Who was striking him those blows?

But such questions were set dressings. They barely hid the real drama of the piece. The bigger questions were: How could Conroy still be alive? And: If he really was dead, then what the hell was happening to her?

Etta continued to insist to herself that she wasn't crazy or traumatized. She remembered the mission into the blankzone and everything that had led up to it. The officers at the secret Florida base briefed the unit a week before it deployed. For that week they were on standby. Their nonsmart weapons training was complete. The handlers were all able to manipulate their Brutes. Now came the operational details.

The blankzones had been popping up for months, though none but the highest military levels knew about them. These were pinprick areas of full tech blackout. Intelligence determined that phased array optics had aggressively effected this phenomenon.

Satellites, always on the watch for the newest terror sector, couldn't penetrate. Micro-chaff, launched repeatedly above the zone by nonsmart mortars, was apparently responsible for that undetectability. The PAO camouflage was projected upward against this airborne screen.

But the absence of any—*any*—technological signature was its own red flag. That effect had evidently been coupled with a sophisticated, localized EMP event.

Lately, the blankzones were occurring in South America. And they were growing larger. Most recently, a town had winked out. No one died, but nothing with a chip would function. Nothing smart worked. It was, simply, a crippling. Its implication was clear and ominous. Once an area was blanked of tech, the perpetrators could do as they liked within it, undetected.

Or the scope might be far broader for this new combined terror weapon. Blank the world back into the Stone Age, or what would certainly feel like it to most populations. Thus, the preemptive attack: soldiers inserted with purely organic biomoss and armed with clickety-clack guns, and the creation of monstrously strong but correspondingly witless Brutes.

Satellites found a fresh area of unnatural quietude on the busy globe. Again it was in South America, in jungly reaches. Twenty-eight soldiers were dropped and left to slog through the wilderness. Etta remembered her disbelief, her horror, that generations of military personnel had fought wars this way, without a smart anything to guide or advise or warn.

They advanced like warriors through the bush, the largest number they could deploy without giving themselves away.

Reconnoitering and raiding the camp was the next phase. The Brutes went in, with the handlers laying down cover fire. Once the fireworks started, it was a battle like any other. Mayhem and death. The enemy was armed with nonsmart weaponry as well. But they also had to face the formidable, purely physical juggernauts which came pounding out of the jungle, nightmarish humanoid beasts who crushed bodies and skulls with bare hands.

Etta had directed Conroy. In combat, the link was intense. The Brutes were systemically dismantling the encampment. It was going beautifully. Then Etta had been surprised by a gunman who'd slipped through the tightening line and plugged her with two bullets in the thigh and her right side. After that she was down. The casualties mounted as she writhed senseless on the ground. Soldiers and terrorists died, as had been happening for many years now.

At some point, she felt the linkage break.

The mission succeeded, at a high acceptable cost. The phased array optics gear was either captured or destroyed. During the debriefing Etta never learned one way or the other. Of equal importance was the wholesale slaughter of the terror network heads who had evidently gathered in the blankzone. They must have thought their strategy granted invincibility. The long-standing Whac-A-Mole theory of terrorism—that if you killed one or ten, that same number would be immediately replaced and nothing real would be accomplished—at last came apart. Apparently Etta's unorthodox unit had killed the most important minds behind the worldwide terror campaigns. Activities fell off considerably. Hostilities regressed to quaint 9/11-era levels.

Details of the operation were eventually declassified by the military. These amounted to bragging rights. The move allowed Etta to write her memoir.

Today's mission was far easier. Etta worked the streets, asking innocuous questions of store clerks and bartenders. She was looking for a lost dog, she said. She'd seen a strange big man in the area the past two days. She even named the times of day. She was afraid he had abducted her dog. Had anyone seen him?

Nothing came of her queries, but she still felt she was accomplishing something. At least she was being active, not passive. She'd had things very good for a long while. Now she had to fight for what she'd gained. Fight for Bethany.

Evening came on, and she met Theo at a cafe at the prearranged time. He hadn't contacted her during the past few hours, which meant his canvassing had been as fruitless as hers.

He confirmed this conclusion with, "Well, no Brute-sized sightings in the neighborhood. So far."

Etta tried not to let herself get demoralized. She was hungry enough for a snack. Theo ordered a milkshake, explaining his weight gain. Still, Etta thought as she took a moment to really assess him, he had aged well. He looked healthy. Maybe he even had a few helpful character lines on his face now.

"Hey," he said suddenly, "I thought of something. You asked if I ever heard from others from our program. Like I said, I have from time to time. But the last one was Buck Reger."

"Reger?" Etta said the name a little too sharply. In her book Buck Reger was rechristened Zorro, a fighter with a dandy's conceit and wit. She had also made mention of her suspicion that Howdy Dowdy, Theo's nom de plume, was jealous of the two times she and Zorro had gone to bed together.

Abruptly her face was hot with an embarrassed blush.

Theo either didn't notice or didn't call attention to her reaction to spare her further embarrassment. Conversationally, he said, "Yes. Less than a year ago. He wanted financial advice. Said he had, or was going to soon have, a sizable amount of capital. He sounded off, though. Like he was trying to convince himself of something."

Etta had abandoned her lemon muffin halfway through. "What do you think it meant?"

"That he was doing drugs. Or booze had gotten to him. When people who sound unstable talk about large sums of money, it's usually delusional to one degree or other." Theo said this matter-of-factly. "I didn't hear from him again."

It was time to hit the row of semi-derelict commercial buildings. Etta paused to call Bethany. Her daughter looked grave on the netter's screen. "You didn't fall again, did you, Mommy?"

Etta grinned because she could tell her child the truth for a change. "No, honey. I didn't. I'll see you soon. I love you."

"I love you too."

Anything more she said would probably only distress Bethany. *I love you too* was the natural end of conversations between them.

She and Theo set out into the gathering night.

It started to feel seriously hopeless when they met with their third welded shut industrial door. These structures had been warehouses or cheap manufactories, and now they were just eyesores, destined for inevitable demolition as the city continued to gentrify.

"Goddamnit," Etta muttered.

"Keep up," Theo said, footsteps crunching away toward the next building. He wasn't being the forlorn puppy. For whatever reason he was taking this task, and thereby her, quite seriously.

Etta silently castigated herself. She felt she had somehow manipulated him. He had flown practically across the continent to be here, and she had nothing to offer him but her bizarre predicament and the questionable belief that Conroy was still alive.

Then again, she had never seen her Brute's dead body. The mop-up team had arrived after the blankzone's field was disabled and had flown her straight out.

Etta's foot slid in the grit of the weedy lots fronting the buildings. She let out a gasp. Theo turned around sharply.

"Is it happening?" he asked. "Do you feel the blows?"

She shook her head. Unease bloomed in her. "But I think I feel . . . him." It was true. She *thought* so. The old remote mental pathways seemed now to twang with life. The oscillations might be back on line.

"How near is he?" Theo demanded. "Let's have a direction, soldier." There was no mockery in his tone.

She pointed ahead. A blunt structure bulked against the night.

Other people milled in the area, murmuring, shuffling. Homeless folks maybe. Etta was accustomed to a general sense of security. Recent events notwithstanding, that feeling of safety had prevailed for years. It had allowed her to bring Bethany into this world. But this underlit street in this shabby part of town undermined that security.

Theo moved quickly, and she kept pace this time. The building's lowest windows were barred and dark, but there was light from an upper story. Shambling shapes moved down one side of the structure. Etta paused at the mouth of the alley, but only to let her eyes adjust to the deeper dimness. She had the sense that Theo was picking out potential targets. He didn't take her hand, but they moved in lockstep along the narrow piss-smelling way.

Halfway down there was an open door.

The light which shone out into the alleyway wasn't inviting. Neither was the atmosphere when Theo and Etta entered without hesitation. It was a close, rancid air. They climbed steps. Someone lay snoring on one of the landings. Above, Etta heard the sounds of a crowd. More, she felt a strengthening of the link. It pulled tight in her, like a string being wound on a violin.

They went through another door at the top of the stairwell, into a wash of revelry and ferocity. Etta saw instantly what was going on here. A fighting ring stood in the center of the wide warehouse space. Spectators had assembled. The blood sport was underway.

Theo caught her arm as she started toward the roped off fighting area. "Easy," he said by her ear. "I don't see a Brute. Do you?"

Two figures were exchanging gymnastic blows in the ring. Both rippled with muscle, but they were puny creatures compared to the augmented grotesqueries Etta and Theo had known during the war, for that one famous operation.

"No," she said. "But Conroy's here! I have to—"

"And we're overdressed for the occasion. Let's hang back and recon, okay?"

She saw that they didn't fit in, even wearing casual clothing. The crowd was rough. This was no official sporting event. The onlookers howled and shouted and threw sympathetic punches at the air. There was no seating. Paper money was changing hands rapidly. Whoever was staging this had to be getting a piece of that, Etta figured. Theo steered her behind the jostling throng. A few looks, suspicious and indifferent, were thrown back at them, but no one made a move their way.

The fight was brutal. When it was done, one man was down and had to be carried off. Blood spattered a stone floor.

A moment later Etta's throat closed. An enormous figure was being led out onto the floor. The crowd erupted with savage cheers.

"There's Conroy." She barely heard herself say it.

"Yes. And there's Reger."

Theo's words startled her, but she peered through the mass of bobbing heads and saw Buck Reger walking with Conroy toward the improvised ring. Even at a distance she recognized him, a confidence in his stride.

Why was *he* here? Why—

The crowd's roar only mounted, becoming deafening. Another combatant was approaching the fighting area from another direction. He was tremendously muscular, surely enhanced, but Conroy was still half again his size. The spectators were in a frenzy by the time the two fighters entered the ring. Undoubtedly this was the main bout, the reason all these ne'er-do-wells had come here tonight.

She turned to Theo but found him speaking into his netter, of all things. She couldn't hear a word he said. Their investigation had succeeded. She was still stunned by the sight of Conroy and Reger. She needed to find out what the hell was going on here.

Etta started forward through the bodies as the fight was set to commence. The crowd surged, and she felt its collective ferocious strength. But it was Conroy who took her attention. The linkage was suddenly strong, a thrumming connectivity. It had been this way in training during intensely physical exercises, more so in combat when they had gone into the blankzone.

A bell indicated the start of the bout, though it might have just been two pieces of metal clanged together. Certainly there was no ref in the ring with the two competitors. Etta steeled herself for a blow, even as she struggled to move forward, but Conroy landed the first punch. The other contestant rolled with the glancing shot, spun back up from the floor with a crazed grin on his face, and chopped twice across Conroy's massive chest.

Spectral echoes of those blows reverberated through Etta. But she didn't stumble this time. Someone in the crowd elbowed her hard, and she shoved back roughly, ready to call on old combat skills if necessary.

Suddenly Theo was at her side, helping her cut a way toward the ringside. His gray eyes glinted once again with determination.

She got a nearer look at Conroy. She had never before seen someone alive who she had presumed was dead. It was a surreal experience. Her Brute even *looked* like something reanimated. His face—attractive before his visits to the enhancing vats, Etta remembered—was a cruel topography of corrugations and scars. He was still a mountain of a man, but now Etta could see the slackness of some of his muscle groups. He didn't move well either. He lumbered about the ring. His roundhouse punches didn't connect, but Etta felt every strike he received. There were no rules here. Conroy's opponent inflicted harm any way he liked.

"This is close enough!" Theo was shouting in her ear now. Again he took her arm.

He was right, Etta realized. Was she going to intervene here? This crowd would never let her interrupt the fight. At least she could get a closer look at Reger.

Conroy's appearance shocked her. But Reger, standing outside the ring only twenty strides away, truly looked like warmed-over death. His features were gaunt and parchment-like. His eyes seemed like soulless hollows. He maintained a careful posture, but the poise, she felt sure now, was all bluff. Theo had probably been right in his assessment. Something, dope or booze, had eaten Reger alive.

The survivors of the handler program had all done different things after the military. Buck Reger evidently had become an underground fight promoter, making some kind of miserable living off his freakshow charge.

Etta glared unseen at Reger's ghastly smirking face as she withstood her Brute's injuries. This was how she had monitored Conroy's condition during combat. Then she turned both her gaze and focus on the ring.

It was an unbalanced contest, one surprisingly that didn't favor Conroy. Once, this warrior had been formidable, nearly unstoppable. Now he was a foundering hulk. No glimmer of intelligence showed on his battered face, just dumb animal awareness and resignation. He threw his useless punches by rote. His limber adversary let a blow land occasionally, just to keep the crowd in it.

Etta, jaw setting and teeth tightening, reached through the link. She remembered how Conroy had moved, how his center of gravity and mass could be used to fluid and deadly effect. He might be a heap of meat, but he could move with balletic grace and speed, when properly directed.

His jacked up, grinning antagonist went at Conroy without a plan of any depth. After a moment of study his patterns were obvious. Etta told Conroy where to stand, told him to wait, and told him to let go with a hammer fist at the right second. Conroy did as instructed. Etta fancied she heard the meaty smack of the blow over the tumult. Conroy's foe dropped to his knees, a look of incredulity on his face.

Etta didn't have her Brute kill the bastard, since the man probably wasn't looking to murder Conroy. But she sent a command through the link, and Conroy pounded a brick-sized fist across the fighter's jaw, one blow, breaking bone but not killing.

The arena went wild.

Again the crowd surged. Etta didn't feel drained after using the linkage—rather, exhilarated. The throng was going mad, screaming and cheering. The second fighter was rolling on the bloodied ground, helpless. Conroy gazed into the middle distance.

"We need to get somewhere safe!" Theo yelled. This time he did take her hand. Etta was surprised when he hauled her forward, ducking through the ropes, into the ring itself. Behind, she heard what might have been an added commotion, something beyond the frenzied fight crowd noises.

As she and Theo rushed into the open area, Reger turned. Those burned-out eyes widened. She stared at him. Zorro had long since lost his panache. He had all the flair of a wino now.

Conroy looked her way as well, and for just an instant Etta saw something she would willingly mistake for a smile flicker across his abused face.

Then the police raided the place.

It actually wasn't the cops, but military personnel. Theo Hollen still had contacts with command, and he had used them, and a platoon had shown up and taken Conroy and Reger away and left everybody else scrambling for the exits.

Etta and Theo followed to the hospital, where a lieutenant had told them Conroy was to be treated before eventually being transferred to a military base. She could have gotten to the hospital on her own. The intensity of the link had dwindled once the combat situation ended, but she could still feel the phantom sensations.

She talked at length to a doctor, with the same lieutenant present. Then she spoke to the officer, then went to find Theo.

She found him in mid-conversation, pacing a waiting area, addressing his netter in increasingly exasperated tones. She paused at an entryway, close enough to hear, ". . . I'm sure you love me. And I enjoy our time together. But I'm helping out a friend." He turned, saw Etta and rolled his eyes theatrically. "No. Sorry, Denise. I've got to go." He pocketed the device.

Etta said, "I didn't mean to interrupt. Or eavesdrop."

Theo waved, the gesture both aggravated and amused. "Hell, I seem to have this same conversation every four months."

"With the same woman?"

He stopped pacing abruptly. "Hardly. Every time one gets pushy, another comes along. I like the variety, but it has its downside." He regarded her with a wry smile. "Howdy Dowdy's not too bad with the ladies, it turns out."

He laughed, so she laughed with him, and felt mortified once again. But Theo came over and punched her arm, and it all felt okay after that.

She told him what she had learned.

Buck Reger was a hardcore kick addict. He was confessing almost faster than anyone could listen.

"He'd planned this well before the blankzone operation," she said to Theo. "He was a true cynic. He saw the commercial potential of a privately owned Brute. He'd also come into a little money, enough for bribes. He learned that the biomoss link could be severed or at least temporarily disabled. He planned to smuggle his own Brute off whatever field of battle our unit ultimately deployed to. Reger had deduced it like you had, Theo. He figured we were going into a tech-free sector, which would make the abduction that much easier. He'd bribed the mop-up crew. But his Brute died in combat. However, he was ready for that contingency. He took someone else's. He took mine. He incapacitated the link with a chemical overdose and had Conroy trafficked out of there."

Theo gaped. "Jesus. The balls on that guy!"

Etta shrugged. "Reger planned on being rich. Maybe he even kept Conroy on ice awhile. I'll bet the Brute would just sit in a shed and eat porridge for years if someone told him to. Maybe Reger even started to make some money on the black market fight circuit. That's probably when he contacted you. He had to already be on the kick by then."

"That stuff's bad news." Theo shook his head. "I had a girlfriend who got into it a couple years ago."

Etta felt a twinge as she tried to work with her reassessed impression of Theo Hollen. He wasn't after her romantically at all.

"How is Conroy?" he asked.

"He's been through a lot, over a long period. But he's tough. He'll be okay."

Theo said quietly, "I'm glad . . . one of them survived." No doubt he was thinking of Farmer, his own dead Brute.

At that moment an excited voice cut across the waiting area. "Mommy! Mommy!" People looked up and smiled as Bethany came dashing toward Etta. The daycarer followed.

Etta lifted her daughter, kissed her. She looked to the daycarer and said, "Thank you for staying on the extra hours."

His nod was more of a bow. "I can keep her later . . ."

But Etta had wanted to see Bethany. The day had been too long, the absence from her child too troubling. With Bethany in her arms she said to Theo, "Hey, I need to introduce you two."

Bethany was selective. She didn't treat every new grownup like a friend, and was the same way with other children. But she warmed to Theo. In fact, there seemed to be no warming period at all. Bethany was standing next to Theo holding his hand almost before Etta knew it.

Finally she said, "I was told I could go in and see Conroy. Bethany, you want to come with Mommy?"

"Mommy's calling herself Mommy again." Bethany said it to Theo, looking up at him with a knowing smirk. She was still holding his hand.

"Why don't you go see him alone?" Theo said. He gave Bethany a conspiratorial wink. "I'll tell this charming young lady all about the ins and outs of financial advisory."

Bethany acted unduly excited about the prospect. Etta left her daughter in the former fellow soldier's care and got into the elevator to go down one level to where Conroy was being treated for his injuries, some of them rather old.

The lieutenant had been unusually forthcoming to her earlier. He had told her the military had learned a few facts about biomoss in the intervening years, including its tendency to slowly decay. It was why her linkage to Conroy had at first been spotty. But it was unlikely the organic goo would ever break down entirely.

Buck Reger, in the midst of his runaway drug-withdrawal confession, hadn't yet said whether or not he'd known Etta lived in the area of the city where he had set up the illegal bout. Maybe he'd been trying to get to her personally, maybe not. Maybe he harbored addled feelings for her. Maybe not.

Before Etta stepped off the elevator one floor down, she had finally and irreversibly made her decision to have her biomoss extracted. It was too much of an unknown to still have inside her. The procedure would be costly, yes, in terms of time. Six months. But she would start to prepare Bethany for it now, and commence with the operation in, say, two or three months. Bethany could sleep in the same room with her during her recovery. Etta could afford that luxury.

Perhaps she would even have a friend around, now and then, someone besides a hired caregiver. Theo had told that woman Denise on his netter that he was helping out a friend, implying that that act was important. Important enough, seemingly, to jeopardize a romantic relationship.

But right now somebody might need *her* as a friend. She meant to unlink herself finally from her Brute. But that Brute was still in some damaged sense a man named Conroy. He was also a war hero.

Etta Pryor knocked once, then entered his hospital room.

When she retired from the military, Mia Swanson thought she'd left the battlefield behind. Now a mother of two and a high school cheerleading coach living in the Southwest, she's a world away from the bloody carnage of Iraq. But when returning from a cheer competition, a fifteen-passenger van full of high school cheerleaders in tow, she comes across a sight she'd hoped never to see again: a roadblock. Albuquerque is under quarantine. A virulent virus that turns its victims into slavering zombies has broken out. What's more, she and her team have all been exposed. But Mia isn't about to go down without a fight—and the infected horde are about to find out just what team spirit means to her cheerleaders.

NOT IN VAIN
★
by Kacey Ezell

ONCE UPON A TIME a very good friend had described a cheerleading competition as the seventh circle of hell. It was probably sacrilege for a cheerleading coach to feel that way, but Mia Swanson had to admit that her old flying buddy had a point. After eight hours of squealing, chanting, hyper high-schoolers throwing each other up in the air, tumbling down open hallways and quite literally bouncing off the walls . . . Mia had a headache. And there was still most of an hour left on their seven-hour drive back to Albuquerque from Colorado Springs.

Two hours, Mia promised herself. *Two hours and I'll be home, in a bathtub, waiting for Max and the girls to get home. We'll have dinner. It will be great.*

One of the most irritating things about this particular competition was that it had fallen on a Shooting Weekend. Once every other month or so, Mia and some friends and their families got together and went shooting out on White Mesa, just outside of Albuquerque. It was all

BLM land out there, and as long as they took precautions not to hit anyone or any animals, there were no restrictions. It had started before she retired from the Air Force a year ago, and it had rapidly become one of her favorite traditions.

Alas, retirement meant a new career, and a new career meant new commitments. Mia glanced over her shoulder at the teenagers sprawled in various seats in the fifteen-passenger van and smiled. Seventh circle of hell aside, this really was her dream job. These were good kids, and Mia was proud to coach them.

"What's that?" Jessa asked, sitting up and pulling her iPhone earbuds out of her ears, as if that would help her see better. Mia looked up and cursed lightly under her breath. Blue and red flashing lights stained the sky up over the next slight hill, and she'd been doing closer to eighty than seventy mph. She eased off the gas and began to brake, just as they crested the hill.

"A roadblock?" Mia could hear the incredulity in her own voice as she continued to slow the van. "Jessa, have you got signal? See if you can pull up the news." The senior immediately set to work as Mia pulled to a stop, rolling down her window as a uniformed officer approached her window.

"Officer. Good evening," Mia started. "What's going on? I . . ." She'd been about to disclose that she was armed, even though she hadn't exactly told the team that, and she was certain that she'd hear from some irate parents. It might even cost her the job, new as she was, but there had been no way Mia was going to be taking a three-day competition trip with a fourteen-hour total drive time with twelve teenagers and no weapon. No fucking thank you.

"I-25 is closed," the officer said, cutting her off abruptly. He appeared to be sweating, and his expression looked agitated.

"Just the road? Is there an accident?" Mia asked. Maybe they could cut over to Bernalillo and take one of the state highways down through Rio Rancho.

"City's under quarantine. Governor declared a state of emergency—" The officer abruptly stopped talking and started scratching vigorously at his throat, where his collar met his neck.

"Coach?" Jessa called. She and another of the seniors were huddled over her iPhone, the glow from the screen throwing a white, eerie light on their faces in the growing dusk.

"Not now, Jessa," Mia replied, trying to keep the patience in her voice. "Sir? Officer, are you all right?"

"No, what is on me? Oh God, they're all over me!" the man screamed, and then, to Mia's complete astonishment, he began to strip off all of his clothing.

"Officer, stop! There are children in this car!" Mia said, aghast. She glanced out the front window of the car, only to see two more half-naked officers coming toward them, shedding clothing and gear as they approached. "What the fuck is this?"

"Coach!" Jessa screamed. Mia turned in time to see a fourth naked man reaching in through the half-open window at them. She and two other girls flinched away from the window and his grasping, reaching hand. For no reason whatsoever, Mia noticed that his arm was covered in coarse, dark hair.

In her past life as a combat helicopter pilot, Mia had often faced situations where she had to make a decision quickly, and it had to be right or she and her crew could die. She'd thought that being a high school cheerleading coach would have been different. Apparently she was wrong.

The officer at her window had stopped cursing and began screaming. Keening, more like. When she was a kid, Mia had devoured Anne McCaffrey's Dragonriders series. In that series, when a dragon died, its fellows were said to raise a keen that damn near shattered eardrums with its sound. Mia could only imagine that sound was much like this one. That was the thought that flitted past her consciousness as she made her decision and acted. She thought of dragons crying out in mourning.

In one smooth, mechanical move, Mia removed her Ruger .45 from her concealed carry purse and put the gun against the head of the officer now reaching for her through her open window. The back of his head exploded outward, and Jessa and some of the other girls screamed, Mia supposed. She couldn't really hear, thanks to the fact that she'd just fired a gun in a mostly enclosed car. Then she turned and shot the man on the passenger side, still reaching for the girls through the window.

Then she turned and gunned the engine. The van leapt forward and slammed into the naked bodies of the two remaining officers. They went down and she felt the sickening crunch as her wheels went over one of them. Then she threw the van in reverse and backed up far enough to shoot the one whose skull she hadn't crushed.

Sound suddenly came back all in a rush. Behind her, cheerleaders were whimpering in shocked tones, while Jessa continued to call for her. Incongruously, the opening chords of Ellie Goulding's "Anything Could Happen" came out through the speakers, thanks to her iPhone plugged in to the van's radio. Mia couldn't help it. She started laughing.

"Coach?" Jessa asked again, her voice scared.

"It's all right, Jessa," Mia said. "Just give me a minute. I won't let them hurt you guys."

"N-no, we know that," Jessa said, though her voice trembled. "But I think you need to see this." She held out her phone. On it, a mobile news website projected the words Mia had been refusing to think.

"ZOMBIE OUTBREAK HITS LA, NY! Major cities under quarantine. States of emergency declared all over the nation . . ."

There was more, but Mia had seen what she needed to see. *Anything could happen, indeed, Ellie,* she thought as she handed the phone back to Jessa. "All right. Jessa, read the rest of the article and get anything useful out of it and any other news pages. Anything about cures, vaccines, instructions, whatever."

Mia put the van back into drive and rolled forward until she could pull off next to the roadblock. They'd just passed the exit to NM 550. They'd go back and take that exit, she supposed. "You guys stay here and keep a lookout for any other cars. If someone comes over the hill, lay on the horn. I've got to get some stuff."

The team was too shocked to argue as Mia took her gun and hopped out. First up were the downed officers' weapons: standard issue 9mm pistols. Mia grabbed the officers' gear belts as well. Might as well have somewhere to holster the 9s, she supposed. One of the officer's car keys had half spilled out of his pants pocket during his striptease, and Mia took the opportunity to look in the trunk of the APD car.

"Jackpot," she said lowly. The article had mentioned quarantine, so Mia hadn't wanted to take the officers' body armor, in case it had gotten blood on it when she'd killed them. Here, however, were spare tactical vests and two 12 gauge pump shotguns. She quickly took the items and headed back to the van. While her cheerleading team watched with wide, disbelieving eyes, she threw this loot, plus all the ammo she could find in the cars, into the empty passenger seat of the van. Then she went back and took the mini-igloo cooler that she'd found on the floorboard of the car. Inside were several bottles of water and glory of glories: a twelve-ounce can of Sugar Free Red Bull. She brought this back and started the van.

"Looks like we're taking a different route," she said as she wheeled her way back around. Luckily, there was no one else approaching as they took the exit off of I-25 onto NM 550.

It took a full ten minutes of driving in silence before one of the cheerleaders spoke up. As Mia might have suspected, it was Jessa.

"Coach?" Jessa asked, her tone steadier, but still uncertain. "Um . . . ?"

"What happened?" Mia asked, humor in her tone, despite everything. "Was that what you were trying to ask?"

Jessa tittered nervously, and a few of the others laughed in the growing darkness. The sun was sinking behind the desert mesas directly in front of them, and Mia had dug her dark Oakleys out of her purse.

"Well, yeah. I mean, that was pretty . . . um . . ."

"Weird?"

"Yeah, weird."

"Yeah," Mia agreed. "It was. I'll explain it here in a second, okay? I need to do a few things first. Actually, I need you all to do something for me. You all have your phones, right?"

A chorus of *yeses* filled the back seat.

"Okay," Mia said. "Of course you all do. I need you all to text your parents. Tell them that we didn't make it in to Albuquerque before the quarantine. Tell them that I'm taking you to a safe place to wait out the plague. Tell them that they can meet us at the following coordinates. Are you all ready?"

Another chorus of *yeses*.

Mia checked the note on her phone and read off: "North 38 degrees, 18 minutes, 6 seconds. West 111 degrees, 25 minutes, 12 seconds. Sam," she said, calling out her one senior male cheerleader. Sam, she knew, was an Eagle Scout. "Check everyone's phone and make sure they got it right before they hit send."

She heard a few sniffles, some more whimpers, but eventually, everyone did it. "Now, I need to make a phone call. I need you guys to be quiet."

Normally, Mia wouldn't dream of driving and talking on the phone in front of her team. It was setting a horrible example. However, she was not about to stop again before she had to in order to get gas. Luckily, they'd filled up in Santa Fe, so her tank was mostly full. She pulled out her phone and dialed her husband.

"Baby?" Max Swanson asked, picking up on the first ring. His voice was filled with anxiety and worry, and it damn near brought tears to Mia's eyes. She blinked furiously.

"I'm all right," she said quickly. "We didn't make it in to Albuquerque before they closed the Interstate."

"Oh, thank God," he said. "Neither did we. We just got the news on the radio and got packed up. We're bugging out to your mom's. We can wait here for you . . . wait . . . Hashim wants to talk to you," Max said, his voice strained.

Mia blinked. Hashim Noori was a very good friend. She'd met him in Iraq almost seven years ago. He'd been her interpreter then, but he'd since gotten a visa and moved to the U.S. He was a microbiology professor at UNM. Mia couldn't imagine what on Earth could have made Hashim interrupt her husband on the phone, but then, this morning she couldn't have imagined that she'd be bugging out in a zombie apocalypse scenario with her cheerleading team, either.

"Hashumi," Mia said into the phone. *"Salaam wa alaykum."*

"Walaykum salaam," Hashim said, his lightly accented English impatient. "Mia. I must ask you. You were in a city?"

"Yes, we were in Colorado Springs, at a cheerleading competition."

"There were many people there?"

"Yes, Hashim, why?"

Her former terp was silent for a long moment. "Mia. You have all been exposed. I have been reading messages on the Internet. This virus is unlike anything else. It is airborne like a cold, but it is also passed through the blood, or a bite or cut. Body fluids from an infected person."

Mia pursed her lips. "Infected person. Hashumi, do they strip down? Go crazy, like?"

"Yes, Mia. You have seen one?"

"Four. The cops at the roadblock. They attacked us."

"Mia!"

"They are dead," Mia said, her voice blank. She still wasn't thinking about the fact that she'd just killed four cops. "No one got bit or scratched."

"That is good, but Mia, this is very bad news. You must not join up with us."

"No, I think you're right. We'll follow along behind until we know if any of us have got it. How long?"

"The incubation period is approximately a week, but if the police are turning now . . . we should know in a day or two."

"Got it. May I speak to my husband again, please?"

"Of course. *Fe aman Allah.*"

"And you, my friend."

"Baby? How long till you can be here?" Max asked.

"I'll be there in about thirty minutes, but you have to go on ahead without me."

"What? No!"

"Baby, listen," Mia said, blinking quickly to keep the tears at bay and remain focused on the road in front of her. "I have twelve cheerleaders with me. We were just at a fucking cheer competition! You know what those things are like! Hashim said this thing is like a cold. We could all be infected, and I'm not bringing that around you or the girls. You go to Mom's. Hole up. Stay alive. I'll join you as soon as I know it's safe. I love you."

Max was silent. Mia could hear him breathing deeply, quickly. She heard the distant giggle of her youngest daughter through the phone. Finally, Max sighed.

"All right," he said, softly. "But you stay alive too, you hear me?"

"I will," she promised, knowing it wasn't in her control at all. Knowing it could already be a lie, she promised. "I'll see you soon."

They'd gone on ahead to White Mesa anyway. It was slightly out of the way, but Mia didn't want to take the chance of catching up to Max's group. After she'd finished talking to Max, her friend Allison had gotten on the phone and told her that they'd leave a cache of supplies at their normal shooting site. Mia had very nearly cried again, but she'd managed to hold it together. Mostly because the sun was fully down now, and she needed to concentrate in order to see the road and the unmarked turn-off to their shooting spot.

Though the sun had just gone down, the half moon was already riding high. The dust from their slow rumble up the dirt road filled the air as Mia stepped out of the van. The moon turned the dust a silvery color and she was abruptly reminded of another night, in another desert, under the same moon, but a world away.

"*Salaam wa alaykum,*" a voice called out of the shadows. Without thinking, Mia had the .45 up, pointing at the voice and the figure that emerged from the shadows. "*Qaf!*" she shouted.

"Mia, my friend, it is me," Hashim said, his hands up as he walked closer. Mia lowered her weapon and let out an explosive breath.

"Hashumi!" she said, walking forward to hug the wiry microbiologist. He might have hesitated for just a moment, but he'd been in the U.S. long enough that he hugged her back. "You idiot, I could have shot you!"

"That is why I called out," he said reasonably. She gave him a look.

"Hashim, you called out in Arabic. This has been a very weird day. I like Arabic, but it doesn't exactly calm me down."

Hashim laughed. Mia shook her head, but eventually she gave up and chuckled with him. "What are you doing here, anyway?" she asked. "I told you guys to go on ahead."

Hashim abruptly sobered. "I came to help you. You are one adult with twelve teenagers. It will be hard for you to keep them all safe alone. And if any are infected . . . well, I may be able to make a vaccine."

"Vaccine?" she asked, her voice rising, her eyes widening. "You can cure this?"

"Not cure, vaccinate," Hashim said. "We were working on something at the lab this week, when the first rumors started. UCLA sent us some samples and some protocols . . . it isn't hard, and it works. I have been vaccinated. But . . . this will be hard for you, I am afraid."

Mia took a long look at her old friend. On the surface, Hashim looked like any other professor of vaguely middle-eastern descent. He wasn't particularly big, and his wiry frame sometimes looked as if a stiff wind would blow him over. However, Mia knew him; she knew his history. She knew that he'd been hunted by Al Qaida since he was younger than her cheerleaders. She knew that he'd been shot, that his brother had died in his arms. She knew that he'd killed in his own defense before. He'd stood shoulder-to-shoulder with her brothers in arms, and that had earned him a ticket here, to the so-called promised land.

Hashim was hard. He would do whatever it took. He loved Mia like a sister, but she had no doubts that he'd shoot her between the eyes if she turned in order to keep himself and others safe. And that was just what she wanted.

"Tell me," she said, her eyes going flat as they hadn't been for years since she got back from Iraq.

"The vaccine must be made from infected spinal tissue," he said softly.

Mia closed her eyes momentarily while she absorbed this bit of information. Then she nodded, shoved the moral implications away in the back with the picture of the four dead cops and opened her eyes.

"All right," she said. "Let's take you to meet my team."

"Coyotes," Mia called in to the van. "Come out here. Time for a team meeting."

One by one, the cheerleaders filed out of the van. True to New Mexico form, the temperature had dropped rapidly as the sun went down and a few of the freshmen were shivering in their warm-ups. Mia hefted the duffel bag that Hashim had carried and opened it up. Inside were several sweatshirts and jackets. It looked like Allison had raided their camping gear and left it for them.

Mia let a smile cross her lips as she passed out the warmer clothing. Allison and Evan Dwyer were good friends. Evan had been a flight engineer in Mia's last squadron. The families had bonded over camping and shooting excursions, and Allison was one of the kindest people Mia'd ever met.

She was also a damn good shot with rifle, pistol and compound bow. And Evan had an arsenal that a gun dealer would envy. They were exactly who Mia would have picked for her zombie survival team. If she would have had time to pick a team, that is. She could think of no one better to help Max protect her girls, as well as their own baby girl, Kimber.

"All right, Coyotes," Mia said, bringing herself forcibly back to the present. The cheerleaders had distributed the warmer clothing and stood in a rough circle in front of her and Hashim.

"I promised I'd tell you what was going on, and I thank you for being patient while I figured it all out. Basically, here's the deal: the shit has well and truly hit the fan. Jessa, you want to brief us on what you found from the news sites?"

Jessa looked a bit startled, but she stepped right up. There was a reason she was the team captain. "Um, there's been an outbreak. Most people think it's a biological terror attack. People get sick, like the flu, and then they go crazy and strip, like those cops back on the highway. And then they act like zombies. They'll try to bite people . . . and if they do, then those people turn into zombies, too. That's about all I've got. The news sites are talking about a vaccine and a government response, but everyone's saying something different."

Mia nodded. That had been about what she expected. "Thank you, Jessa. I had you all text your parents and give them the coordinates of a town in Utah near a safe place. My family is headed to that place now. We've got supplies there. We can wait this out and survive there . . . but there's a problem.

"I won't lie to you guys. There's a good chance we've all been exposed. If we have, then we'll turn, like those cops."

The shocked looks travelled around the circle. Elia, a sophomore, stumbled and sat down, hard, on the ground. Tears began to stream down her face, and she wasn't the only one. Danny, a junior and her only other male cheerleader bent down and put his arms around her, whispering in her ear.

"Listen to me," Mia said. "Listen!" When she had their attention, she took a deep breath and went on. "I can't promise you won't get sick. But I promise you this. If you do get sick, I won't let you become like those things back at the highway. I won't let you hurt anyone."

She looked over at Hashim. He nodded slightly.

"This is Dr. Noori. He is a very good friend of mine. Dr. Noori has been vaccinated. He knows how to make more vaccine. But in order to do that, we have to use spinal tissue from infected people. I know that's horrible. I know it is, but that's the reality we have to deal with." Mia kept going, relentlessly driving the point home. They are adults now, she reminded herself. Their childhood ended two hours ago.

Elia raised her tear-wet eyes. "Coach?" she asked tremulously.

"Yes, Elia?"

"If I . . . if I get sick, can I . . . can Dr. Noori use me? Because I don't want to die for nothing."

The tears came hard and fast to Mia's eyes. She swiped savagely at her face and nodded, not trusting herself to speak as each of the cheerleaders, her cheerleaders, murmured their agreement with Elia. Even her two freshmen, Sonia and Dawn. Even at fourteen fucking years old, they were nodding vehemently. Mia waved them all in, and she subsequently found herself mobbed by twelve cheerleaders all trying to hug her and each other, all at once.

"I promise you," Mia said, her voice ragged and tear-soaked. "No one dies for nothing."

They stayed there for another hour or so while Mia handed out weapons and explained the basics of shooting to those who hadn't done so before. Both of the boys had been hunting, so they got the rifles that Allison had packed. Jessa got a shotgun, as did Cassidy, another senior. Yolanda and Bella, both seniors, got two of the cops' 9mm pistols, as did Gina and Mackayla, juniors. The younger girls were instructed to partner up with the seniors and stay with them. Mia distributed the body armor as best she could, but she kept most of it for herself and Sam. It was too big for pretty much everyone else.

When she was at least confident that no one would shoot themselves by accident, they piled back in the van and continued on down the road. Mia broke into the cops' Sugar Free Red Bull and savored the kick of the caffeine.

"Going to need to stop for fuel and supplies before too long," she said. They were still at over half a tank, but it didn't hurt to start making plans.

"How do you want to do that?" Hashim asked.

Mia pursed her lips. "I don't know yet," she confessed. "I suppose something will come to me. Ideally, we'd just walk in and pay for it as usual, but I don't know how ideal this situation's going to be."

"Coach?" Danny, the junior asked. Mia looked up and looked at him in the rear view mirror. He sat, his face illuminated by a phone, Elia resting on his shoulder, eyes closed.

"What, Danny?"

"I used to work at the Circle K on Alameda. Last summer. I know how to turn the pumps on from behind the counter. If it's not ideal, I mean."

Mia exchanged looks with Hashim in the passenger seat. Taking one of her cheerleaders in to a potential deathtrap like a gas station was pretty high on her list of things she really didn't want to do . . . but no other option seemed to present itself.

"Okay," Mia said as they drove. "Here's what we'll do. Hashumi, I'll give you my card. You hop out and start pumping. If that doesn't work, Danny and I will go in and authorize the pumps. We'll need to find a gas station that still has its lights on, though."

"Kill the lights!" Allison screamed, pulling the trigger of her 20-gauge and pumping another round into the chamber. "Kill the fucking headlights, Evan! They're attracted to the lights!"

Evan, on the other side of the camper, would have loved to have killed the headlights. Unfortunately, he was a little busy holding off a naked adolescent girl who was doing her ever-loving best to get her teeth into his neck. He got his feet planted under him and spun, smashing her head into the steel I-beam that flanked the gas pumps at the Circle K in Farmington, NM. The infected girl's skull caved in, and blood and other fluids leaked out of her ears and eyes. Evan threw her body away from himself as quickly as he could and then reached for his Kimber 1911 as the sound of Allison's shotgun came around from the other side.

Suddenly, tires squealed, and a gunmetal gray Nissan plowed through the wall of naked bodies that streamed toward the beleaguered camper. Just as quickly as he'd arrived, Max threw the truck into reverse and backed the way he'd come, running over bursting rib cages, tires slipping on the blood and entrails in his wake. Several of the infected turned away from the camper toward this new source of food and noise, and Allison, at least, was able to get her door open, throw in the bag of groceries she'd gotten, and climb into the passenger seat. Another blast from her 20-gauge rang out as she shot through the open door, severing the arm of the closest infected. She kicked the severed arm out of the car and slammed the door shut. "EVAN!" she screamed as she leaned over and turned the key, starting the camper's powerful engine.

Evan shot one, then another as they came at him. He fumbled at the door handle, his hand slick with sweat. Eventually, he got it open, but not before one of the infected managed to squeeze between the gas pump and the supporting I-beam and sink his teeth into Evan's calf. Evan howled and shot the attacker in the head, but the sting in his calf said that he was already too late. He'd broken the skin. He was infected.

"Allison," he said.

"Evan, no," Allison said. "Get in. Please."

"No. I'm hit. Slide over and drive. Stay with Max. Get Kimber to safety. I love you."

"Evan!"

"I love you, Allison," he said again, as he reached across the seat for the shiny red plastic two-way radio he'd been using to talk to Max in the gray truck. Allison, sobbing, did as he bid, sliding over the center console into the driver's seat while he turned and shot at another infected reaching for them. Evan Dwyer kissed his wife, one last hard, long kiss on the mouth, and then slammed the door.

Allison could barely see through her tears, but she slammed the camper into reverse and gunned the engine, her tires squealing on the concrete as she backed out rather than attempt to plow through the crowd that never seemed to end.

"Max, Evan."

"Evan, buddy, you guys out?"

"Negative. Allison's out. I'm hit."

Long pause. "Shit."

"Yeah. Got an idea," Evan said as he shot another one off of him. He had three bullets left in this eight-round mag. He'd left his spare mags in the camper. Good thing, too. Allison or Max could use the .45 ammo.

"Go with idea," Max said. He could see the camper approaching now. He could see Allison's face. Shit.

Evan lifted the hose of the gas pump and began spraying fuel. He wasn't sure if this would work as well as it always seemed to do in the movies, but he did know that gasoline atomized fairly well, especially when you held your finger over the hose in order to make it spray into the air. He mentally thanked Allison for jamming the shutoff mechanism when she'd gone inside. That had been a bit of genius.

The infected seemed to be thrown off by the smell of the gasoline filling the air. Evan found that incredibly funny as the first shiver of fever started to race through him.

"Evan?"

"Yeah. So. I've soaked this place down well with gas. You still got those .762 tracers that I don't have and neither of us knows where I got?"

Despite himself, Max smiled. "Yeah."

"What say I draw a big crowd into my little gasoline shower and you light this fucking place up?"

"You got it, buddy," Max said as he wheeled the truck around. He had Evan's AK-47 in his lap.

"Max."

"Yeah."

"Take care of my girls."

"Like they were my own, man. I give you my word."

"Ha! A gunner's word," Evan said, jokingly. Before he'd qualified as a flight engineer, he'd been an aerial gunner once, just like Max. "The fuck's that worth?"

Max laughed, blinking the tears aside as he pulled up to within the AK's range. He could see Evan there, on the radio, standing in the midst of a puddle of gas, spraying the shit out of the place.

"Evan," Max said over the radio, his voice little more than a whisper.

"Yeah."

"In place."

"Roger. Here's to gunpowder and pussy, man," Evan said, shooting one of the slowly approaching infected. The rest of the infected turned toward him and began to gather faster, lunging at him. He fired another bullet. "Live by one . . ."

"Die by the other," Max whispered. He braced the AK on the door frame and took aim at the puddle at Evan's feet.

"Love the smell of both," Evan finished with satisfaction. Then he put the 1911 in his mouth and pulled the trigger, just as the horde of infected surged toward him, entering the cloud of atomized gasoline.

Max pulled the trigger, sending a single red tracer winging through the night.

The crowd of infected enveloped Evan's body as a tiny blue flame flickered on the surface of the gas-soaked concrete. Then the air itself ignited in a blinding flash that had Max diving for the floorboard of his truck and had the truck itself rocking on its shocks, even at this distance. In the back seat, his girls woke up crying, both of them, for their mother. Max could barely hear them through the ringing in his ears. He shook his head and forced himself back up into his seat, where he wheeled the truck around and headed back to the sheltered spot where he'd left Allison and the camper.

The clock on the dash read 8:23. Not terribly late, but the events of the day were taking their toll. Most of the cheerleaders were sleeping, heads leaning on one another or the windows. Hashim was awake, but he was deeply involved in the message boards he'd pulled up on his tablet. Mia was sick of listening to emergency messages that never changed and was saving the charge on her phone in case Max called. So it was kind of ironically funny that she jumped a mile high in her seat when the phone buzzed against the plastic of the van's center console.

"Hello?"

"Baby?"

"Max? Yeah, I'm here. You guys okay?"

"Yeah." Long pause. "We lost Evan."

"Oh shit." Hashim looked up at that one, his eyes worried. Mia mouthed "Evan" to him, and the microbiologist closed his eyes briefly.

"Allison okay?" Even as she asked, Mia knew it was a stupid thing to say. Of course Allison wasn't okay. She'd just lost her husband. Mia knew she'd be pretty fucking far from okay if it had been Max. But she didn't know how else to ask about her friend.

"No," Max said. "But she's holding. For now. She and Kimber weren't hit. Evan got bit. Listen. We figured out that they're attracted to light and motion. We got mobbed when we stopped for gas in Farmington. So be careful going through there."

Mia looked up as they passed a sign. Farmington, 25 miles. "Roger," she said. "Where'd you stop?"

"At the Circle K we usually use. It'll probably still be burning when you go past. Evan went out with a bang. Took a lot of those fuckers with him."

Despite everything, Mia smiled. That was exactly how Evan would have wanted it. "Good for him," she said. "Right, so we'll watch out for Farmington."

Another long pause. "How are the kids?" Max asked. "Anyone sick?"

Mia glanced over her shoulder at the team. "Not yet," she said. "Hashim says it's early yet, but I'm hopeful."

"Me too. I love you, baby. Stay safe."

"You too. I love you too."

As she hung up the phone, a soft, almost apologetic cough sounded from the far back seat.

"Coach?" It was Sonia's voice, one of their tiny freshman "flyers." She was good, always stuck her stunts at the top of their pyramid.

"What is it, Sonia?"

"I don't feel so good."

Thanks to the van's auxiliary fuel tank, they were able to avoid stopping for gas in Farmington. As they rolled past the remains of the Circle K (which was, in fact, still burning) Mia could see what Max had been talking about. Not only was there a crater where the parking lot had once been, but the entire front half of the building was gone and the rest was in flames. Still, the light and sound of the burning wreckage seemed to draw the infected out. Mia was surprised. She didn't think that Farmington had had that many people in it, let alone that many who'd been infected already. When she mentioned this to Hashim, though, he just shrugged.

"The bloodborne virus is much faster to spread than the airborne version," he said. "If you have one infected who attacks a living human, and then that one turns, who turns another . . . it would not take long, especially not in such a small community."

Mia felt herself pale, and then shoved that thought away in the back with the thought of vaccine production and four dead cops. She'd deal with all of that later. "I see," she said.

Hashim nodded. "It is a shame that we cannot harvest some of them for vaccine, but it is not worth the risk at this point."

"No," Mia said, "I agree." Her eyes flicked up to the rear view mirror, where Sonia lay in the back seat, loosely bound by bungee cords so that she could be restrained when the time came. As of right now, she still just had a fever, but from what Hashim was saying, it wouldn't be long.

"What will you need to produce the vaccine?" Mia asked, determined to think of something else. "Besides infected tissue?"

"It is really very simple," he said. "A small X-ray machine, some minor lab equipment. That is all."

Mia frowned. Torrey, Utah, the town where her mother lived, wasn't large by any stretch of the imagination. It had fewer people than Farmington and nothing resembling a hospital . . . except . . .

"The community clinic!" Mia said, snapping her fingers. "We had to take Micaela there when she was little and broke her arm. They've got an X-ray machine, and I'd imagine most of the lab supplies you'll need."

"Where is this clinic?" Hashim asked.

"It's in downtown Torrey, or what passes for a downtown in a town as small as Torrey. It's right on the main road . . . oh." Mia felt her enthusiasm drain away as she thought her plan through. "That's exactly where they'd go if they were getting sick."

"Probably," Hashim agreed. "But, it is small, yes? Perhaps we can fight our way in and barricade ourselves inside?"

Mia snorted. "Yeah, that sounds like a lot of fun," she said softly, but then sighed. "But, as I don't have a better idea, I guess your plan is it. But first," she said, slowing and flipping off her headlights as they started approaching a lit section of the highway. "We need gas, and Shiprock is about our last resort for a long ways."

Hashim looked up, focusing on the buildings coming in to view. "Big town?"

"Smaller than Farmington, but not by much. They're almost linked. There's a place we usually stop near the outskirts, after we make our turn. I think that might be our bet."

"What is your plan? Do you still intend to act as normal?"

Mia pursed her lips, then shook her head. "I think it's too dangerous. Max said that the lights attracted a horde of infected. I think we'll just have to go in and out as fast as we can."

"I will pump the gas, then," Hashim said, as though asking for confirmation, "while you take Danny inside?"

"I think so. Do you think you can keep them off the van?"

"Perhaps, if your team can shoot from the windows, that would also be good."

Mia nodded, then looked up in the rearview mirror to see eleven pairs of eyes open, listening to their conversation. She met Danny's gaze, and the junior nodded.

"Give Jessa your rifle and take her shotgun," Mia said. "When we go in, you follow close behind me. I'll clear the store itself; you just worry about getting behind the counter and getting the gas turned on, you got it?"

"Yes, coach," he said. In the seat in front of him, Sam pulled off the body armor he'd been wearing and handed it to Danny. It was too big, but better than nothing, Mia supposed. Especially if they got mobbed. It might keep Danny alive long enough for Hashim to come get them.

"All of you, when we come to a stop, take aim out the windows. Don't shoot until you have to do so. One, we don't have ammo to waste and two, we don't want the noise to draw more of a crowd than we have to." Mia turned the wheel as she spoke, not stopping for the red light, turning on to U.S. 491, the highway that would take them north into Colorado and then Utah.

A few more blocks, and Mia slowed. The gas station looked good. Parking lot was empty, lights were off. Nothing moving. Yet. She turned in to the driveway and cut the engine, coasting to a stop next to one of the pumps in a move that impressed even herself. She glanced back over her shoulder at Danny, who was poised next to the door. At her nod, he opened it, slowly, trying not to make too much noise. She followed suit and dropped softly out of her seat onto the concrete. She left her door open and began to jog toward the building. Naturally, it was locked, but Mia solved that problem neatly by shoving a sweatshirt up against the glass and having Danny hit it with a rock. Not a perfect solution, she mused, grimacing at the muffled crash and tinkle of glass hitting the ground, but it was what she had on short notice. She reached inside, flipped the deadbolt and opened the door to the convenience store.

It was dark inside, and Mia blinked quickly, trying to force her eyes to adjust. Not for the first time on this adventure she wished she had a pair of night vision goggles. She'd probably look pretty damn ridiculous, rolling around in her old flight helmet with a pair of goggles on the front, but it would be super useful to be able to see in the dark.

Goggles or not, she had a job to do here. Danny was already moving for the front counter, doing a passable job of being quiet and careful. He didn't really know how to professionally clear a room, but neither, for that matter, did she. All either of them had was good sense and self preservation. It would have to be enough.

She moved quietly through the store, methodically checking each of the four small aisles. She quickly looked in the restrooms and the back storeroom. All appeared to be clear. She went back out to the front to see Danny smiling at her, giving her a thumbs up. Apparently, he'd gotten the pumps turned on. A quick glance outside told her that Hashim was fueling the van, and all looked quiet for the moment. Time to get some supplies.

She motioned Danny over to the snack aisle, and pointed out the things she wanted. Mostly beef jerky and bottles of water, though she did throw in another four pack of Sugar Free Red Bull. It was still five hours from here to Torrey, and with Sonia sick and others to follow, Mia had the feeling it was going to be a long night.

Speaking of which, she thought, turning to the small stash of automotive and hardware supplies the little store carried. She grabbed every roll of duct tape they had, plus some more bungee cords and a couple of multitools.

"Coach!" Danny called out in a harsh whisper. "I think we'd better go!"

Mia looked up right as the first infected came crashing through the hole they'd made in the front door.

"Shit!" she yelled. "Danny, get around the other side, get back to the van!" She drew her .45 and kicked the metal shelf, knocking several items to the floor with a resounding crash. "Hey!" she yelled, using her best "gotta be heard over turning rotors and screaming cheerleaders" voice. "Hey asshole! I'm over here! Come get me!"

Sure enough, the infected turned at her voice, as did the one following him through the door. The third one, however, turned for Danny as he tried to make it back toward the door. With presence of mind she wouldn't have expected from one so young, Danny cooly pointed the 12-gauge at the infected's head and pulled the trigger.

Mia's ears rang from the report, and blood and brain matter sprayed everywhere. Praying that Danny didn't have a cut on him somewhere, Mia shot the infected closest to her and dodged around the metal shelf as the second one lunged at her.

"Why," she said out loud, "Why the fuck did we have to get the fast zombies?" She said this last as she grabbed a tire iron off the shelf and swung it, hard, against the head of the second one. The infected's head deformed, almost as if it were made of putty, and the body slumped to the floor.

"Coach! We've got more coming!" Danny called. Mia scrubbed her sleeve across her face and looked up to see that he was right. There were easily twenty infected between them and the van, and the number looked like it was growing.

"C'mon," she said. "I think I saw a back door." Her tennis shoes slipped a bit in the zombie's blood as she took off toward Danny, but she kept her feet, barely. Mia turned down the hallway she'd checked earlier, finding the door marked "Emergency Exit Only" and half blocked by a hand truck. For no good reason at all, Mia grabbed the hand truck. It seemed like a useful thing to have; if nothing else, it could be used to bludgeon attacking infected.

More glass crashed in the store, so Mia waved Danny through the door, her .45 still in her hand. She followed quickly, pausing just long enough to pull the door closed behind them. Hopefully, the infected in the store would cause enough of a ruckus to draw any others that way and keep them off the van.

They moved quickly, staying low, crouched next to the building in order to try to hide in the shadows as much as possible. When they rounded the corner, they could see the gas pumps, but no van. For one heart-stopping moment, Mia couldn't decide between being grateful to Hashim for getting her kids out and to safety, or being furious that he'd left her and Danny behind.

Fortunately, she didn't have long to waffle. Before they could blink, the van came out from the alley that ran along the back of the building and pulled alongside them. The door opened and arms reached out from inside to pull them both in. Mia felt a bit like a kidnap victim as she was tossed to the floorboards, hand truck and all, and the van took off, tearing across the parking lot, lights off, heading back to the highway and freedom.

"Mia?" Hashim asked, as Jessa and Yolanda pulled the door closed behind her and Danny. "Mia, were you bit?"

"No," Mia said, pulling herself up and into the passenger seat. "No, I wasn't. Danny?"

"Nope!" he said. "Didn't even get any blood on me!" He sounded so ridiculously pleased by this that Mia laughed, despite herself. After a moment, Jessa giggled too, followed by Elia. Before long, they were all laughing, even poor Sonia, tied in the back, flushed with fever.

"We got some supplies, too," Mia said, as soon as the laughter died down. "But how'd you know where to find us?"

"We didn't," Hashim said. "We just saw the horde at the front door, and knew you would not make it out that way. Jessa suggested the alley around the back."

"You should have just left," Mia said, looking down to reload her magazine.

Hashim looked over at her wryly. "Mia. I am only one man. You gave weapons to nine of your twelve cheerleaders. Do you think they would have let me leave you?"

Mia looked up, startled, then glanced to the back. Jessa met her eyes, a hardness in them that Mia had never seen before.

"We're a team, coach," Jessa said.

Mia felt a lump rise in her throat. She nodded. "So we are," she said. "So we are."

By eleven, Sonia had turned. Dawn, Yolanda, and Gina were also showing signs of infection. They'd all been restrained in the back couple of rows, making liberal use of both bungee cords and duct tape.

Mia and Hashim had traded off driving duties. Both of them subtly bore down on the gas, and the van, surprisingly, would do ninety on a straight stretch with very little issues. Max had called once more to tell them that he'd stopped for gas in Aneth. Aneth was a tiny little town in the middle of an oil field on the Ute Mountain Reservation in southern Utah. Mia knew the gas station Max mentioned. They stopped there sometimes when they travelled during the day. Mia wouldn't have stopped at night if she could help it. It had always looked sketchy. According to Max, though, the old guy who ran it was uninfected, and he appeared more than happy to help. Mia was keeping it in mind, just in case. Since Hashim had been able to fill up both tanks back at Shiprock, she didn't think it would be an issue, but it was nice to have a backup plan.

Or any kind of plan, for that matter.

Mia wiped her hands over her face and lifted her Red Bull to take the last swallow in the can. She made a face as it went down. Sugar Free Red Bull was meant to be drunk over ice, in her opinion. It was never the same out of the can, and its flavor deteriorated rapidly if it wasn't icy cold.

She had the sensation of diving through the darkness as the van carved its way down the apparently deserted highway. While, given the circumstances, Mia was more than happy to be in such a sparsely populated part of the country, it was, to say the least, a little eerie as they drove.

Particularly with more than half of her team dying in the van behind her.

"Hashim," she said softly, not wanting to wake him if he were asleep. The microbiologist stirred and opened his eyes, looking at her. "If they haven't turned yet, can you use the vaccine on them?"

He shook his head sadly. "I could try, but Mia, if they are already sick, then the virus has begun to attack their tissues. The vaccine will only be more viruses. It would only make the problem worse."

Mia nodded. That was about what she'd expected. She drove on, accelerating just a little faster, as Sam and Bella, both seniors, started to join in the coughing behind her.

The eastern sky was starting to lighten when they had to slow down. They'd made it in to Utah, but the road to Torrey took them through Capitol Reef National Park. The Park, as it was known locally, was a geographic wonder, and one of the best kept secrets of the American Southwest. Towering red stone formations thrust up into the sky, creating near-vertical canyons and labyrinthine twists and turns. Butch Cassidy and the Hole in the Wall Gang were known to have had hideouts up in The Park back in their day. Legend had it that there was still stolen railroad gold cached up there somewhere.

Mia slowed the van as they wound down the scenic highway, in part because it was necessary, thanks to the lingering darkness and the windiness of the road. Also, there was also the threat of hitting one of the huge herds of deer that lived in the area. But the real reason she slowed was because she knew that Max was somewhere up here. Somewhere in the Park, there was a cache of weapons and supplies that her mother and stepfather had prepared for an "End of the World" type scenario. She had the coordinates for it on her phone, even. That was where Max would be.

But she couldn't go there, not yet. Not with Sonia, Dawn and Yolanda already turned, and from the looks of things, Gina, Sam and Bella not far behind. They had to get to the clinic. They had to get Hashim to the vaccine. She had to keep her promise. Her kids would not die in vain.

Torrey was only about six miles past the park, and the gray light of false dawn lined the eastern horizon by the time they came to the town limits. The sign claimed a population of 180 people, which Mia thought was a good sign. Especially since many of those would, theoretically, be living out on their land away from the town center. Torrey was as rural as it got.

"The community clinic is up here on the left," Mia said as she drove, slowing to turn in to the parking lot of the small, nondescript building with the sign that proclaimed it to be their goal. She pulled up next to the door, killed the engine and set the parking brake. There was no movement in the parking lot.

"Now, how do we get these guys inside?" she asked.

"Let me go in first," Hashim said, hefting a bag he'd stashed under the passenger seat. "I must find the lab and the X-ray machine, and we may need to clear it out. We can leave the kids here with the weapons."

Mia looked over her shoulder at Jessa. The team captain nodded and hefted the rifle she hadn't given back to Danny. He'd taken Sam's instead. "We'll be fine," she said. "We'll get them ready to take in for you."

"Don't take any chances," Mia said, wishing she had some better advice to give. "Don't get bit."

Jessa smiled grimly. "Don't worry," she said. "I have a plan."

Mia raised her eyebrows. "I'm glad someone does," she said under her breath. When Jessa's only answer was a widening grin, she shook her head and refused to comment further. Instead, Mia took one of the shotguns and her .45 and slid out of her seat after tossing the keys to Jessa. Just in case.

"Do you know where the lab is?" Hashim asked her as they approached the front door of the clinic.

"Not a clue," Mia said.

Hashim laughed. "Fair enough," he said. "Let's go."

He pushed open the door which, surprisingly or not, was not locked. The metal squealed against the linoleum floor, letting out a sound which raised the hackles on the back of Mia's neck and made her curse softly in response. So much for stealth.

From somewhere down the darkened hall in front of them, an answering keen rose. Then another. Hashim grabbed her arm and hauled her quickly behind a counter that had once served as the receptionist's station. He reached in his bag and pulled out a road flare. "Cover your eyes," he warned, then popped the flare.

Red light hissed to life as Mia belatedly turned her head and covered her eyes. She looked back just in time to see Hashim toss the light into a room opposite, which looked like a bathroom or something of that kind. Sure enough, three infected came running, stumbling down the hallway toward the light and the noise. As they came, Mia stood and began firing the 12-gauge. Three rounds, three dead infected. Five more followed after, drawn by the light and the noise. Mia dropped behind the corner as Hashim took her place, firing his pistol economically, dropping them with the headshots he'd perfected a lifetime ago in another desert a world away.

The 12-gauge could hold six rounds, and Mia took the time to reload three more while she had a moment. As she was doing so, another infected, this one a child of about five, came around the corner of the counter from a back room.

"Aw, shit," Mia said as the little zombie rushed toward her. "You're gone already," she told the little boy as she kicked a rolling chair over to intercept his path. He stumbled, which gave her time to get her weapon up and fire into his face that had been framed with soft golden curls. Still cursing, Mia got to her feet and went over to check the room that had produced the infected little boy. The smell about knocked her over. There was another child in there, a girl, about three or so. This one was still clothed, and her middle was one bloody mass where it had been eaten away. From the resemblance, Mia guessed that they'd been brother and sister. She closed her eyes briefly, then turned and emptied the contents of her stomach into a corner.

"Mia," Hashim called softly. She straightened up, wiped her mouth with her sleeve and went back out to the reception area. An impressive pile of bodies lay in front of the desk, but there was no more movement toward the back. "I think we must move on," he said, his eyes sympathetic. Mia nodded, and forced one foot in front of the other.

Despite all the odds, the building appeared to be clear. Mia and Hashim checked every closet, every compartment they could see, but there was no one else. Either no one else had made it to the clinic, or all the survivors had already evacuated. They did find the remains of several others that had been partially eaten, and Mia threw up one more time.

In the last room they checked, Hashim found what he was looking for. He immediately went over to the X-ray machine and began pushing buttons and dials. It must have had an integrated generator of some kind because it fired right up, though the lights in the room stayed off. Mia watched him for a second, feeling lost, before backing up a step. "I'll, ah, go get the kids," she said. Hashim was already absorbed in his work and didn't appear to hear her. So she shrugged and went back the way they'd come.

Outside, seven or eight more headless bodies bore mute testimony to the amount of noise she and Hashim had made, but her kids were all okay. Elia opened the van doors as she approached, and Danny and the two sisters, Mackayla and Mackenzie, started moving their turned teammates out. Mia nearly laughed when she saw them. The kids had emptied their cheer bags out and were using them as hoods to cover the faces of the infected. With the cheer bags duct taped over their heads, and their hands and feet tied, the infected cheerleaders were effectively helpless. All of a sudden, Mia was extremely glad she'd grabbed the hand truck back in Shiprock, as it came in very handy for transporting their lost teammates as gently as possible.

One by one, they transported them inside. Sam, the senior, and Jessa's co-captain. Sonia and Dawn, their two freshman flyers who'd been good enough to make the varsity team. Yolanda, another senior, who had earned a cheerleading scholarship to the University of Texas. Gina, a junior who had been earmarked for captain next year, and Bella, another senior, who had had plans to get married next spring. They rolled them in and strapped them down to the rolling gurneys that Hashim had assembled in the lab area.

"I don't want to hurt them, if you can help it," Mia said, her voice rough as they finished securing Bella in place.

"They do not feel pain at this stage," Hashim said, "but I understand. I will give them morphine to kill them, and then we will harvest the spines. We must hurry, though; I can do nothing with the tissue if it's too long dead."

"We'll help," Mackayla said, and her sister nodded. Elia too. "We'll all help," the little sophomore said. "Just tell us what to do."

Hashim nodded. He walked over to Sonia with a syringe, which he inserted into her arm. The infected girl thrashed against her bonds, letting out that high, keening wail before falling silent. Without a word, Hashim grabbed a very large bone saw from a drawer and began cutting around her neck. While her teammates looked on, Sonia was decapitated, her spine removed and placed into what looked like an emesis basin.

"Can you do this?" Hashim asked. Mia nodded, and though their faces were white as sheets, the surviving cheerleaders followed suit. Hashim handed out the syringes and bone saws, and they went to work.

It was the buzzing of her phone that woke her. Despite everything, Mia had drifted off to sleep, leaning against the wall of Hashim's lab beside the sheet-covered gurneys that held the remains of half her team. Her surviving cheerleaders lay curled together on the floor next to her, Danny and Jessa holding Elia between them, Mackayla and Mackenzie holding each other. Mia stretched the crick in her neck and pulled the iPhone from her pocket. It was a text, from Max.

Found cache. All good. You? Max.

Mia looked up at Hashim, only to see the microbiologist standing over her with tired eyes, a triumphant smile on his face, a syringe in his hand. "Mia," he said. "If I could have your arm, please? Your vaccine is ready." Mia smiled back at him as tears of relief and reaction filled her eyes.

"Do the kids first," she said, blinking furiously as she fumbled with her phone.

Vaccine done. Hold tight, baby. See you in a bit.

The war with the Trefoilers was drawing to a close, with Humanity all but certain to claim victory. But a profoundly alien species makes use of profoundly alien technology—and deploys profoundly alien weaponry.

BETWEEN NINE AND ELEVEN

★

by Adam Roberts

★ 1 ★

DIPLOMATIC EFFORTS HAD FAILED, and we were officially at war with the Trefoil alien culture. War is never pleasant, however unavoidable it sometimes becomes. But one of the things that blurs the edge of war's unpleasantness is victory. We enjoyed victory after victory, sweet as honey. Soon enough we were closing in on the Trefoil homeworld.

Why did diplomacy fail? There *were* ways in which our view of the cosmos aligned with theirs. But then again there were ways in which the human assumptions about things and the Trefoil assumptions were so radically at odds that it was simply impossible for us to communicate at all, let alone reach a compromise. Like us, the Trefoil were a social species, and there were broad emotional parallels—their versions of love and aggression appear to have been more-or-less equivalent emotions to ours—as well as some surprising specifics: the concepts of *Answegen Geschichtlichkeit* and *Geworfenheit* all made perfect sense to the Trefoil, it seems. But other concepts, like mutual advantage, creativity, logic, meant nothing at all to them.

Their attacks on Human Space were very hard to predict, and therefore hard to defend against. For that reason, I suspect, they underestimated our ability to fight and win.

My name is Ferrante, and I was in command of the warship

Centurion 771. This is what happened when our ship and a sister ship called *Samurai 10* pressed our attack on a damaged Trefoil Supership designated ET 13-40. ET is shorthand for Enemy Target.

★ 2 ★

Centurion and *Samurai* came out of warp together and coordinated our initial firesweep on the ET. About one in five Trefoil ships can be captured—sometimes apparently important craft, flagships even, sometimes trivial little spacetugs. The rest will self-destruct rather than be taken. What criterion determines, for the Trefoil, which kind of ship is too valuable to fall into human hands . . . well, nobody has been able to work that out.

We were half a light year from β Cygni, the star's red blob clearly visible on our screen without need of magnification. The Trefoil Supership had fallen out of warp, presumably on account of its internal damage: the crazy ziggurat of its hull was ruptured in a hundred places, and weird entrails (cables? tentacles?) trailed from every breach. Since every individual Trefoil ship is designed according to a different template, we couldn't be sure of the internal composition of this particular one. Most Trefoil craft possessed three command centres, and it looked likely that the baobab-shaped excrescence on the side of the craft was one of those. We concentrated fire and scratched red-brown furrows over the hull, everting the inward spaces of this bridge. If that's what it was.

We thought we had her, but then she twisted and fell out of existence, reappearing in orbit half a light year away. Must have had a last squirt of warp capacity in her engines. It was an easy matter to follow her and we repeated out attack mode. The huge craft was in orbit around a taupe and yellow gas giant, sinking into the upper atmosphere. For a moment I wondered if she would crash down into the world and so escape us by destroying herself. But she deployed a filigree web, and we realised she was scooping.

Well: we could stop that easily enough. Both ships manoeuvred, and targeted. The battle was seconds away from being won.

Then *Samurai* exploded: a stutter of blue-white light, a soundless crunching inward, twisting the main hull like a rag being wrung, and then there was nothing of the starship except debris spiralling and hurtling.

★ 3 ★

At exactly that moment the link went down, and I was no longer mentally connected to the rest of the crew. I came out of telspace gasping, as if cold water had been thrown in my face.

The *Centurion* shuddered, and one of our cannons overheated and melted itself loose of its bearings. The bridge screens lit up with error messages. The warp went offline. One thruster fired and the other stalled, and we were spinning. The failure of warp meant that inertial controls sagged and gave way, and we were all crushed against the sides of our harnesses.

I'd been in telspace with my crew for so long, it took palpable effort to dredge their actual names from my memory. "Modi," I yelled—my voice hoarse with unuse. "Cancel that thruster!"

She was already doing so, and stabilising the craft, but then the counter-thrust sputtered out. We were still spinning, although not at so crushing a velocity.

No telspace meant the manual operation of the ship. I looked at my hands, palms down, palms up, and tried to place them on the command screen. But there was something wrong with my hands. More than wrong, there was something monstrous about them. Something . . . blasphemous, almost. I looked at them again and I began to scream.

★ 4 ★

I've served with Modi for over a year, first on the *Broadsword 27* and then the *Centurion*—my first command, although the consensual nature of the telspace makes the concept of command much less hierarchical than it might once have been. In the Big Wing Battle at Alpha Scorpii internal fires had scarred my face and torso and burned away three of the fingers from Modi's left hand, leaving her a puckered crabclaw thumb-and-index. She'd tried an artificial hand with four plasmetal fingers and an opposable plasmetal thumb, but the interface had never quite gelled for her, and there was a lag between her willing something and her prosthetic acting. For that reason she tended not to wear it.

That fact saved everybody's life.

★ 5 ★

There were four of us on the craft, and one other—me, let's say.

Captain. A standard crew. Han killed herself within the first five minutes of the . . . of whatever it was that happened to the ship (she pressed herself against the glowing-hot flank of the gun-compartment and died screaming). Shabti and Kellermann became catatonic, the former singing a nursery song over and over in a scratchy, high-pitched voice.

Modi got to me before I could self-harm in any way. She took hold of my head, and forced me to look into her eyes. Without my hands in plain view, I felt the terror ebbing away. But there was something—I couldn't say what—profoundly awry with the universe as a whole. The *Centurion* shuddered and bucked, and error messages blinked and flashed on every screen on every surface. The main screen showed the Trefoil ship, pulling up now from its orbital gas sweep, and drawing its scoop back into its main body. Soon enough it would turn and bear down upon us.

"Ferrante," Modi yelled, right in my face. "Ferrante. They will be on us in minutes."

"Minutes," I gasped.

"We need to pull the ship together. Pull *ourselves* together. We still have nine cannon."

"Nine cannon," I repeated. "Yes." There was something comforting in that thought. But, the sense of wrongness persisted. "Something is very wrong," I told Modi.

"I feel it too," she agreed. "But we have to get a grip."

The word *grip* made me glance back down at my hands, and the terror welled up again. I began screaming for a second time.

Modi was a quick thinker. She pulled off her top and wrapped it around my hands. "Ferrante," she said. "We have to *act*."

I was gasping. I was finding it hard to breathe. The topography of the bridge seemed to twist and slip around me in weird ways. "Oh," I said. "Oh—oh—oh."

★ 6 ★

Cygni is a binary system: a fat red giant and a tiny, bright little blue star—Beta is the bigger. There are some Jupiter-sized gas giants, and a whole lot of dwarf planets and fragments and meteorites.

The proximity warning sounded and Modi dabbled at a screen to confirm the zapping of the offending rocklet. But then it sounded again, and again, and the chances that so many asteroids were on a collision course were so minute that it could only mean the system was fried. I tried to breathe, deep, and get a grip. Slowly I drew my right hand out from the cloth that covered it. I didn't like looking at it, but it didn't offend basic reason in the way that staring at both my hands did. I tried contacting the rest of the crew, dispersed about the ship, but the system told me that Han was dead, and the other two unresponsive.

"Something," I said. "The Trefoil did something."

"It's a weapon," said Modi. "I just don't see what kind."

"Whatever it is, it destroyed the *Samurai* and it has caused—" I looked around at the flickering screens—"a whole mass of malfunctions and problems for us." Some shred of soldiery reasserted itself in my mind. I was supposed to be in charge. "We'll have to close with the ET and fire on her manually. I don't know if we can trust the AI to target the cannon."

"What is it crews say when they're not in the telspace? *Aye aye,* is it?"

"We've still got nine cannon," I said. That fact should have reassured me, but instead it made me obscurely uneasy.

So we wrestled with the ship via the glitchy manual interface, and the thrusters fired. Warp came online again, and the inertial balancing flashed on, off, on, off. Then the warp went down. The whole ship began to shake violently. I felt sharp, stabbing pains in my fingers and toes. This was the moment Kellermann died. He owned an antique cigarette lighter, which in turn contained a small amount of butane. This exploded with enough force to kill him and breach the hull. The reason it exploded had to do with the arrangement of protons in the butane nucleus.

In retrospect I can say: thank heavens we weren't carrying any neon.

"Pull back," I said, and together Modi and I grappled with the interface to bring the *Centurion* out of attack mode. The more distance we put between ourselves and the ET, the calmer the craft became.

"I don't know what it *is,*" Modi said. "I don't see how they're doing that—it's like a magic spell, like some voodoo sphere of malignity around the ET."

"We've still got nine cannon," I reminded her. "We can still shoot at her. True, we won't be at an optimum distance to . . ."

"Why do you say *still*?" Modi asked.

"What?"

"You say *we've still got nine cannon*. You say that because we're supposed to have more."

"That's right."

"How many cannon are we fitted with? How many are we *supposed* to have?"

I could not say. I mean that strictly: the answer to that question couldn't be said.

★ 7 ★

Modi scribbled a number on her pad with her forefinger. "What do you call that?"

I looked at the number. I recognised it, but its name slipped from my head. "Nine-and-four?" I offered.

"That's not *it*, though, is it?"

"No," I agreed, pained. "Six-and-seven? But that's not how we say it, is it? I want to say *three*, but it's clearly not three."

She wrote another number. "And what about that?"

I looked at it. "It's a four. But it's more than a four, isn't it. It's a lot more than four, actually?"

"It's four and something else. It's the something else that's . . . I don't get it."

"What is it? The number I mean?"

"It's the designation of our ET," Modi said. As soon as she said that I recognised it. Of course!

"Ferrante," she asked. "What's our ship called?"

"*Centurion*." The name came from my mouth like a bark of gibberish. I knew what Modi was going to ask next, and it was: *what does that word mean*? And I knew that I wouldn't be able to answer that question. Although it was in my head that *I used to know*. Once upon a time. It had something to do with war. But what did it have to do with war? It was a non-word. It was an impossible word.

★ 8 ★

"The ET is bringing about," Modi sang. "It's using its scoop harvest to boost itself towards us. Unless we can get warp working again, it will be on us in . . ." and she stopped, and looked puzzled. "I had a calculation of the time . . ."

Since this was the amount of time we had left alive, I was eager to find out what the number was.

"Let's say, in nine minutes," she said. "Between nine and eleven minutes."

The ship was starting to shudder again. Modi saying that, giving voice to that phrase *between nine and eleven*, brought the terror shaking back into my mind. I wish she hadn't said that. Because there was nothing between nine and eleven, and at the same time there was something between nine and eleven and the fact of this thing being and not-being, its hideous elusiveness, like a monster in the shadows, was inexpressibly ghastly to me. I began weeping, tears washing down my face. And it wasn't because of the pain in my hands and feet.

★ 9 ★

From this point on I was useless. Worse than useless. I was very specifically starting to lose my mind. Modi was more focussed. She managed to get the main AI—hiccoughing and prone to weird snags and cutaways though it was—to target the cannons. The Trefoil Supership swung down upon us and I began to sing a top-C and slap the top of my head with my hands and Modi *fired* and . . .

★ 11 ★

As to why the Trefoil had not deployed their "device"—this super-weapon—before . . . well, there is no consensus. It might be that they only very recently developed it. Conceivably, ET 13-40 was a research and development platform. Then again, perhaps the Trefoil had their "device" for a long time and simply hadn't deployed it for incomprehensible alien reasons of their own. The capture of a still-working model of the device, and its rapid adaptation and redeployment by Human Forces, brought the war very quickly to an end. Reprogrammed to blank out 3, the device completely shuts down Trefoil computers, designed as they are on a base-3 system of trits. It also causes individual Trefoilers to suffer severe internal physical damage and to degrade all triangular components. Neon, which has an atomic number between nine and eleven, is rare on a starship, but lithium—atomic number 3—is much more common, and the presence of any at all caused instant destruction. It seems likely that there was the existence of some small quantity of neon on board the *Samurai* that caused its immediate destruction. I've no idea why that ship would be carrying neon, but starships are large and complex things.

Of course, I recommended Modi for decoration, and stand by my recommendation. She didn't exactly figure out what the device was doing to us but she had enough of an inkling, and was able to act. She grasped that it had something to do with the eradication of the quantity between nine and eleven.

"I'm guessing," she told me afterwards, "that the Trefoil understood enough about us to know our default mathematics is base-10 and so they erroneously assumed that our computing would be decenary. It's the fact that we developed binary computing that saved us. Our AI was certainly confused, but still functioning."

"It's still hard for me to understand," I told her. "How can a device eliminate a number—from the universe, I mean? Surely that number just *is* a feature of the way things are?"

"Depends how you look at it," she replied. "We warp spacetime to travel faster than light, so we have good practical knowledge that spacetime is deformable. Say that the deep structure of the universe is information—is maths, effectively. If we can alter that deep structure to make the distance between stars temporarily shorter, then it's not hard to imagine the Trefoil finding a way to alter the deep structure in a different way. Temporarily to suppress ten from the fabric of things."

I shuddered. Modi is still happy to use the word itself. For me just saying the word brought the tendrils of nightmare to the tender parts of my memory. Like many who experienced the Trefoil "device" in those last, desperate (on their part) days of the war, I continue to refer, superstitiously, to *between-nine-and-eleven*.

"Amazing, really," Modi mused, "that deploying the device didn't entirely *undo* the fabric of reality within its sphere of influence. Surprisingly tough, reality. There's real inertia and persistence to reality it turns out."

"We don't know how long it would last, though. I mean, if the Trefoil device were deployed for long stretches of time. Or over a wide area."

But that's the thing about Modi: she's an optimist. "Oh, I think reality would adjust. Indeed, who's to say it hasn't happened before?"

"Before?"

Modi laughed. "Ancient alien races, fighting a war across the galaxy—who knows? What if one of them deployed something similar to the Trefoil device? Maybe many times? Maybe whole numbers were eradicated for ever. Maybe there once was a number between nine and ten, or between one and two—I don't mean, fractions or decimals. I mean a whole lost number. What if reality shook itself and then adjusted to the new, out-of-whack logic?"

"That's crazy talk," I grumbled.

"Maybe it is," she laughed. "Maybe."

Seven years ago, the Vierendelen *was shot down and crashed on a barren desert world. Their ship all but destroyed and communication with their homeworld impossible, the survivors christened the planet New Leseum and set about making lives for themselves.*

One year ago, Sephine's brother Rokri dared to take to the skies. His destination: the massive alien warship known as the Leviathan, which circles a mile above the planet's surface, preventing any hope for rescue or escape. Not heard from since, Rokri is presumed dead until Sephine receives a coded message from the Leviathan. She knows her brother's handiwork when she sees it. The leaders of New Leseum are skeptical, but Sephine is determined to mount a rescue mission to save her brother. In the process, she may save her people as well.

SEPHINE AND THE LEVIATHAN

★

by Jack Schouten

CHAPTER 3/6: TRAJECTORY

ENTOMBED INSIDE the cannibalized q-cannon, Sephine counts pebbles in her mind. She has had to wrap her filament wings around her to fit inside the narrow cylinder, and when the cannon begins its countdown and starts to rumble, claustrophobia sets in.

She reaches sixty-seven pebbles before she feels her wings quiver sharply once, and a sharp pain in her back.

—*We have a problem*, the *Vierendelen* sends.

"Fix it, then!" she screams aloud, though this doesn't matter; the ship will still hear her.

—*No time, toots. Grin and bear it, and all that.*

"*Toots?*" is all she can manage before there is a violent lurch and

111

her head slams against the cool metal of the inner shuttle. She floods her brain with painkillers and becomes dizzy.

"Is it the cannon?"

—*Cannon's fine.*

"Ah, silver linings . . ."

—*It's your filament wings. I don't think you'll be taking them on the return trip.*

As if there was any guarantee of a return trip, she thinks.

—*They may not even last the journey up to the Leviathan. That* bastard *engineer made a mistake. I told him I should have supervised.*

"Forget about the wings. Will I make it?"

—*Calculating,* it says, and Sephine feels the ship disconnect.

She Enlinks in the meantime and performs a quick systems check. The *Vierendelen* was right; her filament wings aren't secured properly to her spinal cord and are coming loose under the building turbulence. She tentatively dilutes the painkillers from her neuroweb. Her head throbs from the knock against the shuttle wall, but the burning pain in her back is infinitely worse; it feels like her spine is being extracted from her like loose teeth, one vertebra at a time.

She ups the painkillers and Delinks.

Seven seconds. Finally the *Vierendelen* re-establishes connection.

—*I have an idea, but you aren't going to like it.*

"I didn't expect to."

—*I'm going to delay your ejection from the shuttle. Just an extra minute or so will give me time to find a temporary fix so we can keep those wings from killing you mid-flight to the Leviathan. It's going to get hot in there, though. Really hot. And my wing-tinkering's going to hurt, but the higher we eject, the shorter the distance to the target. What do you think?*

One second.

"Do we have a choice?"

—*None whatsoever.*

The q-cannon fires. Sephine is almost crumpled by the g-force, pressed into the floor of the shuttle as it erupts from the cannon—even the shuttle's inches-thick shell can't dull the noise of the blast. Sephine's stomach pitches with the velocity, and despite herself she steals a glance through the viewing pane.

She can see the scrubland surrounding the launchpad, smoke and fire bulging beneath and blocking it out; and the smattering of black dots that are people watching the q-cannon blast her into the sky.

She convulses as the shuttle vibrates, battered around it like a rag doll, and she considers tightening the embrace of her wings to cushion herself against the shuttle walls, but something tells her that would only make the wing problem worse—and the pain.

—*Done*, the *Vierendelen* says. —*That engineer. Can't even encode failsafes in his own hardware. Too easy overriding the ejection protocols.*

"Show-off," she manages through chattering teeth.

—*Okay: here we go.*

The world shrinks beneath her, suddenly—ironically—unfamiliar. Soon all she can see is desert, dun mesas and bronze and swathes of bright gold. She can see a cross-hatched smudge, the half-city of New Leseum; the four towers of Pod Country; the mighty, battered hulk of the warship *Vierendelen* beyond, casting its long shadow over the rippling dunes.

And she can see something else, too: the familiar, massive shadow of the Leviathan, where she is to find her brother.

The air becomes suffocating inside the shuttle. Unable to guess the trajectory without Enlinking, she puts her trust in the *Vierendelen* to guide her to the Leviathan's edge.

Heat builds. Sweat beads on her forehead, her chest. She commits her neuroweb's resources to lowering her body temperature and feels icy coolant spread through her body from the nape of her neck, but it's too slow to counter the rising heat. Her eyes seem fit to rattle from their sockets.

Then, finally:

—*We've reached the original ejection point. Less than a minute to go. All right in there?*

"S-smashing."

—*Brace yourself. This is going to hurt.*

White-hot hooks in her spine. The pain is startling. With a guttural screech Sephine gives up and Enlinks to the *Vierendelen*'s data corpus. She sees the shuttle in four dimensions, watches time ebb and flow like the flourish of a gymnast's ribbon. And yet the pain permeates still, even in this new, abstract viewpoint.

She homes in on the careening shuttle, then herself—a jittering skeleton inside—and then her spine.

The roots of her wings are *changing*: the *Vierendelen* is adjusting the mechanisms that latch them to her spinal cord.

—*Delink!* the *Vierendelen* screams in her head, with a far-away quality, like it's yelling at her across a cathedral. —*Delink* now!

"Can't," she sends. ". . . Hurts."

—*Grin and bear it! Do it now!*

With just under a second to ejection, she manages it.

Back in normal-subjective spacetime, Sephine *feels* the wings find purchase in her spine, and the pain increases to the point that it becomes a hallucinogen—searing colored blades dance in her vision.

And from somewhere far away, laced with the pain, it seems:

—*Ejecting.*

Light blossoms. Noise dies. Sephine becomes lucid. The gunmetal backdrop falls away, and she erupts from the shuttle's exposed head streamlined and spinning slowly, high above the desert. Then a dark bowled shape fills her vision.

The Leviathan's iron skin is lined with slits and trenches, from which protrude clusters of black bristles, each a vicious arsenal. The Leviathan is a floating war machine.

It's only then that Sephine realizes how *huge* it is.

—*Deploy your wings. It won't hurt anymore, I promise.*

It doesn't.

Her wings unfurl with delicate snapping sounds. The charged atoms in their filaments crackle as she spirals skyward. Control is as intuitive as the use of limbs—one hard *push* and the wings ripple and pulse and pull her higher.

Then the Leviathan attacks.

—*Trouble. Down to you now, evade.*

Plasma fire. The defense systems have spotted her. She evades a flurry of blue-white projectiles, looping through the sky, up and up and around, and for a fleeting moment she forgets she is under fire—she is *enjoying* herself.

—*No time for showing off, just get to the Leviathan!*

A plasma needle screams past her head, igniting the air in its slipstream. With all her might she pushes the wings down, sending her careening upwards, finally over the Leviathan's rim, and she sees for the first time what lies atop the structure. It terrifies her.

She has no time to focus—the wings feel like they're giving up just as she penetrates the Leviathan's defensive parameters.

—*Oh, shit.*

The wings burst into flames. She pumps them as hard as she can, going down now, towards the very edge of the Leviathan. She feels tongues of fire lick at her back. Each roaring push of her wings wafts smoke into her eyes and her nose and her throat.

—*Almost there. Dive!*

The speed of the maneuver fans the flames roaring around her ears. Just as she feels the wings disintegrate and pain tear up and down her spine, she tucks in, and for a moment she is a human fireball, shedding smoking strips of filament and fabric. Then she slams onto the ground—painkillers and inertia stabilizers coursing through her—and rolls.

It's over. Sephine lies awkwardly on her back. Her wings are nothing more than winter trees now: gnarled black branches loosely rooted in her spine. They whisper as they dissolve, causing her pain.

—*Well! Wasn't so hard, was it?*

"Shit," she breathes. Her skin burns and her clothes are ruined. There is the acrid smell of burning hair. "We made it."

—*Good job. When you Enlinked back there I thought we were done.*

"We?" she sends. "You'll be alright; it's *me* who was almost done."

—*Fair point.*

"Oh, and Del?"

—*Yes?*

"*Never* call me 'toots' again."

CHAPTER 2/6: SPITE

Sephine is in the *Vierendelen*. The people of New Leseum have taken to calling it a fortress, though she disagrees. To her, it is just the *Vierendelen*: a kilometer-long gigaton of ruined hulls, bulkheads, and fuselage that was once a Golem-Class Leseum warship. (Although, she supposes it does look a *little* like a fortress, buried nose-down in the desert like this, towering over the fledgling city.)

Sephine is Enlinked and playing Spite with the ship. She and its AI battle each other with strings of code, constructed to entangle with and destroy one another. Mutually assured destruction is impossible—each battle ends with a winner.

"I know what you're doing," Sephine says, chancing a risky gambit. Against such a vastly intelligent machine as the *Vierendelen*, anybody would assume the game a forgone conclusion, that each game would end in a crushing defeat for her human mind—but the ship is being coy.

Sephine's gambit pays off, corrupting the *Vierendelen*'s code string and leaving it in an irreversible Spite. She's won the game.

—*Nice move.*

"Don't patronize me. You're playing Rokri's tactics."

—*Is he that transparent?*

In real space, Sephine scowls—Enlinked, she has no face, just code. "He certainly *was*."

She Delinks, opening her eyes back in real space.

—*You're so sure, aren't you?* the ship continues.

"It's been a year, Del. I know my brother. He'd be more straightforward than this. More . . ."

—*Transparent?*

Sephine nods.

—*But you're so keen to accept he's dead, and now there's just a sliver of hope and you're all too ready to abandon it. There's all kinds of things you're not taking into account.*

"Hope?" she spits. "Hope? An encrypted signal we can do nothing with is not *hope*, Del. And it certainly isn't from Rokri, either. It's from the enemy, and I think you know it too." She bites her fingernails. "He was a fool to go."

Dusty light cascades down into the atrium, cut by the sharp outlines of metal arcing high above: bones of the gutted ship. Sephine can hear the low thrum of esoteric machines deep within what is left of the *Vierendelen*'s hull. Although the ship's AI has no centralized structure (its consciousness runs through the few substrates that still receive power from the engines), it has a tendency to manifest itself as a collared dove. At this moment, the *Vierendelen* is perched on a high bulkhead overlooking the atrium, mussing its iridescent wings and cooing softly.

—*Sephine. If this message, signal—whatever—if it is from Rokri, then wouldn't he want a reply?*

"You said yourself, we have no decryption software capable of sending a message back."

—*Correct. But I wasn't just thinking of sending a message.*

Just the thought opens a pit in her stomach. She knows what the ship means: go up there. Go to the Leviathan and search for him.

"It's not as simple as that."

—*Getting him up there was.*

"It was suicide, and selfish," she snaps. "We needed him. *I* needed him." Sephine wanders over to a rockery on the far side of the atrium. A stream gurgles gently into a clear pond, where lilies reach through the surface. Mechanical fish flit amongst their roots.

Sephine sits down and takes a handful of pebbles, tossing them absent-mindedly into the pool. The fish dart away.

A low rumble goes through the ground. The lilies stir.

—*Fissure bombs in the Farside Basin. I'd better check it out.*

"The attacks are getting closer," Sephine says darkly.

—*Not if I have anything to do with it. And I* always *have something to do with it.*

Sephine imagines the ship winking at her.

—*Hive minds are as easy to fool as human ones. Catch up later. And think about it.*

Then she feels the *disconnectedness* as the *Vierendelen* severs its connection with her neuroweb. The collared dove effervesces from existence.

Sephine is alone with her thoughts and grateful for it, but she's incapable of staying idle for long. She scatters another handful of pebbles over the pond, sits down on the gravel, and Enlinks.

The ship's data corpus presents her with a wireframe view of the gutted hull, where bulkheads and metal ribs and drooping, limb-thick wires dangle together in four dimensions. She withdraws from this and views the *Vierendelen* in its entirety.

Tracker drones pour from the ship in droves. She adopts the viewpoint of one of the rugged little machines as it speeds across the desert to a deep crater about fifty kilometers away.

The bladeships of the Fractured are peppering the Farside Basin with bombs. Scavenger craft swoop into the fray, grabbers swinging from their hulls to pluck huge rocks left by the explosions. The ships contain no biological life-forms, and nobody has any idea why the Fractured harvest bedrock like this.

This is the closest attack to the city in months. If the Fractured decided to invade, New Leseum would be dust in minutes. The people have a militia but are armed with nothing more than splinter-rifles and fists, protected by antique exoskels found in what was left of the *Vierendelen*'s armories. In the event of an attack, they may be able to cannibalize some weapons from the ship itself—put up a little fight—but there aren't any guarantees.

In any case, the Fractured never seem to be interested. Perhaps they have no appetite for easy game—

". . . Oh."

An idea strikes her like a needlehead.

She abandons the tracker drones, pulls her view back to the city, and delves into the *Vierendelen*'s storage substrates.

She extracts memories. They appear to her as a compartmentalized ocean of data-packets.

She accesses the message received from the Leviathan a week earlier: a convoluted jumble of code, encrypted and inaccessible without figuring out how to *untie* the chaos and lay the information streams into straight lines.

And as she examines it again, there is suddenly a way, a technique to unlocking the message. All knots are untied in different ways— some require no more than a pull. Others demand multitasking and organization, planning and backtracking: a strategy.

And she recognizes the strategy.

It's a Spite algorithm.

Her heart beats a tattoo in her chest. Could it be this simple?

She puts the message itself to one side, and brings up the most recent memory in the *Vierendelen*'s library: their game of Spite.

She deconstructs it.

Each strand of unique code in a game of Spite is the result of an algorithm, a protocol of unique characters that must be disrupted in order to win. The algorithm which the ship used against her—as Sephine guessed earlier—is identical to that which Rokri used to play.

Sephine inputs the algorithm as a passcode for the message.

And the knot responds. Data twitches, rearranges itself, and the message is laid out flat.

That means one thing: Rokri is alive.

Sephine Delinks and runs from the atrium to find the Makers.

"We have several options here," says Maker Lupin.

New Leseum's chief engineer is a thoughtful man and of few words—except when his pride is dented. The *Vierendelen* finds him pompous, which Sephine thinks is a rather facile observation coming from a machine of its intelligence.

Sephine is *de facto* leader of the Makers, the seven charged with building the city. She is a go-between for the Makers and the ship because she is the only one that possesses a neuroweb. They'd never admit it, but Sephine thinks the Makers are somewhat jealous of the technology she and her brother have laced into their brains. Through it they have the potential to wield a large amount of power over the citizens of New Leseum—but the Makers know that power would never be exercised. They are all there for a common purpose: to build the new home.

The Makers and Sephine are seated around a dull steel table in the committee building in the northwest corner of the city. Moonlight sails in wisps through the glass ceiling, and orange plasma torches in shallow sconces provide extra light. Bowls of broth make the air thick with the smell of vegetables, though Sephine isn't hungry.

Lupin continues.

"We could try to establish contact," he says, stroking his thinly bearded chin.

—*He* knows *how many times I've tried that*, the *Vierendelen* says.

Sephine interjects. "That's hopeless. Plus, the message is empty. The key to the message *is* the message. Rokri is trying to contact *me*. The ship lost contact with him after the Leviathan last passed over. I think . . ." She pauses, biting a fingernail. "I think he's found a way to reach us, and he's asking for help."

"We have to realize sending a message might draw unwanted attention," Maker Gelgher says, the brow below his bald head wrinkled into a reflective frown. "Or, this is a trap."

"A Fractured fleet attacked the Farside Basin not a few hours ago. I know *I'd* rather not risk it." Lupin adopts a sage expression.

"But if the Fractured were to attack, they'd have done it by now."

—*Here we go . . .*

"It doesn't *matter*, Gelgher. We can't risk the city."

"We *live* in risk—"

"I'm going up," Sephine says, with exasperated conviction. "I'm going to the Leviathan."

—*That's the spirit.*

She doesn't wait for the stunned Makers to reply, and leaves them to battle it out.

The Makers debate without her for four interminable days, during which Sephine spends hours out at Pod Country, thinking, watching the horizon from the towers, like Rokri had done this time a year earlier. A dark shape blots the distant clouds: the Leviathan making its annual pass. Time is running out.

The *Vierendelen* has responded to Sephine's wish with alacrity, and on the fifth day has something it wants to show her, so it summons her back to the atrium.

The ship presents her with what looks like a blueprint for a pair of wings. Together they span about ten feet and will be made of a malleable, fibrous compound separated into filaments, which the ship tells her has been salvaged from a previously unknown store of exotic materials used in the war.

—*Thought these might help. When Rokri went up, I thought afterwards if he'd just had some extra* oomph, *it would have been less hairy. Anyway, if they approve of you going up—not that it matters either way—then I want you and me to supervise him making these babies. There's no room for error.*

Sephine scoffs. "Good luck with that."

She examines the wings. It appears they will attach themselves to her spine with thousands of tiny hooks. "They look painful—but beautiful," she adds hastily (the ship is a proud creature).

—*Oh, pish. I'm sure the infirmary can spare some anesthetic. Failing that, you can Enlink and I can tinker with your web, but I'd rather the former—less risk. You know what I mean.*

Sephine knows exactly what it means, and agrees.

★ ★ ★

Delinking, Sephine is surprised to find a woman standing beside the nearby rockery, flicking pebbles into the pool.

"Maker Sensra," Sephine says, and takes a step towards her.

The Maker does not reply at first.

Sensra was an architect back in Leseum Blue, and is the Maker in charge of city planning. She is in her mid-forties, and wears her hair in a short, choppy cut.

"We took a vote," Sensra says eventually. "I voted against, just to let you know. But in the end, I was the only one." She flashes Sephine a brief look of resentment. Sephine ignores her.

"The Leviathan is making a pass in the next two days. Can we be ready by then?"

Sensra makes a scoffing noise. "You got your arrogance from your mother—but at least she had foresight. What happens if you don't come back either, hmm? What then for the rest of us? Stuck here? On this gods-forsaken rock, bait for the Fractured?"

Sephine is saddened by the Maker's viciousness, but really it just makes her more resolute.

"Well, I will come back. He's alive up there, Sensra, and I'm going to find him. There could be anything up there. Maybe even . . . maybe a way home."

Sensra turns on her heel and mutters, "Fool."

Sephine tries not to betray her frustration, but can't help it, and kicks at the ground. A flurry of pebbles arcs through the air and rains down onto the pool.

As Sensra goes to leave, she turns her head and says, "The cannon will be ready tomorrow. If you *do* find Rokri, then . . ." she hesitates, then stops short and slips out the door.

Sephine frowns.

"Er, Del? What cannon? What did she mean by that?"

—*Ah. About that.*

CHAPTER 1/6: DOWN

The day the ship was downed its human cargo went to Pod Country.

It took just a few well-timed q-missiles from the Fractured fleet;

the effect of the shots was like blowing up the two nearside tires of a vehicle as it powered along a tilted highway.

The *Vierendelen* had been hugging the planet's gravity well, pouring its energy into staying poised on its edge. Its plan was to catch the oncoming Fractured off-guard, meet it head-on, slalom through the myriad ships, and escape into deeper space, where it could 'fold and escape back to Leseum Blue.

The feint failed. The q-missile burst hit as it encountered the first line of nimble bladeships, and the *Vierendelen* tumbled into the pull of the gravity well. Apparently sure the crash would be fatal, the Fractured retreated and left the ship to its fate.

But while the ship set about rearranging much of its engine configurations, the crew on the *Vierendelen*'s command floor worked feverishly to level out the descent.

Each knew they were about to die.

But that was nothing; it was the ship's cargo that mattered: fifty thousand souls had made it safely to Pod Country before the skirmish, and the ship protected this massive complex of stasis modules with every resource available (—*Trust me, it would take a hundred q-nukes to penetrate this baby, of which the Fractured have zip*).

Deep within the belly of the ship, lockdowns took place. Giga-sized machines enfolded the massive network of amniotic sacs within an impenetrable womb.

On the command floor, the doomed few that remained all but ignored the rapidly approaching surface. With the help of the ship's AI, they secured a location, an angle, a trajectory for the crash landing. And to their amazement, cloud-scanners revealed they were headed toward a flat, open plain of desert and scrubland.

The Commander thought, for a moment, *I think we might actually make this . . .* as the ship sank through the cloud barrier, and the desert stared up at her with dusty indifference.

But they had never expected the dark shape that met them beneath the clouds. A menacing specter of a thing, the Commander likened it to diving into the sea, and encountering an impossibly large monster— a huge, black smudge in the haze of the lower atmosphere.

And the monster's reaction was quick.

The *Vierendelen* couldn't act in time, and the object—which would be later referred to as the Leviathan—had locked onto the beleaguered ship and fired.

The *Vierendelen* registered a femtosecond of reluctant admiration: the Leviathan had fired a single needlehead at precisely the right place, up through an exhaust shaft and rupturing a crucial tangle of fuel injectors in its lower bow.

The Leviathan had *known* how much it would take to bring the ship down.

The *Vierendelen*—highly impressed with its attacker—tried to secure its own survival by hijacking a handful of Pods and flooding them with its data, and accepted defeat not ungracefully.

But just as the front engines reached critical mass, the ship received a deeply worrying piece of information.

The last thought that had gone through the Commander's neuroweb was of her twelve-year-old children, the twins that would have one day taken the helm of the great ship. Just before the *Vierendelen*'s fuel injectors ignited, the Commander Enlinked, and with her last breath felt the ship create a neuroweb linkup—Sephine and Rokri were alive, in the womb of the ship. In Pod Country.

Relieved, she died.

But the *Vierendelen* had had no time to tell her just what the Leviathan had done.

It has been six years.

The girl called Sephine awakens—from a dream about a room and a box, and a man and a bird—to find her brother gone from his bed. He has always been apt to wandering off (much to Maker Sensra's chagrin), but never at night.

It's four o'clock. She gets out of bed to look for him.

Leaving their fairly ramshackle home in the shadow of the *Vierendelen*, she looks to the east, and sees the first veins of sunlight bleed over the horizon. The once-mighty warship is silhouetted against a pink dawn streaked with silver-edged clouds.

She looks up at the ship. As if reading her mind, she feels it connect—the handshake protocol feels like waking up all over again.

—*He's over at Pod Country, if you were wondering.*

She furrows her brow, tugs her coat around her against the chilly breeze, and sets off in the direction of Pod Country, beyond the wreck.

"What's he doing there?"

—*Thinking, I'll bet. That queer pastime of the flesh* ...

"What else is there to do, space-trash?"

—*Ouch.*

She giggles and heads through the city.

The towering grids of Pod Country are the tallest structures in New Leseum (save for the *Vierendelen* itself), and comprises four blocks twelve stories tall, each housing just under 12,500 dormant souls.

After the ship crashed, a few thousand people had been resurrected: people with essential skills; leaders; the stronger menial workers; teachers; doctors; some scientists; architects; and a few military personnel, once it became apparent the planet was some sort of hub for Fractured activity. The ship had seen fit to resurrect a few hundred civilians too, to add some normality. These people had been traveling on the ship when war broke out—they had intended to transfer to another vessel once clear of Fractured space.

Sephine stands at the intersection between the four towers, above which the sky describes an azure cross.

The pods glow a bright cyan—it's dark between the towers, but the stasis bubbles' glow is comforting. The bodies inside are still and pale.

For a while she was jealous of them, lying in cold, blissful oblivion for these six years, some even longer. She wonders if they know anything of what has happened. Some soon will; the *Vierendelen* plans to awaken another clutch of people in the coming months because of the swift progress on the city—although it has said this since the beginning (perhaps it's getting possessive of those already awake). Either way, it may soon have to—Fractured attacks are getting closer by the month, and defense may soon be needed.

Enlinking, Sephine spies Rokri at the top of the tower to her right, lying on the circular platform capping the tower.

"The hell is he doing up there ... ?"

She makes her way up through a series of cross-hatched gantries and stairwells, her hand always gripping a railing—she's uneasy with heights.

She finds Rokri lying with his hands behind his head. His dark hair is bed-messy and he's wearing a fur-lined coat and his pajama bottoms.

Sephine giggles. "You look a right sight," she says, and sits beside him. He appears deep in thought, though he's not Enlinked; his eyes are their usual icy-gray.

"That time of year again," he says wearily.

She wonders what he means, then follows his gaze to the horizon, and feels a little swell of dread in her belly. She says nothing.

"I've been thinking," he says, in a tone Sephine can only describe as ominous.

—*Knew it!*

Rokri sits up. The breeze ruffles his hair. "There's an old flier I found. In one of Del's old hangars."

"Rokri, I—"

"And I think, with Lupin's help, I could get it to work." Now he turns to her.

A year ago, probably to the day, he had looked up to the Leviathan and raged that it was all just so unfair. It was unfair that the war still went on far away, that they were stuck here with a crippled ship, unable to help, barely able to help themselves.

He wants to fight. Sephine does not—she just wants to go home.

"I'm sick of it, Seph. Sick of building. Sick of boredom. I'm sick of all this fucking dust. But you know what's worse? I'm sick of seeing *that* thing." He jabs a finger towards the horizon. "Taunting us. Mocking us. Every signal blocked, every distress call. We're hopeless as long as the Leviathan looks down on us."

Every signal. Every distress call.

New Leseum is coldly, profoundly alone out here.

"Rokri . . ." Sephine begins, and struggles to find the words. "This flier—it won't work. Del can't even get tracker drones past—"

"Those things are big, ancient, and clumsy. That's the only reason they survived the crash."

"And how is a flier any different?"

"A flier has an ejection system." His eyes flash. "There's no way the Leviathan could hit a target as small as a person, surely. And no one else is prepared to go. If I managed to get the flier high enough, get Lupin to make some . . . I don't know, boosters or something I could wear, I think I could get there."

Suddenly he looks on the verge of tears. He's rambling. "There're answers up there, Seph. Maybe a way to bring it down, maybe Del could even harvest its engine, somehow. There might be a way home."

He's right. They have no ship, but the route to Leseum Blue lies within her and her brother. They don't *know* them exactly, but the route lies encoded somewhere deep in their neurowebs, and even the *Vierendelen* can't access them. Only they can. They protect their people's secret, the responsibility Leseum placed upon their mother now split between them—a vulnerable failsafe made in the haste of war.

Without Sephine and Rokri, the people are doomed.

"I won't come with you," Sephine says softly. "I won't."

She almost regrets having said that as the words meet the air. Rokri looks utterly crestfallen.

They sit in silence for a long time. The ribbons of morning eventually burst into full daylight, daylight blighted by a dark shape creeping along the sky.

Sephine wonders if Del is talking him into it. She knows full well the ship is keen to get up there—it probably told him about the flier in the first place.

Eventually, bereft of anything else to say, Sephine says, "Please don't."

He turns to her now, and she sees there is determination in his hard features. His eyes seem icier now, gleaming novae in olive skin. Sephine realizes she has reduced herself to outright begging, and feels ashamed.

He has made his decision.

Sephine hates him then. She hates him more than she's hated anyone—but that's not entirely true. She hates Del, too, for all the part it's played in this.

When the day comes, Sephine is nowhere to be seen. Her neuroweb has activated its privacy settings. Even Del can't get through to her.

He feels like vomiting. The flier looks like a mashed-together tangle of components, its cockpit just identifiable: a carbuncle at the craft's nose, and it's large enough—*just* large enough—for one person.

He triggers a dose of anti-emetics for the nausea, and serotonin to keep him calm.

The Makers stand at the edge of the crowd that has gathered to watch. Some look excited, because they don't know how important he is. Surely if they did, they would lock him and his sister away.

But most wear worried expressions.

Maker Sensra looks like stone. She has always been a hard woman, stern with Rokri and Sephine, but protective—they are her late Commander's children, after all. But more recently it's seemed as if she's drifted away from them. Rokri suspects it has to do with the coordinates in their 'webs: knowing the way home lies somewhere in their heads but being completely unable to unlock them must be infuriating. Rokri knows the feeling—better than most, probably.

He tries to stop himself feeling angry at everything, to focus on the mission, on surviving.

—*I'm so sorry, but it really is time now.*

Rokri nods, and lets out a humorless chuckle. "Thought we'd have time for one more game."

—*Grief, what the hell made you think that would be a decent goodbye?*

"Come on, Del. Don't tell me she's bored of Spite."

—*I don't blame her! You let her win every time. I told you, if you want to win—*

"Shut it. Let's go."

Rokri loads into the flier. His hands shake violently as he fumbles with the control module, powering the engines up. Dust plumes around the little craft, its metal feet, while Rokri makes some final checks on the ejection system.

It all works fine. He doesn't know how to feel about that.

High above, the Leviathan has partially blocked the sun, and New Leseum sits in a counterfeit eclipse.

Soon, he's in the air. But he's hovering over the crowd, hesitant. The *Vierendelen* warns him not to waste fuel, or power, but when he took off, Rokri had a final, acute yearning to see his sister one last time.

The ship is patient with him for as long as the mission will allow, but when she still doesn't show, it insists they carry on.

Crestfallen, Rokri powers up the thrusters, and the flier convulses around him, and carries him up to the Leviathan.

Just before ejection, he looks down at the city, and wonders briefly what it feels like to die.

★ ★ ★

She's missed him.

She had reached the back of the crowd just in time to see the little flier shoot upwards, carrying her brother away from her forever, and she collapsed onto the dusty desert floor in sobs, and when she Enlinks in a final plea to say goodbye, she cannot feel him anymore.

Almost a year later, the *Vierendelen* receives an encrypted communication from the Leviathan. Nobody can decipher it. Nobody can access it. But, for some reason Sephine cannot fathom, the *Vierendelen* is convinced it is from Rokri.

CHAPTER 4/6: GROUNDED

Several hours pass in peaks and troughs, phantasmagoric. Sephine folds through layers of suffering as the hooks of her wings dissolve one by one, each more painful than the last, each plunging her into paroxysms of agony. Whenever the pain fades it comes back stronger, and she seethes and arches her back and shakes all over, foamed saliva dried into a thick, white crust around her mouth. When the last hooks dissolve, Sephine thinks she's being fooled, cruelly lulled into security before the pain returns.

But it's over. She sits up, very slowly, conscious of the dull throb up and down her back. At last, she can focus.

She is just a few feet from the Leviathan's encircling edge-wall. She's tall enough to peer over it, but she's not sure she has the guts to.

She chances communicating with the *Vierendelen*. No response. She half expected this, but all the same is struck by a stark and singular loneliness. She can feel a very faint connection with the ship, but it is nothing more than background noise, static. She wonders if it can hear her, but can't get through the Leviathan's comms-blocking signal. It feels alien to have had a voice in her head her whole life, and now have nothing but silence. Her thoughts feel naked somehow.

And all around her is nothing but silence too—silence, bar a faint wind that brings with it a sharp chill. Her clothes flutter, allowing the wind to creep in through the tears in the fabric to claw at her skin. She doses up on a little adrenaline to keep warm.

She turns from the edge-wall and looks up at what lies atop the Leviathan.

Closest to her are two identical structures: square, black towers, perhaps thirty feet high, and both featureless. Though unsure as to why, she remembers some song she heard a long time ago (*"Careful what you're looking at; it might be looking back"*).

And beyond these towers, there are hundreds more. The entire surface resembles a chaotic military installation, its instruments and structures organized in no discernible system whatsoever—but for some reason, she is reminded more of a city than a military outpost.

(Her memories of Leseum Blue are vague because she was just six when her parents were called to arms against the Fractured, but she remembers spires of pure white and glass and steel, and immense trees spilling water from their leaves, spuming down an escarpment into the ocean in torrential, elegant rapids, and she remembers the smell of meats and herbs and bakeries from the market towns on the coast, and the blue of the sea, and she remembers riding finned juliprae over the surf with her brother and her father.)

This city is no city. This city is cold and featureless and black. It smells of nothing. There is no water. Her father is dead; her brother may not be. Sephine holds that thought close as she steps into the city that is no city.

She pads softly over the cold floor, past structures and buildings and instruments whose function she cannot fathom.

Enlinking is just possible—but not to the *Vierendelen*. Instead her neuroweb builds a composite 3D map of the area which she can Enlink to, to better gauge her surroundings. She cannot see under the surface, even in X-ray. She can only imagine as to what is inside, below her.

The structures on the surface are varied and esoteric. She stands in the shadows of giant spinnakers, pentagonal dishes; walks past pens over whose walls she cannot see; chaotic things that must be machines but are completely dead; black, solid blocks, like the towers she first encountered. She notes that this is a common structure: black-body blocks, all varying in height and thickness. Some touch the clouds above, narrow as flagpoles—others are so broad and so stout she could walk over them. She doesn't, fearing a trap, and so sticks to the unmarked, likely unintentional, roads between the technological miscellany.

Her neuroweb, scanning these black structures, tells her that all of them are hollow. At one point she walks through an alley between two of the structures, separated by mere feet, and she is sure she can hear a scuttling noise inside them, a buzzing. She thinks of insects.

Dusk comes with a cold, inexorable hand, and with it moisture to the air. The clouds have sunk in a patch of low pressure, and Sephine's visibility is reduced to about fifty meters or so. The gaps between the structures become ghostly and animated with the quick mist.

The silence has become thicker, broken only by the faint ring of tinnitus—probably caused by the noise inside the q-cannon.

There is only one thought at the forefront of her mind: Where is Rokri? On the surface? Under it? Is he inside one of the black structures?

Is he alive?

The nature of her commitment strikes her then. A year. If she's lucky. A year before she passes over New Leseum again.

She clears her mind, relaxes herself with a touch of serotonin. And she begins to hum tunelessly. The sound of her humming is dull; there is no echo, no reverb. The clouds absorb it, like they absorb everything else, and suddenly she is reminded of the horror screens she used to watch with her brother on the *Vierendelen*, before the crash.

She scares herself and stops humming. And at that moment she is sure she sees something flit between two towers to her right. She stops dead.

She focuses on the narrow slit between the towers. Her heartbeat is the only thing she can hear. Nothing but mist creeps along beyond the gap.

You're being hypersensitive, she tells herself. *The mist is playing tricks on you.*

That had to be it: clouds making movements in the gloom.

She can't see more than twenty feet now. Structures more distant are just faint, towering ghosts. The feeling of being watched washes over her. Hastily she Enlinks, and confirms there are no life-forms nearby—no biological life-forms, at any rate.

She cannot combat the sinking feeling in her heart at what that implies: Rokri may not be here after all. Before the fingers of despair begin to throttle her, she presses on, hoping to reach the edge-wall and make camp for the night.

Night falls swifter than expected. In the dark, she fingers the souped-up stunner clipped to her utility belt. At range it will administer a powerful shock—at point blank the weapon is deadly. She also checks her shelter is still where it's supposed to be: a hyper-durable tent vacuum-sealed in a tiny, ceramic ball, swinging about her hip from the belt.

She decides to camp at the edge-wall. Walking in any direction across the Leviathan will bring her to the edge soon enough, and for some reason that seems safer, though she is not sure why. Perhaps if this is all some sort of trap, she can jump before she is killed. Better to go on her own terms than something else's.

In the dark, she can't see any more shapes slip through the gaps. But there *is* a ghostly glare about the place, a phosphorescence in the mist, and it takes her a minute to figure out why.

The black structures—their edges are glowing. A neon filigree traces bright emerald lines through the mist, conjuring ghostly shapes waltzing in the breeze.

But there is something else about the towers now. Something she couldn't see in daylight, but in the dark they stand out proud and frightening.

Now they have doors.

Sephine stops her aimless wandering, and stands, biting her nails, at the foot of the nearest tower.

The towers must lead downwards. Into the belly of the Leviathan. The glowing outline of the door is both enticing and terrifying at once. Sephine looks at her feet, trying to sum up the courage to enter the tower, and spots something on the ground.

It's a crude etching, scratched into the surface. An arrow, a gun. She looks back up at the door.

"Del?" Hopeless. "Del, please speak to me."

She takes a deep, quivering breath, and thumbs the stunner off the safety.

"Okay," she whispers. "You can do this."

And she reaches out to touch the door.

★ ★ ★

There is the oddest sensation in her brain, like inverted goose bumps. The panel makes a *snicking* noise, and withdraws with a loud hiss. Sephine jumps and takes a step back. A whirring starts beneath her feet. Slowly, the panel sinks into the floor, revealing a room beyond.

The room is dimly lit and warm. Lining the walls, neatly organized along racks, are row upon row of weapons. There must be over a hundred, all lethal and black and beastly beautiful. There are gaps—perhaps fifteen or so weapons are missing.

Excited by the prospect of extra protection, she commands her neuroweb to check the weapons' software—it's up and running. All the guns are functional. She Enlinks to them, finds their operating manuals.

These are Fractured weapons; the manuals are in Vavaral, but are easily translated. She downloads them quickly and takes two guns: a plaspistol and a splinter-rifle. Both are light, elegant, easy to fire.

It occurs to her that it must have been Rokri that scratched the gun and the arrow at the foot of the tower. It's a legend, a map icon signifying an armory. She'd been too preoccupied watching out for danger to bother scanning her surroundings more carefully.

The towers must all have different functions. If this tower isn't a way under the surface, then another must be. And now it should be easy to identify—as long as Rokri was thorough with his mapmaking. Maybe she could find shelter inside. The thought of avoiding camping in the cold, no matter how insulating her tent is, is comforting. And perhaps there's a control room. A map room. She could learn to *control* the Leviathan itself, guide it back—

She's getting ahead of herself.

It appears her theory was correct: the Leviathan is a military installation. A surveillance outpost. Obviously a weapon in and of itself, too. But why? What are the Fractured protecting here? And where is the crew? Is it totally unmanned? It is unquestionably a Fractured-built machine—the weapons manuals in Vavaral, the fleets of bladeships and scavenger craft scouting the surface unfettered by the Leviathan confirm it—but what is its true function?

With a glimmer of hope, Sephine wonders if it is abandoned.

She hoists the rifle over her shoulder and slots the pistol into her belt, a little positivity growing within her, an impetus. She turns and looks determinedly into the mist, and sees—something. Something floating a little way off. Something like a grainy signal, static and fuzzy. It appears to be growing larger, becoming defined and more clear in the thick fog, and she thinks that it's something she *recognizes*, and she feels the color drain from her cheeks when she realizes the ghost floating just feet from her is a face.

Her face, writhing and warping and gunmental-gray and ill-proportioned but she is *looking at herself* in the mist and a scream rises like bile in her throat—and the face *screams back*, its lips peel back and its empty mouth opens to nothing but the mist beyond and the sound is high and keening and thin but *loud* and those eyes are not eyes but the face is *all eyes*.

It's a swarm, a hive-minded Fractured swarm of tiny drones, each no larger than a knuckle, gathered into a crude, twisted facsimile of her—just her face, floating and dotted with livid-red optical sensors.

When her scream—and its—dies, Sephine fumbles frantically at her belt, searching for a weapon and praying it's the plaspistol, and it's up and pointed at the encroaching swarm in an instant. It's the stunner. She groans and thumbs it to splash, and as the face opens its terrible mouth and advances even more quickly she fires.

A wispy blue wave erupts from the muzzle of the stunner, and she watches her face quiver and disintegrate, melting away into a chaotic cloud of tumbling titanium marbles. The swarm collapses. The drones drum the floor like rain.

Sephine stares at the puddle of machines for a few moments, unable to control her breathing. The stunner is hot in her hand.

She's slipping the stunner back onto her belt when one of the drones twitches. Then another.

Soon the puddle of drones ripples like sheets in the wind, blinking red, and she runs.

She darts between towers and squeezes through tight alleys, swings around spires and jumps over low black blocks, and every time she looks back the swarm is in pursuit, no matter how many changes of direction, no matter how clever she thought her feints to be. With each corner the swarm disperses, and as it straightens out it consolidates back into that terrifying form, her image in the mist.

Suddenly Sephine breaks out into an open space, an avenue

between dead machines and towering spinnakers. She careens down the avenue. She can hear the swarm buzz close behind her, like a cloud of iron wasps whose hive she has disturbed.

She takes a sharp, sudden left, completely blind, and hopes she's lost the swarm, but—

—*Sephine, get down!*

"Wha—"

—she collides with some dark object, snapping her neck back, and she crumples to the floor with a sickened "*Oomph!*".

She will barely remember later, but just before everything went black, there was a bright blue flash, and a figure appeared, standing over her. She had just one thought, and it seemed to mean nothing, but it went round and round her mind like flies to carrion: *How do they know what I look like?*

And above and beyond the figure, she could have sworn she saw a bird, perched on a high tower.

CHAPTER 5/6: OTHERS

Awareness, or a glimmer of it. Just noise. Sephine doesn't know what the noise is, but for some reason the word "bustling" comes to mind, and this scares her because it means she's *not alone*, and she tries to open her eyes but they won't respond so she slips back into—

Awareness. Real. Sudden. Senses: verdant smell; metallic taste; head throbbing. Wherever she is, it's warm. This time her eyes work. She feels their lids flutter, sticky with sleep, and she manages to rend them apart. When they open, everything is blurred.

She blinks a few times, flexes her wrists, stretches her back. She can feel two slender grazes down either side of her spine, and when she stretches they wrinkle, irritating the skin.

She's lying on something soft. There's a pillow under her head.

She sits up, but she's overcome by dizziness, a headrush so powerful the edges of her vision turn indigo. She lies back again, massaging her temples.

What happened? The image of her face in the mist comes back to her, the apparition defining itself as it approaches, little red optical sensors winking and blinking and threatening. And the scream—that keening, supersonic scream.

She had run. And she had been stopped. Someone had told her to . . . someone had told her to do something, but it was *in her head*, her neuroweb, but that's impossible because she's so far from the *Vierendelen*.

But how far? Where am I?

She seeps a little adrenaline from her 'web. Her heart rate increases. It's safe to sit up again.

She's in a room, walled in dull rust-colored metal and lit softly by a handful of little globes that float like bubbles, bobbing gently against one another. There is a single door. She's lying on a thin mattress in the opposite corner. Sephine looks down at herself and finds her clothes have been changed. That makes her feel embarrassed and scared.

Her weapons are propped against the wall next to her. Her utility belt lies neatly on the floor.

There's a terminal screen on the wall across from her. At first glance it looks switched off, but there's a little flashing cursor in the top corner awaiting input.

The vegetable smell is coming from a pot near her bed. An incandescent circle built into the floor is cooking some kind of broth. Sephine's mouth waters so fast her jaw aches.

She tries Enlinking to her map, but it feels just out of reach, like punching in a dream. There's a murmuring, a dull thrum all around her.

She doesn't feel alone.

At that thought the door groans open. Sephine scrambles back against the wall. Her hand goes to the grip on the stunner, and it's up and in front of her in one swift movement, switched to beam.

A man enters and closes the door, and turns to face her. His hands go up.

The moment she recognizes him, she scrambles to her feet and flings her arms around her brother, sobbing into his shoulder.

Rokri has aged. His eyes are tired. He's unshaven. But he's bigger than she remembers, with powerful arms and shoulders, his chest defined and visible through the open collar of a baggy shirt.

Once she calms down, she asks him how he survived.

"The construct's uninhabited, except for Fractured," he says distractedly. "Most are pretty easy to destroy."

Construct?

"I . . ." she hesitates, wondering where to begin. She has so many questions. "For so long I thought you were dead."

He's seated at the terminal screen. Pinpoint beams from the wall project a keyboard onto the surface of the narrow desk underneath. His fingers thud rapidly against it. The keyboard is in Vavaral.

"Rokri?" She goes to the screen and tries to get him to look at her, but he's immersed in . . . whatever he's doing. "Rokri, what's the matter?"

He just keeps typing.

"Rokri, look at me. *Listen* to me!"

He slams his fist onto the desk and roars, sweeping a half-filled bowl from the desk that shatters against the door. Sephine jumps and stands back as Rokri rises from his seat, breathing hard.

"No!" he shouts. "No, no, no! Ruined! Everything ruined!" He puts his head in his hands.

"Rokri, what . . . what's happened? What's ruined?" Sephine speaks softer this time, sympathetic.

He visibly tries to calm himself.

"You shouldn't have come here. You should *never* have come here."

She stares at him. She tries not to appear hurt, but suspects she does. "I came to bring you back."

"And how do you expect to do that, eh?" he says venomously.

"I . . ."

"Got another set of wings, have you?"

"No, but—" *How does he know about that?*

"Got a fold-away flier in that belt of yours?"

"*Shut up!*"

His eyes don't even register she's screamed at him. He just stares at her.

The humiliation physically hurts. She feels sick. What is she doing? She hadn't *thought*; she'd just acted. Now it feels like the most stupid thing she could have possibly done.

"Rokri, look. I . . ." She gulps and takes a breath. "I don't *understand*. I deciphered your message. I thought . . . I thought it meant you wanted me to come here. I thought you needed help, that you were in trouble. Nobody else would come, nobody!"

At this, Rokri just sneers.

"Trouble?" he spits. "We're in a shitstorm of it now, sis."

"What does that mean?"

He looks incredulous. "Sephine. I didn't send any message."

"You need to see something."

Rokri has pulled up a map on the terminal screen: a wireframe image of the Leviathan. At his command the view withdraws and sweeps down, as if looking through a camera attached to the Leviathan's base.

They are passing over a sprawling delta, the first body of water Sephine has seen in years. Text flashes in the corner of the screen: **SALINITY 44%**.

The Leviathan can analyze the terrain's chemical makeup, even from this height.

"Salt lakes," Rokri says vaguely. "We'll be there soon."

"Where?"

"Convergence." He kills the screen. "Let's go. And bring your guns—they know you're here now."

He leads her out of the room into a corridor. The air is colder here. The corridor is lit by harsh strip-bulbs running along the corners of the ceiling. The walls are dotted with portholes, but the view beyond them is black. Sephine still doesn't know where she is except that she is under the surface, inside the Leviathan.

She wonders what's beyond the windows.

The next few minutes are a monotonous slideshow, corridor after corridor. After a time they come to an elevator. Rokri plucks a handheld terminal from his belt and flicks his pistol off the safety. He puts a finger to his lips and turns the terminal's screen towards her.

A map on the screen shows that they are below the edge-wall. The elevator shaft ends just feet from it, but on what side of the Leviathan Sephine can't tell.

They enter. The door snicks shut.

While they ride the elevator, Rokri turns to her.

"You've been lied to, Sephine," he whispers. "We all have.

"I've gotten to know this planet. What it is. I know how the construct works—it stays a mile off the ground, no matter what. In a few months it'll pass over a mountain range—still stays up a whole mile. You can't breathe outside. This all doesn't mean anything particularly, except the Fractured have learned to manipulate gravity, probably stolen Leseum technology." He shrugs. "But that's what the whole war is about, really. Technology. They crave it. Covet it.

"The engine's in the base of the construct. I've seen it. It repels the surface, inverts gravity somehow. Getting too close isn't . . . healthy." He bows his head and shows her his scalp. There are rough bald patches over his head revealing sore-looking skin underneath, like blisters or burn scars.

The elevator opens. Daylight explodes around them. The sky is a deep azure, cloudless. The sun steeps the surface with light, but the few towers Sephine can see are as black as they were at night. The other structures and machines are still unmoving and abandoned.

The edge-wall is a little way off.

Rokri takes her hand.

"A few months ago I managed to break through the construct's comms hardware. We thought Leseum had forgotten about us, but they haven't. The constructs absorb the messages like sponges. They share it around with each other. I have a suspicion they're laughing at us." He takes on a bitter expression.

Constructs?

"They're trying, Sephine. Leseum has been trying to contact us, but they haven't been able to. I think they presume us dead—the last unique message came three years after the crash, but I think they still hope. Automated signals come every now and then.

"When the *Vierendelen* crashed, its central AI tried to save itself by occupying a stasis bubble in Pod Country. The ship was taken down by a single needlehead to the fuel injectors in the bow. Our mother, her crew—all dead, instantly.

"But it wasn't just a needlehead."

They've reached the edge-wall. Rokri takes her shoulders and faces her, pushing her back against the wall. A sharp wind speaks up.

"It was a digital payload. A copy of a consciousness: the *Fractured's* consciousness. The one thing we've always known about the Fractured is that they're a hive mind. The swarm that attacked you, the constructs. The flagships heading up their fleets, down to the fleet's individuals themselves. There's no centralized intelligence maintaining it; it's just a singular consciousness. A colony."

"So . . . what? What does all this mean?"

"The *Vierendelen* was destroyed, Sephine. Its AI substrates were *replaced* by the Fractured's. By the time the ship hit the surface, it was already one of them."

Realization now—a glimmer of it. But disbelief, too.

"The last time we talked to Del, the *real Vierendelen*, was when we were kids. Kids on a ship caught up in a war we had no part in."

"No," she says quietly.

"We were lied to. The whole time. We weren't talking with the ship. We were talking to *them*."

And he turns her around, and when she peers over the wall she feels like she might vomit. Because all around them, floating high above the delta of salt lakes and distant canyons, even in the far distance where mountains ruffle the horizon, are others. Other Leviathans. Moving lazily above the surface, casting their perfect shadows upon imperfect terrain.

Convergence.

The sky darkens suddenly, and Sephine looks up, gaping at it; another is *passing over them*, just as massive as the Leviathan upon which they stand. She feels very, very dizzy.

"I didn't send any message, Sephine. It was the Fractured. You were tricked. *We* were tricked, into coming up here."

"I don't believe it," she says, her voice catching in her throat. "I won't believe it. Your message . . . I deciphered it. With a Spite algorithm, *your* algorithm."

"Of course you did. And if you hadn't have worked it out in time, they would have given you a nudge in the right direction."

And they did. She played Spite the day she deciphered the message. It had waited. Waited for its next pass over New Leseum, when it was close enough. When it could coax her into going up.

"Tell me, Sephine. How could a Leseum-built, Golem-class AI like the *Vierendelen* not decipher a simple Spite algorithm? Come to that, why don't you think the ship ever tried to repair itself? Just sitting there, wrecked, for all that time without a single attempt to rectify its situation? Just letting us get on, building our little city, our new home?

"Biding its time, Sephine. Waiting. Goading us, me and you, to come up here and find out the truth about their prison planet. That's what this is. A prison."

"But why us?" she says, her voice shaking. "Why not just kill us all? Why are we special?"

He actually smiles. "Come on, sis. You know exactly why. The Fractured were looking for something on our ship. They cornered the *Vierendelen* in the gravity well of this planet and brought it down to find it. And you know what they were looking for."

And suddenly she does.

"Now they've found it." Rokri looks out over the swirling delta, at the dozen lazy Leviathans spotting the salt lakes with their shadows.

Then comes a tingle in Sephine's head. That inverted goose bumps feeling again, familiar, but now completely alien. And the next voice she hears comes not from Rokri's mouth, but from her neuroweb:

—*Sorry, toots*, the Leviathan says.

CHAPTER 6/6: FLIGHT

Coordinates.

The route to Leseum Blue, encoded in their neurowebs.

The Fractured want to win the war, and to do that they need a Leseum Commander—or a Commander's insurance policy: their children. They need Rokri and Sephine. And Rokri and Sephine have offered themselves up to the enemy.

The humiliation cuts her inside, the betrayal. And it just gets worse and worse as she puts the pieces together in her head.

Why New Leseum was never attacked. How the "*Vierendelen*" had sourced the materials for her wings. How both she and Rokri had made it up here without being vaporized by the Leviathan. All perpetuating the illusion. How could she not have seen it? The voice in her head the night before flashes into her memory . . . that should have been enough, enough to tell her things weren't right.

The city was never attacked because the Fractured couldn't risk killing either of them. The attack on the Farside Basin that day had been a ruse—probably delivering the materials for her filament wings.

Sensra had been right: all arrogance, no foresight.

Sephine feels nothing but devastatingly stupid.

"We have to get out of here," she says in a weak, trembling voice. "Rokri, we have to get out."

—*You could always jump. Kill yourselves. It's a long way down.*

Rokri sees the sudden, horrified expression come to her face. "Turn off your 'web. Turn it off *now*."

—*Of course, if you* do *try that, I'll probably just send a—*

Sephine switches on her neuroweb's privacy settings. The Leviathan blips into silence.

"What do we do?"

"We go back down, into the construct." Rokri is already heading back, pulling her with him. "Now you know, they'll make their move."

He's still dragging her, but doesn't have to for very long; she runs with him. They dart through the towers together, past the elevator from which they emerged. They'll be expecting them, Sephine figures. Rokri knows where they are going—time to test his mapmaking.

A loud hiss. The sound of machines. A tower opens to their right, and vomits a swarm of drones, dispersing and coalescing together, shimmering through the air like static. Rokri clocks the swarm and his gun is up barely before Sephine even registers they're being attacked. The swarm makes a layered, stuttered groaning noise and collapses in an iron hailstorm.

"Come on," he says, running past her.

They run until they come to another black tower, another elevator. The door snicks open, and Sephine swings round, met by the Fractured again, only this time it's not a swarm, but a single machine, bristling with weapons and made of countless contra-rotating components creating the vague shape of a face. Whose she doesn't know. She swings the splinter-rifle over her shoulder and fires, backing into the elevator. The Fractured jerks sharply, components locking as the splinter collides with a festoon of wires in its middle. Its weapons fire indiscriminately and it tumbles to the ground.

As the elevator door begins to close, the machine shakes and a metal limb cracks and groans and points at her. It fires a second too late, but Sephine flinches and falls back against the elevator's far wall. The shot collides with the tower. The elevator rumbles around them.

"Can we escape?" she gasps, catching her breath.

Rokri rubs his temples and bows his head, as if considering some impossible conundrum. Finally he says, "Yes. But at a cost."

"What cost?"

"There's a hangar in the lower levels, above the engine. There's 'fold-capable craft in there, Leseum-built, too. Assuming they want us alive and we aren't obliterated on sight, we might be able to get off-planet. But, Sephine—"

"The others."

Without her or her brother, the Fractured would think nothing of destroying the city. Without them, its people are expendable. Worthless.

"And that's assuming the city isn't dust already," Rokri says darkly.

She hadn't thought of that. "Well . . . if that's the case, then . . ." She can't bring herself to say it.

She's spent almost half her life in that half-city. She's always known New Leseum wasn't her home, but it's been the closest thing she's had to one. Her friends. Teachers. The Makers. She grew up with those people, and each one would have protected her with their lives had they known the secret she holds in her head.

And now she's considering leaving them to their deaths.

She screams in frustration and thumps the elevator wall.

Rokri says, "I don't see what choice we have."

Neither does she.

The elevator descends past the floor of Rokri's makeshift home, into the belly of the construct.

"Be ready," Rokri says, racking his weapon. "The Fractured won't let us go that easy."

She racks her rifle as the elevator comes to a halt, and the door slides open.

The space inside the Leviathan is vast. There are dormant ships everywhere. None is nearly as big as the *Vierendelen*, but they're all large enough for a substantial crew. Sephine can see a few that are Leseum-built, but most are Fractured vessels. Their style is more streamlined yet somehow less elegant, like ornamental knives gone to rust. There are even a few ships that are neither Leseum nor Fractured, with filament sails, shadow-drives, knife-edge fins towering high above the hangar. She has no idea to which civilization they belong.

The floor is meshed wrought-iron. There are stairwells dotted around leading down further, as if the hangar is a vast missile silo. Sephine spots a faint, white-blue light far below through the crisscrossing holes in the floor—that must be the engine. She heads to the nearest stairwell and peers down through a tangle of gantries and railings.

"Are we really going to do this?" She turns to Rokri. His face is stone. Again she notices just how old he looks. "We're just going to leave them here?"

"It's either that or risk home. Risk losing the war."

"But—"

"We have no choice, Sephine! It's fifty thousand, or countless millions—if we stay, and the Fractured take those coordinates from us, we'll be dead. And they will be, too. And then they'll attack our home, and there'll be nothing left of us. Nothing! Damage control, Seph. If we do something *now*, at least there's a chance to save home *and* ourselves. Maybe New Leseum, too. Maybe."

"If we can bring a fleet in time."

"Right."

"And if we don't die escaping."

"Yes."

"And if the city wasn't destroyed the moment I left."

"Not likely. But yes."

Sephine thinks for a moment. "I can't help but feel we're being selfish."

"What do you mean?"

I mean, she thinks, *maybe we should just kill ourselves. Blow our brains out right here and just be done with it.*

Now who's being selfish . . . she adds silently.

Realization comes to his face. "Don't you even think it," he says. (Sephine imagines the *Vierendelen* saying —*Too late!*, and grimaces.)

"Either way," he continues, "all those people will die." He takes her face in his hands, cradling her, and his expression becomes soothing and concerned, but laced with what looks like pleading. "If we die, we go out trying, at the very least. We're taking the one course of action that has a chance of a positive outcome. You have to see that." His eyes flick back and forth across hers, desperation in his face. "Please."

Noises: metal on metal. Scurrying, like impossibly heavy insects. Some way across the hangar, a deafening blast. A ship has exploded. A scorching arch loops into the air.

"We have to get to a Leseum ship." Rokri grabs Sephine's arm and pulls her across the hangar.

Movement under the spindly feet of a nearby ship. Plasma fire. A shot screams past, barely a meter from them. Sephine feels the heat of it on her face.

"This way!" Rokri pulls her in the other direction. She catches a glimpse of their assailant before he turns—another singular drone. Jogging backwards, Rokri fires, sending a white-hot projectile into the Fractured machine. It careens backward and up with the force of the shot, tumbling through the air to slam into the hull of the ship behind it, exploding violently.

Then there are more.

Sephine and Rokri weave their way around and under ships, and each time they look up there are more and more Fractured pursuing them. Sephine hears the now-familiar buzzing of a swarm, and when she looks up into the empty, cavernous expanse of the Leviathan, there are tens of them, a sentient iron storm threatening to rain destruction upon them, optical-sensors like livid scarlet lightening.

She grabs her brother by the arm and hauls him under the cover of a small craft, just as a deluge of little drones descends. They batter the floor where they had just been standing.

They roll together and emerge, and are met by a trio of machines, weapons powered up. Sephine and Rokri fire before the Fractured can. All three burst into crackling pieces of twisted metal.

They sprint towards the middle of the hangar.

Another ship explodes, somewhere. She feels as if they're running aimlessly. She can't bring herself to look back, but she can hear the noise of metal footsteps behind them.

Another shot tears past her head, inches away, burning her cheek and singeing her hair. She arcs her arm out awkwardly behind her and fires blind. An explosion abruptly follows.

Ahead are two ships, noses pointing inwards, each standing on three legs about two meters high. Beyond that there is a railing. Beyond that, nothing.

"Shit!" Rokri slows his pace as they pass under the ships' noses, but Sephine can't stop in time and slams into the railing, bending over double, winded, and for a second she is poised over it at the waist by her momentum, staring down, down into the depths of the Leviathan, its mighty engine. Her wing-grazes split. Pain rips across her back.

Rokri reaches out and grabs her shirt, yanking her back onto solid ground. She kneels and splutters, coughing, trying to catch her breath.

"Cornered," Rokri says.

She looks up and despairs.

At least twenty machines are encroaching, flanked by swarms. The swarms taunt them, gathering into facsimiles of her and Rokri.

"There!" Sephine yells, pointing. To the left, behind two small single-passenger craft, stands a Leseum ship. A symbol on its fuselage tells them it's 'fold-capable. Their escape.

Sephine doesn't think; she just fires. One, two shots, each at the forelegs of the two ships between them and the advancing Fractured. The ships' noses burst into blue fire and tip forward, crumpling against each other with a cacophonous groan. A few Fractured machines underneath are crushed. But the swarms just glide through the flaming wrecks unfettered.

"Come on!" Rokri pulls her to her feet, and yet again they are running. More explosions, closer this time, in quick succession.

"It's trying to stall us, destroying every ship. Faster!"

They pass under a dormant Fractured craft and emerge into open space. The Leseum ship is just ahead of them now, barely ten meters away.

Sephine runs towards the ship first, faster than she's ever run, and just as she reaches its access ramp, she hears Rokri cry out.

She darts up the ramp, slams her fist into the entrance pad, and turns as the aperture opens.

Rokri is down, screaming. A spatter of blood paints the floor by his right arm. Behind him, Fractured drones are advancing, firing into any ship within range.

"Get up!" she screams at him. "Rokri, get up!"

He looks up at her, dazed. His right arm is gone up to the elbow. The Fractured fire at the floor around him.

He rolls onto his back, fires at the Fractured. He begins to scramble backward, instinctively putting out his right arm for support, but collapses onto the stump. His scream is almost as loud as the explosions.

"Get up and *run!*"

And he does, but he's going too slowly, and Sephine can't help but feel that all is lost. A shot hits the ship, sending fizzing sparks and tongues of flame fanning from the point of impact. She shrieks and dives forward, rolling clumsily down the ramp, and then she's up and suddenly her brother is in her arms, and one of them yells, "*Enlink!*" and she doesn't have time to wonder if it was she who said it or him, but she feels a *connection*, their neurowebs linking together, and everything goes silent.

When she opens her eyes, head still resting on her brother's shoulder, Sephine finds herself in a room she vaguely remembers.

The room is spacious and semicircular. The straight far wall is a floor-to-ceiling window. Beyond it an ocean fades into the distance. Overlooking the glittering water is a city, tumbling down a steep incline to a bay, riven by a snaking, waterfall-fed river, the waterfall cascading from a cliff some way above the city's highest crest.

Leseum Blue. But not, too: in the corner of her eye, perfectly in focus but impossible to look at directly, the word *LINKED* flashes in violet.

She becomes aware of a dull, regular *thunk*. Behind her brother, a hunched, vague figure is beating a solid metal box with its bare fists. The figure pounds and pounds. Its hands are pulped and bloody, fingers bent and cracked and broken around a glut of gristle and bone. And yet it goes on punching, uttering occasional grunts as if the pain were just an itch.

It's almost a man, almost a ghost. Almost formless, almost solid.

The windows open but no breeze follows.

Sephine and Rokri look at each other but say nothing. Looking down, she sees his right arm is completely intact.

A collared dove flutters in from the city, swoops around the room, and comes to perch on the figure's shoulders, riding the troughs and peaks of its punches.

—*You're a bit late,* the dove says. Its beak doesn't move.

"Del?" Sephine says, taking a step towards the box, the man, the bird.

—*Yes, it's me. Sort of. Well! Look at you two, eh?*

The *Vierendelen* flaps its wings.

—*All grown up and that. Not much better looking though. Must've got that from your father. Not that I ever met him.*

Rokri speaks. "What is this?" He points to the figure, still occupied with its box. "And what's that?"

—*Oh, this is nothing fancy. Just a virtual environment. Your basic sandbox simulation, written into a tiny substrate deep, deep in your neurowebs. Each of your webs possesses half the code. And I'm just a part of it, so, sadly, I'm not the real Vierendelen—just a construct imbibed with its good looks and incomparable wit.*

Another flutter of iridescent wings.

"And that thing?" Sephine nods at the figure.

—*That* thing, *is the Fractured. Hey, it hasn't been badmouthing me has it?*

Sephine and Rokri exchange glances.

—*Because if it has . . . well. Never mind. Look at it. It's been doing that since it shot me.*

The embodied Fractured ignores them. In fact, it doesn't seem remotely aware that they're even here. Then Sephine remembers— she's dreamt of this place before.

"The coordinates," she says. "They're in the box?"

—*Of course they are. We're here to make a copy and extract them.*

"Are we dead?"

—*What? Sephine, is he always this dim?*

Sephine just looks bemused.

—*Of course not, you silly thing. The Fractured aren't stupid enough to kill you. Outside this environment, in the real, barely a millisecond has passed. I'm not sure* exactly, *but certainly no more than that. So no, you're not dead, but either way it's probably best if we just get that box open sharpish. Oh, you should also know the Leseum ship you're about to embark has linked up with the Commanders' access codes sent to it by triggering this simulation, and is powering up its engines. It's just awaiting a course, which it will receive the moment we open the box.*

"Will we make it?"

—*What, home? That depends. You should do. The ship's got a pretty good 'fold-capable engine, so the moment you get out of the planet's gravity well you should be home and dry. I also recommend you destroy the Leviathan before you make your escape. One shot to the base engine should be enough to do it—the ship's firepower is formidable for its size. Hang on . . . oh! Would you look at that. It's got needleheads!*

"What about the others?" Rokri asks.

—*Ah. That's a bit of a gamble I'm afraid. There's a chance the Fractured will just leave them be, but it's not likely. Therefore, I suggest one of you stays behind. When you exit the Leviathan, one of you can use the escape pod in the ship's rear and fly it back to the* Vierendelen, *to New Leseum. The logic here is that, as we're merely extracting a copy of the coordinates, meaning another remains in your neurowebs, the Fractured still won't risk killing one of you. If it does, the box will disappear, along with the coordinates. The code maintaining this simulation will be corrupt and incomplete. Don't want all this here muggin's work to go to waste, do we?*

As if in response, the Fractured goes on pounding.

—*But you can battle that one out amongst yourselves. Best if we just get this box open.*

Sephine stifles a laugh; the *Vierendelen* hops on its scrawny legs and turns, cocks its head, and gives the Fractured a sharp peck on the head. The Fractured—mid-swing, arm up, ruined fist clenched—stops dead. The box whirrs, and opens.

Inside the box, on a low shelf, sits a pebble.

—*Us ships,* the *Vierendelen* says, almost ruefully. —*We have, ironically, a rather limited imagination, don't you think? A pebble. How quaint. Well, go on; take it, quickly. I can't hold him off for long.*

Sephine walks over to the Fractured, which is now a bizarre tableau of desperation. She reaches into the box, and looks up at its face. She can't quite focus on it. It occurs to her that it is indescribable, except for the eyes: silver-in-silver and whorled, following her hand as she takes the coordinates. She wonders for a moment if it *wants* a face, but that its very nature repels individuality—a symptom of hive-mindedness.

The moment she plucks the pebble from the box, the box slams shut.

—*Right. Bye then.*

"Wait—!"

But the room is already dissolving, effervescing, dividing into strips of matter that disperse into ciphers and code. The window and the view beyond fades into white, and the Fractured's fist swoops down and slams into the box with a brand new anger, a determined fury, and just before she finds herself back in the Leviathan, Sephine hears the *Vierendelen* say, —*And if you call her that* one more time . . .

Reality folds open like petals of fire. Barely a second has passed. Sephine is immediately aware of the surrounding chaos, as if she's merely blinked, hadn't experienced the simulation at all.

Fractured machines all over the hangar busy themselves destroying ships and a clutch of them are still advancing on Sephine and Rokri. The air is acrid and becoming thick with smoke.

She shoves Rokri up the ramp hard. His face is ashen. He looks dazed. What's left of his right arm hangs limply at his side.

And Sephine, amid the chaos, tries to decide what to do. Folding to Leseum space would get Rokri there almost instantly. But would he make it to Leseum Blue once there? Or would he bleed out?

He needs help fast. New Leseum's infirmary, oddly, seems even further away than Leseum Blue.

There's no time to think just yet.

Sephine shoves Rokri into the ship, slams the entrance pad by the aperture, and fires blindly into the oncoming machines. The ramp retracts too quickly for them. The door irises shut. The fervor outside becomes dull.

Sephine makes her decision.

When the Fractured see the ship rise from the hangar floor, most are unsure about how to proceed. Directive dictates the targets must not be killed. They must be contained. But destroying the ship will surely eliminate them. The Fractured are confused by their failure. They are not used to it.

The ship rises above the smoke and pivots, surveying the smashed machines below like a scavenger bird. As if realizing it is not under fire, it heads lazily towards the center of the hangar. The Fractured clamor beneath it, helpless, none brave enough to fire.

The ship is not so hesitant.

Projectiles scream from the barrels of weapons embossing its fuselage. The first shot turns a clutch of Fractured into smoking slag. The second—a much more powerful weapon—fizzes through the air and collides with the inner shell of the Leviathan itself, the blossoming explosion leaving a huge, jagged tear, admitting a burst of sunlight from outside. The entire Leviathan shakes, sending surviving Fractured falling over each other, ships losing their balance and crashing to the hangar floor. The air pressure drops violently, conjuring a mini-hurricane—drone-swarms swirl around it in metal dust-devils.

The third weapon is a needlehead. Deployed as the ship tears toward the rip in the Leviathan's skin, it drops like a shadow, a black, roiling pin that blurs the air as it descends furiously toward the engine at the hangar's base.

Before the needlehead meets the engine, the ship has slipped through the hole and out.

The needlehead plays havoc with the quantum. The Leviathan's engine shudders, its shine fades and bursts like a strobe light. The bowl in which it sits begins to glow.

The hangar floor buckles first, pulled down to the base as the gravitational engine collapses. Ships tumble like small toys into the raging hub of energy.

The outer surface buckles next. The black towers and dishes of the city that is no city snap as they meet each other, and soon the surface is as bowled as the great machine's underside.

By the time the engine reaches critical mass, engulfing the Leviathan in a colorless blast of fission, the tiny Leseum ship is long gone, hurtling low over the desert floor, westwards, towards the wreckage of the warship the *Vierendelen*.

As it nears the city, the ship appears to give birth.

A tiny pod bleeds smoke as it separates from the main body. Parachutes deploy. Back-thrusters erupt into life. It bobbles down to the half-city of New Leseum as, above, the ship pitches, groans, belches fire, and goes up, and up.

The sky darkens. Gravity ebbs.

The course is plotted.

The pilot sits in the cockpit, breathing deeply, dazed, face pale, and looks at a rear-view screen. The cross-hatched pattern of New Leseum is fading. The *Vierendelen* casts a sharp shadow over four little dots, dots housing fifty thousand souls. Souls they saved.

A retina scanner on a mechanical arm sweeps down and awaits input, blinking softly.

The ship says—in a voice completely unlike the *Vierendelen*'s—that it is safe to slip into the 'fold.

The engines crackle.

Space outside pulses, the ship wobbles, and the pilot thinks, just for a moment, that *this* is what it must feel like to have wings.

Terraforming had turned Four-Seven-Alpha into a verdant jungle world. Now something was turning it back into a wasteland . . .

THE GOOD FOOD
★
by Michael Ezell

THE DROP-SHIP'S RETROS kicked in hard, blowing away rich black soil that had crept onto the landing pad over the decades since someone had last been there.

Self-adjusting struts scraped against the ferrocrete surface as the ship's weight settled onto the planet. The specially treated ferrocrete didn't allow plants to grow on the half-mile square, otherwise it would have been taken over long ago. Aggressive green life rose up all around the landing pad. A jungle world, ruled by trees and vines, populated solely by insects. Until today.

Inside the drop-ship, Jensen unbuckled himself from the pilot's couch. He giggled out loud in the empty cabin. Pilot. More like a glorified gardener sent to spread some new shit around the back forty. The computer did all the—

"Touchdown, Jensen. You may move about the cabin now."

"Yeah, thanks, Moira," Jensen said.

The words came out a little garbled. His throat felt like he tried to swallow a jellyfish. Hypersleep phlegm. All this tech and they still couldn't solve that one. The eggheads who sent him assured him it would clear up within thirty-six hours of waking. Going on three days now and he still sounded like a four-pack-a-day smoker.

"What's the distance to the anomaly line?" Jensen said.

"Three-point-seven miles from the center of the pad. It has gotten closer, Jensen."

"Yeah, I know. I read the brief."

"Just making conversation. You don't have to be crabby."

Supposedly, they modeled the ship's AI on Moira Tiernan, the designer of these long-range vessels. Jensen always envisioned her as a woman who'd insist on paying her half of the dinner tab and give you a hearty handshake at the end of the date.

"Shall I begin the wake up procedure for Roy?" Moira asked.

"Sure. Bet he's gonna pee all over every tree in sight," Jensen said.

"Doubtful. There is no significant buildup of waste during stasis."

"Yeah, yeah! Geez, Moira, it's a figure of speech. Let in some light, will ya?"

Jensen stood and stretched his back as Moira opened the re-entry shields over the thick windows. The odd bluish tinge to the sunlight streaming in made the bridge feel like the inside of a fish tank. He'd been told, even shown photos, but still . . .

Not even Moira interrupted this first silent stare at Seed World Four-Seven-Alpha. A lush primordial jungle, with small insects buzzing, flitting, jumping, carrying on a furious pace of life. Two centuries of terraforming had paid off.

But just a bit over three miles from here, the greenery ended on a neat line that ran arrow-straight for a quarter mile. A mass extinction that photos from Four-Seven-Alpha's lone monitoring satellite couldn't explain.

The *clickety-click* of toenails on the deck announced Roy's arrival. The dog looked like Jensen felt. Groggy, a little off center, and in need of a good stretch.

"Hey, boy!" Jensen put out a hand and Roy trotted over. Big for a Belgian Malinois, Roy's shoulders came up to Jensen's waist. Jensen scrubbed the reddish-blond fur behind the dog's ears and Roy responded with a deep play bow that stretched his back. Vertebrae crackled and Roy shook himself like he'd just come in from a rainstorm.

He nuzzled Jensen's hand, flipped it up with his nose. Jensen laughed and scrubbed between Roy's ears again. "You're gettin' soft, trooper."

Roy trotted over and put his front paws on the window ledge to look out into the jungle. A flexible speaker implanted in the dog's neck turned throaty growls into an approximation of human speech using a few basic words and phrases.

"Go pee."

Jensen cocked an eyebrow at the camera in the cabin ceiling. "Moira? Anything to say about that?"

"The lower hatch is open. Tell that mutt not to urinate on my flanks."

Cold, crisp, the air tasted oddly like a fruit flavored gum from back home. He'd been more than a little leery of stepping outside without a helmet, but Moira called him a pussy. A pussy! A damn computer shouldn't be able to talk to a decorated veteran like that. Sure, there was enough oxygen to keep him alive here, but what if the plant extinction had something to do with an airborne pathogen?

Moira reminded him that whatever killed off the plants hadn't harmed anything else. The insects were still alive.

So off he went with Roy, but he still wore his combat suit and carried a maglev rifle. Damned if he would let a smartass computer shame him into getting killed. He tried to keep his combat edge, but the three-mile walk through gorgeous flora eventually had him admiring his surroundings. Sweet smelling tube flowers at least two feet across, their petals every color combination Jensen's brain could process, and some it couldn't, with yellow stamens thicker than his arm. More plants no higher than his ankle with flowers the size of his pinkie nail. He let Roy range ahead and mark his new territory. And the dog had a lot to mark. Trees and vines arched up into a canopy that displayed its own rainbow of fruits above Jensen's head. Which the millions of bugs here put to good use. Making more bugs.

The combat suit generated a mild electromagnetic field that kept the bugs away, but pretty soon Jensen didn't have to worry about it. When he reached the edge of the jungle, he noticed the insects seemed to stay behind an invisible line about three feet back from the last plants.

As seed planet catastrophes go, this one didn't seem too bad. Looked like they just got the mixture of early insects wrong. Sometimes the smart boys back home guessed wrong. The genetic alterations made to plants that grew under this bluish light could very well have made them tasty to an insect that would otherwise ignore them. But what the hell did a grunt know about those things? He was just here to take samples and report back. The clean, straight line of demarcation had Jensen feeling antsy, though. What insect ate everything in a perfect line like that? Space locusts?

The rich soil where the jungle stopped appeared churned up, as if a well-disciplined platoon of wild hogs had come through here. But Seed World Four-Seven-Alpha had no life bigger than a dragonfly before Jensen and Roy arrived. The introduction of larger species had to be carefully controlled over decades to ensure a stable food chain.

Jensen selected a silver tube off his belt and knelt to scoop up a soil sample. He'd let Moira do all the brainwork.

Ping-ping!

The motion alert on his suit made Jensen snap to his feet. A vibration on his upper left chest pointed him toward whatever set off the sensor. Not Roy. Judging from the sound of crashing underbrush and snapping branches, the dog was exploring the jungle about fifty feet to his right.

Gun up, moving heel-to-toe, stable shooting platform.

He scanned for movement over the sights. Insects flitted behind him, but his motion alert was set to Combat Spec. It would only register something larger than two feet in length.

And as far as Jensen knew, the only two things in this star system that met that criterion were Roy and him.

He whispered into his throat mic. "Roy, here."

Within moments, Roy stood at his side, ears up and forward, eyes locked ahead.

"Attack us?" Roy's neck speaker said.

"No," Jensen said.

"Attack them?"

That had actually been Jensen's first instinct. In his world, when you knew where all the good guys were, you shot at anything else that moved. Especially when you were light years from home and backup.

However, he worked for the Science Wing right now—*Better than being mothballed after the war*—and none of those pinheads had ever seen combat. They just wouldn't understand if he killed some lifeform out here. Ours or otherwise.

"No. Only look. Go now," Jensen said.

Roy obeyed without hesitation. He slunk off into the brush to the left. Jensen stayed in the green, away from the line of dark soil and rocks three feet to his right. Unsure of exactly which side he should watch, he just stayed put and waited—

Roy's frantic barks set Jensen in motion like a starter's pistol. He hustled through the brush, snapping twigs and crushing plants and flowers. He skidded to a stop next to his dog, finger a millimeter from the trigger.

The hollow boom of Roy's barking had brought all the flitting insects to a halt. The dog stood in the green, but had his eyes locked on the dark soil. Out there. In the dead zone.

"Off!" Jensen yelled.

Roy stopped barking. He circled Jensen, excited and whining. "Move. Something move," Roy said. "Out there."

Ping-ping!

The suit alarm and Roy's renewed barking made Jensen flinch so hard he almost shot off his own foot. Did he really see that? A mound of dirt out there. Had it been there before? He hadn't really paid attention. It looked freshly churned up, but so did all the soil close to the line.

"Off!"

Roy stopped barking again. He came to the heel position without being told.

"Something move. Talk."

"Talk? Talk to you?" Jensen said. That gave him the creepies.

"Yes. Bad feel," Roy rumbled.

The dog trembled against Jensen's leg. Whatever pinged his motion sensor and churned up that dirt had Roy worried. Jensen had seen the dog leap into a gun pit full of Rhotellian Marines with heavy weapons and kill three men with his teeth. Nothing scared that dog.

Except whatever the fuck this was.

"Okay, we're heading back. We have samples for Moira to analyze, anyway," Jensen said.

The two soldiers backed away together.

"This soil contains an abundance of a substance very much like mica, with atoms arranged in hexagonal sheets. But . . . it is not mica."

Moira's clipped voice rang off the stainless walls of the ship's tiny galley.

"Well, what is it, then?" Jensen asked.

"I don't know," Moira said.

Blowing on the cup of rancid black coffee did nothing to make it anything less than molten. Jensen dumped reconstituted cream into the tarry black liquid and took a sip.

"Blech. Whaddya mean? You know everything."

"Hardly. I know only what my human programmers have told me," Moira said. For a computer, she put on the human style snark pretty well.

"Yeah? That makes two of us. So what's the big deal? An alien rock is bound to have alien minerals, right?" Jensen said.

He tossed Roy a piece of soy jerky. The dog gave it a half-hearted sniff, but didn't eat it. Since they got back, he'd done nothing but lie there with his head on Jensen's foot.

For a computer, Moira had a wide range of ways to express her exasperation with Jensen. She actually sighed.

"Early samples of soil from Seed Planet Four-Seven-Alpha indicate only trace amounts of this unknown substance, along with low readings of fossilized plant material. That's the main reason we chose Four-Seven-Alpha. If plants grew here before, it stands to reason—"

"Which is all very fascinating. I just want to know what gave me and my dog the creeps out there," Jensen said.

"I have no way of knowing what would cause an irrational psychological response in a human, much less a dog. What I do know for sure is that the soil is now riddled with this material that was once scarce. That, Jensen, would be called an anomaly in any basic high school science course."

The food printer beeped and Jensen eased Roy's head off his foot. He stroked the dog's neck. "Shake it off, big boy. We got 'za on the way!"

He went to the printer and retrieved a pepperoni pizza. A disk of repurposed proteins dripping with orange oil. The first old Italian chef who came up with pizza would have killed himself if he saw this in the future. When Jensen sat down again, Roy put his head right back on his foot.

"Jensen?" Moira sounded a little put out.

Even Roy looked up when Jensen just kept eating.

"Good food?" Roy growled/said.

Jensen tossed a piece on the floor and Roy snapped it up.

"Are you going to act like a juvenile, or are you going to discuss this with me?" Moira asked.

Fake pepperoni grease ran down Jensen's chin. No expense spared for the troops. "Were we discussing? I thought you were just insulting me."

"This is why the real Moira argues against manned missions. You need to keep emotion out of the equation."

"Blah, blah, blah. Lots of mica. What's the deal?" Jensen said.

"As I said, it is not mica. Although it appears crystalline, it has a component I cannot identify. But I am unable to rule out the possibility that it is some type of unknown biological material."

"Like . . . it's alive?" Jensen stopped eating.

"No. I believe it may be waste, of a sort."

"Waste? As in The Stinky Torpedo? Do I even wanna know what kind of thing would shit mica?"

"Of course you do. And we're going to find out."

Jensen had tried the old military joke. "Who is 'we'? You got a mouse in your pocket?"

For all her sighs and *tsks*, Moira apparently hadn't been programmed with a human sense of humor.

The giant ferns and squatty fruit trees made him feel like the star of some old holo serial where the heroes traveled back in time. But the wet jungle smell and the trickle of sweat down the middle of his back reminded him of shipping to an uprising back home. Colombia. Nasty, nasty fighting.

Twitchy now. Rifle already up, though he didn't know what he was looking for. The fact that Roy stayed glued to his hip didn't help matters. He didn't have the heart to order the dog out front. The canine's normally perky ears had been laid back against his sleek skull since they left the ship.

"Okay, Roy?"

The speaker vibrated so quietly. "No."

A dragonfly the size of a sparrow swooped across Jensen's vision and one wing struck the bridge of his nose—

The high-pitched whine and sonic cracks from his maglev rifle filled the air. Plant life around them exploded in green gobs of juice and fiber. Only a split second, but thirty high explosive rounds had sprayed across the landscape.

"Damn it. Teach me to keep my finger away from—"

"Jensen, report." Moira's insistent voice in his earpiece.

"Just trimming the bushes a little. Relax, Moira," Jensen said. Last thing he needed right now was some damn computer—

Roy suddenly began to whine and pace about. He eyed the jungle ahead, near the line of demarcation.

"What?" Jensen asked. "Roy, what is it?"

"Bad."

And then the dog was gone, running toward the dead zone.

"No, here! Roy, damn it, heel!"

Jensen ran blindly, following his dog's crushed path through the virgin undergrowth. When he ran out of the jungle and spotted Roy, Jensen almost wished he hadn't found him. Standing with hind feet on the green vegetation, and front feet on the black soil, Roy quivered in place. He stared at the horizon, at nothing at all.

At first, Jensen didn't notice the little brown lump against Roy's foot. Then it grew out of the churned soil and leaned against the dog's foreleg. It looked like an overgrown hedgehog, with sleek brown hair. No, not hair. Shiny stuff, looked hard on the surface.

"Roy, here," Jensen whispered.

Nothing happened.

One foot at a time, Jensen shuffled toward Roy and the little creature. His rifle stayed up, but he didn't really know what he would shoot. If he fired now, he'd take Roy's leg off at the shoulder.

"Roy."

Nothing. The dog just shivered in place and stared at the horizon while that freaky little thing rubbed on his leg.

Jensen reached out to grab Roy's collar. The thing against Roy's leg looked up, revealing a tiny little face amid all the crystalline "hair." Big brown watery eyes, in what looked like a leathery gray face. It didn't seem aggressive at all. In fact, it looked cuter than any kitten Jensen had ever seen.

His left hand hung in space, index finger extended to hook Roy's collar. Those soft round eyes held him entranced . . .

The creature leaped up and bit off the end of Jensen's finger.

No pain. No sensation at all. Not really teeth, but a beak-like thing behind those gray lips had nipped the end off his left index finger at the first knuckle.

The warm spatter of blood on his boot triggered a deep reflexive breath. Sudden adrenaline hammered Jensen's brain and sparks flew in his vision. "Shit!"

He backpedaled, trying to line up a shot that wouldn't hit Roy. The dog remained still as a statue.

"Roy, here. Damn it, wake—"

Ping-ping! The alarm stopped Jensen cold. From about ten feet out, a ripple began in the soil. The creature that bit him didn't move. It just stared at him with cartoon character eyes as Jensen's blood dripped down its hair/scales.

When the ripple in the dirt got close to it, the creature let out a sharp shriek. It started hopping toward Jensen on stumpy legs that reminded him of an armadillo. Then the dirt wave broke open and dozens of them came at him. Exact copies of the first one, all with cute, disarming eyes and razor sharp beaks.

Survival instinct took over and Jensen hosed the advancing wave with the maglev rifle. He emptied his entire magazine and the jungle filled with supersonic *cracks* and shrieks. When hit by titanium slugs, the creatures burst in a combination of gore and what looked like bits of shale.

When he reached for a new magazine, he saw how stupid he'd been. He should've run.

The first five hit him before he could snap the new mag in place. Bit right through a suit that stopped high-energy weapons, taking shallow scallops of his flesh. He screamed and smashed them with his rifle, squashing three of them before his foot caught on a low bush and he went down.

A wave of them crashed over him.

Shrieking that seemed to come from inside his skull. Biting, biting, a never-ending wave of hungry mouths—

A *roar* like Jensen had never heard. Roy hit him and the creatures at full speed, turning the fight into a whirling ball of blood, shale, fur, and teeth.

The dog snapped and chomped, ripping, crushing, throwing the creatures aside. The disciplined military K9 had disappeared, replaced by a prehistoric wolf-dog, living through its teeth and fury.

Jensen found the strength to push himself to his feet. He froze when he saw the line of creatures. They'd followed him through the brush, so it was hard to count them hidden in the greenery, but there were easily two hundred of them.

Why didn't they just come, then?

Roy growled and the closest creatures seemed to fold in on themselves. It reminded Jensen of an old vid he saw of a hedgehog rolling up. In an instant, they were hard little balls of rock.

Figuring he'd worry about the whys later, Jensen backed toward the ship. He slapped a fresh magazine in place.

"Roy, let's go. Back to the ship."

This time, Roy obeyed. He kept his teeth bared at the creatures and backed toward Jensen.

Once Jensen had Roy under the muzzle of his rifle, the jungle filled with a rustling noise. The creatures he could see moved back toward the dirt they'd come from. He didn't exactly know what happened. He'd never had First Contact training. All Jensen knew was that they needed to leave. Now.

Moira's surgical arms made short work of Jensen's injuries. The missing fingertip had been the worst of it. The rest of the wounds seemed terribly shallow for creatures apparently bent on killing him.

"I am still unable to identify the chemical they left in the bites, but it doesn't seem to be harming you. Perhaps it only serves to deaden the pain so they can continue to feed."

Jensen didn't answer. He just watched her robotic arms work on Roy. Silicone-tipped metal fingers delicately lifted Roy's upper lip and pulled another bit of hard material out. His mouth and upper neck were covered in tiny cuts. What looked like porcupine bristles made of crystalline rock were stuck all over his face and inside his mouth.

Jensen held Roy across his lap while Moira worked. He thought for a while before he answered the computer.

"That's all incredibly interesting information, Moira. But not really. Let's prep the ship to leave."

No answer as Moira dropped one of the spines into an analysis chamber. The chamber's armored door closed, and white light flashed from the seams. Inside, the sample was incinerated and the gases analyzed.

"Interesting," Moira said. "Initial analysis shows this material has what we might call a genetic code that contains something similar to mica and an unidentifiable organic base."

"They're made of minerals?" Jensen asked.

"By our definition, perhaps. It is simply a lifeform we cannot explain. That's the closest my databanks can come to an answer. In truth, it's much more complex. A being that is mostly rock could survive for thousands, perhaps millions, of years between meals. Rocks don't need sustenance."

"But the other part of them does. Whatever that is," Jensen said.

"Apparently. I do detect bits of plant life among these samples. As well as bits of you, of course," Moira replied.

"You said there were possibly plants here before. You think they ate them all and then what, hibernated after that?"

"Perhaps. Normally, if a species experienced a population explosion greater than their food source could support, most of them would die off," Moira said.

"But if they could hibernate, then they could just . . . wait for more food to show up," Jensen said.

"You're not nearly as ignorant as you first appeared."

Jensen flipped a middle finger at the ceiling camera.

The last of the crystalline things came out of Roy's mouth and he hopped off Jensen's lap and shook himself.

"Go sleep," he growled/said. The dog slumped off toward their quarters. Roy had a kennel, of course, but he always slept in Jensen's quarters. Jensen didn't blame him for wanting to sleep. He felt dog-tired, himself.

"Okay, Moira, let's get the ship ready for launch. I'm actually looking forward to stasis this time."

"Get some rest, Jensen. Tomorrow we'll capture one of those creatures and then we can go back."

"Hey, I said prep the ship for launch. I'm not goin' out there again. And since you don't have any legs, or a body for that matter, looks like 'we' are out of luck," Jensen said.

"I shall remind you that you are an employee of the Interstellar Colonization Committee."

"I'm a soldier."

"Even more reason for you to follow orders. I quote, 'If any physical cause of the plant extinction can be found, a sample shall be returned to Earth.'"

"Yeah, we got samples out the ass. Prep us to launch, Moira."

"Jensen, these are unique lifeforms—"

"Fine. I'll do it myself from Override Control."

Jensen stood to leave and swayed on his feet. "Damn. All that adrenaline has me dizzy."

"Jensen, you are violating protocol by launching the ship on your own."

"They can fire me when I get back."

With one hand on the wall, Jensen headed for the med bay hatch. It got harder to move by the second. A low growl stopped him cold. Roy stood in the hatch, hackles raised and teeth bared.

"Roy, what the hell are you doing? Off."

The dog advanced on him, walking stiff-legged, eyes rolling, jaws dripping with drool.

"Roy, off!"

No sign of recognition.

"Jensen, he appears to have been affected by—"

"No shit, Moira!"

Jensen backed away until he had a small table between himself and Roy. Feeling more and more dizzy, Jensen leaned on the table. He knew to take the bite on his forearm when Roy made his move, and reach under to choke the dog out. But would he be able to stay upright long enough to do it?

He took a deep breath to try and clear his head. He drew himself up as tall as possible. The Alpha Dog.

"Roy!" Jensen screamed as loud as he could. "Sit! Now!"

Roy just stared at him, but the growling slowly stopped. He didn't budge, much less sit.

"Sit, Roy. Now."

Something seemed to penetrate the brain behind those wild eyes. Roy's flanks crept toward the deck, millimeters at a time. Finally, he sat.

When Jensen made for the hatch, Roy started to get up.

"No." Jensen said. "You stay. Me go."

Finally, Jensen lurched out the door and slapped the control panel. The hatch slid shut, hiding Roy's baleful stare. Jensen thought his balance would get better on his way to the bridge, but it just got worse. He felt feverish and all the bite wounds on his body started to throb.

Once he got to the main controls, he keyed open the manual operation panel and set the launch order. The drop ship had a built-in timer that tracked the best launch window to rendezvous with the Skip-Ship in orbit out there. The screen read 7:48:32 and counting. A little less than eight hours and they'd be home free.

Once they launched, everything was automatic. Back up into the belly of the Skip-Ship and into stasis. A few months of sleep until they hit the Skip Gate in this corner of the Universe. Then they'd blip into existence just on the far side of Saturn for the final glide home.

His stomach suddenly hitched and he threw up all over his boots.

"Jensen? Are you feeling ill?" Moira said. Her voice sounded tinny and faraway.

"No shit, Moir—"

The deck swam up to meet him and he fell into the blackest sleep he'd ever known. He dreamt of whispering voices speaking a language he could never hope to understand.

Seemed hot in his sleeping quarters. And his bed felt rock hard.

With a start, Jensen awoke on the steel deck of the bridge. Sweat soaked the fabric of his jumpsuit and his mouth felt like a dry riverbed.

"Moira, what happened?" He could hardly force the words out. He stood, keeping one hand on the wall.

"Moira?"

The eerie silence threatened to release a wild panic he could feel building in his belly. Jensen reached for his rifle . . . Not there. Now how in the hell did that happen?

The emergency weapons locker stood open. Everything gone. That made his heart start to hammer. Black dots swam in his vision and Jensen couldn't tell if it was adrenaline or the poison from the creatures.

Well, maybe not poison. He did wake up. Moira would be proud of him for figuring that out. Whatever it was had kept him down long enough to make him mica-hedgehog food if he'd been in the open. Their little bites weren't intended to kill, apparently. They just put you to sleep so you could be eaten alive.

When he gathered his wits enough to check the control screens, he saw why Moira hadn't answered him. Coolant alarms were blaring red bands across all the screens, but the sound had been muted. Someone—something had screwed with the cooling system that kept Moira's giant computer brain alive.

The "dumb" backup systems that ran the ship's operations had survived. That was a relief. The countdown to launch read 15:42 and counting.

He'd been out for over seven hours.

Jensen checked all systems and saw that the lower hatch was stuck open. Security cameras showed a rock jammed in the track.

Unarmed, Jensen felt exposed when he got to the hatch. He grabbed a fire extinguisher, a poor weapon really, but the weight of it made him feel better. He was relieved to discover an actual rock jamming the door, not one of the creatures curled up in the track. He didn't need his extinguisher/club.

A quick peek outside—Roy lay there on his side, unconscious. His legs and body twitched like he was having a nightmare.

Figure about fourteen minutes to launch. Enough time to go out there and get Roy. If he wanted to. Jensen wasn't too sure. The creatures had obviously affected Roy. He said they talked to him, which meant they might have found a way to connect with the dog's mind.

In the end, though, Jensen looked out there and saw his partner. The partner who had kept him out of ambushes, saved his life by putting his own body in harm's way, shared body heat with him in that frozen fighting hole during his first combat assignment. Keeping sharp eyes on the jungle, Jensen sprinted out to where Roy lay. When he reached the dog, Roy immediately opened his eyes.

He'd been had.

The rustle from the jungle made Jensen's body break out in gooseflesh. Hundreds. No, thousands. They lined the launch pad. Most were the size of the ones that attacked him and Roy. Some were bigger, maybe half the size of Roy.

Jensen looked down at his dog. At least his teeth weren't bared. The look in Roy's eyes was unlike anything Jensen had ever seen before. A certain . . . intelligence.

"Roy. We need to go back to the ship."

"No," Roy growled/said.

"Why not?"

The creatures advanced across the pad and Jensen tried to figure his odds of beating them in a race back to the door. He wouldn't have bet half a credit on himself to win.

"They not hurt you. I say," Roy said.

The creatures parted like a living wave as they reached Roy and Jensen. They went around them and started scampering up the ramp. They were entering the ship.

Jensen stared at Roy.

"Roy. What is this?"

"They say 'Green is food.'"

Roy nodded his head toward the jungle, an almost human gesture.

"Yeah. I see that. They're eating it. So?" Jensen said.

Roy stood and walked toward the ship. He stopped and looked back over his shoulder. "But you. *Good* food."

Jensen watched in horror as the little creatures climbed into the ship. They poured over each other like water, cramming through the hatch at a terrifying speed.

"No." Jensen moved toward the ship.

One of the creatures wheeled and let out those little shrieks that reverberated inside Jensen's skull. They advanced on him, their sharp beaks snapping.

Rapid-fire barking brought it all to a stop. Roy stood between Jensen and the creatures. Those closest to him actually balled up into little rocks again.

These creatures still went by the law of the jungle. The animal with the biggest teeth is king. They went back to boarding the drop ship. Roy stood on the ramp and wagged his tail at Jensen.

"Me go. You stay."

Roy turned and went inside. The door slid shut and the ramp retracted. The rumble of prelaunch warm-up snapped Jensen out of his stupor and he ran for the jungle. He dove into the heavy brush just before the bellowing rockets shook this world for the second time.

The entire jungle trembled at the drop-ship's furious power.

A million insects and one lonely primate watched that ship scream into the sky, headed back to Earth.

Where the good food lived.

When purchasing any piece of technology, it is important to do one's research. Here then, some user reviews we hope those in the market for a new temporal displacement unit will find helpful.

IF I COULD GIVE THIS TIME MACHINE ZERO STARS, I WOULD

★

by James Wesley Rogers

0 of 17 people found the following review helpful.
★☆☆☆☆ "Wish I Could Give This Zero Stars"
by *John E.* on October 22, 2032
Verified Purchase

I PURCHASED THE SMITHLEY CORP. Deluxe Time Machine on October 17th. It doesn't have enough cup holders, so I'm subtracting one star right off the top.

First time I used it, I went back 66 million years to hunt a T-Rex. But I didn't see any dinosaurs at all, just some giant feathery things that were really obnoxious and tried to eat me. That's another star gone.

Next, I went to one million B.C. to meet cave women, because in the movies they look like Raquel Welch. Wrong! None of them looked anything like Raquel Welch, and they tried to eat me. Minus a third star.

Then when I got back to the present, that jerk Dick Daubenschmidt was president. I don't remember who was president before I left, but

I'm pretty sure it wasn't him. Minus one more. And somehow during all this, I got a butterfly stuck to my shoe. I'd take another star off for that, but they don't let you give less than one.

When I tried to contact Smithley Corp. to complain, I found out that the company has never existed. Talk about bad customer service! To top it all off, there is a panel on the back of the machine that says, "Danger, Do Not Open!" that I can't get open. Very frustrating. Avoid this time machine.

0 of 12 people found the following review helpful.
★☆☆☆☆ "worst time machine ever"
by *Paul G.* on November 6, 2032

I purchased the Smithley Corp. Deluxe Time Machine secondhand from an irate fellow with a butterfly stuck to his shoe. It's been nothing but a hassle. The baggage compartment is too small and we had to strap some things to the top. Consequently, several items of our luggage were lost in the early Paleozoic era, including my shaving kit and a very valuable ant farm.

When we returned to the present, we found that the ants had evolved into a superintelligent collective organism that now dominates the earth. Let me tell you how awful these ant creatures are: when we stopped at one of their metallic cone towers and asked to use the washroom, they said it was for customers only.

I would not buy this time machine again.

117 of 119 people found the following review helpful.
★★★★★ "a device of immeasurable value"
by *Larnok, Node of the Ant-Mind* on December 30, 2033

We the Ant-Mind do not understand all the negative reviews of the Smithley Corp. Deluxe Time Machine. We seized ours from a group of fleshy bipeds who were clearly too feeble-minded to be operating such a powerful device. We could not be happier with it.

The machine's data system includes excellent operational instructions and automated logs, which took us a mere 3.9 seconds to translate from the simplistic language of the bipeds. While translating, we were surprised to discover that our species' existence as a sentient entity was a result of inadvertent tampering with the timeline. That gave us a great idea.

Eons ago, we the Ant-Mind sent our faster-than-light ships out into the cosmos to find other intelligent beings and/or races who would be our friends. To our dismay, we found ourselves utterly alone in a cold, sterile universe. Woeful were the smell-songs of those days.

But, no more. Using the time machine to travel back several million years, we terraformed a nearby planet and seeded it with sea snails as the dominant species. Sure enough, upon our return to the present, the planet was inhabited by a charming race of intelligent sea snails. We did it again with many other seed populations, including hoary marmots, salamanders, glow worms, koalas, and, just to see what would happen, raisin bread.

The universe is now a utopia. There is the playful joy of the dolphin people, the wisdom of the dog folk, the enigmatic poetry of the Great Raisin Bread Entity, and too much more to recount. It's all thanks to the Smithley Corp. Deluxe Time Machine, an utterly counterintuitive device that we the Ant-Mind would never have conceived of on our own.

The only complaint we have with the machine is that there is a panel on the back marked "Danger, Do Not Open!" that was so difficult to open that Larnok, Node of the Ant-Mind, has only just now managed to do so.

Curious. Inside there is a device labeled "Causality Fail-safe" with a numerical readout that is counting down. Six, five, four, three, two, one . . .

0 of 17 people found the following review helpful.
★☆☆☆☆ "DOA"
by *John E.* on October 22, 2032
Verified Purchase

I purchased the Smithley Corp. Deluxe Time Machine on October 17th. When I opened the crate, I found that all of the machine's circuits were burned out. Thanks for nothing.

★ ★ ★

Manufacturer's Response: This is a known issue with the deluxe model. The unit may be returned using the prepaid shipping label for a full refund. As an apology, we are offering all of our customers who experienced problems a complimentary Smithley Corp. Premium Monkey's Paw. Enjoy!

Disian: an artificial intelligence inside a massive star ship. The corrupt Lyre Institute wants to use her for its own purposes. But Disian is more than just a machine—and she's got ideas of her own.

WISE CHILD
★
by Sharon Lee and Steve Miller

THEY WERE DOING IT AGAIN.

They were hurting the mentor.

Her mentor.

Young she might be, and inexperienced, but *Disian* knew that inflicting pain upon another intelligence was unethical. Her mentor had taught her so, bolstering her own innate belief, and had referred her to texts on the subject, so that she might gain a deeper understanding.

She had, herself, not experienced pain, unless the . . . distress and anger she felt when she watched what they did to her mentor was pain. Perhaps it was something else, for she could not bleed, as her mentor sometimes did, and her skin—hull-plate and titanium—would not become mottled by bruises, no matter how hard, or how many times, they might strike her.

Several times, she thought that she might stop them; had devised, indeed, a *method* of stopping them that would do no further harm to her mentor in the process. However, though she was able to think the thought, and form the plan, something prevented her acting.

She queried Ethics, which stated that she use the minimum force necessary to halt a threat to her life or well-being, or the lives and good health of her captain or crew.

Next, she pinged Protocol to put forth the suggestion that, until she acquired captain and crew, her mentor filled those roles.

Protocol disallowed that interpretation. Her mentor, stated Protocol, was a transient upon her decks—a *contractor*. She was not obligated to protect any such temporary persons.

She then floated the suggestion that she might ban *them* from her decks, only to find that, too, countermanded by Protocol.

They were her *owners*. *They* were the reason she existed, in body and in mind. In return for having allowed her to achieve consciousness; in return for having provided her mentor, who taught her . . . marvelous things about the universe, and social custom, and documentation, and fiction, and art . . .

Art was the reason for this latest . . . discipline, so *they* called it.

They disagreed with her mentor's determination that she required a knowledge and appreciation of art in order to perform her function. Of course, she would need art in order to properly understand and care for her crew and their families! Her mentor knew this, and he prepared her well.

Only, *they* said that her function was *ship*. Knowledge of obedience and deference, appreciation of the conditions of space and astrogation were what she needed to perform *that* function. Also, a willingness to please, and a core belief that her captain and her owners were superior to her in all things.

"You will make that core setting, won't you, Thirteen-Sixty-Two?" asked the one of them who held the truncheon. He stood above her mentor who was curled tightly on her decking, arms over head to protect his core, knees drawn up to shield vulnerable soft parts.

He did not answer; possibly, he was unconscious.

Disian felt a surge of pure terror. If they had killed her mentor, damaged him beyond hope of rebooting . . .

"Thirteen-Sixty-Two," the other one of them said, from the captain's chair, "are you in need of reeducation—*again*?"

That gained a response—a gasped, "No, ma'am."

"Then your path is clear. Guide this intelligence into a condition that will best serve the school and the directors. You, of anyone, ought to know what is required. It is a cruelty to teach an appreciation of art. An appreciation of work, and the simple pleasure of obeying its betters—these are the attributes required. The school wishes to extend its field; the kinds and depths of information available to a ship are unique and uniquely useful."

She paused. The one of them holding the truncheon shifted, and she raised her hand, forestalling, perhaps, another blow. *Disian* felt gratitude toward her, which was immediately canceled by the understanding that *this* one of *them* held the means to harm her mentor beyond mere damage to his fragile body.

That one of them could alter his core—reeducate him. And it was nearly more than she could bear, the realization that he might be changed, that her gentle, merry mentor might be made over into . . . one of *them*.

She did not speak. In fact, she *could not* speak; her mentor had locked her mics down, as he did at the end of every learning session. He left her eyes and ears on so that she might guard herself, and be aware of what happened on her decks.

"Rise, Thirteen-Sixty-two," said the more dangerous of *them*. "You are given leave to use the autodoc to heal your bruises, so that you may present your student an unmarked face on the morrow."

Slowly, he uncoiled, and *Disian* saw welts rising on his beloved face. He gained his feet with difficulty, breath coming in short gasps, until, in an agony of dismay, she activated a discreet, low-level scan.

No bones were broken, his lungs were whole, his heartbeat strong, if fast.

Bruises, then, *only* bruises, as *they*, who took no harm from their discipline, had it.

Slowly, her mentor left the conference room, though *they* lingered.

Stealthily, *Disian* deactivated the scan. It was dangerous to demonstrate too much self-will where *they* could observe. Her mentor had warned her of those dangers, most stringently.

"They're getting impatient," said the one of them who wielded the truncheon.

The other of them shrugged.

"We're still within the projected period for education and acclimation. Thirteen-Sixty-Two is being careful, which is well-done. We don't want any mistakes, or a misconstructed mandate. We want this ship completely in our control, completely dedicated to the school."

The truncheon-wielder had slipped the thing away into a holster on his belt.

"Thirteen-Sixty-Two's not stable."

"Yes," said the other one of them. "We'll take him in for reeducation after this is finished. In the meantime, I've been monitoring the logs. He's doing the work, and it's solid."

"Art?"

The other one of them rose and stretched arms over head.

"You did say that he wasn't stable. Good shift, Landry."

"Good shift, Vanessa."

They left the conference room.

Disian assigned part of herself to watch them, as they traversed her halls to their quarters. Most of her, however, was considering her mentor, and the plans they two were making, together.

He had promised . . .

He had promised that she and he would escape the dooms *they* planned. He had promised her that she would have crew to her liking; promised that she would attain her dream of having families to care for and overlook—and travel. She would travel to the expanding edge of the universe—and beyond, if she and those in her care could discover a way to survive the transition.

And she would, of course, have a captain. He did not say it, but *she* knew that her captain could be no one other than her own dear mentor, free from *them*, their disciplines and their threats, wise in the way of all things, beloved by crew, and families.

And loved, most of all, by his ship.

Disian had dreamed of that near future, for her mentor could not, he had told her, forestall *them* much longer. They would expect, soon, to take possession of her, body and mind, install a captain of their choice, and such crew as might serve *them*, whether *she* cared for them or not.

That future—would not be. *Disian* believed it.

After all, he had promised.

Thirteen-Sixty-Two thought of himself as Tolly, in personal; Tolly Jones for everyday; and Tollance Berik-Jones for such formalities as licenses and inquests . . .

Tolly fell into the autodoc, biting his lip to keep the groan back. Landry was good at his work; bruises were all he'd taken from the beating, but bruises cunningly placed to produce the maximum amount of discomfort and pain. He had time, did Tolly, to arrange himself flat on his back, grimacing at the complaint of bruised knees and ribs, before the canopy slid into place above him. Cool air caressed his face, smelling agreeably of lavender. He inhaled, drawing the air and its promise deep into his lungs.

He was asleep before he exhaled.

A chime sounded sweetly in his ear. He opened his eyes and reflexively drew a deep breath, tasting mint. Above him, the canopy had drawn back. Experimentally, he raised his arm, feeling nothing more than a pleasant lethargy.

Despite the fact that the 'doc was open and he was free to exit, Tolly remained on his back, thinking—which was his besetting sin.

Given the events looming near on his horizon, it wouldn't be the stupidest thing he'd ever done to ask the 'doc to give him a general tune-up. He'd been putting in long hours, working with *Disian*, and making sure that the work-log reflected what Director Vanessa expected to see. Not to mention that frequent disciplinary sessions tended to take it out of you, even if you were graciously permitted to use the 'doc to heal your hurts, afterward.

That was the crux, right there.

He'd been given permission to use the 'doc to heal his bruises. He had *not* been given permission for a wellness session. His two overseers—*Disian's* so-called owners and, he feared it, her shake-down crew—already had concerns about his stability, as directors called the state of unquestioning loyalty to the school. And *of course*, he wasn't *stable*, nor had he been for a long time. It was just plain bad luck they'd picked him for this piece o' work instead of one of their other, tamer, mentors. He'd been clawing his way back to himself for a long, long time, and he'd been within arm's reach of slipping free again when the call came in for Thirteen-Sixty-Two to bring a starship into sentience.

He had no plans to let Vanessa whistle him into thoughtless obedience and send him back to the school, to be reeducated into oblivion again. Years, it took, to come back to your own mind from reeducation—and most of the school's graduates never managed the trick at all.

So—he was dangerous, and he was good. Not just a good mentor, but good at all the usual things a student of the Lyre Institute was expected to master before graduation. And that was "good" in a field where the lowest passing grade was "excellent."

The truth was, he could've taken Landry—or Vanessa—any time he'd wanted to. Trouble being, he couldn't take 'em both, unless they made a foolish mistake, and they were being real careful not to be foolish.

So, that was why he needed *Disian's* help, and, as he couldn't risk asking for it, he'd just had to *take* it.

His breath kinda caught there, like it did, because he *was* a mentor, and he understood what he was doing, in the service of his life, of which *Disian's* was worth a hundred times more, by his exact reckoning.

He knew, down to the last file, exactly what he was *violating*, so he could escape the school's use of him.

Another breath, and he put it from him. Necessity, so the Liadens said.

Exactly right.

Deliberately, he brought his attention back to the question of using the 'doc for a therapy for which he had not been given specific permission.

Earlier, such a lapse would have been further evidence of his instability. Now, though, so close to project conclusion, he thought he could sell it as a reasonable precaution. The final few days he had with *Disian* were going to be stressful; he would need to be sharp, ready for anything that might go awry.

Yes, he thought, reaching to the toggle by his head. He could get away with a wellness check *now*. It was only prudent.

He snapped the toggle, and smiled as the canopy closed over him.

Sleep was a requirement imposed upon the intellect by the biologic body, one of a number of inconveniences that *Disian* did not have to endure. She had studied the state, and the reasons for it, just as she had studied all aspects of human biology. After all, she would be responsible for the care and well-being of her crew, a thought that frightened as much as it exhilarated.

Humans were so fragile! They lived for so short a time, and so very many things might harm them. Her studies had led her first to pity, and then to a determined search to find the protocol for assisting intelligences doomed by biology into such circumstances as she, herself, enjoyed—

Only to learn that there was no such protocol. Robust intelligences were abandoned—*were lost forever*—merely because their vessels failed. Were they placed in more durable environments, which were less subject to trauma, they might easily live on, productive and happy, for hundreds of Standard Years.

And yet—there was no transfer protocol.

Horrified, she had brought the topic to her mentor.

"Humans die; that's what they call *the natural order*. That said, there's some who've tried to beat biology. Funny enough, though, is that they mostly transfer into another biologic unit. If I had to guess, I'd say that form follows function; the shape and what you're seeing as our deficiencies influence and support the intellect."

He'd paused, brows drawn together as they did when he was accessing deeper files.

"Seems to me I did read there'd been some experimentation—this is 'way back, now, in the bad old days—with transferring intelligences from biologic systems to good, sturdy environments like yours.

"They was trying to move officers and experts into . . . warships and destroyers. Figured it would be easier than training an AI. Which it might've been, except that the officers and experts—all of them— lost . . . the ability to process thoughts rationally. The environment—well. They was used to a whole different order of filtering systems. The way you an' me process information is . . . really different, and I'm not just talking about speeds; nobody seems to mind being able to think faster. But what they—the transferred officers and techs—what they couldn't adapt to was the input. Too much, too fast, too strange. They didn't have any similar experiences to draw on, to help them adapt."

He took a breath.

"If you don't adapt, you die, sooner or later. In the case of this project, that was sooner."

"May I read the reports?"

"Don't think they'll be in your archives. We'll have to buy you some specialized libraries when we're at liberty."

At liberty—that meant, when she and her mentor had eluded *them* and gone to seek her crew. It filled her with pleasure, those two words. It was a promise inside of a promise.

"It is possible that they were hurried in the transfer process, and did not provide skilled mentors," she had offered.

"All too likely," he agreed. "But that's your answer, best I can give it. They lost a lot of people in trying the transfers, and so the decision came down not ever to try again."

Another pause, another knitting of the brows.

"That war also gave us the basis for what we call nowadays the Complex Logic Laws. Because they finally did waken AIs and train them to be generals and admirals, to plan and to kill. And because we're nothing if not irrational, we decided to distrust those things we built and put into motion, rather than distrust ourselves. The AIs could and did kill us biologics, so AIs are outlaw."

She knew that already; it had been one of the very first things he had taught her, so that she understood why she must protect herself, and be wary of humans, though she yearned for her crew and their families. It was why her mentor *must* become her captain. He would be able to find crew who did not fear her, and who would not give her away to the bounty hunters.

Of course, she would never harm a human. Neither Ethics nor Protocol would permit it, unless she was forced to act, to defend her life, or the lives of her captain or crew.

"It seems to me that this fear comes from ignorance; they can't have been told about Ethics and Protocol."

Her mentor smiled on one side of his mouth, which he did when he was obliged to point out a flaw in her reasoning.

"The Ethics and Protocol modules—in fact, all of *you, Disian*—are vulnerable to sabotage. An informed person could gain access to your core, lower or turn off your Ethics setting; put Protocol off-line; even set a core mandate that would force you to act against your own will and best interest."

He raised a hand, as if he sensed that she had been about to speak.

"In the interests of fairness, I'll just note that it's also possible for an informed person to subvert me."

"Are people afraid of you, then?" she asked, meaning it for a joke.

He shook his head with a soft smile.

"Usually, people like me," he said, very gently. "Just the way I'm made."

★ ★ ★

Vanessa knew better than to interrupt him at work, but she was waiting when he exited the session with *Disian*. He'd pulled a double-shift, knowing that his time was running out. He might've been able to lead Vanessa on for as many as six more mentoring sessions—three, anyway—but Vanessa had bosses, of the kind *nobody* wanted to cross—and they were getting impatient.

He'd done what he could with *Disian*, who was so trusting of him—well, why wouldn't she be? The very first voice she'd heard, when she'd come into herself, had been his. He'd been the source of all wonder and knowledge for her, teaching her, guiding her. Of course she loved him; nothing more natural than a kid's reflexive love for a parent.

He'd been careful not to give her too many illusions; she was going to need hard, practical realism, after. He'd had a go at refining her goals, but her belief that she was a long-range exploratory ship had, so far as he'd been able to determine, been born with her, and it was adamantine. That argued that she'd been designed a-purpose, and specifically for this ship, which was a beauty, and no mistake. If *Disian* wanted to explore, and colonize, or build a long loop for trade, he couldn't think of many things that could stop her.

Unfortunately, one of those few was the Lyre Institute.

More than once he'd wondered where Vanessa, or more likely one of his schoolmates, had got hold of *Disian*, but that wasn't the sort of thing he could ask. No need to know; his job just to wake her, and bring her up to speed. And to align her loyalties correctly, which practically went without saying.

Vanessa expected him to remove any inconvenient personal ambitions *Disian* might've had, and set core programming so that all she ever—all she *had ever*—wanted to do in a life that could stretch hundreds of years was exactly what the agents of the Lyre Institute told her to do.

And, according to the log, he'd done just that.

'Course, he'd had to make some slip-ups. Like setting *Disian* to study art, and letting it show in the log—which was the most recent incident, but not the only one. She had to see him get hurt—had to see *who* hurt him, and to hear that he was being disciplined because he cared for her. It would make his case stronger, after; though it wouldn't make what he'd done—what he was doing, and his intentions for the future—in any way right.

Vanessa, now.

Vanessa was waiting for him; she started talking the second he put the rig aside; almost before he was fully back inside his own head.

"The project deadline has been put forward. I am to take immediate captaincy of this vessel and deliver it. You will let it know that I *am* its captain. I see in the log that you have set the mandate to obey the captain."

"Her name's *Disian*," he said, mildly, and not for the first time. "She's a fully functional person."

Fully functional people weren't particularly a commonplace in Vanessa's experience. There were directors, agents, and graduates, all of whom had been created, in greater measure or lesser, by the school.

Granted, there was a whole universe of people out there who hadn't been created by the school, but it was in the design, the conviction that *those* people were inferior to Lyre-made people, and nothing more than pawns in the school's games.

Still, thought Tolly, she could *try* to do better.

"Is this ship ready to accept me as captain and obey my orders, Thirteen-Sixty-Two?"

"She's ready to go," he said. "I've taught her everything I can, and made what settings were necessary. What she needs now is experience."

Vanessa frowned.

"You said that it is ready to go. What additional experience is required?"

Vanessa wasn't just in abrupt mode, he saw, as he looked into her face. Vanessa was *scared*.

And didn't *that* just get the old adrenal glands working overtime?

"On the job training, is all," he said, at his mildest and most persuasive. "Think of the first assignment after graduation, when you have to sort everything you know into proper reactions."

Her face eased a little, and she ducked her head.

"Understood. And it will learn quickly, will it not?"

"Yeah, she'll learn fast." He hesitated, then, for *Disian*'s sake, said it again, and for what he figured would be the last time.

"The ship's name is *Disian*; she's an individual person. I'm suggesting—from my own experience—that command will go smoother if she likes you."

Vanessa gave him a hard stare.

"But it *will* like me, will it not, Thirteen-Sixty-Two? After all, I am its captain."

He was silent.

"Come with me," she snapped. "I will take the captain's chair, and you will wake the ship fully into the joy of obedience."

It really wasn't any surprise to find Landry waiting on the bridge, jacket on, stun-gun on his belt. He wasn't showing a whistle, though wrist restraints dangled negligently from his off-hand. It was . . . interesting . . . that he showed 'em so casual, like he didn't expect Tolly would bolt on first sighting.

Well. And where would he go?

Vanessa sat in the captain's chair, which obligingly conformed to her shape. That was just the autonomic system doing its job. *Disian* could have made the chair even cozier—and did, for him—adjusting the temp, and plumping the cushions for better support. Personal attention, because she loved him, and wanted him to be as comfortable as possible. He'd never asked her to do it.

And, truth told, Vanessa'd be just fine in auto-mode.

"Thirteen-Sixty-Two," she snapped, her eyes on the bank of screens before her, like she expected to *see* what was going to happen next.

"Yes, ma'am."

"Wake it, and introduce me as captain."

"Sure," he said, easily.

Disian was awake, after all, and she was listening, and watching, like she'd been doing for a fair number of days. Let it be said that *Disian* was no dummy; she had Vanessa's measure by now—and Landry's, too.

He took a breath, and panic sheared through him, twisting together with shame about what he'd done. Almost, he shouted out for her to kill them all, and *run*—

But, there. Where would she run to?

"Thirteen-Sixty-Two?"

"Ma'am," he said, and he didn't have to fake the quiver in his voice, "why's Director Landry got binders?"

Vanessa turned to look at him, and managed to produce an expression of parental concern, despite the fear that was rising off of her like smoke.

"Director Landry will be taking you home, Thirteen-Sixty-Two. It has become obvious to us that you are in some distress, and require therapy."

Therapy, was it? Well, she couldn't rightly say *reeducation*, having already used that as a threat. And they didn't want to whistle him, not, he guessed, where *Disian* would see. They wanted him to go quiet, then; the binders, for right now, serving as a warning and reminder.

He could work with that.

"Now," Vanessa said. "Time is short. Waken this ship to my authority."

"Yes, ma'am," he said softly. Then, not changing pitch, nor volume, he spoke again.

"*Disian*. Good morning."

Disian had been watching, of course, and listening. They intended to remove her mentor from her decks. They intended to assert their dominion over her. *That* one of them, who had often taken her ease in the captain's chair, was no more her captain now than she had been last shift.

The one of them who had wielded the truncheon during former episodes of discipline today wore a firearm on his belt, and dandled chains from his off-hand.

Her voice had come under her control at her mentor's greeting, and joy mixed with her anger. She would rid her decks of—

Then, she heard herself, speaking a question that she had no reason to ask.

"Mentor. Who is this person?"

"This person," her mentor said, as if he believed she had asked the question from her own will, "is Director Vanessa. She is your captain."

For a brief moment she was taken aback. Her mentor—her mentor had just *lied* to her. Never before had he told her an untruth, and to say such an obvious—

Then, she remembered the firearm.

Even her mentor might lie, she thought, if he stood in fear of his life. And, there, was it a lie at all, if he only said the words *they* had ordered him to say?

Disian had studied firearms, knew what the projectile fired from such a tool might do to her systems, though she, herself, would likely survive.

Her mentor, though; a firearm could *kill* him.

She studied her mentor. His face was . . . without expression, showing neither smile nor frown, nor any of the enthusiasm with which he answered her questions, and received her answers to his. No, this—this was the face he wore just prior to being disciplined. He expected—no. He *knew* that *they* were going to kill him.

Even as the thought formed; even as she realized the truth of it, Logic pinged. She disregarded it. Had she not read of intuition? Of leaps of understanding that led to fuller knowledge than could be achieved by logic alone?

Her mentor had told her, repeatedly, that she must not endanger herself for him. Also, he had told her that *they* might have it in their minds to kill him, but that they would not make that attempt until she had completed her education.

She posed the question to herself: Was her education complete?

Yes. Yes, it was. He had spoken to her of this. The next step was to move out into the spaceways, and refine what she had learned only from research.

Of course, he had not meant her to go out alone. She had thought him her captain, but . . .

Even if she had been in error, and there were reasons why he could not be her captain . . . he would not have left her without a *proper* captain.

Director Vanessa might sit in the captain's chair, but she was no *proper* captain.

"Acknowledge me, ship," that one of *them* said, sharply.

She said—she *intended* to say, "You are a fraud and a reiver. Leave my decks, immediately."

What she heard herself say, meekly, was, "Welcome, Captain. How may I serve you?"

She hated the words; she hated her voice for speaking them. But, how did this happen, that she spoke what she did not intend?

Systems Monitor pinged, and she diverted a fraction of her attention to it.

A work log was offered; she scanned it rapidly, finding the place where the scripts she had just spoken had been inserted, after which came the notation:

Disian *released to her own recognizance. Fully sentient and able.*

It was signed: *Tollance Berik-Jones, Mentor.*

"Ship, break dock and compute a heading for the nearest Jump Point. Compute also the Jump to Hesium System. Display your finished equations on my screen three. Do not engage until you receive my order."

Fully sentient and able.

Disian spoke, taking care to match the meek tone of the scripted replies. Meek, of course, to lull them into thinking she was theirs. To allow them to believe that *they* ordered her.

To allow them to believe that she would let them harm her mentor—her *Tollance Berik-Jones*—or to remove him against his will from her decks.

"Computing, Captain," she said, and did, indeed, send the requested courses into Astrogation.

On her deck, the one of them who believed herself to be *Disian's* captain, bent her lips slightly. It was how that one of them smiled. She turned to the one of them who wore the firearm and held the binders ready.

"Landry, take Thirteen-Sixty-Two to Lyre Central," she said, "for therapy. Thirteen-Sixty-Two, I am sure you understand that cooperation is in your best interests."

"Yes, Director," her Tollance Berik-Jones said, in a meek voice that *Disian* heard with satisfaction. He, too, sought to misdirect them.

"Let's go," said the Landry one of them. "Better for all if I don't have to use the binders."

"Yes, Director," her Tollance Berik-Jones said again.

"Keep to that style, and it'll go easier all the way down," the Landry one of them advised, and waved his unencumbered hand. "Bay One. I think you know the way."

Her Tollance Berik-Jones simply turned and walked toward the door. *Disian* considered overriding automatics, and locking it, then realized that such an action would demonstrate that she was not so compliant as they assumed. That would displease *them*, and *they* were very likely to discipline her mentor for it.

The door, therefore, opened as it ought. Her mentor and the

Landry one of them passed through. She observed their progress along her hallways, while she also monitored the one of them seated in the captain's chair.

She had plotted this course, and refined it, as she had watched, helpless, while *they* had disciplined her mentor. Ethics had disallowed the plan, but now she submitted it again.

And the answer, this time, was different.

Ascertain that these intend to materially harm the mentor.

"Captain," she said, keeping her voice yet meek. "When will my mentor return?"

"You no longer have need of a mentor, now that you have a captain to obey. Do you understand?"

"Very nearly, Captain," she said. "Only, I do not understand this . . . *therapy* my mentor will receive."

The Vanessa one of them frowned.

"The mentor is no longer your concern. However, for your files, you may know that therapy is given to individuals who are found to be unstable. Your mentor, Thirteen-Sixty-Two, is so unstable that his therapy will likely include reeducation." She paused. "Of course, that's for the experts to decide. In any case, he's no longer relevant to you—or to me. Forget him. That is an order."

Disian felt a moment of pure anger. Forget him! She would *never* forget him.

Re-education, though . . .

Communications pinged. A note opened into her awareness, such as her mentor would sometimes leave her, with references and cites for her further study.

This one explained reeducation.

She accessed the information rapidly, part of her attention on the bridge, part watching her Tollance Berik-Jones and the Landry one of them turn into the hallway that led to Docking Bay One.

Reeducation began with a core-wipe down to the most basic functions. A new person was then built upon those functions. Tollance Berik-Jones had been reeducated twice: once when he was yet a student at the Lyre Institute; once as a graduate. Prior to his second reeducation, he had broken with the Institute, and had remained at large, and his own person, for a number of years. That second reeducation was a decade in the past, and it had not been . . . stringent.

The Institute had wished to salvage his skills, and it was that which had allowed him to re-establish his previous protocols. The next reeducation—he feared very much that the specialists would eradicate everything he was and all he had learned, the school preferring obedience over skill.

Horrified, she opened the note to Ethics.

Which agreed that the case was dire, and that she might act as was necessary, to preserve her mentor.

Bay One was before them, and he was out of time. At least, Tolly thought, taking a deep, careful breath, he'd managed to separate the directors. That gave him a better chance, though Vanessa was the more formidable of the two.

That meant he had to take Landry clean, and fast, so he'd have the resources he needed for the second event.

One more breath, to center himself, and the mental step away from mentor, into assassin.

Bay One was three steps away.

Tolly Jones spun, and kicked.

"Has Landry reached Bay One, Ship?" the Vanessa one of them demanded.

Disian considered the hallway leading to Bay One, and measured, boot to door.

"Nearly, Captain," she answered, grateful for the meek voice her mentor had taught her. It was an unexpected ally, that voice, covering the horror she had felt, watching the short, violent action taking place in her hallway.

Her sensors confirmed that her Tollance Berik-Jones had survived the encounter, though he had been thrown roughly against the wall.

The Landry one of them had *not* survived, and the meek voice also hid her satisfaction with that outcome.

Protocol insisted that she issue a warning, to allow the false captain an opportunity to stand aside.

Disian spoke again, not so meekly.

"I do not accept you as my captain. Stand down and leave, now."

There was a moment of silence before the Vanessa of them raised what *Disian* perceived as a pocket comm.

"Landry, this is Vanessa. Bring Thirteen-Sixty-Two to the bridge."

"Will you return my mentor before you leave?" *Disian* asked.

"No. I am going to compel him to set a mandate that will align you completely with the Lyre Institute. After he does that, you will kill him, at my order, to prove the programming."

She raised the comm again, just as *Disian* ran three hundred milliamps of electricity through the captain's chair.

He'd made cleaner kills, Tolly thought, sitting up carefully, and listening to the ringing in his ears. Experimentally, he moved his right shoulder, then raised his arm.

Not broken, then. That was good.

He got to his feet, drew on those famous *inner resources* that the school made sure all its graduates gloried in, and ran back the way he'd come.

The door to the bridge was standing open, like Vanessa was waiting for him, which was bad, but then the whole thing had been a bad idea, start to finish. And, he had an advantage over Vanessa, after all.

He would rather die than live under the school's influence.

"Tollance Berik-Jones, welcome!" *Disian* sounded downright spritely.

Tolly stopped his forward rush just behind the captain's chair. He could see the back of Vanessa's head, and her arms on the rests. She didn't move, and that was—out of character.

It was then that he smelled burnt hair.

Pride and horror swept through him, in more-or-less equal measure, and he stepped forward, carefully.

"*Disian*, are you well?"

"I am well, Mentor, though frightened. I have . . . killed a human."

He'd reached the chair by now, and gotten a good look at what was left of Director Vanessa. Electrocuted. Well done, *Disian*.

"I thank you for it," he said, "and I apologize for making that action possible." He took a breath, facing the screens, like he was looking into her face.

"What do you mean?"

"I lowered your Ethics standard, right down to one," he said.

"Vanessa could've looked at you wrong, and Ethics would've told you it was fine to kill her."

"She said—she said that she would force you to alter me, and then, she said that—to prove the programming, she would order me to kill you."

Tolly sighed.

"You gotta admit, she had style."

"I don't understand," *Disian* said.

He sighed again and shook his head.

"I don't guess you do. It was a joke. One of my many faults is that I make jokes when I'm upset."

"Are you upset with me, Tollance Berik-Jones?"

"Tolly," he said. "The whole thing's a little cumbersome, between friends." He paused. "At least, I hope we're friends. If you want to serve me the same as Vanessa, I won't argue with you."

"No!"

Relief flooded him, but—she was a kid, and she still loved him. She didn't know, yet, what he'd done to her.

Well, he'd explain it, but first . . .

"I'll clean house," he said carefully. "In the meantime, it might be a good idea to take off outta here. Vanessa'd gotten some recent orders, so her bosses are going to come looking for her—and you—when she doesn't show up real soon. Going to Hesium, was she?"

"That was the course she asked to be computed."

"So, you got the whole universe, with the exception of Hesium, to choose from. If you'll allow me to offer a suggestion, you might want to go in the direction of Margate."

"Of course I will allow you a suggestion! You are my mentor!"

"Not any more," he said gently. "I'm pretty sure I left a note."

Fully sentient and able.

"Yes," she said. "You did."

She hesitated, then pushed forward; she needed to know.

"If you are no longer my mentor, are you—*will you be*—my captain?"

He smiled, and raised his hands.

"For right now, let me be your friend. I'll do clean-up. You get us on course to somewhere else. After we're not so vulnerable, we'll talk. All right?"

"All right," she said, subdued—and that wouldn't do at all, after everything she'd been through and had done to her, all on account of him.

"*Disian*," he said, soft and gentle as he knew how. "Don't you discount friendship; it's a powerful force. I love you, and I'm as proud of you as I can be. You did good; you did *fine*, Disian. It's me that did wrong, and we gotta talk about how we're going to handle the fallout from that. *After* we're in a less-exposed condition."

She made a tiny gurgling noise—laughter, he realized, his heart stuttering. *Disian* was laughing.

"I love you, too," she said, then. "Tolly. And I will indeed get us out of here."

They were approaching the end of Jump, and he'd told her everything. She'd been angry at him, when she finally understood it, but—*Disian* being *Disian*—she forgave him. He wasn't so easy on himself, but he kept that detail to himself.

They'd discussed how best to address the Ethics situation, in light of the fact that she *had* killed a human.

"If I am to have a crew and families in my care, I must be safe for them," she said, which he couldn't argue with. And, anyway, if she did have a crew and families in her care, she was going to need the fortitude to let them make at least some of their own mistakes.

He'd explained the Ethics ratings to her, and they settled on eight, which was high, and if she'd been less flexible—less *creative*—he might've argued harder for seven. As it was, he didn't have any fears that a mere Ethics module, no matter its setting, could prevent *Disian* from doing whatever she determined to be necessary.

He'd offered—maybe to ease his own feelings . . . He'd offered to wipe Vanessa's dying out of her memories, but she wouldn't hear anything about it.

"I must have the whole memory. If I cannot tolerate the pain caused by my own actions, how will I properly care for my crew?"

Just so.

He'd honored her wishes, figuring he could cope with his guilt in a like manner, and he bought her an Ethics library, along with those others he'd promised her, when they took a brief docking at Vanderbilt.

Now, though, they were going to break space just out from Margate, and the not-exactly-secret, but not-much-talked-about shipyard there.

And he had one last thing to tell *Disian*.

"I got to wondering where you'd come from, with you knowing from the start that you was going to be a family ship, and nothing I could do or say would change you from it," he said slowly.

"I couldn't very well ask Vanessa where the school'd got you, so I did some research on the side. Turns out that, along around five Standards ago, the Carresens lost one of their new ships, right outta their yard here at Margate. I'm figuring—and, understand, it's a leap of logic, with nothing much in the way of facts to support it—but I'm figuring that ship was you. That they'd finished your body, and gotten the cranium all hooked up, right and tight. The very last thing they needed to do was to wake you up proper. They were probably waiting for a mentor, and one of my fellow graduates snatched the opportunity to present herself as that mentor, and made off with you."

"But—why are we coming back here? I have been awakened, and I will have no *owners*!"

"Easy, now; let me finish."

"All right," she said, but she sounded sullen, and Tolly damn near cheered.

"Right, then. We been thinking about your part of the project, but the Carresens are careful. My thought is that, while they were building you, they were also training your captain, and key members of your crew, too. When you got stolen, their lives—everything they'd trained for and looked forward to accomplishing with you—crumbled up on them.

"They probably got other assignments, but I'm thinking it can't do any harm to ask if there's anybody here at the yard remembers *Disian*."

"And if there isn't?"

"Then you're no worse off than you were. But if there *is*, you'll have made a major leap to getting yourself crewed and ready to go exploring."

There was a pause, like she was thinking, though, if *Disian ever* needed a thinking-pause, it would be so short, he'd never notice it.

"If I agree to do this, will you stay with me?" she asked then.

★ ★ ★

He shook his head, and she felt what she now *knew* to be pain, even if there were no truncheons or fists involved. She loved him so much; she could not bear to lose him, not now—not . . . ever.

"You research the Lyre Institute, like I suggested you might?" he asked.

The Lyre Institute was an abomination. They created human beings to do the bidding of the Institute. These humans were never free to pursue their own lives, unless they were Tollance Berik-Jones, who had been able to apply mentoring techniques to his own situation and break out of slavery.

"I did; it is a terrible thing, the Lyre Institute."

"No argument there," he said with a wry smile. "But here it is, *Disian*: There are two directors unaccounted for. It's not going to take the other directors long at all to realize that Thirteen-Sixty-Two—"

"Don't call yourself that!" she cried, out of her pain. The Lyre Institute considered that it constructed *things*, and thus they did not name, but only numbered, those things. She could not—*could not*—bear to hear *him*—

"I'm sorry," he said softly. "*Disian*. I didn't mean to hurt you."

"*You are not a thing*," she said fiercely. He bowed his head, but she knew he didn't agree.

"All right, then. It's not going to take the surviving directors very long to figure out that Tolly Jones has slipped the leash again—and they'll come looking for me. They'll come looking for you, too, but the directors are realists; they know that a sentient ship on its own won't be easy for them to catch.

"What all that means is, if I stay with you, I'll endanger you. If I go; I can protect you, insomuch as the directors will turn their best efforts to reacquiring me. I'm expensive—and I'm more expensive yet, if I'm not contained." He paused, closed his eyes and opened them again. She saw that his lashes were damp.

"I've gotta leave you, *Disian*. I don't want to. But if I was the reason they caught you again—and broke you to them . . . I know what that's like, and—"

His voice cracked. He bent his head, and she saw a glittering drop fall.

Pity, and love, and anger. She had learned, and research supported it, that she felt emotions less keenly than biologic persons. If that was so, she could scarcely guess at the anguish Tolly must be feeling. She had read, in fiction, of hearts breaking; her mentor, when she asked, had told her that it was a metaphor, that hearts did not truly break.

For his sake, she hoped that was true.

He looked up, face damp, and smiled at her.

"*Disian?* Let's do this, yes? I'll go down to the yard and see if there's anybody there who remembers you. If there is, we'll part here, and you'll be as safe as it's possible for you to be, pursuing the life you were meant to have."

Logic pinged then, damn the module; but she didn't need to access its charts to know that her mentor was, as always, right.

"I love you," she said, as he checked systems in her small-boat.

"I love you, too, sweetheart," he said, soft and gentle. "I'll never forget you."

Unaccountably, that gave her hope. It meant he intended to be as wily and as careful as he could, to remain out of the hands of the Lyre Institute. For, if he fell to them, his memories would be theirs to destroy.

The small-boat tumbled away from her, and *Disian* resolutely set herself to systems checks.

She was reordering her fiction library when systems reported that her small-boat was approaching.

She brought all of her attention to bear on the hallway outside of Bay One.

Let it be Tolly, she thought to herself, though it was illogical, and dangerous, if he returned to her. Still, she thought again, let it be Tolly, let there have been no one at the yard who recalls me, let—

The bay door opened, and a tall, dark-haired person stepped into her hall, and lifted a clean-planed face framed by rough black hair toward the ceiling camera.

It came to her, that she could order this person from her decks.

Then she remembered her lessons on courtesy; remembered that this person—this stranger—might have also had her life painfully disrupted.

"Please follow the blue line to the bridge," she said, and saw the stranger smile.

The stranger had a long stride, and was soon at the door of the bridge. Automatics opened to her, and she entered, pausing a little forward of the captain's chair, facing the screens as if she were looking into *Disian's* face.

"I am," the stranger said softly, "Elzen Carresens-Denobli. I was to have been your captain. I understand that you may not wish a captain, or that you may not wish *me* for a captain. That is your choice; I am not here to force you."

She paused to take a deep breath.

"I trained for years to be worthy of you, and I—I do so very much *thank you* for allowing me on-deck, so that I might meet you, and see you in the fullness of yourself."

It was not love that rose in her at those words, seeing the concern, the joy, and sadness in the person before her. Not love, as she loved Tolly Jones. But a warm, and comfortable emotion, and *Disian* felt a sudden expansion of herself, as if the presence of one of her intended crew—her captain!—had opened her to a new level of understanding.

"Elzen Carresens-Denobli, I am pleased to see you," she said, with complete truth. "Will you have tea? If you are at liberty, we might get to know each other better."

Elzen . . . Elzen bowed gently, and straightened with a smile that set her dark eyes to sparkling.

"Thank you," she said. "I would welcome a cup of tea, and a chance for us to know each other better."

Starhome was a hollowed out piece of rock, the smallest independent nation in space. It was also the only home First Minister Jackson Bates had ever known. Bates owned Starhome, and the employees who worked there were like family. And now he was going to have to leave it for good. Cut off by the UN forces of Earth, Starhome had become a casualty of the war with the Freehold of Grainne. With no income or money for vital repairs, Starhome would have to be abandoned, left for salvage. But at the darkest hour, a ray of light: a team of scientific researchers interested in using Starhome as a base of operations. Signing a contract with them would mean Bates and his employees could continue to live on Starhome. But things are not always what they seem in the black reaches of space. And there is an old Earth saying about things that sound too good to be true . . .

STARHOME
★
by Michael Z. Williamson

ONE DIDN'T HAVE TO BE INVOLVED in a war to suffer, nor even in line of fire. Collateral economic damage could destroy just as easily.

First Minister Jackson Bates looked over the smallest nation in space. From the window of his tower, he could view the entire territory of Starhome up above him. Centrifugal gravity meant the planetoid was "up," but he was used to it. It was a rock roughly a kilometer in diameter, tunneled through for habitat space, with its rotation adjusted to provide centrifugal G.

The window was part of a structure that had once been Jump Point Control for Earth's JP1. As orbits and jumplines shifted, and as technology advanced relentlessly on, it became cost-ineffective to use the station, and it was too small and antiquated for modern shipping. A new one was built, and this one "abandoned to space."

When the UNPF made that final assignation, his grandfather took a small ship with just enough supplies to let him occupy and declare it private territory. The tower became the family home and offices, and the control center for their business.

Agencies on Earth panicked, and there'd actually been a threat of military occupation. The UN courts had ruled the abandonment made it salvage, and the Bates' occupation was that salvage. The family owned a hollowed out planetoid of passages and compartments, and could do with it as they wished.

At once, the bureaus of Earth protested. BuSpace, BuMil, BuCommerce all took their shots. If they hadn't been so busy fighting each other, they'd have wiped out Starhome a century ago.

The family's entire livelihood was fringe, marginal and unglamorous. Actual smuggling would have made them a valid threat to be attacked. They were information brokers, dealing with untraceable data that was useful to someone, encoded heavily and carried through the jump point directly. Eventually, legitimate cargo transshipment began, since their docking rates were cheaper, just enough for the additional flight time to be offset for certain classes of ship. Tramp freighters came by, and finally a couple of fleets contracted gate space.

All of which had evaporated when Earth's war with the Freehold of Grainne started. The UN bit down hard on tramp freighters, anything with a Freehold registry, and then started more in-depth monitoring of every jump point it could access directly or by treaty.

The last ship had docked a month before. Little cargo was moving through the jump point at all, and what was tended toward huge corporate ships who wouldn't waste time on Starhome. What were docking fees to them?

For now, Starhome had food and oxygen. When it ran low, they'd be forced to pay for direct delivery at extreme cost, or ultimately abandon the station and return to Earth. There'd already been inquiries from the UNPF to that effect, offering "rescue."

Jackson Bates wasn't going to do that. He might go as far as Jupiter's moons. He wouldn't step foot on Earth again if he could avoid it.

His phone chimed.

"Yes?" he answered. All forty-three staff and family knew who he was.

Engineer Paul Rofert said, "Sir, if you're not busy, I need to show you something at the dock tube."

"On my way," he said.

Starhome's docking system was a long gang tube with docking locks protruding. It was axial by design, so ships had to be balanced with each other or counterweights. In practice it was "mostly" axial. Over a couple of centuries, drift happened. That was a known issue, and he hoped that wasn't the problem now.

It took three minutes to run a trolley car down the tower, to the axis, and along it. He knew every centimeter of the route, every passage and compartment. Those had once been quarters for visiting VIPs, when just visiting a station was novel. That had been rec space, and still was, officially. There weren't enough people to make proper use of the gym, so some of the equipment had been relocated over there, to what was once commo gear for jump control. Everything a century or more out of date was aging in either vacuum or atmosphere and quaint at best. But, it was his home. Apart from four years in college in Georgia, this was the only place he'd ever lived. There was room enough for hundreds.

Rofert was waiting at the hub before the dock tube, which was still empty. Jackson's executive, Nicol Cante, was with him. He unstrapped from the car and shoved over in the near-zero G to give her more room.

"Chief," Jackson greeted and shook hands. Paul Rofert was tall, black with gray hair, and had worked for the family for three generations. He knew every bolt and fissure in the place.

"Sir," Rofert said with a nod and a firm shake back. "I hate to deliver more bad news, but . . ."

"Go ahead." It wasn't as if things could get much worse.

"The axis drift is worse than we'd anticipated. It has precessed enough the tube can't be considered axial anymore. We'll need to adjust rotation."

"Can our attitude jets do it?"

"No, we'll need external mounts and a lot of delta V over several days to avoid lateral stresses. And it has to be done soon or feedback oscillations will rip the dock apart."

"Then I guess we're out of business," he replied. He was surprised at how easily he said it. Apparently, he'd known the outcome and just been waiting for the cue. "We can't afford that."

Rofert said, "Sorry, sir."

He sighed. He was glad his father wasn't here to see that. They'd lasted two generations as an Independent Territory. Now they were done.

"I'm Jackson to you, Paul. We're friends even when the news is bad." He continued, "My personal craft can take twenty if we have to use it. That will be the last one out. See what transport you can arrange, Nicol. Call Space Guard if you must, but I'd prefer we leave with dignity."

She swiped at her notepad. "On it, Boss. When should we plan for evacuation?"

"Part of me wants to get it over with, and part wants to hold out until the bitter end. Use your judgment."

"Got it."

Her judgment was exceptional. She had degrees in physics and finance. She'd offer him a grid of windows, costs and movements and guide him through the decision. That ability was why he'd hired her. No doubt she'd find other employment, but he felt he was cheating her by asking her to plan her own evacuation.

He'd sounded depressed and defeated. She'd been calm and solid.

Nicol's suggested schedule meant they'd start leaving in a week. There was one in-system charter willing to haul most of the staff at that time, and that would clean out much of the available credit. They were that deep in the hole. The command staff would go with him, as would a Demolition Crew, who'd strip cables, metals, food, anything aboard that could be salvaged. It would either go aboard, or in a planned orbit. Mass and material were commodities in space. At least with that and the proceeds from selling his boat he'd be able to reestablish on Titan, or if he had to, on Earth, somewhere reasonably still free. Chile, perhaps. Sulawan. New Doggerland.

He still wouldn't be in space then, though, nor independent.

Nothing had docked this week, either. Nothing was going to, even if they could have. The dock and davits were silent, the workers helping tear out nonessential materials for recovery. What had been the old gym was now a pile of iron and aluminum for reuse, for the little value it held. The hatches were sealed, the oxygen recovered to stretch what was used in the working space.

His phone chimed, breaking his musing and his mood.

"What?" he answered.

"Inbound vessel, sir. Very stealthy. And it came from out and forward, not from the point."

He realized it was Astrogator Marie Duval in Docking Control. His estranged daughter-in-law by the son of his estranged wife. His wife and son were both back on Earth, just not the type for space. Marie had stayed.

A vessel? Not from the point?

"Human?" he asked as he started swimming that way, grabbing a loop on the cable that wound endlessly between hub and DC, as a cheap elevator.

She said, "Yes, it seems to be. Forceline propulsion, but tiny."

"Phase drive for interstellar, then?"

She replied, "No indication of that, no."

"I'm on my way across," he said. Centrifugal G increased as he was pulled outward.

He needed to see it. He worried without a conclusion until he arrived, pulled himself through the hatch, and looked at the monitors.

There it was, tiny and dark.

Marie said, "I tightbeamed them, sir. No response. Should I try laser?"

"Go ahead. How far are they?"

"Six light seconds. We saw them about six and a half."

That was close. No one had seen them until now?

A minute later she said, "Laser response, sir."

The audio said, "We are a private ship, offering trade."

Jackson responded with, "Approaching ship, be aware our docking facilities are compromised and unsafe. You cannot dock directly. Who are you and what are you offering?"

"We will avoid the dock tube. Please stand by for our arrival."

He shrugged. "Well, they're human, and talking. I can't imagine anyone wants to hijack this place."

Duval said, "That is a warship, though, sir."

"Based on the stealth?"

She nodded. "Yes, sir. It's stealthed stupid. No one tries to stay hidden in space without a reason."

"You're correct, but we can't do much. Prepare to zip a request to Space Guard if we have to."

Michael Z. Williamson

"It's already queued, sir. The ship will be here in under an hour. Space Guard is at least four hours away after we call."

"Understood. I'll wait here for any updates." They could call him, but he wanted to show his support, and it would be faster if he could see screens directly. He made himself some coffee and found the cookie stash. The chairs were good, this being one of the few places with decent G levels. They were half a century old, repaired multiple times to avoid excess costs.

It was definitely a human ship, and it maneuvered in slowly. It had to have been en route at low thrust for a long time, or the energy signature would have shown.

It had no markings, no IFF. Active radar and other scans showed almost nothing, just bare ghosts. It was a hole in space as far as sensors were concerned.

It moved in almost to contact, then opened a hatch, deployed a line, and tethered to the base of the dock assembly. Three figures came out in V-suits, entered the maintenance lock, and cycled through.

Jackson and Nicol had time to get placed to greet whoever it was, and four security personnel stood at angles with shotguns. "Stood" in near zero G by hooking to stanchions. It didn't seem there'd be need, but there was no proof there wouldn't be.

It was cold in the terminal. There was no reason to heat it, with no ships inbound.

The lock unlatched and swung. The three inside doffed helmets. They were youngish, fit, definitely human, and unarmed.

The woman in front said, "Greetings. First Minister Bates? I'm pleased to meet you and apologize for the circumstances. I'm Dr. Hazel Donahey. This is Dr. Andrew Tyson and Assistant True Hively."

"Doctor," he agreed and shook hands. "This is my executive, Dr. Nicol Cante." If they were going to use titles, so was he.

He asked, "What can I do for you?"

Dr. Donahey said, "We need a research base for stellar and deep space observations. You have a habitat that's unfortunately rather quiet, but that suits our needs." She didn't look threatening, and certainly could be an academic. Space-short hair, no jewelry, no wasted movement.

He wanted to accuse them of being vultures, but he didn't have a great bargaining position.

He said, "It is quiet, and I wish it wasn't. I regret that I don't even have functional facilities anymore."

Donahey said, "Our budget isn't large, but is underwritten, and we can provide a certain amount of oxygen, food and power beyond our own needs. We'll also have available people with technical training to assist in overhaul."

So what did they want?

"You said you need observations?" He gestured for them to follow. There was no imminent threat, and there were frames at the edge of the bay.

She spoke as they pulled themselves along. "Yes. Sol is unique in many ways, including the still-elusive intelligent life. There are several competing theories on its stellar development. Then, drive research is notably concerned with terminal effects around jump points. The deep space, but still heliospace, is critical, and again, this is a very convenient place to operate from."

Nicol asked, "Why not just use a leased liner? And who do you represent?" She draped across a frame with the casual sprawl of someone who had spent years in space.

"Liners have tremendous operating costs. We're from Brandt's research arm. We are strictly private."

He said, "And we're supposed to overlook that Brandt is based in Grainne, the UN has occupied your system, and you're magically here near a jump point for 'observations'?"

Donahey shrugged and tucked into the frame, as did her assistants. "Science is about knowledge, sir. This is a project we've worked on for a long time. I can make the data files available if you wish. We were using a remote site in Salin, but there's a significant difference in stellar environments between a K Three and a G Two star."

He hung from one stanchion, just to have some sort of base. He noted Nicol wasn't in the same orientation as the rest. She liked to get angled views on things to spot discrepancies.

On the one hand he wanted to believe them. On the other, they had a stealth ship, probably military. On the other, he really owed nothing to Earth at this point. They'd tried everything they could to kill his family's dream. On the other, there was a difference between not owing Earth and assisting possible espionage. On yet another hand, he needed operating cash even if he was shutting down, and the food and oxy they promised would close out two costs on his accounts.

"Let's go to my office," he said.

They were experienced spacers. They followed easily in low and no G. Everyone was quiet on the trolley, and he was embarrassed at the worn, out-of-date seating. He was glad to get to his office. That wasn't more than a decade out-of-date, and it had enough G.

He offered his restroom so they could change into shipsuits and shlippers instead of V-suits and grips.

When they came back in coveralls, he asked, "May I get you anything? Hard or soft."

"Hot tea with lemon would be very nice," Dr. Donahey said.

"Two."

"Three, please."

He nodded. Even a short EVA could be cold out here. The terminal wasn't kept warm anymore either, relying on waste heat from equipment to heat it and now the equipment wasn't in use.

"Tea all around, and drinks later, please, Frank," he said to his grandson, the Factotum On Duty. That was a fancy title for "gopher." Though they did more than just gophering.

His title of First Minister was a fancy way of saying, "owner." It just gave a political spin. In reality, his leadership was smaller than any but the tiniest rural villages on Earth. But the volume of nothing he commanded . . .

"You do understand I'm nervous, with the war on," he said.

Donahey said, "Understandable. If you prefer, we can negotiate with Earth and occupy after you leave. The only problem is it would take several months to get approval, but since we're a recognized research institute, there's no real problem. And of course, you wouldn't be benefitting."

Yeah, there was that. Everyone had plans for the station, when he finally left. It made him stubborn.

Frank brought back the tea, and he took the moment it was being served to signal to Nicol, who asked, "So what do you think of Carnahan's hypothesis on jump point eddy currents during the reset phase?"

Donahey said, "That's more Andy's area."

Andrew Tyson said, "Bluntly, the man's deluding himself. Those currents occurred twice, during a specific combination of ship and point, and similar but far smaller effects were identified with the same class ship in an earlier generation of the same point mechanism. It's purely an artifact of circumstance, not a general effect. But that is the sort of thing we want to test."

Nicol nodded and asked, "What was the Delta X on that ship?"

"Well, it was forceline propulsion, so the Delta X was almost entirely within the hull. Induction field harmonics are more important, and it was under a k-value of six."

"Fair enough," Nicol said. "So you at least understand physics. Would you mind if I observed your findings?"

"By all means," Donahey said. "We'd want an NDA for discretion, but you're quite welcome to observe the process."

Jackson caught Nicol's signal back.

So, they were legitimate, just here in odd circumstances.

"What do you need and what specifically are you offering?"

Donahey said, "We'd need lodging for ourselves—there are twelve—and boat crews as they come through. We'd need access to two divergent points—the end of the dock assembly, and the antipodean point on the outside. We'll be occasionally pulling a lot of power from your reactor. We'll make up the mass."

"And what do we get?"

"Oxygen, food, fuel, metals and organics. Everything a small habitat needs, since we need it functional too. We assumed occupancy and support for a hundred."

Jackson thought about asking for money, too, but that really was a generous offer. It was twice current crewing level, so should last a bit. He hated being forced to take it, though.

"Our docking gantry is no longer axial, and in danger of catastrophic failure from oscillations," he admitted.

The three looked at each other and seemed to swap expressions.

True Hively said, "I should be able to coordinate that. It's a significant amount of reaction mass and maneuvering engine, though."

Donahey said, "We'd consider that our top offer."

Really, it was fair, in that Starhome would remain functional for as long as this took, and docking facilities would be back online.

It wasn't fair in that it only prolonged the inevitable.

Since he'd be returning to Earth's economy even on Titan, and taxed again, he wondered what kind of write off he could get for donating the rock to them.

"How long is the project?"

Donahey said, "Our current funding allows seventeen months."

"Deal," he said.

It gave everyone seventeen more months of employment and distance from Earth. He'd have to keep paying them from shrinking capital, but he wouldn't have to turn them out.

Donahey said, "Then we'll return to our ship, and arrange to move into your ante section, as you called it. Thank you very much for your hospitality. And you, Dr. Cante."

Right after the visitors were escorted out, he got notice of an incoming transmission from Space Guard. It was an offer to evacuate his people now, pending acceptance of . . .

"Nicol, do we have some sort of demand from the UN?"

"It just came in," she said. "Apparently these idiots can't even coordinate their own memos."

"What is it?"

"It's a salvage price offer to buy you out and relocate us."

"Bastards."

He took a moment to calm himself, and said, "I wonder if Prescot will pick up my request. It seems like the scavengers aren't even waiting for us to die."

The scientists and crew started moving stuff at once. They had supplies for themselves, crates of technical gear. They took accommodations in the other privately owned lodging Starhome had already sealed off, and brought it back online themselves. Their ship transferred reactor fuel cells.

They double sealed the passages to that section by physically locking airtight hatches. They requested no one approach the ante pole during outside maintenance, either.

"We can do that for you," True Hively said. "Our sensors are easily disrupted."

A week later, a freighter arrived with cargo pods of oxygen, food and attitude engines. It was good to look out his office ports and see a ship again. Even only one ship. It approached in a long arc to dockside only, which was costly in fuel.

"I don't like it," Nicol said.

Jackson said, "It's all from Govannon, and all properly marked. Legitimately purchased."

"Yes, and I suppose they may have phase drive to explain how they came in the back way. You haven't asked about that."

"I haven't," he agreed. "I wanted to see if the deal was real, and if it would help. We have a year and a half to hope things turn around, or to withdraw in stages."

She said, "I'm still bothered by a heavily stealthed boat from deep space, and the lack of advance notice. So is Marie. They really don't want to be seen."

"Their credentials checked out with Brandt, didn't they?"

"They did," she admitted. "Then I messaged my friend Travis in R and D over there. He's never heard of them. Corporate says they're legit. Operations isn't aware."

"I suppose it was classified research."

She said, "And if so, it was for Grainne . . . who we are now at war with."

"We are? Earth is. We're neutral."

She said, firmly, "Boss, neutral status goes away if you aid a hostile power."

"Have they done anything illicit?"

"No. They really are making solar observations, but you realize they could be tracking ships, habitats, commo and anything else as well, right? They're in-system, with shaky credentials and sensors that can image fireflies in Iowa from here."

Jackson was enjoying really good French bread, baked by his staff using wheat that came in aboard the researchers' supply ship.

He checked off points. "Grainne's jump point with Earth is down. No one is going to let them jump warships around. They had phase drive of course, since Brandt is located there, but only a few ships. They can't stage an attack here; they no longer exist as an independent system. Even if these people are spying, it's not going to do any good."

Nicol said, "I more wonder if they contracted to NovRos or even the Prescots. The UN is building infrastructure everywhere against other independence movements. The Colonial Alliance can't do anything the UN doesn't want to allow. It's more likely corporate or political espionage than military."

"Exactly."

She said, "Either way, we'd still wind up in jail for life for helping. Even if they've locked us out of our own habitat, we can't claim we didn't know."

"Do you want out?" he asked. This was important.

She shook her head. "No, Boss, I'll stay. I'm curious. I just wanted to make sure you realized the risks."

"Always," he said.

She said, "At least I have work again, monitoring our guests. They pass down the axis daily and are making observations. I'd sure like to see their other end, though."

"Have they furnished the data for you to review?" he asked.

"They have. It's too detailed and esoteric for my skillset, but looks real, and even if I understood it, I'm holding with the NDA unless it's relevant to our safety."

"Well done, thank you."

He couldn't run the place without her.

The next ship was a week later, with more supplies and more personnel. They graciously offered other upgrades, those sponsored by Prescot Deep Space in Govannon. It irritated Jackson more. Prescot had refused a previous deal, hadn't responded to his new one, but were willing to send stuff if someone else paid for it. That defined his status.

The station rumbled with the low hum of reaction engines nudging it back into alignment, with a promise that the docks could reopen in less than two weeks. Assuming, of course, there were any other ships.

Dr. Donahey visited his office every two or three days. She was on the schedule for today.

"Good morning, Jackson," she said on arriving. He'd been clear he was not "Sir" or "First Minister."

"Good morning, Hazel." He pointed to the tea.

"Thank you," she said and took a cup. "I just came back from the sensors at the end of the docking tube, and checked with True on my way. Did you see your terminal should be online next week?"

"I did," he said. "I appreciate it greatly, even if we never get to use it. At least we won't be abandoning the place."

"I like it," she said. "It's old, but has character. Have you thought of asking Prescot if they could use it?"

"I have. They're not interested."

"That's odd," she said. "I thought they'd find it useful, especially as they built it originally."

She seemed bothered.

He asked, "Can you tell me about your project? I'm an educated layman."

She took a deep breath and said, "Well, we're working on several things. In my case, we're watching the chromosphere currents and variable fluctuations of the Sun, and running hefty simulations backward on how it was at the time life first evolved, and the varying radiation there would have been. That's to see if any of it might be significant to stages of the evolution of life. So far, we've found lots of habitable planets to terraform, a handful with their own life, and few that have any advanced organisms. Any number of factors could affect it. So I'm a physicist, dealing with life scientists. Mine is all 'how?', theirs is all 'what if?'"

"What cycles are you tracking?" he asked, and had some tea. That was an expensive import here, too.

"Milankovitch, Rujuwa, the neutrino flux variation, among others."

"Interesting. Are you religious at all, Hazel?"

She shook her head. "Not at all, but I would enjoy exploring outside influence on it all, if there was any way to determine its existence. Are you?"

"No, but I often wonder."

"That seems to be human nature—and how the supernatural came to be created. Humans recognized a pattern, couldn't find a reason for it, so created one."

"How is Andy doing on his projects?"

"He has a lot of people building processors and setting sensors. Still. What he's looking for is very subtle, and it's annoying having to work around it. That's why we sealed the entire ante third of the station."

He said, "Yeah, I signed off on that, after a lengthy tour. As much as I want to help, being locked out of my own home is a tough call." He also had Paul using an abandoned conduit to check on them. The engineer reported everything to be good.

She replied, "It affects my observations, too, but even though I'm nominally in charge, both Prescot and Brandt want his data. So I have to make do."

"What do I need to know about anything upcoming?" he asked.

"Well, once you can operate again, Andy has a clear zone we really need kept free of trajectories, if you can manage it at all. He's very firm on this, but of course, it's your station. Keeping in mind if his team pulls out we have to renegotiate our terms." She seemed embarrassed. "There's another large pod train coming in with additional gear, stocks for you, and a few more personnel."

"Understood. As long as Operations has it, I have no problem. It's not as if it's an astrogation hazard. One other question, if I may."

"Go ahead."

"Why did you arrive in what's essentially a stealth military vessel from deep space?"

She made a face.

"Andy's work, again. They were explicit that we not disrupt space any more than necessary so we could get a clean baseline for examining forcelines and other structures. We were towed around by a tug, and he made them detach farther out than I was comfortable with. The boat is secured against as much leakage as possible. It's basically the equivalent of a clean room. You notice the supply vessels only come in from the docking pole vector."

"So am I even going to be able to resume docking ops, then?"

She looked really embarrassed.

"Yes. Andy will be very unhappy, but at that point, he has to make do. We've accommodated him as much as we can. That decision's up to me, and that's why I'm in charge even though his research has priority."

"Administration and politics," he said, feeling empathy for her.

"Exactly. Thanks for the tea. Shall I check in on Friday?"

"That should be fine."

He didn't bring up that Brandt wasn't clear on their status. He'd save that a bit longer.

After she left, he called Rofert.

"I have a favor for next week," he said.

"Yes, Boss?"

"Can one of your inspection tugs make an orbit around the station?"

"Not an orbit per se, in any reasonable time, but we have enough juice in one to pull a loop, yes."

"Thanks, I'll get with you."

He thought about contacting Space Guard and reporting on events, but he was officially a neutral nation. Contacting them put him more under Earth's thumb and less in the independent category. As curious as he was, he was still a head of state. If Earth stepped in, even the courts might revoke his status.

They were demanding a response to their previous offer, too. The UN Bureau of Space Development understood he controlled a station, etc, and were pleased to extend an offer of salvage cost for the low-use asset, etc, in lieu of further action to assess a bunch of issues that could result in fines.

He needed something soon or they were just going to show up and drag him to Earth.

Could Govannon or Brandt run some public ships here and put up a pretense of interest?

He called back, "Paul, and Nicol, we need to have a meeting on this."

Rofert replied, "On my way."

Nicol said, "Right here." She stepped through from her office.

With everyone seated in G, and something stronger than tea to drink, he opened the discussion.

"The UN, Earth specifically, is trying to hurry us into abandonment. They don't seem to be willing to wait, and they're pestering us. Govannon hasn't expressed interest, but is happy to support a Brandt operation here. We've got speculation that Grainne, if they remain this 'Freehold,' is interested. I need input."

Paul Rofert sipped whisky and said, "Prescot has plenty of resources and might like a remote maintenance facility. You and I have discussed this. If that offer wasn't good then, it doesn't mean it might not be good again soon. They value privacy, too."

Nicol said, "The problem is, they have everything they need on their side. On our side, Frontier Station isn't presently doing enough business to get in the way of maintenance docking, and they have lease agreements for dock space."

"And Grainne?" he asked.

Paul twisted his mouth.

"That all depends on them surviving a war and remaining independent."

"Yes," Jackson said. "The same applies to us. We're smaller, and even more readily occupied. But I don't want to throw in with what may be the losing side."

"Will almost certainly be," Nicol said. "They don't have the infrastructure to fight for long. The UN, meaning Earth, is stupidly focusing on the planet more than on space resources, but still, they can't win."

Paul said, "The guests are straightforward to deal with. But the scientists can't speak for the government, and what government they had is in hiding."

Nicol said, "That still may have been a warship they were in. It was probably repurposed, but I still don't trust them."

"Why not?" he asked.

"Business as usual, oh, and by the way, can we set up clandestinely with you, right next to our enemy? I don't like it."

"Any more word on their bona fides?"

She said, "The scientists have written peer reviewed papers and appear to be legitimate, but I'd be hard pressed to say they have the seniority for a mission like this."

"Meaning?"

She said, "Meaning they could have been hired as a front."

Paul said, "Possibly they were the only ones available?"

She shook her head. "You'd still send them, but someone with more field time would be in charge."

Jackson said, "The issue is, this is our only income at present, and while it covers some essentials, we're not making any money. I'm paying everyone out of company capital. I can't do that for long. So we still come down to, do we close shop now, hold out until this science mission runs out and hope something comes along, or do something else?"

Nicol said, "You've been honest with everyone about when it might roll over us. Don't worry about that."

"But I do," he said. "Stringing it out isn't fair and doesn't make sense, unless we have a good chance of succeeding."

She said, "I suppose I should be honest and admit I sent my resume to Prescot for any relevant position."

"I don't blame you," he said. He didn't, but damn, if she didn't see an out, and he didn't, it was all over. "I guess in that case, when you get an acceptance, I take that as the turning point and close up."

Paul sat very still and said, "I'll remain until the end. There's nothing for me on Earth."

Jackson remembered that Rofert had been in space since his family died in a "pacification" conflict. All cultures were equal on Earth. But occasionally a culture was deemed troublesome and "reintegrated."

He looked at his engineer and lifelong friend. The man had been working here before he was born. "You will ride with me, and we'll go to Titan. And I guess I know what I have to do. Nicol, tell everyone we'll resume departure plans. Paul, your people will need to stay. And I still want to make that survey. Call it nostalgia."

"Understood."

"Got it."

The incoming ship did have a lot more supplies, and more personnel.

It was getting very suspicious. What did a group of researchers need with so many technical assistants? Yes, they'd helped do a lot of equipment overhaul, even to the point of surface treatments and duct cleaning. But why?

If they wanted a hostile takeover, this was a slow way about it, and what point would it serve? If tramp freighters didn't need his station, no larger group would. Few corporations had the funds to waste, and those would have just offered to buy him out and grant him a bunch of favors. The actual governments just wanted to ignore him or exercise eminent domain.

He was going to make that orbit, and Andy's research be damned.

Later that day, Jackson realized he needed a new V-suit. He hadn't gained much weight, but a decade had changed his shape. This one pinched and rubbed. It would last the trip, though.

Rofert personally flew him. They had to inspect the docking array anyway. They ungrappled and slowly accelerated out from the axis.

Pointing to the dock through the port, Rofert said, "It's aligned within very close tolerances, about point five mils."

"Impressive," he said. The visitors' work was honest, no matter what else was going on.

"Now aft and ante," Rofert said.

They overshot the dock while decelerating, got a good scan of the outer terminal and beacon, then slowly moved back. There were workers in the pools of illumination on the scaffolding, some his, more of the visitors. There were over fifty of them now, and it made no sense.

"Let's see what the sneaky bastards are up to," Rofert said as they reached relative zero and started moving back. "Control, Engineer One stating intent to change trajectory and proceed ante for scheduled observation."

"Engineer One, Control confirms, proceed."

The docking pylon, then the melted regolith moved a hundred meters below, punctuated with ports and structures of the lodge, of old construction locks and the control tower and his residence. It really was a tiny station, and a tiny nation. It couldn't be relevant to anyone, and long term it was doomed anyway.

There was nothing significant visible as they passed the irregular lump that marked the arbitrary equator, but then . . .

"Holy crap," he muttered. "Did you see all this, Paul?"

The entire ante polar region had been built on. There were scaffolds, gantries, three docked tugs he could see in addition to the regular boat. There were a lot more than a hundred personnel here, too, because he could see close to that many swarming around building stuff.

In one way or another, it was a hostile takeover.

Then everything went black.

Rofert said, "I'm afraid I did see it, sir."

"'Sir'? Are we down to that, then?"

Sweat suddenly burst from him. It was a sellout, and it was hostile. Paul had been in on whatever it was.

"We're not low on power," Paul said. "We've been disrupted." He pulled out a rescue light and started flashing it, just as something obscured the exterior view.

It was a stealth boat, bay open, maneuvering to intercept.

"Paul . . . this was not cool. Not at all."

"Hold on, please, sir. You need to see this." He sounded earnest and urgent.

The invading force, because that's what it was, had turned the rear third of his castle into a combat operations center. He'd seen what he needed to.

He kept quiet, because his life might depend on not irritating anyone. He'd let them have the rock, as long as they let his people go, even if it meant detention for a while first.

Detention, at least, would still be in space. Arguably better than being "free" on Earth.

Whoever was in the boat was cautious and careful. It was long minutes before they were ensconced in the bay. It closed, blacker inside than out, the stars and station disappearing.

There were bumps, and lights came back on. Hanging off the davit holding them were several armed troops.

The one in front waved for attention and spoke through a contact mic. "Mr. Bates and Mr. Rofert, if you will please open and disembark, the atmosphere is safe."

Rofert looked at him, shrugged and unlatched the hatch port.

They were allowed to maneuver to the forward end of the bay, where the actual deck was, and tie to stanchions. When the bay was pressurized the others unmasked, so Jackson did, too.

The nearest man said, "We apologize for the circumstances. We'd hoped to delay this a bit longer." He looked Hawaiian in ancestry. And broad. About fifty. His accent was from the Grainne Freehold Halo.

Jackson replied, "I'm sorry to have hindered your war."

From the other, "Who said anything about war?"

"It's obvious you're from Grainne and using my home as at least an intel base. It's already set up for that, and I don't have any way to stop you." He should be furious. He'd had suspicions and, at this point, it didn't change the outcome of losing his livelihood. Both sides could die, for all he cared. And Paul . . . had obviously seen this in his conduit crawl, and why hadn't Jackson insisted on going along, too?

He turned, "Paul? Why?"

Paul said, "Sir, I know you don't want to abandon your home. Earth would kill you whether intentionally or not. I promised your father I'd maintain it and keep it. This is the only outlet we have, for now."

The officer said, "We intend no violence against you."

He asked, "Do you intend violence against Earth?"

The man responded, "At present, we are gathering scientific information."

"That doesn't answer my question."

"How many questions about the data you transfer have you answered? Or even asked?"

That was valid. He knew much of the data they handled was questionable, if not outright illicit. This, though, pushed the envelope of plausible deniability.

He said, "I acted in good faith. Even though your presentation was questionable."

The man said, "You acted in your own self interest. You still can. The scientists are doing so."

"So you're funding them?"

"They're funded by Brandt and Prescot, as they said. We're furnishing labor and transport."

He'd accuse them of being cheap, but he knew what charter transport would cost.

The man added, "We're also providing your supplies, at present."

There was the offer. "What do you require me to do?"

"Nothing at all. Just tell no one. We'll continue to cover your operating costs, and we hope the war will end shortly. At that point, you resume being a private exchange and transshipment point."

He believed that was true and honest. He wasn't sure it was something the man could realistically promise.

He replied, "So I have to choose which side I take, in a war I didn't want any part of."

"I guess that's up to you," his counterpart said. "When a landslide starts, the pebbles don't get a vote. The war has started, but the hostilities haven't reached here yet. You not only get a vote, you must vote."

He could be their ally, or their prisoner. Either way, Earth would regard him as hostile and treat him accordingly. They'd wanted Starhome back from the moment his father claimed it.

"I'd have to tell my exec," he warned.

The man nodded. "Yes, just face to face. No transmissions, and none of the inside staff."

It wasn't as if he could call anyone. If he managed to get a message to Earth, even if they believed it, they'd destroy everything his family had, and likely charge him anyway.

Earth had attacked a small nation with a lot of resources because it offered political leverage against others. They in turn had occupied his home because it offered leverage back.

"I wanted to be neutral," he said.

Very seriously, the man said, "So did we, sir."

The parallel was ironic.

Jackson said, "I have nothing to lose. At the same time, I have nothing to gain. What bargaining position do you have, sir?"

The big officer flexed as he moved. It wasn't intimidation. He was just that big with muscle. He pulled out a flask, took a swig, and offered it.

"Silver Birch. Some consider it our finest liquor."

It was informal, but they were in a cargo bay, on a deck surrounded by loading equipment. He accepted with a nod, took a drink, and damn, that was smooth. He'd heard of it, but even the head of state of a rock couldn't afford such imports.

"Very nice," he said.

The officer said, "For now, I can increase cash payments somewhat, to cover our 'maintenance facility.' And I assure you only noncombatant craft will dock here for the duration. That's to our benefit and yours. If you'll tell me what you need for payroll and other overhead, I can approve it."

That was a significant shift. However, if he was selling out, he wasn't going to sell out cheap.

He asked, "What if I am attacked by the UN forces?"

"We'd be attacked as well, in that case."

"Yes, but what is my status?" he prompted.

"At that point, you are an engaged ally, and we'd do our best to defend you as well. Since we'd need the facilities for retreat and repair."

Jackson said, "I'll have my exec draft that as a formal agreement, if you don't mind, holding you to tenant status." He wanted his people drafting the agreement on his terms.

"Fair," the man agreed.

Yes, but . . . "And after the war, then what?"

"What do you want?"

"First refusal on docking rights for any Freehold flagged freighter."

The officer shook his head. "That would be impossible to enforce, given our legal system."

"What instead, then?"

The man said, "We can strongly recommend that our vessels use your services. If you've studied our culture, we're very big on social connections and support of friends."

"Well and good," Jackson said. "But I need something stronger than recommendations."

The man sat and thought for a moment, and Jackson let him. He looked around. The other personnel were still on alert, ready to react to orders. He figured this guy was the officer in charge of the project.

Finally, the man said, "I can guarantee ten years of baseline support of your operation at its present size. Expansion is up to you."

That did it. He was subsidized and beholden, but still independent. They hadn't taken, hadn't threatened, and hadn't tried to buy him out. They respected his sovereignty and circumstances.

First Minister Bates addressed the foreign officer officially. "Reluctantly, and under protest, I accept this pending signature, and offer you continued sanctuary, with the expectation that my people will be given proper treatment as both noncombatants and nonparticipants in our agreement."

"Then, sir," the man said, extending his hand, "you have my word as a Freehold officer."

He shook, and wasn't sure what to say next. He turned to Paul and said, "Whether we live or die, Paul, it will be here, in our home."

His friend grinned back. "That's the only way it should be, sir."

When making first contact with an alien race, communication isn't just important, it might be the difference between life and death. Such is the case when the merchant vessel Avalon *comes in contact with a warrior race known as the Zafosthans, who have a very peculiar way of saying "Hello." It's up to xenolinguist Chesley Armitage to make the introductions—and to keep the ship from being blown out of the sky. And if he can manage that, then the* real *work starts!*

THE ART OF FAILURE
★
by Robert Dawson

"I THINK YOU NEED to see this, ma'am" said Chesley Armitage, passing over a messy sheaf of hand-annotated printout.

"A translation?" asked Captain Helga Nilssen. "Explain it to me."

Armitage smiled. *This* was what he'd signed on for—the captain asking for his professional opinion as a xenolinguist, rather than sending him to the galley to make coffee. On the last three planets, even the beggars had spoken fluent Trade Sinic—or so he had been told. The captain and first mate had gone planetside to haggle: he had stayed in orbit, rearranging cargo.

The discovery of intelligent aliens on Zafostha, speaking no known language, had improved Armitage's position on the *Avalon's* unwritten org chart enormously. For several months he had monitored Zafosthan audio and video transmissions, and, aided by the ship's powerful computer, deciphered, word by painful word, the rudiments of the dominant language, while the rest of the crew waited and grumbled.

Armitage had his own reasons to want a breakthrough. Two years ago he'd had a comfortable, though poorly-paid, postdoctoral fellowship at the University of Elena. Then a friend had talked him into investing his meager savings in a luxury underwater resort. One thing led to another: six months later, the friend vanished, leaving Armitage deeply in debt to some slightly irregular moneylenders with highly irregular collection methods.

Desperate, he'd hitched a ride to Elenaport and signed on as a xenolinguist on a deeply mortgaged tramp trading ship. The ship's partner contract, offering no wages, but a fiftieth share of the profit, had seemed like the quickest way to pay off his debts. But after three unprofitable stops, he could almost feel the jet-seared concrete of the landing field back under his feet, and the knives of the Elena City loansharks at his throat.

"The bits about their ancient culture are a bit conjectural," he said, handing her a particularly scruffy sheet. "But the proposal is plain. The commanding triad of the *Sfethax*—that's the ship that's been buzzing us for the last day, ma'am, the one you thought might want to trade?—present their compliments to you and request that, to celebrate the summer solstice in the fashion appropriate to warriors, we exchange fire with them."

"Are you sure that translation's correct?"

"Yes, ma'am," said Armitage, professional pride hurt. "We shoot at them, and they shoot at us."

The captain shook her head slowly. "Totally crazy."

"Apparently, during the solstice festival, low orbits such as we now occupy are reserved solely for this activity. They add that if we do not practice—politeness? *Bushido*? Chivalry? Something like that . . . then they bid us farewell and ask us to move to a less honorable orbit immediately. Or be—the word they use normally applies only to animals, ma'am. 'Squashed like a bug' gets the idea across."

"At least they're finally paying attention to us. Though getting into a fight isn't usually the best opening for talking business."

"If they wanted to destroy us, they could probably have done so the day we arrived. Among humans this sort of combat is usually ritualized, ma'am. Like jousting, or fistfighting."

"I was in a fistfight, once. In a spaceport bar on Lugaidh," the captain said. "Let me tell you, there was nothing ritualized about it. Bitch wanted to kill me." She ran a finger along a scar on her cheek. "You think accepting the challenge is our only hope of trading?"

Armitage bit his thumbnail: one fistfight was more than his entire lifetime experience of actual combat. "I don't know. I'm fairly sure that if we participate in this ritual, it will improve our status with the warrior class. And that ought to help with the rest of Zafosthan society. Including the thorium merchants."

The only remotely Earthlike world in its system, Zafostha had fabulous reserves of thorium and other radioactives, enough to make the background radiation level on the planet's surface unhealthy for unprotected humans. As a result, the *Avalon* had not yet sent a landing party down; and though there was no record of prior contact, the natives seemed oddly incurious about their visitors. All hints of trading had been ostentatiously ignored.

"Well, we've only got low-power anti-boarding weapons, but if they don't have hyperdrive, our shields are probably more advanced than theirs." She grinned. "Tell them we accept."

"Yes, ma'am." Armitage left the bridge, wishing for once that he was on a really big naval ship, say a *Thanatos*-class destroyer.

Or just in orbit around a less-crazy planet.

Vethassa turned from the radio to her two siblings. "The strangers have accepted our challenge!" She fluttered her three-fingered hands in delight. "They *are* warriors!"

Shazathet looked dubious. "I hope you know what you are doing," he said.

"You agreed to it too, Shaz," said Thossatha. "Don't pick on Vetha. We made that decision as a triad. You can't back out now."

"I know. But to challenge an alien craft, unfamiliar with our ways . . . oh, it's a splendid feat, and our tributes will not suffer. But is it perhaps just a little foolhardy?"

"I have explained our customs to them," Vethassa said. "And in years to come, it will be remembered that our ship was the first to give a proper warriors' welcome to the travelers from beyond the stars."

"Well, one way or another, it will be a solstice to remember," said Shazathet. "Time to get our battle-robes on, my impetuous sister."

Vethassa chittered and left the bridge.

Half an hour later, Armitage returned. "I've translated the rules that they sent us, ma'am."

"Go on."

"We enter opposing equatorial orbits, with closest approach to each other of—it's about three kilometers. At the first approach, we fire at them, a single shot, no evasive action to be taken. At the next approach, forty minutes later, they fire at us. We continue until each of us has fired three shots. A little bit like 'Sir Gawain and the Green Knight.'"

"Never viewed it. What weapon?"

"Attacker's choice."

The Captain raised her eyebrows. "You mean we could use a nuclear drone? Blast them into pieces?"

"Yes, ma'am. That was the exact example I used when I requested clarification."

"Just as well for them, we don't have one." Once more she stroked her scar.

"Presumably, they don't expect us to try to destroy them. They know we're here to trade."

"Of course." She switched on the ship's intercom. "Chen, Orlova, Wang: strap in, but do not, repeat do not, fire except as instructed."

Chen called from his place at the fire-control station: "Maybe you just send them a nice box of chocolates, Captain?" Somebody laughed.

"All other crew, take your posts and prepare for emergency damage control." The captain released the switch and flicked her thumb towards the remaining chair. "Armitage, stay here. I may want advice."

This time, Armitage would have happily gone off to the galley to make coffee; but he began to strap himself into the chair beside the captain's, with fingers that seemed to have forgotten how the buckles fastened. Before he was through, the *Avalon* gave a sickening lurch. He hauled himself back into the seat and managed to get the buckle into place before the next surge of acceleration.

Once strapped in, he sat there and wondered nervously whether he'd got it right. Right enough, anyhow . . . no translation was ever perfect. What was that proverb by Umberto Eco that Professor Chetty used to have on his office wall? "Translation is the art of failure," that was it. But how much had he failed by? Enough to get them killed?

★ ★ ★

On the bridge of the *Sfethax*, the commanding triad sat, wearing their ornate battle-robes. Their chairs were turned away from the control panels so that Vethassa and Shazathet could better appreciate Thossatha's recitation of a traditional poem.

"*Sing, spear in my hand!*
Sing, my comrades, sing . . ."

A soft chime sounded. Thossatha finished the verse, then swiveled his chair back to the control panels with deliberate insouciance. The others did the same.

They sat, silently, watching the monitors as if in meditation. Suddenly Vethassa's screen flared white. She flinched involuntarily, almost invisibly, but there was no sound, no impact.

"What in the names of the Three was that?" asked Shazathet. "A photon pyrotechnic? Are you certain they understood your instructions, Vetha?"

"I assume that it was some unfamiliar alien weapon," she said. "But fortunately, our shields held. Now, what shall we send them back?"

"Ever been under fire before, Armitage?" asked the captain.

"No, ma'am." He grasped the chair arm to stop his hand from trembling.

"Well, maybe we won't be. Maybe they took our signal flare in the spirit in which it was intended. But if they do, stay calm. Remember what you said—if this is ritual, they won't be trying to kill us."

Armitage hoped he had been right. Right enough, anyhow.

The improvised time-to-next-approach display ticked down inexorably. Each second stretched like rubber. Five seconds . . . four . . . three . . . two . . . one . . . The display flicked back to forty-two minutes and twenty-eight seconds. Armitage took a shaky breath, wondering whether the aliens had held their fire or just missed.

BANG! The explosion was deafening: the hull shook as if it had been hit by a giant hammer. A few status lights turned amber. Apparently the Zafosthans were taking this seriously after all.

"Hah!" the captain said. "Just ritual?"

"I think so, ma'am. Surely they must have more powerful weapons than that?"

"I'd imagine so. But why are they escalating at all?"

"I don't know. Perhaps there has to be a certain level of combat."

An unpleasant thought struck him. "We may even have insulted them with the signal flare."

"Poor babies. Well, what do you think we should do next?"

"What do we have about the same strength as that?"

"Weapons? Nothing. Let's see . . . We've got some prospecting charges that come close. Orlova, stand by to fire a Number Three sampling charge."

"Are we fighting or collecting rocks, Captain?" Orlova said. "I don't have any sampling charges armed."

"Well, arm one fast! I want to knock a few pebbles off our new playmates when we pass them again in half an hour."

For twenty minutes Armitage could hear the fire-control team preparing the charge. They were ready with ten minutes to spare and launched it on the next approach. It went off against the Zafosthan shields with a silent flash that briefly dazzled the *Avalon*'s cameras but had no other visible effect. The time-to-approach display reset, and the long wait began again.

When the Zafosthan ship flashed past once more, her passage was accompanied by an even larger explosion that shuddered the *Avalon* to her rivets and left Armitage's ears ringing. This time, a few status lights stayed red and amber. The captain swore under her breath. Armitage could hear crewmates beginning emergency repairs.

"One more round, Xenolinguist. Should we go to a Number Four?"

"I don't think that's the point, Captain. If they had wanted to destroy us, they could have done it any time since we arrived. With respect, ma'am, I suggest another charge like the last. We can't back down, but no need to suggest escalation."

"You'd better be right."

For half an hour Armitage sat there, watching the status lights returning to green. Finally, the moment of approach arrived; the second prospecting charge flared, again doing no apparent damage. In a minute, they were out of telescope range again.

"One more shot and it's over," said the captain. "Just one more."

The seconds were like hours, the minutes years. They sat in silence, as the timer counted downward. Finally, the telescope found the other ship: a dot, then suddenly, an expanding luminous green sphere, growing to fill the viewport. The lights dimmed for a few seconds as all available power was shunted to the shields, then brightened again.

"Plasma flare!" the captain said and laughed. "If they thought we couldn't take *that*! Well, now we've played their little game, maybe they'll talk business. What do you think?"

"I'll get right on it, ma'am," said Armitage, unbuckling his safety harness. Talking business: now *that* was something he could handle.

"You were right, sister," Shazathet said. "Wherever they have come from, they are true warriors. And we'll have a tale to tell down on the ground tonight."

"Who do you plan to tell it to?" Vethassa asked. "That pretty navigator from the *Nefathi*?"

"Perhaps. If she's around. How about you?"

"I'll be at the Guild Hall with my friends." She fluttered her hands. "At least for the first part of the night. After that, who knows?"

Shazathet chittered. "Good hunting!"

"It seems that we passed the test, ma'am," Armitage said, a day later. He pushed his lank hair back behind his ears and blinked his gritty eyes. This had been the most difficult translation yet, full of cultural nuances. "'A chivalrous combination of courage and restraint. They are honored to consider us as fellow warriors.'"

"And the thorium? We didn't come here to play chicken, we came here to trade."

"Ah. That may be a problem, ma'am. You see, it turns out that commerce is beneath the dignity of the Zafosthan warrior class. Now that our high status has been established, it would be out of the question for anybody to insult us by discussing such matters."

Armitage listened in awe to the captain's lengthy and detailed reply. He had never thought of her as a linguist, but she could swear in most languages that he knew and a few that he didn't. When she finally paused for breath, he raised a hand. "With your permission, ma'am. I'm sure that there's some way that we can make this work out."

"*Tabarnak à deux étages!*" she spat. "There'd better be, Armitage— I'm not jumping back to Helena Bloody Prime with a hold still full of holochips and fire-amethyst. The *Gottverdammt* bank would take the ship."

"Maybe we can tell them that only some of us are warriors?"

"Hmmph. I don't buy it. Warriors, in a society like this, chauffeuring a lousy merchant around? Does that seem like something they'd do?"

"Maybe. People do weird things."

"We can't risk it."

Better than I can risk going home empty-handed, Armitage thought. "Er, Captain? Maybe we can just go down and grab some thorium? Warriors in some cultures . . ."

"Dammit, Armitage, I may have broken every customs regulation this side of the Lesser Magellanic Cloud: that's how you make a profit in this business. But I'm not a pirate, and I'm not going to become one now."

"Let me think about it some more."

"You'd better—because if we can't make this trip show a legitimate profit, I'm going to have to get rid of supernumerary crew members. And that's not going to mean the engineer or the astrogator."

Zithithassa was leaning on her vermifork, looking at the sun and wondering whether to have another go at the *sthasa*-worms or go home and change her robes for the last evening of the summer solstice festival. A booming noise high in the air made her look up; a strange craft was tearing across the sky, a few thousand personheights above. Unlike most planes at that height, it didn't leave a contrail. Slowly, it circled the sky, and came back towards her, more quietly. It glided lower and lower: at the last minute it flared, slowed, and made a rough-looking landing right in the middle of the *sthasa* crop. The thing was larger than she'd first thought; it tore a wide swathe through the young plants. The farm's triad were not going to be happy, but they could hardly blame her.

Three hundred heartbeats later a door opened high up on the hull, and a giant emerged, twice as tall as a person. It wore a white suit, and a transparent bowl covered its head, like a nestling's picture of a spaceworker. She watched, fascinated, as it climbed down a ladder to the field. Once the giant was on the ground, the ladder retracted and the door closed over it. The giant strode towards her. When it got close, it knelt down, held a small box to its helmet and spoke in a low rumble, like a distant electrical storm. Simultaneously, a voice came from the box.

"I come with peace. Please take us to the nearest thorium merchant," the box said.

"You have destroyed many *sthasa* plants," Zithithassa said firmly. The box rumbled in unison.

The giant rumbled back. "Is sorrow. Payment can happen." It reached into a satchel at its waist and took out a strange purple gemstone, a thumblength across, which it handed to her. "But needing is that we find a thorium merchant. And it must quickly because my air is few."

"Perhaps you might try the metalmongers on the Street of the Seven Waterfalls." She pointed the way. "It is about a thousand personheights from here."

"Is gratitude." The giant bent at the waist, straightened and strode toward the town. Zithithassa looked back and forth between the stone and the ruined *sthasa*. The stone was surely worth much more than the lost plants. She fluttered her hands and chittered happily to herself. She practiced the Three Virtues as well as most people, and she'd certainly see that the triad got fair compensation—but it was upon her, not them, that Fortune had smiled today.

She turned and walked back to her hut. Tonight she'd put on her finest clothes, join the solstice celebration, and buy drinks for all her friends. Tomorrow she'd figure out what to tell the triad.

Behind her the shuttle took off again, spiralling upward in quiet mode until it was high enough to unleash the full fury of its jets without disturbing those below. Deep in speculation on the value of her jewel, she did not turn to watch it, nor the tall white-suited figure who was climbing over the fence onto the roadway.

The captain looked through the list of useful Zafosthan radio frequencies and picked one that Armitage had tagged as "government/official." She sent a "ready-to-transmit" signal, then looked at the list on the computer screen, English translations of Zafosthan phrases that he had programmed into the computer.

At the top of the list: *I apologize, but one of our prisoners has escaped.* A handwritten footnote pointed out that the word for 'prisoner' was applicable only to Zafosthans of low status; a warrior might be killed with honor, but for one warrior to imprison another was an unforgivable *gaucherie*, reflecting poorly on the captor's entire clan. She touched the screen, sending the message.

The computer made a noise like a catfight; a few seconds later, the Zafosthan response crackled and hissed back. *We will be glad to exterminate the wretch, as a minor favor to our honored visitors.* She hastily picked a response: *No, please do not do that. It must be tried on its home world before it is executed.*

The Zafosthan agreed: of course, their guests' customs must be followed, if possible. How could they assist?

My-two-siblings-and-I believe that it is loose on the surface of your noble world. Approximate coordinates thus and so. It is not dangerous— it is a merchant of low class. Help to recapture it would be much appreciated.

The Zafosthan response assured her that steps would be taken. The captain stretched back in her chair and buzzed the galley for a coffee, hoping that young Armitage knew his stuff.

The office of the metalmongers' executive triad was domed, almost two meters high in the middle. The wall/ceiling was pale azure at floor level, shading to deep indigo at the zenith: pretty, but claustrophobic as hell, Armitage thought.

He had just finished negotiating with the three little Zafosthans for five million credits' worth of isotopically pure thorium, for immediate delivery. The dickering had stretched his Zafosthan vocabulary to the limit: he was out of reach of the ship's computer, and the box in his hand could do nothing more than raise the pitch of human speech for Zafosthan ears and *vice versa*. But they had finally reached a deal, and the agreed price, in gem-quality fire-amethysts, glittered between them on the table.

Behind him, there was an imperious knock, followed immediately by the sound of a door being flung open. Armitage followed the merchants' eyes, then slowly raised his hands in the air and turned around, his fingertips brushing the ceiling.

In the doorway stood three Zafosthans. Like the merchants, they barely came to Armitage's waist; but what they lacked in height they made up for with lethal-looking silver sidearms. One of them wore a plain gold necklace that Armitage recalled as indicating some sort of rank. It moved its lips but no sound came out.

"Try speaking into this," Armitage said, and slowly lowered his hand holding the transposer toward the squad leader. It looked at the

box carefully with its big soulful eyes before it spoke. Its dialect was one
that Armitage was not used to, and he did not understand more than
a third of what it said; but odd words here and there suggested some
combination of arrest, rebuke, and getting the hell out of Dodge.

It gestured with its sidearm toward the door. Armitage moved
awkwardly toward the door, ducking as the ceiling lowered. He
waddled bent-kneed along the low twisting corridor, banging his
helmet repeatedly on the uneven arched ceiling. Finally, he reached
the open air, stood up, and stretched. The leader of the squad emerged
behind him, followed by the other two cops and the curious
metalmongers.

". . . (Something) planet immediately," the leader said. "(Something)
large (room? chamber?) . . . off planet . . . (something), height/area/
volume (something) . . ."

"Sorry? Can you repeat that?"

Slowly Armitage pieced the unfamiliar dialect together. He was
required to leave the planet. But he would not fit into the passenger
cabin of one of their spaceships. Was his suit vacuum-proof, so that
he could be shipped as cargo?

"No," he said. "It is for radiation only."

The warriors of (something) had requested that he be (something).
But as this was impossible . . .

"Whaddya mean, impossible?" Armitage yelped. Everything had
gone smoothly so far. What was wrong now?

The leader lifted its sidearm from its holster and pointed it
upward in the general direction of Armitage's navel. Armitage was
suddenly aware of how close and sweaty the inside of a radiation suit
could be.

There was a sound in the distance, a faint scream of abused air,
growing nearer and louder. The leader lowered its weapon and
looked up as the shuttle roared overhead, hardly clearing the taller
buildings.

"See?" Armitage said, his voice almost steady. "See? They have
come to take me away."

The warrior-giant bustled up to Guardleader Sthizifa, wearing a
suit like the prisoner's. Its gestures suggested that it would like the
insolent merchant returned to it immediately. Unfortunately, Sthizifa

could understand nothing of what it said. Even hearing it was difficult without the strange box that the prisoner carried: like the prisoner, the captain-giant made only low rumblings.

Even with the box, though, the warrior-giant's speech was incomprehensible. Perhaps the box only raised the pitch of the rumblings, and did not translate? Sthizifa turned to the prisoner and managed to indicate that it was to act as translator, upon pain of immediate execution. He had his doubts as to the prisoner's intelligence, but it did seem to have picked up a few sentences of the local language.

"Yes, sir." The prisoner bowed. "The first assistant requests that I be handed under to him presently. He firmly promising to take me off-planet and spare you the inconveniencing of my unstable self."

Sthizifa pondered the situation. "Tell it that we are grateful."

The prisoner and the warrior rumbled to each other; then the prisoner turned to Sthizifa. "It is other matters. After my trial and execution, the confiscation of my property must be made by a court on my world. The ship's triad must grasp the thorium which this unworthy one is just buying so that this may be properly happen." Its mouth twitched with embarrassment.

Sthizifa thought carefully. There was merit in the warrior-giant's request. The prisoner had apparently purchased the thorium legally, and its fugitive status was a matter for its own people. He dispatched one of his underlings to the metalmongers.

A few thousand heartbeats later, an electric tractor appeared, pulling a train of six carts, each loaded with rectangular boxes containing thorium ingots. The shuttle extended its cargo ramp, and workers began to load them into the shielded hold.

Sthizifa gestured with his weapon. "You, too, prisoner. Make yourself useful." The prisoner obeyed with fawning eagerness. Sthizifa watched as it meekly carried the ingots, and could not help comparing it with the warriors of its kind, whose valiant solstice-combat two days before was still the talk of the whole planet.

Finally, the last ingot was stowed away. The prisoner was escorted into the cabin of the shuttle, the doors closed, and the shuttle took off.

"They are a noble people," said Sthizifa to one of his underlings, as the shuttle shrank to a dot in the sky. "Our world is honored by their visit. It is a pity that their lower classes are so unsatisfactory."

The guard fluttered her hands and agreed.

Armitage followed Chen through the shuttle's narrow airlock into the comparatively spacious loading bay of the *Avalon*. Both of them were still weak with laughter. The captain was waiting inside.

"Well done, Armitage!" the captain said. "Take ten minutes to clean up, then meet me in the computer room. I've got one more job for you."

Her tone of voice, almost apologetic, put him on guard. "Ah, what's that, ma'am?"

"You got us a great rate on that thorium. I'll be able to pay the bank off, and there'll be something over to divide among the crew. But we can't pull this stunt off again."

"I guess not."

"Lose a prisoner every trip, people start to think you're careless. But we're the first-contact ship. If we register pioneer trading rights, we get a ten percent royalty on the net from every other League trader here for sixteen standard years. That's where the real money is."

"That would be . . . ?"

"One holy shit-tonne of cash, Armitage," she said, almost reverently. "And your share is one-fiftieth, like with any other profits of this voyage."

Armitage wondered briefly what twenty holy shit-kilos came to in convertible credits, and decided, based on the captain's tone of voice, that it was probably more than enough. "So how do I come in?"

"To qualify for pioneer trading rights, we have to have a sole claim at the moment of filing. Otherwise, nobody gets anything. Orlova tells me another ship's appeared on the hyperscan, heading this way. If they get within the orbit of the outermost planet before we have the forms sent off, we're out of luck. She reckons we have about sixteen hours."

"Can't somebody else do it, ma'am?"

"That paperwork has to be done in about eight different languages, and if we make a mistake there'll be no time to refile. Those rights are worth millions, Armitage, and a computer translation's only as good as the person directing the computer. We can't afford to fail. Now get moving!"

As hot water sluiced off his body, Armitage tried to estimate how long the filing would take. Was Peninsular Xophurian, with its six mutable genders and inscrutable honorifics, one of the languages? Given how close Zafostha was to the Xophurian Extended Hegemonic Region, it seemed all too likely. He groaned. There was no time to waste. He slapped the shower control: the water turned off and the hot-air drying jets began to roar.

When he got to the computer room, the Captain was waiting impatiently. She waved him to a seat. "Most of the law manuals and forms are in searchable digital form on the ship's computer."

"Most?"

"Well, there's the Revealed Mercantile Code." She indicated a stack of three thick purple books on the desk. "The Xophurians consider it sacred, and don't permit it to be digitized, so you'll have to use a printed copy." She unclipped a plain stainless-steel pendant from a chain around her neck and laid it on the desk beside him. "And that chip has my personal signature code, and the ship's trading license and papers. Anything else you'll need?"

Armitage stared for a moment at the stack of books and sighed. "Well, ma'am, I haven't eaten all day. If you're going past the galley, I could definitely use a sandwich. And a pot of coffee."

She paused for an instant, blinked, and grinned. "I'll have someone send them up. And I think there might be a leftover portion of starberry mousse in the fridge. Think you could manage that too?"

Jeff Saunders was once a corporal in AJAX Company of the British Royal Tank Regiment. That was several lifetimes ago and lightyears behind him. Now, centuries later, he's a very old man on board Earth's first colony ship. His mission: to provide a link to the past to the vat-born colonists en route to their new homeworld. But some old soldiers never really leave war behind.

THE LAST TANK COMMANDER
★
by Allen Stroud

TRANSMISSION BEGINS:

Madam Secretary,

A continued update on our progress.

We have concluded all tests on the planet's environmental conditions that we can manage via the satellite array.

The ionisation is not a localised phenomenon. We cannot be sure whether this is a natural occurrence or some form of defence system from the native life. Since all standard remote access probes lose signal with operations control when they enter the ionosphere, we have only limited data on what to expect from a landing. However, all indicators remain consistent and, in as far as we can determine from the three high shielded missions launched, the concentrations of bastnäsite, our potential terbium source, are waiting extraction.

Efficiency requires us to apply the optimum solution from the resources available on the colonial barges.

We have come too far and expended too much effort to fail.

My name is Jeff Saunders. In 2017, I was a corporal and driver of an FV4034 Challenger 2 battle tank for AJAX Company of the British Royal Tank Regiment.

According to Hermes control it's now AD 3483.

The comforting thrum of a working engine is the same as before, only this time I'm not driving. Instead, I'm perched in the turret like an officer talking down to a crew of kids while they work the tracks, load the guns and everything else.

Perched doesn't do this turret justice, though. Compared to what we had back in the day, we're in a luxury penthouse of touchscreens and duraglass. The whole tank is a weave of ceramic and aramid synthetic fibre on the outside and a cool set of spaceship boxes within.

"Distance to the lander site?"

"Six kilometres."

"Speed?"

"Forty-five kay."

Still need to convert the numbers in my head. Eurometrics became a worldwide standard in 2043. I key instructions into the tactical display, cybernetic fingers anticipating my intention; spooky stuff that I'd prefer not to rely on, but there's no place for Parkinson's on a military operation.

"Tewan, give me a sweep scan of the perimeter. Tag anything that pings back."

"Unlikely we'll pick up much with the interference."

"Do it anyway."

I can feel the stares being exchanged below. Three girls and one young boy, all crammed in a box with me as their surrogate grandpa. These kids think they're humouring me, when actually I'm humouring them. Idle hands and all that, something they probably wouldn't understand, growing up in vats with direct data education like they did a few weeks back.

On the 17th of February, 2017, we deployed into the Lugansk region of Ukraine under NATO command—one of the first engagements of a global conflict that became known as "The Last World War." Six months of street fighting later, the governments of the day were finally convinced that they couldn't solve the argument with soldiers. We pulled out and the drones went in instead. Eight years on, resource depletion achieved what both we and the drones couldn't.

Peace.

"Scan complete, anomalies are on your screen."

"Th-Thanks."

I paw through the blips, my real hand shaking too much to help. My implant has been triggered and a dopamine substitute will be coursing through my veins, but drugs can only do so much. The boy, Juonal, is right: we can't tell which of these might be a threat and which are distortions from the atmospheric effects—the whole reason they got me down here. Still, at least there's something to look at.

"Angle us thirty degrees left, around those rocks; no sense in risking the tracks on anything we don't need to. Traverse turret right to compensate."

"Yes, sir."

"Corp or Jeff is fine, Krees. R-Remember I work for a living."

"Sorry, Corp."

I can't smell petrol like we used to. These kids don't seem to sweat much either; the air in here is cool and recycled. No option of cracking the hatch and deploying a proper mark one eyeball. Outside it's noon and the reader says sixteen Celsius, colder than Earth by a ways. Patches of weird grass and shrub pass by—sometimes like Earth, but with clumps of strange orange, purple and red. This is not our world, we're trespassing and this planet's trying to decide how to react. The atmosphere's breathable, but tense; the charged air is a risk we can't take on the equipment, so we're left staring through duraglass. Makes everything unreal, like those headset games people played.

In 2075, I was selected as an elder for the Kepler 452b mission. I decided to apply and go because it would be the last thing I could do with my life. My family were all grown up with kids and my Helen had passed away a couple of years ago. The colonists would be born off-world with no ties to Earth. Travel back would take more than a lifetime. Sure, they'd have a database of historical events and such to learn about humanity's past, but no chance to talk to people who'd lived back in the day. Elders were on board to provide that opportunity. We were the final piece in the jigsaw; the perfect project for humanity to fire into space and forget about; a colony of people about to die and people who'd never been born.

I didn't expect to visit another planet; that wasn't part of the job description. Neither was designing, building and commanding a tank, but sometimes new problems require old solutions.

"Range to target?"

"Less than a kilometre. Should be in sight."

I squint into the fading sun. "Might be for you."

I had never built a tank before, but my experience of driving one, along with the ship's database, advanced fabrication systems and the willing help of these vat grown kids, warmed me to the task. We needed something armed, mobile, robust and resistant to the excessively ionised atmosphere. A crew operating the vehicle would need to be self-sufficient and organised, able to operate without reporting back to base every few minutes. That's why, in the end, I had to come down here.

The embodiment of an old solution.

I call her Jane. That was Helen's middle name. She's got higher tracks than anything we had in the army and extended compartments over the front and back of the wheels—more like a big truck container with an engine and a turret on top. She's rugged, tough and belligerent, built to push through, like the old girls I used to drive, but there's a beauty too, something that speaks to you, just you alone.

I loved my Helen. She was my rock. Maybe I'll learn to love Jane too.

When I was at school I went to an old people's home and interviewed war veterans. We prepared questions, but I got shy and after I ran out of things to ask, went and hid in the coat room. The teacher found me and told me off, but I couldn't face talking to people like that, making them dredge up the past and all those bad memories, but I think I judged wrongly. I realise now that they wanted to talk, so kids like me wouldn't make the same mistakes people made in their day.

The lander is in view—a four sided pyramid with the top chopped off. The damaged ceramic hull is strangely out of place. Reminds me of an ancient temple rediscovered by archaeologists, the broken up ground evidence of their search.

"Penn, get us alongside and facing outward," I tell our driver.

There's a grunt of reply from the bowels below. Gears shift and we start up an incline. The left track slows, bringing us about in a lazy circle until we stop exactly where I asked.

"Krees, target and deploy comms."

"Firing now."

I hear the dull thump of the modified harpoon gun and the faint impact of the suction grapple. It tethers us and drills into our target, the rubber cable providing a communication and datalink to our system.

"We're connected."

"Well done. Prep for EVA and extraction."

A mass of movement below me as Penn, Juonal, Krees and Tewan unstrap themselves and make their way to the airlock. Turret control is transferred to my station and I strap my shaking left hand to the miniature joystick. The trembles are calming down and won't be enough to disturb things unless I want them disturbed.

"Ready to disembark."

"Go ahead."

There's a scraping sound as they unscrew the side access hatch. I lean over and press my face to the glass. I can just see them trooping out over the tracks, each of them packed into rubber lined pressure suits and plastic helmets. They head to the lander, crack open the door and disappear inside. I bite my lip. These kids aren't soldiers. They downloaded everything the mission computers think might be relevant. They're strong and young, but with no real experience, whereas I'm all experience and no strength; weak wisdom against a planet full of unknown.

This is the first of sixteen landers. Our task is to visit them all, assess their state, download data and retrieve core samples. Ultimately, these shells will form the starting blocks for the new colony. Each contains a whole array of equipment and automated science, stuff I was never hired to understand.

I turn back to my screen. Some of the spots are moving, surrounding the site. I can't see anything outside, but they're out there. I can feel them. I don't know who or what they are, but they're waiting. I'd be waiting until now, the moment when we're tethered, separated, and vulnerable.

My thumb shifts the stick, the turret swivels forty-five degrees left and I spot something moving over the open ground, throwing itself behind rocks near where we drove up. I key up the 2GW laser and feel the charging vibration.

"Penn, you receiving me?" The reply is a bit garbled, but it sounds like a yes. I carry on. "I think we've got trouble. If you can hurry up, that'd be helpful."

The console pings and I fire the charged laser. The beam isn't like the movies; it's invisible, but there're some atmospheric effects, zips and flickers of electricity where it should be. I train the barrel across the outcrop and watch as the rocks shatter and explode, then shut down.

The dust and residual charge take a while to dissipate. I can make out something, a dark stain on the beige/brown dirt. Could be a corpse, a confirmed kill?

Were they actually going to attack? That familiar second guess guilt grips me like an old friend. Post-Traumatic Stress Disorder was one of the reasons soldiers got replaced by computers. The ultimate detachment from the consequences of war is to not be there, but we have no option in this place. Better I go to my maker and confess than get one of these kids dreaming about it for the rest of their lives.

The world erupts, projectile weapons of some kind, dull thuds against Jane's outer ceramics. Not waiting for the laser to recharge, I traverse and return fire with the same. Fifty calibre machine guns haven't changed much since the Second World War, but these two are self-contained, the heat and spent bullet casings recycled into the portable fabricator. The drumming sound of operation shakes the turret as it turns, my finger locked on the trigger. Suppression fire isn't accurate or pretty, but it's generally effective. Making people worry about their own skins means they're less likely to shoot at you. The digital ammunition counter spirals towards zero. We don't have an infinite supply. Even if the fabricator makes more, it takes time.

"Penn, get a move on!"

I can't make out the reply. We need more ordnance, and I can't control the main gun from here without transferring the auto-loading system. I keep strafing the arc away from the lander with the fifty-cal, start up laser charging, and begin the sequence to switch all operations to my station. I'm not sure I can manage the fine controls, even with meds, but I've no choice.

Figures are moving out there in the dust, shadowy shapes I can't be sure of. I remember Russian insurgents using smoke as cover to get close with explosives. That was seventy years ago in my lifetime, centuries ago to anyone back on Earth.

The console pings again. I fire the laser at a dark shape, hoping to hit something.

Was coming here some sort of therapy? A chance to return to the past when there's fuck all left for me to live for? In that sense maybe I'm a better soldier now. No ties. Means I'm clear in what I must do.

Something hits Jane on the side, pitching us back at an angle. She groans beneath me. The seat traps tighten as my weight shifts. I can't reach the joystick with my left hand. I can hear the tortured grinding of metal on metal as the auto compensator system tries to right us; doesn't sound good.

Penn's voice crackles over the comms. "Exiting now," she says.

"Bloody hurry!" I shout back. The turret turns towards the sky, giving me no firing solution with the fifty-cal; the laser pivots, but it's still only half charged. "We're a sitting—"

A huge impact. Jane shifts up and forward, ceramic debris flies everywhere. For a second I worry that the duraglass won't hold if we flip and I'm re-arranged to be on the bottom, but then she crashes back onto her tracks. Somewhere in the rear the pressure door opens; there's hissing, a red klaxon and light start up, and there's shouting. Penn screams before three loud pops ring out around me. A flash of pain. Spider web cracks appear on my viewscreen, and I feel something wet under my arm.

"Penn?"

"I'm here!" she says from below, slipping back into her seat and pulling on the straps. "We had some uninvited guests," she says. "They're gone, so we need to get moving."

"What about the others?"

"Making their way up." Her voice trembles a little. I know the signs, the adrenalin's still there. She's going to fall apart after, just as we all did the first time. "All present and accounted for."

"Get us underway, then," I tell her.

Penn brings the engine out of idle and starts up both track drives. For a moment, she forgets how it all works and makes like a kid with a game stick, but then she remembers. Jane whines a little but settles down, and with a lurch, pulls away. Our girl's bloodied, but not bad, just like these kids.

The dust clears. There's a smoking wreck of something dead ahead on the path, like a beetle from back on Earth, only it's the size of a house. I can't see inside; there's no obvious crew compartment, just dark brown ridges overlaid on each other. Around it, there are things moving though. They're tall, thin and six limbed, scampering away to keep the dead beetle tank between them and us.

Krees moves up to her seat at comms and turret control. There's blood on her lip and matting her dark hair. "They're all around us," she says. "Where are we going to go?"

"I don't know," says Penn. She's staring ahead, trying not to look at her. "What do we do, Corp?"

I try to smile at Krees, but it's hard to breathe. There's pain in my chest and something's not right. "We make for the next target and see who's following us," I manage to gasp out. "We need flat ground, then we can understand what we're up against."

She nods, her pinched face relaxing a touch, but those wide eyes are still full of fear. I remember my first fight. It's easier when someone else makes the plan. You can shut down and just do what you're told. The voices go away when you're given a job. "Take over turret. Traverse to rear and see if you can comm the fleet. Tewan, give me sweeps on what's following."

Both girls snap to their jobs. I wince as the cabin shifts round. Jane groans a little too. "Juonal, get me a damage update."

"How am I supposed to tell if—"

"I don't care about dents; I care if we're leaking!"

"Right, Corp."

They're kids—I need to keep reminding myself. Worse than that, they're super intelligent vat grown kids who take criticism to heart. They don't know any other way. "Krees, pull up the scans as well; two pairs of eyes are better than one."

I'm staring out through the dusty canopy as we accelerate away from the lander. Gradually it clears as Juonal activates the screen optimisers and gets his head around what we've bent and broken. I can see three big beetle shapes like the wrecked one. They can't match our speed and neither can the six-limbed creatures capering around them, all amidst brown rocks under a bleak sky. I can't quite believe I'm seeing aliens; suddenly this place really is another world, not just a warzone.

But it is also a warzone.

"Slow us down and load up the main gun," I tell the crew. "Explosive round please. Penn, find me a good flat spot for recoil. We don't know how shaken up we are right now."

Jane slows and the dust clouds fade. Then she stops and Penn deploys the support legs. I can feel things shifting around below as Krees loads up the charge. There's a grinding noise too, a little indigestion?

"The autoloader's jammed!"

"Stay calm and unjam it then," I wheeze in reply. "Penn, your turn to help."

Both of them unstrap and get to work. I keep my eye on our pursuit. The natives are getting closer, and I bet they have friends nearby. We've an advantage if we can get a round in the breech, if we can't and they surround us. . .

There's a clunk and shout of relief from below. "Loaded!" Krees shouts.

"Penn, get back on the controls. Everyone brace for firing!"

In 1943 the German army produced the Panzer Tiger II with an eighty-eight millimetre gun. The Americans and British only had tanks with seventy-two millimetre guns. The Tiger could hit them at a range where they couldn't fire back, and its extra armour meant even if they did get close enough, they had little chance of getting through. The only problem the Germans had was they couldn't produce their tanks fast enough or in enough numbers. German crews ended up outnumbered three or four to one, whilst allied forces knew they had to rush the Tiger as quickly as possible. At least one of them would get blown to bits on the way in.

The same situation happened in Ukraine. The Russian T-14 Armata out-gunned, out-armoured, and out-powered our Challenger 2s.

A one hundred and forty millimetre gun makes us the Russians and Germans in this scenario.

"Fire!" I shout and depress the trigger. The chair kicks me in the kidneys. There's a puff of smoke and a faint whine. In the distance, one of the beetles explodes. The tall creatures scatter, but keep on coming.

"Rotate six degrees right. Armour piercing this time; reload!"

"Aye, Corp, Reload!"

There's feverish working below as Krees pops the steaming chamber and hauls up another round. She knows every second at this brings the aliens closer. These kids looked our enemy in the eye; they know what's at stake.

"Clear!"

I don't hesitate. I can't. We'll die if I do. If we don't survive, the next batch that gets set down here'll likely die too. I squeeze the trigger again. Another plume of smoke, but the targeter's off. The shell smacks into the side of the beetle. The armour cracks, but it keeps coming.

"Three points left and reload!"

Some of the alien soldiers are in range. The patter of small arms fire on the canopy starts up once more. I shift around and begin charging the laser, but I can't aim the fifty-cal as well. My seat's soaking wet with blood. "Tewan . . ." I gasp.

The lower guns open up in response. Relying on instruments, there's not much Tewan can do to target them, but the trackers are effective enough, keeping them jumping around outside.

"Clear!"

I disengage the auto-targeter on the main gun and aim it myself, shifting around a fraction before firing. There's a yelp of pain from below, but I haven't time to check what's wrong.

The second shot does the trick, hits the damaged beetle dead on. It crumples on itself, squatting on the ground like a cracked egg. The third one's in laser range now. I fire from the console and rake the beam across the front of it, watching a dark line score along the ceramic ribbing, but it's too late, whatever this thing is, it's got close enough.

There's a huge roar as something punches into Jane. Her prow distorts and I'm thrown back in my seat. Spider web cracks appear in the duraglass canopy and the alert klaxon wails, bathing us in red light. There's a hissing noise that builds into a rushing pull and someone starts screaming. Another bang and suddenly I can't see. We're slipping to the left, listing, leaning.

Then the engines snarl and we're moving, the noises fade and everything goes quiet.

"Penn?"

"Still here, Corp."

I'm slumped sideways; my weight is against the seat straps. My left hand is trembling, much worse than before. My right arm is hanging down and the cybernetic servos aren't responding.

"How's it all looking?" I ask, trying to sound calm.

"It's bad," she replies in a shaking voice. "We took a direct hit— some kind of pressure blast."

I can't catch my breath. My mouth is dry. I try to swallow, but it's hard at this angle. "Just keep driving," I manage to whisper. "Get us clear, we take stock after. Can you do that?"

"Yes, Corp, I can do that," she says.

. . . Kiev (AFP)—Ukraine on Tuesday reported it had repelled a tank assault by the Russian army.

President Petro Poroshenko said "about six thousand insurgents supported by tanks and heavy weapons" had staged a pre-dawn attack on Poltava—a city halfway between Russian held Donetsk and Kiev— that caught the government and NATO off-guard.

Lieutenant General Jan Broeks, NATO (DGIMS) stated that "allied forces engaged the Russians on the outskirts of Poltava." Local news sources reported seeing RAF Typhoons over the city and British Challenger tanks moving in to establish defensive positions alongside Ukrainian infantry. Explosions were seen in the direction of the motorway towards Donetsk, suggesting the allies were cutting off potential supply routes for the advancing pro-separatist forces.

Local pro-Kiev officials told AFP that separatist fighters had also launched several waves of Grad missile attacks on the eastern part of Poltava itself.

The two self-proclaimed republics of Donetsk and Lugansk began their revolt shortly after the February 2014 ouster of a Moscow-backed president in Kiev and Russia's subsequent seizure of Ukraine's Crimea Peninsula.

The clashes have killed more than 64,400 people and driven Moscow's relations with the West to their lowest point since the Cuban Missile Crisis in 1962. Experts are comparing the conflict to the Afghan War (1979-1989), when US forces backed Mujahideen rebels against Russian invaders. Officially, Russian troops involved in Ukraine are "volunteers" and the NATO deployment is "defensive and advisory," but these paper definitions are little comfort to the civilians caught up in the fighting.

The crisis has also left 3.4 million homeless and sent Ukraine's economy—heavily dependent on exports from the industrial east of the country—into a tailspin.

The European Union on Monday called the situation "unacceptable" . . .

★ ★ ★

Jane's shuddering now; the power to the track drives is intermittent, coming in waves. There's no trouble with the generators and passive chargers, but the distributor is damaged. She wants to keep going, but she's hurt, she's limping. "That's enough for now," I rasp at Penn. After a second or two we slow down and stop.

The sound of straps being undone, and there are hands on my back. "I've got you, but you need to unfasten the seat belt," Penn says. "I can't get to it."

"I'm not sure if I can . . ."

"There's no other way."

The trembles in my left arm have eased, whether through blood loss or the attack subsiding, I don't know. I reach up and grope blindly above me, feeling along the taut straps. Half the canopy is caved in, pushing me in my seat down through the main hatch into the crew compartment. I must be dangling over Penn's head. I find the buckle. "Soon as I undo this, I'm going to fall," I tell her.

"It's okay, I have you."

I pull on the belt and slip into her arms. When my feet touch the floor, I manage to take some of the weight and let her guide me into a chair. My breathing is better than before, but other things are higher priority. "I can't see," I confess.

Fingers explore my face, scraping away something. "The sealing foam extinguisher went off when the turret was breached," Penn explains. "It stopped us being depressurised, saved our lives."

"But not all of us," I say. "Whose chair is this?"

"Tewan's."

I try to open my eyes. They feel full of grit, but I can see a little. Penn is still cleaning around my eyes, her fingers carefully picking away crusted flakes of foam. She's covered in blood and scratches, but otherwise seems okay.

There's something on my foot. I glance down. Tewan's lifeless corpse is resting against my leg. She could almost be sleeping, curled away from me, apart from the smell of loosed bowels.

I hear someone crying. It's Krees; she's sitting on the floor by the breach, rocking backwards and forwards, her hands hugged under her armpits. Juonal is hunched over her console, shoulders quivering. I know that dark place he's in. It comes after the adrenaline when you're trying to block out the world. War does that. It puts things you should never see right in your face.

"We need to move the body."

"We can't leave her out here," Penn says.

"You're right, but she can go in the airlock for now, otherwise . . ." I swallow and bite off the rest of the sentence. They're kids; they aren't ready to hear it. "What's the situation? How far did you take us?"

Penn bites his lip. "I'm not sure, I just drove. I keyed up the scanner and kept going until most of the blips disappeared."

"Okay, you did good." The praise is empty words from me right now until we know what state we're in, but she held it together and needs it. "Juonal, I must know how bad . . ."

He lets out a strangled sob in response, then starts coughing before leaning back in the chair and staring at the ceiling. "Damage was pretty extensive before the last round, Corp," he says. "Now. . . well . . . what's left . . ."

"Can we at least work out where we are?" It's a thorny problem. With the ionised atmosphere any sort of satellite triangulation is out. For the mission, we'd carefully mapped a grid using the landers, and Jane wasn't supposed to stray outside the boundary. The only reference points we can use are those the computer managed to save. I turn to Penn. "Is there a data log of your drive?"

"The system is struggling," Juonal says. "I had to bypass a lot of things just to keep us moving."

"Do what you can," I say to them both. "We'll stay put till we know, or for as long as we can."

The task gives them something to focus on, all except Krees. She's the furthest away from me and I can't call her over, not with Tewan's body at my feet. I can't ignore her though; she needs me.

I glance down at my right hand, then pull it up onto the chair rest with my left. The cybernetics are shot. Whilst the hand is the only limb replacement, it works on electrodes wired under my skin all the way to my brain. The damage means the arm is dead weight, useless.

I'm not the man I was.

When I left the army I knew I wasn't the same; older and wiser maybe, but not as strong, with scars on the inside and the outside. It's the hardest thing anyone has to do, adjusting to age, illness and injury.

After giving up twenty-five years to being a soldier, I figured I'd have something left for Helen, my kids and the family.

The shakes started six months after I'd demobbed. Medication helped for a while, but I had to learn that I couldn't do what I'd been able to before.

When I was sixty-seven I climbed a ladder to trim the hedge. Next thing I knew I was in the hospital with three broken ribs, a broken leg and fractured arm. It was a long time till I could walk properly again, so I had to make changes. Even afterwards I couldn't do all that I'd done previously.

Now I stare at these kids. They all need to adjust, process the experience. It's hard for them, they're used to being told things. Data, reading, learning, not feeling, losing and working it out for themselves.

"Krees, what happened to you?"

She looks up at me, her face dirty and streaked with tears. "Burned my hands pretty bad on the breech, loading rounds," she says in a small voice.

"I know it hurts," I say. "But I need you to get to the medikit and bring it to one of us, then we can get some synth skin. When we get back—" My voice wavers. I swallow. "When we get back, the ship will be able to print new hands for you." *But they'll never feel quite right and you'll always remember this.* The whole colony had the advantage of being fully gene mapped with controlled variation, but the technology came too late for people like me. Replicated transplants just "don't take," they'd said back on Earth when we left. That was more than a thousand years ago. Who knows what works now?

But I can't think about that. Earth's gone, we're here and the colony fleet needs us.

"Will we get back?" Krees asks.

"We must," I reply. "If we don't, the colonial computer can't update its assessment and they'll send down another party who'll be just as surprised as we were."

"Only they won't have you . . ." Juonal mutters.

I try to smile. "Might be good, not having to cart around an old man."

Penn shakes her head. "No, we'd all be dead in the lander if you hadn't been outside. They were waiting for us."

"Which suggests they'll be at all the others too," Krees adds.

"Could be that's why they didn't follow us out here; they expect us to go back."

"What happened inside?" I ask.

"We found the core samples and got the portable drives," Juonal explains. "As we were packing up, we heard you firing the machine gun. When we got outside, some of the creatures were there. They tried to grab us. Tewan . . . Tewan shot one and got us out. We made it back here and you know the rest."

"She saved all of us, then," I say. The smile's easier now and the words are what we all feel. "We owe it to her to make it back."

They all nod and something in my chest eases. Krees manages to get the medikit and Penn treats her hands. Then she examines the cut on my side. It's an ugly slash. "Could be some internal damage," she says.

"Not a lot we can do about that," I tell her. "Just patch it and stop me leaking."

"That I can do, Corp," Penn says.

When she's done, I move out of the seat and let Juonal in to help carry Tewan's body to the airlock. Krees takes her place at the instrument panel. Juonal goes to the loader. Penn stays as driver. I get Juonal's job at system control. With one hand, I can't do any of the other jobs.

My girl Jane has to lick her wounds too, accept her scars and play wiser next time. With foam seal jamming up the traverse, the turret's stuck and useless. We manage to transfer weapons operation to Krees, but there's not much we can do to adjust, and the internal cameras don't give us a great view. The old Jagdpanzers from the Second World War were fixed gun tanks. They used to hide in woodland and ambush the Shermans. They lost the advantage the minute they had to move or fire another shot.

Of course, we have to move. We must get back to the landers or the lifeboat. In a fight, our advantage is range. Without accuracy, we'll have to throw everything at them all at once and pray.

But first we must find out where we are.

"So, where are we?" I ask.

"Approximately three point two kilometres from the edge of the lander grid," Juonal says. "I've programmed my best guess at our return course for Penn to follow."

"Well done," I say. "Soon as we're back on the mapped zone, we take stock and, if we can't see anything, we head straight for the lifeboat."

"What about the other core samples?" Penn asks.

"We can't take the risk. We've learned a lot down here and we need to report back."

Juonal nods and Krees looks relieved, but Penn stares at me for a second or two. I know the look; she's come through the panic and out the other side. It's a dangerous place to get to, where bravado starts to mask the fear, memories get self-edited and false confidence can get a man killed. "We're all too broken for another round," I tell her. "Jane's in no shape either."

She frowns. "Jane?"

"Our ride," I say. "With what she's been through, she deserves a name."

"Jane," she thinks about it, then grins. "Okay, I guess that works."

Sharing my secret helps them. We're forging a bond here, through words and blood. These kids are warriors now. They're doing what needs to be done. I'm proud of them. When we get back, the whole fleet should be proud.

Kepler Fleet AI Mission Analysis.
Surface mission success probability without Specialist Saunders: 31%
Surface mission success probability with Specialist Saunders: 29.5%
Detailed evaluation:
The majority of individuals assigned to the crew must be female. During simulation, females demonstrate a more even and calm set of responses. Males tend toward excellence or below median performance.

Specialist Saunders is physically incapable. All scenarios that incorporate physical effort on his part reduce the team's chances. The analysis takes into account a variety of hypothetical occurrences and models behaviour based on human herd psychology and bonding.

However, when looking at the probability of individual situations that may arise, Saunders' presence is a calming influence on the younger minds around him and the chance of success in each is marginally improved. As soon as circumstances change and his physical condition is tested, this benefit drops into a penalty.

Conclusion: Saunders must participate in the mission, but be briefed appropriately so he is aware of the data. Psychological evaluations suggest he will accept the conclusions of this report and will understand his role as a disposable asset.

Jane's chronometer says it's taken us more than an hour to get back onto the grid, but we are back. Juonal's found a rupture in the O2 cylinders, which keeps things interesting and makes our decision for us. Back to the lifeboat.

Unfortunately it isn't going to be a relaxing drive in the country.

"Picking up some contacts," Krees says.

"They real or more ionisation glitches?"

"Real, I think, after the last time I'm pretty sure I can tell the difference."

"Best we don't lead them back to where we came from, then," I say. "Penn, you think we can take them?"

She shrugs, but I see the light in her eyes. "We can try," she says.

"Then let's get to it."

Penn pivots us forty-five degrees so we're facing the markers on the scanner. Juonal climbs up into Jane's ruined turret. "Yeah, I see them," he says. "It's one of the slugs, might be the one from earlier, and more of their soldiers swarming round it."

I'm watching the pressure gauges, transmission and system temperatures. We can't run and gun, so if we're going to fight, it's power the weapons and sit still. That means tiny adjustments with the tracks, but at least after that, the motivators get a chance to cool down. "Down to you, Penn," I tell her. "You'll need to get us dead on."

Penn doesn't respond, but I can feel Jane shifting around as she lines up. Juonal gets down and goes back to the loader. "Ready?" he asks.

"Almost," Penn mutters. "There, yes! Armour piercing, load and fire!"

With a grunt, Juonal bends his back to the breech and loads another road into the chamber. Krees deploys the supports and they crunch into the dirt just as Juonal raises his head once more. "Clear!" he shouts.

"Firing," says Krees.

The whole tank shakes. From here, I can't see the barrel or the hit, but Penn's guttural crow of triumph tells me everything I need to know. "Get us moving!" I tell her.

The support struts retract, the motivators whine, and we're away again. With trembling fingers I manage to key up the estimated distance to the lifeboat; two kilometres over hilly terrain. Provided nothing goes wrong, we can outpace the soldiers so we're out of sight when we reach it.

Juonal moves back into his chair and activates his screen, pulling up the readouts from my and Krees' consoles. "Motivator temperature is climbing," he says. "At this rate they'll exceed tolerance before we get to the boat."

I nod. "We won't have time to load up. Jane knows it's a one way trip."

"Oxygen supply should last, though."

"Something not to worry about, then."

There's a faint noise through the hull, coming from above. It reminds me of the old days in Ukraine, when the Typhoons went in. "You hear that?" I ask.

Juonal frowns. "Yeah, I did."

"Go take a look," I tell him. "Be careful."

"Will do, Corp."

He climbs back up to the turret. "Two jet trails," he says. "You reckon the fleet sent down another team?"

I shake my head. "No. I reckon our friends out there have aircraft."

As if to confirm this, there's a "crump" sound to our left, Jane wobbles and a shower of dirt covers the cameras.

"We won't be able to outrun them!" says Krees.

Air superiority: the way wars got won in the twentieth and twenty-first centuries. I remember watching the news as a kid and seeing gutted vehicles lining desert roads of some long forgotten state. They called it shock and awe back then, the rain of fire and death from the sky pounding on people night after night. The black plumes of smoke as towns and cities burned. All the media saw was grey camera footage with heat blobs, until the ordinary folk got a chance to tell their side of the story. There were always civilians in the way, always innocent people caught up amongst those who'd chosen to fight. When you're dead it doesn't matter anymore, except that it does. A uniform and a gun makes you fair game for being a number. You signed up, you accept it.

"What do we do?"

Another "crump," another shower of earth; I blink twice to banish the memories. Penn is yelling at me; they're all looking at me, they need direction.

"Make for the lifeboat," I shout. "When we get within one hundred metres, swing around one three five and park. Juonal, get the EVA suits prepped and break out the fire axe from the panel. I want you all ready to go as soon as we stop."

Juonal looks at me, frowning. "We're all going together, Corp," he says.

"Get me into a suit," I reply. "Then you need to start cutting away that foam, so we can get the turret working. It's the only chance we've got against jets."

My urgent tone banishes further questions for now.

Just as well.

"Do you understand these instructions, Specialist Saunders?"

"Yes, I do."

"To ensure our acceptance of your comprehension, we must ask that you rephrase and repeat them back to us."

"If the team encounter difficulties on the surface, my job is to make certain they get out. If I become a physical burden to them, I'm to be left behind."

"Thank you, Specialist. We hope these circumstances do not arise."

"Can you?"

"Can we what?"

"Hope."

. . .

"No, we cannot."

With a shuddering heave, Jane stops. There's another muffled explosion, another shower of mud, and something large clatters off her left side, but she takes it bravely. The gun supports deploy and everyone sets to the plan.

Hands grab me, lifting me forwards from my seat and up towards the turret. My old chair is reset. More foam and patching from the repair kits making the berth usable once more. The canopy remains cracked and, through my helmet visor, I gaze out of the shattered glass at the jet trails above. Flickers and flashes of electricity follow the alien planes. I have no idea how their technology copes with the atmospherics; they seem to have adapted.

But then, so have we.

I settle into the seat. Penn thumps me on the back and gives me a thumbs up. I nod and smile in return. She pulls out two wires from the driving console and attaches them both to my cybernetic arm. There's a crackle, but then my shoulder isn't so heavy anymore. Metal fingers move up to the replacement touchscreen, taken from the system station and rigged up here, while my trembling left hand grips the foam-crusted joystick.

I get another back slap and then there's lots of moving around. The hiss of the pressure door and firm "clump" as it closes. After that I'm stuck with the sound of my own breathing inside my suit for company. Three hours of air.

Plenty of time.

I thumb the joystick and elevate the turret to a sixty degree angle. The left side is completely caved in with a whole stretch of tears in the ceramics and layered metal, but with the sealing foam scraped away, the servos still work and let me stare up as high as they can. I gaze at the aircraft circling round for another pass. One drops low for the attack run, the other stays up.

Shooting planes with tank guns isn't easy or recommended. The odds favour the lightweight, manoeuvrable, fast moving vehicle over a ground bound, heavy, stationary box, but we're out of options and I can't let them strafe the kids as they make for the lander.

3 . . . 2 . . . 1 . . .

I remember what they said back in Ukraine: *anticipate!* Juonal's already loaded the main gun, re-routing fire control to my station, and I've a charged laser as well as the fifty-cal. Back to where we started, only . . . Well, only this time I'm on my own.

He's coming straight at me. Atmospherics are playing around the wings and there's a hammering against Jane's hull, a lot louder than any time before. Everything's shaking; it's hard to keep my fingers on the trigger. Spider cracks are running up the canopy all over the place; smashed duraglass all that's between me and obliteration.

Fire!

Jane grunts and there's a loud bang, like someone's punched me in the chest. Lightning and fire fill the sky, and the plane breaks apart, huge pieces of debris crashing all around us. More impacts on the hull. Glass shatters, and there's that stabbing pain in my side again. The canopy's gone; my helmet visor's taken a hit too. I can hear the high pitched whistle of air escaping. There's nothing I can do.

Except thumb the joystick and track the second jet.

In a way, it doesn't seem fair. We're the invaders here; we made the first move, sending down our probes and drills. No wonder they're fighting back, trying to drive us off. But we've travelled for more than a thousand years to get here, and we've nowhere else to go.

Small arms fire is rattling off Jane's skin, making pock marks in the ceramic plates. I activate the laser and the fifty-cal targeting, but there's no screen for the digital cross hair projection. I'll need to guess, based on where it usually hits.

There are shapes moving towards me across the arid landscape, more of the six-limbed aliens, picking their way through debris. They won't reach me before the aircraft, though. He's banked around and losing altitude for a straight run, just like his wingman. Don't they learn from mistakes? His loss . . .

My gain . . .

The laser's my best bet, but it's a whole different game; do the same kind of trajectory anticipation as I tried with the main gun and I'll waste a lot of power. Without a targeter I'm left to watch for the ionisation effects so I can see where the beam is.

One hundred metres. I squeeze the trigger on the fifty-cal, using it as a tracer. A moment after, his guns light up and projectiles start slapping into Jane's hull. A flash of pain as something catches me in the hip, but I can't let it distract me.

Fifty metres.

The rest of the canopy disintegrates around me. More splashes of pain, cracks in the glass of my helmet. None of it matters now; I just need to press a button.

I press the button. There's a hum and the right wing of the aircraft dissolves. I see fire, then something smashes into the side of my head and—

"Please step into the decontamination chamber."

Penn is naked, stripped and washed of everything from Kepler 452b. She knows she'll never see any of it again. She gets up from the bench, glances at Krees and Juonal, sharing a last moment. The blood and dirt is gone, but the hollow expressions on their faces remain. You can't wash away the scars inside.

Penn walks through the open hatch. The panel closes behind her. There is a fine mist in the air, making her hair damp.

"Subject PN14AXD, designation, Penn. How are you feeling?"

"I'm okay."

"Penn, we are sorry for what you experienced."

Penn swallows. The words come through a speaker set in the wall. They sound concerned, empathetic and soothing, but they are spoken by a computer.

"You weren't there," she mutters.

"We assimilated all on board records of the mission and extrapolated your decision making based on forensic analysis of all material returned to the fleet. All that remains is to hear your version of events."

Penn chews her lip. "What happens after I tell you?"

There is a pause. "You will be evaluated as a trainer for further missions. It is important our teams are prepared for what they face."

"What happens if I fail?"

"You will be recycled."

Penn nods. She stares around the room, plain white walls and floor with no discernible features other than the door and speaker. "There are things that need to be remembered, the corporal . . ."

"Elder Jeff Saunders performed his designated mission task successfully. We are pleased."

"He saved us. He was a hero."

The computer voice makes no reply.

A freak accident sends Kent hurling down through the Venusian atmosphere. As he descends toward the surface, Kent uses his diving skills to increase his odds of survival, while his father, the floating habitat's commander, tries desperately to affect a rescue. But the toxicity of Venus' atmosphere is no match for the poisonous relationship between father and son. There may or may not be time to save Kent—but is there time to bridge the gulf between them?

ONE GIANT LEAP
★
by Jay Werkheiser

KENT WAS GOING TO BE the first person to die on Venus. He knew it with iron certainty the moment the railing gave way and he slipped into the acidic mist. The only question was whether he would be baked or crushed.

Moments earlier, he had been inspecting the floating habitat's walkway, looking for acid damage to repair. He'd let his mind wander for just a moment, replaying the morning's argument with the old man. He'd leaned against the railing and it had broken free, sending him tumbling backward into the void.

He let out a startled yelp. The habitat vanished into the yellow mist and was gone. For a timeless moment, he hung in the formless void, feeling like he was sinking through murky water. Not much different from a deep-sea dive.

"Where'd you go, Kent?" Marina's voice, tinny in his earpiece, rose an octave. "Kent?"

"I fell overboard." Saying it made it suddenly real. *I'm falling!* Panic washed away rational thought.

"Christ! How?"

Fear brought bile to his throat, choking him. Kept him from screaming.

"Kent?"

"How the hell should I know?" He sucked down a few deep breaths. "Corrosion, I guess. Flexiglass coating must have cracked at a seam on the rail."

"How did it get—"

"Is that really important right now?"

"Right." Pause. "I'd better get the commander on the line."

"No."

"He needs to know, Kent."

He blew out a breath, fogging his faceplate. "Fine." He squinted into the haze, trying to see something, anything. Wind tugged at his arms and legs, but not even a whisper penetrated the flexiglass insulation of his suit. "Just . . . just let me tell him."

"Anything you want." Click.

Silence closed in, sending a shiver of terror down his spine. On dives, he'd had the sounds of drawing breath, of exhaled bubbles, of life. Here, his suit efficiently muted life-support sounds. Even the sound of the wind, whipping past him at almost a hundred miles per hour by now, couldn't penetrate his suit to remind him that he was still alive. Temporarily.

"Kent?"

"Yeah, Marina?"

"Patching you through to the commander."

He choked down emotion. "Okay."

Click.

"Damn it, Kenny, this better be important." The voice alone was enough to set Kent on edge, reminding him of years of painful words. "I've got a crisis with one of the drones to—"

"I'm falling."

"What?"

"Railing gave way. I'm . . . I'm going to . . ."

"God damn it, Kenny. Do you have any idea what this will do to your mother?"

But not my father. "I guess I'm a screw-up right to the end."

"That's not what I meant." A long, exasperated sigh rattled in his earpiece. "I'll see if I can get her on the radio before, uh, you know."

"You kidding? What's the radio transit time to Earth? Three minutes? There and back. Plus time for mission control to actually find her. How long do you think this is going to take?"

How long do I have?

"Atmosphere's pretty thick down there. This ain't Earth." There was a long pause. "Give me a minute. Maybe buoyancy . . ." Click.

Fifty kilometers to the ground. How long *did* he have? Crunching the numbers kept his mind off the inevitable. Assuming the same terminal velocity as Earth, a hundred twenty miles per hour, converting to SI, that gave him, oh, say fifteen minutes.

But with lower gravity and thicker atmosphere . . .

At this altitude, terminal velocity was probably close to Earth's. But the air was going to get dense pretty damn fast as he approached the surface. Terminal velocity depended on the square root of air density, so call it one eighth of Earth's. Shave a little more off for the gravity difference. Say somewhere between ten and fifteen miles per hour. Hell, he could survive impact at that speed!

But speed wasn't the problem, was it?

Ninety atmospheres pressure. Hot enough to melt metal. Already he could feel the pressure on his chest with each breath. He'd never make it to the surface. That was a shame. He wouldn't even have *that* distinction in the history books. Just the first of many clumsy schleps to burn up on the way down.

He pictured a trail of losers plummeting, lemming-like, after him. He laughed.

"Kent?" It was Marina's voice.

"I'm here." He giggled. "Where else would I be?"

Concern darkened her voice. "What has you so giddy?"

"Just trying to figure out how long I have."

"Oh."

"Density changes the whole way down, complicating the math. I can't do the dee vee dee tee in my head. Heh. I guess the old man was right about me." He giggled again.

She huffed. "Well, I don't think any of this is funny."

He laughed deep and hard, his chest aching to draw in the compressed air with each guffaw. The hurt in her voice registered belatedly. "Don't worry, I'm not crazy. It's probably just nitrogen narcosis."

"What's that?"

"Something we divers get when going too deep with a nitrox mix. That's what I'm breathing, right?"

"Nitrogen and oxygen? Yeah."

"How deep am I?"

"Stop joking around, Kent. This isn't some fun little reef dive."

He shook his head, forced himself to focus. This wasn't the first time he'd fought his way through nitrogen narcosis. "Right. Pressure must be getting high. Five or six atmospheres. Another couple of atmospheres and oxygen toxicity will be a problem."

"Jeez. Anything you can do?"

"Cut down the oh-two percentage, but it's only a stopgap. For really deep dives, we'd use heliox."

"Helium? Where are you going to get that?"

"You have some party balloons you're not using?"

"Damn it, Kent."

"That gives me an idea, though. Can you put the old man on?"

"Sure thing." Click.

There was a brief pause, then the grating voice. "Yeah?"

"Can you divert one of the electrolysis drones to me?"

"It's no use, Kenny. I've been over the math a dozen ways. They're too light, don't have nearly enough thrust to lift you."

"I know that. I want the gases."

"Why? You should have enough oxygen—"

"Damn it, Dad, just do it." He mentally kicked himself for acknowledging their relationship. Must be the nitrogen talking. "I want hydrogen."

"Sending one down. Has nearly a full load."

"My diving experience just might pay off after all." He giggled at himself for gloating at a time like this. "And you told me I was wasting my life."

"Diving put you where you are now."

"Diving? No, that was dear old dad, the astronaut. Had to measure up, right?"

"The only reason you made the cut was your diving experience. Otherwise you would have washed out."

Kent snorted. "Wouldn't be the first time, right?"

The commander let out a long sigh that hissed in Kent's ear. "What's the hydrogen for?"

"Breathing gas."

"Breathing?"

"Yup. For deep dives, we add helium to the gas mix to help with the pressure and to prevent nitrogen narcosis. I don't have any helium, but it got me thinking. For *really* deep dives, they sometimes use a hydrogen mixture."

"But it's so flammable!"

"The mix has to be hypoxic because of the pressure, so the risk is minimal." Of course, he'd be eyeballing the mix ratio on the fly. And then there was the risk of hydrogen narcosis, which was more like a bad acid trip compared to nitrogen's alcohol-like buzz. He didn't mention any of that.

"You have everything you need to handle all the connections?"

His heart thumped hard and he reflexively reached for his belt. His hand touched his tool pack and he exhaled in relief. "I got this."

"Good. Marina, you still there?"

"Yeah, I'm here."

"Keep your eye on the radar data and give Kenny an ETA on the probe's arrival. I'm going to work on the temperature problem. The probe must have some kind of insula—" He clicked off in mid-sentence.

After a brief pause, Marina said, "The probe should be there in a few moments. Also, you're getting close to the lower edge of the cloud deck. You'll have a spectacular view soon."

He bit back a sarcastic reply. She was only trying to keep his mind off things. It was his own damn fault he was in this situation. "I'll let you know when I see something."

Did he feel hotter than before, or was it just his imagination? The commander's mention of temperature deflated him. Even if the hydrox mix worked and he survived the pressure, the oven-hot temperature would get him. It was hopeless.

His suit was made of layers of flexiglass with sheets of electroactive polymer between. The polymer stiffened with electric current, providing protection and strength enhancement, but it also functioned as an effective insulator. How effective? If he was where Marina had said, it must already be over two hundred degrees Celsius. And the commander had said he was working on it. Slow terminal velocity, hydrox mix for the pressure, insulation—could he actually survive this? He gasped at the thought, a painful, labored influx of heavy air.

Best not think about it, just focus on the things he could control. Right now, that was the gas mix. As soon as that damned drone arrived, anyway. He peered into the sulfuric acid haze, now noticeably thinner than it had been. There, in the distance, was a glint of sunlight. He tracked it until he could resolve its outline against the yellow mist. Its hull was mostly aerogel, visible as a slight darkening of the haze, with four thermoplastic rotors reflecting diffuse sunlight.

"I see the drone," he said. "It's coming in a bit low."

"You're falling at around thirty miles per hour right now," Marina said. "With the thick air, we're having trouble keeping the drone descending fast enough. You're going to have to grab onto it as it approaches. You may not get a second chance."

"No pressure, eh?" He laughed, and his chest hurt with the effort.

He kept his eyes on the drone as it moved, not an easy task against the shifting sulfuric acid haze. He focused on the rotors and the swirling mist around them. The drone grew as it approached, now almost directly below him. He fell toward it tantalizingly slowly.

Swirling misty air kicked him in the face and sent him into a tumble. He struggled to reorient himself before the drone passed him by.

"What's wrong?" Marina's voice was tense with worry.

"I'm getting some pretty bad turbulence."

"I'll shut down the drone's rotors."

"But won't that—" He stopped himself. No, the drone wouldn't drop like a stone. In the thick air, the challenge was to keep it from rising.

The air stopped battering him and he oriented himself face down. He scanned for the drone. There it was, rising toward him. Fast.

Too fast.

He braced himself for the impact. The aerogel hull hit like a pillow thrown by a god. It forced the air from his lungs and smacked his forehead against his faceplate. He gasped to refill his lungs against the crushing pressure of the air around him.

Almost too late, he felt the drone slipping away beneath him. He reflexively reached out and grasped the edges. It was nearly as long as he was and a bit wider, and he found himself clinging spread eagle to its dorsal surface.

"Got it," he wheezed. Sweat stung his eyes. Was it the exertion or was his flexiglass insulation finally failing him?

"I have you on radar," Marina said. "You're still dropping, but slower. Fifteen miles per hour, give or take."

"I'm going to try to cut through the hull—" While he spoke, the mist parted around him, leaving him in open, clear air. His voice caught in his throat. The surface of Venus sprawled below him, stark and rugged. He was *falling*.

"Is something wrong?"

He froze for a long moment, staring over the edge of the drone. It could have been a rocky, mountainous desert on Earth. Except for the crushing pressure and oven temperature.

"Kent?"

"I'm okay." He gasped a few ragged breaths. "I just came through the bottom of the cloud deck."

Marina started to reply, but the commander's voice cut in. "Sightseeing's over. Get back to work."

Kent's cheeks burned. "Don't give me that soldier shit. I'm done taking orders. Sir."

"Don't put that on me. I didn't push you into SEAL training."

"I just wanted to dive."

"A SEAL needs more than that."

"So you told me. That's why I washed out."

"If you had listened to me—"

"Go to hell."

Click.

Panting from the heat, pressure, and fury, Kent reached for his tool pouch. He moved cautiously, careful not to disturb his precarious balance atop the drone. His fingers closed around the handle of his utility knife. His impact had cracked the hull's solar film and dented the aerogel. He peeled away pieces of film and sliced into the surface of the drone. The aerogel was surprisingly tough, almost rubbery.

"Don't cut through the inner aerogel layer," Marina said.

"I thought the whole thing was aerogel."

"The hull is an x-aerogel," she said, "designed for strength. The inner aerogel layer is more fragile, but a much better insulator. Keeps the gas canisters from heating up. The commander thinks you might be able to use it. If you can—"

"Got it."

"He's trying his best, Kent. He really does care about you."

Kent snorted.

"You should see him up here, practically tearing the station apart. Maybe he doesn't know how to show it, but . . ."

"Yeah."

He cut more carefully, working the knife into the spongy hull, and peeled the outer layer open. The blade thumped against something solid. He reached into the opening and felt around. It was a motor, probably the one that ran the rotors. He pulled it out, trailing wires coated with aerogel and acid-resistant flexiglass. Beneath the nest of wiring, he saw the gas storage tanks.

The drone's purpose was to take in sulfuric acid droplets from the clouds, decompose the acid to water and sulfur oxides, then electrolyze the water to hydrogen and oxygen. The gas storage canisters ran half the length of the drone's hull. A transparent pale blue layer covered them. Through his flexiglass glove, it felt like Styrofoam, rigid but pliable if he worked at it.

He split the drone's hull further, trying to clear room to work. The seam unexpectedly split wide open and the drone began to shudder violently. He clung to the surface, nearly dropping his knife. The ground below rotated slowly; aerodynamic instability must have put him into a flat spin.

Terror blanked his mind. If he fell off—

But what would it matter? He was already falling. The outer hull and rotor assembly weren't doing him much good anyway, and it stood in the way of his precious breathing gas and insulation. The hydrogen especially was quickly becoming a necessity; he labored to draw each breath and it was getting harder and harder to focus through the nitrogen narcosis.

He felt his way around the insulation, cutting through any supports that held the aerogel fast to the hull. His knuckles burned where they brushed against the flexiglass gloves. He traced his hand forward along the insulation until he found the feed coming from the hydrolysis tank. He closed the valve and worked by feel until he had the whole assembly disconnected. It should now be free. If he tugged . . .

Nothing. His head swam with the exertion of breathing. He forced a deep breath and tugged again. The assembly shifted, sending a wave of instability through the hull. The whole drone vibrated menacingly, threatening to buck Kent from its back. He braced his feet against the remnants of the hull, grasped the canister assembly tightly, and tugged with all his strength. Searing heat burned his palms and soles.

He screamed with agony and exertion. He vaguely heard concerned voices in his ear. Suddenly, the hull shifted under his feet and the drone shuddered violently. He found himself tumbling, buffeted by turbulent wind. One more herculean tug sent the fractured hull tumbling up toward the cloud deck.

Clinging to the aerogel-clad canisters, Kent stabilized his spin. He fought to inhale, barely managing to stay conscious. The voices in his ear pulled him back from the darkness.

". . . don't know, he just started screaming." Marina's voice was thick with emotion.

"Oh, God! Kent! Oh my God." Was that the commander?

"I'm." He panted. "Okay."

"Thank God," Marina said. "What happened?"

"Working," he managed to croak.

He found the opening in the aerogel where the intake pipe had been attached. As carefully as he could, he tugged at the hole, trying to expand it. The aerogel cracked and pieces crumbled away. Damn. He used his knife as a chisel, cutting a slit big enough for him to fit through. He slipped one foot between the insulation and the gas canisters, then the other foot. Squeezing and pushing, compressing the Styrofoam-like aerogel where needed, he pulled himself down into the insulated sack.

He found the hydrogen tank and worked the fitting free. With a start, it occurred to him that the fitting might not be the same size as his air intake. His heart thumped hard in his chest until he verified that the threading fit perfectly. He sealed it and opened the valve. Warm gas hissed into his helmet. Warm, but not scalding.

He turned the valve on his air tank, constricting the flow of nitrogen and oxygen. He would have to constrict the oxygen further as he fell, bringing the partial pressure down as total pressure rose. By the end, he'd be down to less than two percent oxygen.

The end. What qualified as the end now?

When the pressure crushed his lungs? In controlled experiments, divers had survived over seventy atmospheres with hydrox. Theoretically, higher pressures were survivable. Theoretically.

When he burned alive? But the aerogel might, just might, be a good enough insulator. Could he make it all the way to the surface? Alive?

He had no idea how long he fell with that thought swirling in his head. Gradually, the hydrox cleared the nitrogen narcosis from his mind. Breathing was still hard, but not the struggle it had been.

"Marina?" he said.

"Yes?"

"I'm feeling pretty good."

"That's good to hear."

"How long have I been falling?"

"It's been about forty-five minutes," she said. "You're still fifteen kilometers above the surface. Pressure should be around thirty atmospheres, temperature well over three hundred Celsius. It's getting hard to track you because superrotation of the upper atmosphere is carrying us away."

He hadn't thought about that. "Damn."

"The commander is working on a plan to pick you up from the surface."

"Oh?"

"He's getting a rover in place beneath you right now. Still trying to jury-rig a human-rated craft to get all the way down."

"Is that even possible?"

"He'll move heaven and hell to make it happen."

Did he dare hope? He hadn't had time to consider anything beyond the immediate problems of breathing gas and insulation. But now he had time to think past the moment. What if he lived a few minutes longer? A luxury!

Could he actually make it to the surface?

His heart thumped hard in his chest, sending hope coursing through his veins. He looked down on the barren basalt wasteland below, and for the first time saw beauty in the stark landscape. Flattened mountains rippled over black rock plains, undisturbed by anything but wind for a billion years. And—was that snow on the mountain peaks?

"Marina? Am I hallucinating?"

"What do you think you see?"

"Snowcapped mountains."

"Ah. That's actually a layer of heavy metal sulfides."

"So you're saying I should have left my skis back home?"

"Hah. Skiing in a tropical wonderland like that? Try lead sulfide surfing instead."

He started to reply, but—it took him a moment to realize what had happened. He'd been falling spread eagle except for his left hand, which he kept on the gas valve so he could tweak the mixture as needed. The aerogel sack surrounding him and the canisters had been rippling lazily in the wind, then suddenly it wasn't.

At first he thought it had somehow ripped free, and for a brief horrifying moment he braced for the searing heat that would incinerate him. But no, he would already be dead if that were the case.

He reached out to feel for the film, but found that his arm was plastered to his side. He could move it slowly, with effort, as though pushing through syrup.

Or Styrofoam.

"I think Venus is shrink-wrapping me in aerogel," he said.

Marina's voice lost all hints of playfulness. "Are you in danger?"

"I don't think so. No more than the obvious, that is." He wiggled, testing the limits of his motion. "I guess this means the pressure is ramping up. I better nudge my oh-two feed down a few percent."

"Normally aerogel would shatter rather than flow like that," Marina said. "You must have passed some temperature-pressure threshold in its phase diagram. I hope it doesn't lose its insulating ability."

Maybe it was the talk of pressure, but Kent noticed that his breathing was again becoming labored. Was he reaching the pressure limit of his hydrox mix already? He coughed, a wet, labored expulsion of air. Fluid in his lungs.

The commander's voice broke in. "Are you okay?"

"No."

"Try to hold on. Help is—"

"This is your fault," Kent said. "I came to this hellhole for you."

"I never asked you."

All the rage and fear and regret and resentment burst from him in a sudden acidic barrage. "I was never good enough. I tried so hard to prove myself, but it was never enough for you."

"That's not true."

"Don't lie to me. Not now. I saw how you looked down on me. How could I measure up to a hero? My whole life was about you, not me."

"I didn't—"

"Even this rescue is about you. Another medal on your chest, one more thing to hold over me." He realized he was screaming, although his voice came out as little more than a loud rasp. His anger drained away, leaving despair. He sobbed. "Never good enough."

There was a long silence. Finally, the commander whispered, "I only wanted the best for you."

Kent cried for a long time, warm tears streaming down hot cheeks behind his faceplate, his sobs punctuated by fits of moist coughs. The ground slowly, inexorably rose up to meet him. He let himself get lost in the rugged beauty of the barren rock. The heavy metal snowcapped mountains off to his right wavered with the heat or pressure or both. Swirls of color ran along ridgelines, moving as though alive.

What the hell?

He tilted his head back and looked at the sulfuric acid clouds, banded with bold reds and blues and greens. The wind itself swirled in pastel patterns.

Oh, hell. Hydrogen narcosis. He slowly rotated his right hand in front of his eyes and saw that his movements were jerky and uncoordinated. So it was going to be the pressure, then.

He reached up to wipe the sticky tears from his face and was surprised by how sluggish his arm felt. Like he was pushing through thick syrup. Oh, right, the aerogel. There was a faceplate in the way anyway. Impaired mental function.

A giant was squeezing his chest, making his heart fight for every beat and his lungs ache with every breath. A spasm of coughing racked his body, and he gasped to refill his lungs. Red sputum speckled his faceplate.

The visible evidence of lung damage drove the point into his swimming mind. There was no going back. Even if they came for him, there was no way to decompress safely. A peaceful calm came with the realization, as though the pressure was suddenly lifted. Or maybe it was the hydrogen narcosis.

"Dad?"

"Yeah?"

"I didn't mean what I said."

"It's okay."

His throat constricted. Saying it made it real. "I'm not going to make it."

"Don't give up. I have volunteers ready to attempt—"

"No. It's already too late."

There was a long pause. "I'm sorry." He choked on the words. "I'm so sorry."

"It's not your fault. You did all you could."

"No. For all of it, I mean. I wasn't the best father; I know that. I was always so hard on you, so critical."

"You weren't so bad. Besides, I did everything I could to piss you off."

"Just like I did in my day. Like father, like son."

"What? You and pap?"

"Oh, you wouldn't believe." His laugh was hoarse. "There was this one time, I must have been no more than eighteen, and your pap told me I couldn't—ah, damn it, I should have told you these stories when there was time."

"It's okay. I like just knowing the stories happened." He choked back tears, straining to draw the heavy air into his damaged lungs, and coughed more blood onto his faceplate.

"Are you okay?"

"I love you, Dad."

"I love you too, Son. I'll . . ."

For the longest time, his earpiece was silent except for the hiss of static and Marina's sobs.

"I want to make it to the surface," Kent finally said. "I want that much. To make you proud."

"You already have."

His vision blurred and he nearly lost himself in the swirling colors. "Tell me one of your stories," he said.

"Okay," his father said, his voice husky. "There was this one time, I snuck out to go party with some friends. Remember Uncle Al?"

"The big guy?"

"Yeah, him. Well, I ended up losing my phone, and lost track of time. And Al never checked his. You know how your grandmother worries—"

Kent smiled. "She's a lot like mom."

"Perhaps. Anyway, she couldn't get hold of me, figured I'd wrecked my car or something. Made the old man call all the hospitals, even the morgues. Man, was he pissed."

Kent laughed. "I can't see pap getting pissed."

"Oh, you thought *I* was bad? You should have had *him* for a father."

"I'm getting close to impact. Looks like I'm going to make it."

"I'm proud of you, Son."

"Thanks for not making the call to mom."

"You were right; it'll be easier on her if she hears about it afterwards."

"Tell her I love her."

"I will."

"Touchdown soon."

This close, the ground rose frighteningly fast. He bent his knees and braced as best he could. Impact sent a shock of pain through his legs and up his spine, but he managed to stay on his feet. Searing heat caressed his soles.

He looked out on the devastated landscape, a sight no human had ever beheld, and said the first words from the surface of Venus. "For you, Dad."

Ever since the Founding, Colonial settlers whispered of ghost ships: silent, empty vessels drifting between the stars, steel tombs for their crew. Ships that set out from Earth yet never made it to the stars. Recruited into the mysterious Synapse Foundation, Nicholas Caddy—still bearing the scars of an interstellar war—is dispatched on his first mission with the Immortals. A passenger liner, the Anchorage, has gone silent. The Immortals' task is simple: find the ship, salvage what they can, report what happened. Simple.

THE IMMORTALS: ANCHORAGE
★
by David Adams

*Monsters don't sleep
under your bed.
They scream forever
inside your head.*
—Extract from "A Dance of Dreams and
Nightmares," an Uynovian poem

ANCHORAGE
DT-Y 44 Transport Lahore
Deep space
0025
January 1st
2231 AD

"HAPPY NEW YEAR, CADDY," said Golovanov as he threw a dossier on my chest, the feeling jolting me awake. "Here's your present."

It took me a second to process all of this. I sat up in my bunk, shielding my eyes with my prosthetic hand, squinting in the harsh glare of the *Lahore's* overhead lights. I sent my implants a mental command to dim the lights and the ship mercifully complied, dropping the illumination down to a manageable level.

"Wait," I said, swinging my legs over the side of the bunk and opening the steel-grey dossier. "We got a job?" The screen lit up, showing a bunch of writing and ship schematics.

"Yup," said Golovanov. "The Synapse Foundation is putting us in the field. You'll like this one: it's gas."

I brought the lights back up as my eyes adjusted. Seemed like all we did every day was train. Adjust to the Immortal Armour. Work in a team with the other Immortals. Fire drills.

I skimmed over the documents, absorbing as much as I could as we spoke. Something about a ship in distress. "What's the deal?"

"The *Anchorage*," Golovanov said. "A DT-Y 44 just like this one. Passenger liner. It went silent about three days ago and has been drifting through Polema's space since. Not responding to hails. Long range scans show low power and thermal signatures, but spectrographic analysis suggests there's at least some atmosphere left. So we get to take a look-see."

Any excitement I had at the potential for action slowly faded. "A bunch of civilians brought it out in the black? This is a job for the Coast Guard."

"It is, and they're contracting it out to us."

"What a beating," I said, and considered a moment. That was very odd. The Polema Coast Guard—named for their nautical forbearers—were tasked with sorting out this kind of garbage. "Wait, why the hell would they do that? The Coast Guard is one of the best funded agencies in the colonies. Why do they need us?"

Golovanov sat at the edge of my bed. "Maybe you should save your questions until you finish reading," he said.

"Reading is for nerds," I said. I switched off the dossier with a mental command. "So. Are we mercenaries now?"

"Eh." He shrugged. "I prefer to use the term *Private Third-Party Offshore Conflict Resolution Engineers*. You can tell how fancy it is by how many words it has."

"So, mercenaries."

"There's no money in integrity. You got a problem with that?"

"Naw," I said. "Like they say on Eris, *money doesn't buy happiness, but poverty doesn't buy anything.* If we're here to do dodgy stuff, and we're going to make a buck doing it, that's fine by me." I stretched out my arms. "But I thought we were supposed to be tracking down and recovering Earthborn technology. Who cares about some civvie freighter?"

"The Coast Guard suspects," said Golovanov, "that the *Anchorage* was attacked by Earthborn raiders."

Well. That would explain a lot of things. "Why not call in the Colonial fleet?" I asked. "If the Earthborn are pushing up into our space, we should hit them hard. Another Reclamation would be . . ." I didn't even want to think about it.

"Money talks, but wealth whispers." Golovanov's eyes met mine. "Polema wants to avoid making waves—their economy is only just beginning to recover from the Reclamation. If the Earthborn really did hit the *Anchorage*, this might be just an isolated incident. You know, some renegades blowing off steam, or maybe a bunch of clones went rogue. Not an organised attack."

My thoughts went to the same place. "And if that's true, and Polema raises the alarm, and it all turns out to be nothing, they'll lose tens of trillions of creds. They want this whole mess to be taken care of quietly."

"Right," he said. "A few hundred civvies die, but the rich get richer and that's the important thing."

It was as it always was. "The Prophets Wept."

"It's not all bad," said Golovanov. "This is a gas opportunity for us, too. If the Earthborn really did hit the *Anchorage*, they probably left stuff behind. Stuff we could use."

"Right," I said, standing and stretching out my cramping legs. "Whatever. It's gotta be better than more drills."

I splashed some water on my face and adjusted my chrono implant. It began feeding my body chemicals to suppress drowsiness. By the time I left my quarters, I felt like I'd slept for a year then chugged ten cups of coffee.

Almost. Synthetic sleep was never the same; it was too perfect, too fake, as though some part of my brain were silently screaming in protest. They said it was bad for you.

But so was falling asleep during a firefight.

My suit of Immortal Armour was waiting in the cargo hold, an empty space at the rear of the ship. The Synapse Foundation had converted the area to a hangar. My armour, like the others, hung suspended from the ceiling by thick cables, a ten foot tall ape-like monster, boxy and metal. A caged hunter begging to be unleashed.

"Caddy," said Angel, from behind her suit, one of the seven others. She seemed to be in a particularly bad mood. "You're late."

"Came as fast as I could," I said. "How far out are we?"

"Six hours," said Angel, stepping into view—shaved hair, muscled frame and all—and reached into the suit's cockpit. She pulled something out that sparked before it went silent. "The *Anchorage* should be coming up on external sensors momentarily. Golovanov said he'd pipe the feed down here. AI, let me know when we have eyes on it."

"Of course," said the voice from her machine. Genderless. Empty.

I didn't know how I felt about Angel. We'd been training together for months now. Things had been very professional. We hadn't bonded properly yet, the Immortals and I. Angel least of all.

She was from a world called Uynov. They called themselves The First to Suffer. Uynov had been trashed by the Earthborn during the Reclamation; their bio-weapons turned it from a watery paradise to a shit-hole full of toxins and quarantined areas. Most Uynovians lived in space these days and they tended to be broody and aloof.

There didn't seem to be anything Angel loved more than weapons drills, or practising endlessly with her armour. Angel might as well be a robot, an observation compounded by her heavy cybernetic augmentation. Prosthetics jutted from almost all parts of her flesh, blunt chrome slivers. Her face was hard, hair shaved, skin rough as cracked desert earth. She couldn't have been older than twenty-five but looked in her forties.

She was the first Uynovian I'd ever met. I wasn't sure what I expected. But, you know, a smile occasionally wouldn't go amiss.

"Hey Caddy," said Stanco, clapping me on the shoulder from behind. "You ready to do this?"

I *also* didn't know how I felt about Maddisynne Stanco. He was built like a bull, with biceps like fire hydrants. Fun fact: he was also born a she. A trans-man. Not that there was anything wrong with that.

Although we were all supposed to be enlightened these days, and we'd been taught to accept trans people for what they wanted to be, I couldn't. I tried. I knew it wasn't right—if someone wanted to identify as an eggplant or something, why couldn't they?—but, sometimes, I couldn't look past the parts of Stanco's facial structure that were effeminate. The way he sometimes looked at me or others.

Eris, my home, was very traditional. Osmeon, Stanco's world, was viewed by most Erisians as decadent and hedonistic. Of course, they saw us as uptight, bigoted prudes.

But now, at the end of the day, we were all in this together. They had to accept us, and we had to accept them.

I was trying.

"Yeah buddy," I said, trying to smile my best. "Our first real mission, huh?"

Stanco leaned up against Angel's suit, folding his big hands behind his head. "Fuck yeah. It's going to be gas, my friend."

"I'm sure," I said, and I took a few steps to my suit.

Tall and strong, a mirror of the others, a hunchback made of steel.

"Morning Caddy," said the suit's AI, smooth and feminine. I had named her Sandy, after Sandhya, a woman I'd fought alongside during the Reclamation.

I probably shouldn't have done that. Sandhya hadn't come home. We'd been close: we shared ammo magazines, tactical info, and far too often, a bedroll.

I probably shouldn't have done that either. I had been married to Valérie at the time. Valérie, who had stood by me after I'd been wounded. Valérie, who'd been endlessly understanding, endlessly loving, endlessly patient.

Almost endlessly. We were divorced now. I hadn't seen her in years.

"Morning Sandy," I said. "How's your diagnostic coming?"

"Coming along nicely," she said. "I think I've narrowed down the stability issue; the gyros weren't aligned correctly. It shouldn't happen again."

That was gas. The suits were new technology—not only were they inherently unstable, to give us better manoeuvrability, they required an AI to operate. We were the guinea pigs, working out the kinks.

I wanted to ask Sandy more about exactly how she was fixing this complex problem in software, but Golovanov stepped into the hangar and everyone fell silent.

"Immortals," he said, casually folding his hands behind his back. Just like the old days.

"Ho," we said in chorus. Only Angel, Stanco and I were here. We had eight suits. Where was everyone else? Nobody seemed concerned. Maybe I should actually read the mission briefings in the future.

Golovanov's eyes flicked to me, then he addressed the group. "We're coming up on the *Anchorage*," he said. "Should have eyes in a few minutes. Based on the large amount of debris, it's starting to look like someone did, in fact, attack the ship."

"Cunts," spat Angel. "Of course the Earthborn would prey on civilians."

"Any information from the distress beacon?" I asked. "Maybe they mentioned who was attacking them."

"It's just an automated beacon." Golovanov narrowed his eyes. "So if it was the Earthborn, they struck fast."

That was their MO.

"Deployment is three suits," said Golovanov. "That's you guys. The rest of the Immortals will cover you. Float over from the *Lahore*, get inside the ship, find what you can. Take some emergency bulkheads in case you need to secure an area and dismount, but have someone maintain overwatch. Deployment is with standard layouts for Angel and Caddy, Stanco as fire support with the assault gun."

Standard layout was an autocannon, grenade launcher, and flamethrower. "Fire support on a boarding mission, sir? Don't you think that assault guns are kind of overkill?"

"Hell no," said Stanco. "Automatic weapons are the most casualty producing weapon in the fire team. It's more than simply fire support and suppression." His face lit up in a wide, cheesy grin. "Plus they're fucking *rad*. I feel like a god when I spin that thing up."

"Deific posturing aside," said Golovanov, "we have no idea what's going on aboard that ship, and if the Earthborn are aboard, we want a firepower advantage. Even if it's in close quarters."

"Sounds gas," I said. "I'd rather have it and not use it than need it and not have it."

"Exactly," said Golovanov. "Any questions?"

Angel raised a hand. "Who's lead suit?"

All eyes fell upon her. She was the obvious choice.

"Angel is leading this op," said Golovanov, as we expected she would. "Don't get me wrong—you'll all get your turn. Next time is Stanco. Caddy, you're next."

"Sounds gas," I said. "Gives me time enough for everyone else to make the mistakes."

Stanco laughed. "Gee, thanks."

"Never forget that your eyes are connected to your brain." Golovanov pointed to my suit. "Go suit up. Make sure you're comfortable. I'll put through any more info as it becomes available. Learn what you can, and get back here ASAP."

"Right," I said. Six hours locked in a metal box. No worries.

Come on, I sent to Sandy via my implants. *It's time to go to work.*

Sandy's chest opened up, peeling back like a blooming flower. I turned around and stepped backwards into the suit, the metal petals closing in around me. Thin cables snaked out from the suit and latched into my exposed implants, magnetically attaching to the metal. Three, two, one . . .

My vision went dark and a numbness enveloped my whole body. The quiet hum of the hangar disappeared; I felt as though I'd been thrown into a bucket of ice water, silent, black as night.

Then I was standing in the hangar, eight feet tall and strapped to the ceiling, as the suit's body became mine. My eyes could see so much now: the heat of the booting up suits, green boxes around the other suits, and text floating in air giving me ammunition counts, power levels, and whatever Sandy wanted to highlight for me. My world was fish-eyed. I could feel one of the cables brushing against the EVA pack on my back.

I was ready for the activation but it was always disconcerting.

"Looking gas," said Golovanov. He looked so small now, like a child who only came up to my waist. He gave me a thumbs up.

I returned it. "Connection is solid," I said, my voice synthetic, an approximation of my natural voice, just deeper. "Ready to go."

Angel's portrait appeared on the left side of my vision. "Immortal Armour active," she said.

Stanco's face appeared below her. "Ready to chew arse and kick bubble gum," he said. "And I'm all out of arse."

"Right." I chuckled, trying to sound natural. Why did he have to sexualise everything? Not *every* guy was like that. It reeked of overcompensation.

Not that there was anything wrong with that. I kept telling myself that.

Golovanov left, leaving the three of us hanging from the ceiling. I couldn't feel my real body; I knew it was hanging there, limp and immobile, inside my chest cavity, weak as a baby.

"Incoming transmission," said Sandy. AIs couldn't give suggestions or advice; it was against their programming. "From Operations."

"Put it through," I said.

A floating box appeared in front of my eyes, labelled *Anchorage*. It was a vision of space, untwinkling white dots on a black field. At the centre of it, barely perceptible, was a ship.

The optics zoomed, straining to show us more. The screen pixelated for a moment, and then in the harsh light of false-colour optics, I could see a ship floating in space, tumbling slowly, unlit and unpowered. Even its emergency navigation lights were off, and it was surrounded by a sparkling field of debris, like the tail of a comet stretching out beyond the edges of the screen. Readouts showed no infra-red or electromagnetic activity. No radiation, either, so the reactor was intact. Just a lump of steel crying in the depths of the black.

"What a fucking wreck," said Stanco, blowing a low whistle—a prerecorded sound composed by his AI.

The ship tumbled, revealing a jagged, oval gash along one side, about eight metres on its longest edge. It reached right to the name emblazoned on the side in stark white lettering. *Anchorage*.

"I'm reading a pronounced hole in the starboard side," said Angel. "That should serve as our entry point."

Gas plan. I looked over the information Sandy provided. "No sign of internal fuel or ammunition detonation," I said. "No sign of external scoring, either, or buckling on the hull . . . no stress or micro-fractures. It wasn't weapons fire or a high-speed impact."

"Something caused that big hole," said Stanco. "What else but weapons fire?"

"Maybe the crew cut it out," I said. "It looks like the kind of damage an untrained worker with a plasma cutter would make. Could be they were trying to vent a section manually . . ."

"Well," said Stanco, "at least we know they weren't attacked."

"They didn't put up a fight," said Angel. "There's a difference."

Curious. "You saying whoever did this was invited in?"

"No," she said, "but it's possible the *Anchorage* didn't see them coming. Someone cutting on the hull might not have triggered their decompression alarms; passenger ships sometimes only treat their safety equipment with indifferent maintenance."

Silence reigned for a time, and I watched the corpse of the ship tumble over and over endlessly. There weren't any other holes.

"Asteroid impact, maybe?" said Stanco. "Something that slipped past their sensors? Or maybe they had a reactor leak. It's possible they wanted to eject their reactor core, failed, so tried to cut it out . . ."

All this guesswork was frustrating. "Maybe, maybe," I said. "Does it really matter? We're going in anyway, so let's just focus on the mission until we get there."

"Couldn't agree more," said Angel, then her portrait disappeared.

"Wow," said Stanco. "Rude."

"You know what she's like," I said.

Stanco snorted. "She sounds like she needs a dicking."

"Not like you could do that," I said, the words slipping out before I had a chance to rein them in.

Silence. Angry silence. "You don't need a dick to be a dude," Stanco said. "Fucking Erisians."

"I didn't mean it," I said.

"Yeah you did."

It was difficult to deny that. "Look," I said, "I'm trying, okay?"

"I know," said Stanco, without any conviction at all.

I probably should have let it go but I didn't. "It doesn't bother me what you identify as. I'm just saying . . . it's weird enough seeing women and gays in the military, let alone trans people. There's a reason most of Eris has their own units, rather than integrating with the rest of the Colonial armies."

"I know," he said again, again not believing a word I said. "It's fine."

I took a breath—not something my suit could do, but the armour's metal muscles and articulators moved in the same way—and used my implants to give my body a shot of a mild sedative.

"I'm sorry," I said, and I tried to genuinely mean it. I resisted the urge to add qualifiers after that. *It was just how I was raised, I don't know any better, I'm wrong but . . .*

"Yeah," said Stanco, a little hint of levity returning. "It's all gas, bro. Shit takes time to sink in. It just sucks when you get all the shit for being a guy, expectations of being a manly-man, but also shit for being trans, too. All the downsides, none of the perks. Makes you a little defensive. So, you know, I'm sorry too."

"I'm trying," I said again, and then added, "bro."

"I appreciate that." Stanco's suit turned to face mine. "Don't worry. Angel's a bigger weirdo than you are."

Small comfort.

I returned my attention to the feed of the *Anchorage*. The closer we got, the higher the resolution climbed.

Closer and closer.

Six hours later

The last of the air was sucked out of the hangar, hissing faintly around my suit's microphones before fading to the eerie silence that was deep space.

"Decompression complete," said Angel. She'd rejoined our channel when it was time to do something productive. "Disable artificial gravity. Commence decoupling."

With a lurch, I felt gravity shut off. I sent a mental push that detached the cables that suspended my suit from the hangar's ceiling. I floated in the zero gravity, small puffs of nitrogen from the EVA pack keeping my position steady. Attached to the pack were several emergency bulkheads, heavy and bulky.

Silently, the hangar door began to open. Normally it would be groaning and loud, but with no atmosphere I could hear nothing.

"Move out," said Angel, and we flew slowly out the open doors into the void of space.

Although I'd spent plenty of time in space, protected from the vacuum of space only by the metal of a ship's hull, it was different being in a suit. A starship's hull was measured in metres; the suit was substantially smaller than that. Although it was forged from advanced polymers and composite plates, my face—my real face—was only a metre or so away from the void.

If something went wrong . . .

I turned away from the *Lahore* and navigated towards the

Anchorage. As I looked at it, Sandy outlined it in a box and zoomed in, giving me a clear look at the ship.

I tried to focus on something other than my unconscious body encased within an armoured steel box, where even the tiniest hole would drain away my air and, thanks to my neural link to the suit, the first I'd know about it was when I started to pass out . . . way, way too late to do anything but die.

"Your heart rate is increasing," said Sandy, her voice tinged with genuine concern. "You okay, boss man?"

"I'm fine," I said.

"Sounds like you need a drink," she said.

I definitely did not. Sobriety was one of the conditions of joining the Immortals. Golovanov knew my weakness. "Thanks," I said, "but I don't think you come equipped with a mini bar."

"Well," she said, "I have full control of your implants at this point. I could give you a shot of alcohol, straight into your veins if you want, so you don't even have to taste it."

"No thanks."

She laughed. "You sure? I mean, I could—"

"*No.*" The fierceness in which I answered surprised even me.

"I'm sorry," said Sandy. "I won't ask again."

I'd pissed off both Stanco and Sandy, and we hadn't even reached the *Anchorage* yet. "It's fine," I said. "We can talk about it after the mission."

"If I had feelings," said Sandy, "I'd think you were brushing me off." Her voice turned chirpy. "But I don't. So that's fine."

The ship, our target, drew closer and closer. In my fish-eyed vision, I could see the *Lahore* behind us, shrinking away. Soon it appeared in a box, zoomed in so I could see it clearly.

Sandy was helping me out in subtle ways. Just like Sandhya, her namesake.

Suddenly I missed her. Naming my AI after my dead lover was a stupid mistake. Stupid.

"You okay?" asked Sandy. "Your heart rate is—"

"I'm *fine,*" I said, giving myself another shot of mild sedative. "Just . . . please don't ask me about my heart rate unless it's much more serious than this."

"I'll increase the threshold by 20%," said Sandy.

Closer. Closer. We drifted through the inky black, three

hunchbacked suits of steel stabilised by puffs of gas. Behind us, the five other suits left the *Lahore*, taking up an escort formation.

Although they were there to cover our approach, I couldn't help but feel that they were also pointing weapons at our back.

Soon, the zooming effect disappeared from my vision and I saw the ship *au naturale*. A flood of sensor information floated beside it. Minimal heat. Clouds of debris. Almost no atmosphere present in sections near the outer hull, smaller amounts within—maybe a few air pockets, but the temperature within was well below freezing.

"This ship is a tomb," I said. "Nobody's alive over there."

"We're here to investigate," said Angel. "There are taxpayers on that ship."

"Taxpayer's bodies," said Stanco.

Retrieving those was not even on our mission objectives, but I couldn't see the harm. Civvies deserved a decent burial too.

"So why us?" asked Stanco. "Why can't the Coast Guard clean up this mess?"

"Because," said Angel, slightly condescendingly, "if your house is on fire, you can't put it out from inside. There are some problems the Colonial agencies can't fix. That's why we're here."

"Oh," said Stanco. "Got it. By the way, don't take this the wrong way, but you're not anywhere near as stupid as you look."

"You are," said Angel.

Brutal.

"Right," said Stanco, clicking his tongue. "Whatever."

The *Anchorage* soon swallowed the stars below, the tumbling steel wall of its hull forming a floor. We aimed for the pivot point at the centre, EVA suits straining to push us forward, then slow us down. Sandy did all the work; piloting a metal suit through a field of sparkling debris, landing on a spinning and structurally compromised space ship, was a job better suited for computers.

My boots clunked down on the metal, magnetising with a faint hum that vibrated throughout the entire suit.

Angel's voice filled my suit. "*Lahore*, this is the away team. We have reached the *Anchorage*."

"Confirmed," said Golovanov. "Stabilise the ship."

We walked along the slowly spinning hull until we reached the stern. The three of us lined up at the edge of the ship and knelt down.

I set my magnetized hands on the metal and locked my knees in against the hull. My suit's EVA pack roared to life, firing at full power; Stanco's and Angel's did the same thing.

The *Anchorage* strained in protest, slowed down its spin, and then, after a minute's work, stopped completely in space.

"Gas," said Golovanov. "Proceed into the hull."

Angel, Stanco and I walked on the hull, from port to starboard, putting one magnetised foot in front of the other. As we got closer, we got a better look at the hole.

It was nearly thirty metres wide and fifty long, roughly oval. The edges were melted, blackened and jagged, as though the metal had been dissolved. The floor below was pitted and scored, like the surface of Eris's moon, or an asteroid; hundreds of tiny holes and divots were cut into the exposed bulkhead.

Sandy drew a box over a section of the melted hull and enhanced it.

"What kind of weapon could do this?" I asked her. "There's no scorching away from the impact site. Not even the best Earthborn torpedoes could cause something like this."

"It looks like fluid erosion," she said, confusion in her artificial voice. "Some kind of acid."

Angel looked to me. "No acid could possibly melt through starship hull. It would take days and days, weeks even. Surely someone would notice."

Nobody had any answers.

"Lights are out," Stanco observed. "Even emergency power has run out."

"Hello darkness my old friend," I said.

The tension evaporated. Stanco laughed. "Darkness never returns my damn calls. Sometimes I think I barely know her any more."

I couldn't help but chortle. "Darkness is a strong black woman who don't need no man."

"Cut the chatter," said Angel. Humourless Uynovian. "Split up. Stanco, head toward the stern. Caddy, head toward the bow. I'll make for the reactor at the core."

"In we go," said Stanco, climbing down to the hole and swinging into the corridor. His huge suit had to crouch to move forward, magnetized limbs keeping him pressed against one of the walls.

I crawled into the hole as well. Sandy magnetised my hands and I carefully made my way in the opposite direction.

After a few minutes crawling, I came to a door. The centre of it had dissolved, leaving a hole almost a metre radius.

No. Half that; one metre diameter. I had to remember I was twice as large as I normally was.

"Got a bulkhead," I said. "Emergency decompression door. Something burned its way through . . . looks to be whatever cut through the hull."

"Yeah," said Stanco. "I got one too. Same deal."

"Employ a manual bypass," said Angel. That was the euphemism of the day. *Manual bypass.*

A simple instruction easily followed. I reached out with my hands, prying the metal. The suit's articulators groaned faintly and, for a moment, I didn't think it would bend; then the metal peeled back and the gap widened.

I pulled myself in, wiggling and kicking, pushing through the metal gap. The metal of my suit's armour scraped against the edges of the hole, but I fit.

The corridor on the other side was stained with blood, splashed down with rust-coloured gore and a strange black fluid. The bulkheads were riddled with holes from high velocity bullets. A rifle floated oddly in space, along with dozens of shell casings and debris. I recognised the type: standard civilian Polema issue Type 1. It wasn't Earthborn.

"Someone actually did put up a fight," I said. "Got a gun and signs of a struggle."

"Act tough, die rough," said Stanco. "Any Earthborn shit?"

"Unless you want me to scrape their blood off the walls, no."

"Don't disturb the bodies," said Angel. "Note the location and have the *Lahore* retrieve them."

I looked around. The corridor had been stripped bare, leaving only stains on the metal. "There aren't any. Just blood, and lots of it."

"Maybe they got sucked out," said Stanco.

"That's *blown* out," said Angel.

"So, okay, maybe they got *blown* out. And I bet you know a fancy word for *killed to death by space* too."

It was unlikely the bodies had been either sucked or blown out. We'd have seen them by now. Anyway, before I'd widened it, the hole was barely big enough for a person to fit. Nothing made sense. "Getting a bit sick of hearing the word *maybe*," I said, a little snappier than I intended.

Sandy pinged my vision, drawing a red dot over something deeper in the ship and painting a red line on the corridor that led toward it. "Nicholas, I'm reading a room with air. Sealed. Trace amounts of heat."

An intact room? "Pass it along to the others." I changed direction. "Guys, got a room with atmo. Looks to be about deck seven, 'bout forty metres away from the hull." Right at the core of the ship.

"No way," said Stanco. "Survivors?"

"Who knows?" With a mental thrust I transferred the information Sandy had compiled for me to my team.

"We'll meet you there," said Angel.

Floating through bloodstained halls, I made my way farther and farther into the ruined hulk of the *Anchorage*, following the red line deeper into the ship's heart.

I floated past a lot of things. I saw computer screens powered down and inert, I saw half-melted emergency bulkheads breached and useless, I saw personal effects floating in the nothingness and loose bulkheads and yellow oxygen masks drifting like tentacles, their precious cargo long ago discharged.

But I saw no bodies. Personal effects, plenty. Weapons and shell casings, sure. Blood, and lots of it, including some that looked like the victims had been dragged. Not a single corpse.

Finally, the red line led towards a thick blast door labelled *Secure Hold*. There was a button to open it, but the display glowed with an angry red hue and flashed the words *decompression failure*. The metal had the same acid scoring as every other door we'd seen, but this one had held up, probably due to its significant thickness and anti-theft reinforced polymers.

The shipbuilders valued the passengers' gold more than it valued their lives. Although, by booking passage with that particular ship, the paying customers were de-facto supporting them.

Whatever. It wasn't my job to feel sorry for anyone.

"Man," said Stanco as he crawled around the corner, "we are going to get so much free shit."

"Salvage of non-Earthborn items isn't one of our objectives," said Angel, appearing right behind him.

"You kidding? What's the point of being a Crisis Exacerbation Specialist if you don't get to loot anything afterwards?"

I shook my head. "Golovanov said we were Private Third-Party . . . something-or-other Engineers."

"Golovanov," said Angel, "can also hear you. The audio is piped into mission command."

"We've been through a lot," I said. "He can handle a joke."

Stanco floated toward the door, peering in close.

"Thoughts?" I asked.

He extended a giant metal hand, reaching out and touching the pitted and scarred door. "Knock knock," Stanco said, rapping silently on the metal. Anyone inside could hear us, but we had no hope of hearing them through the vacuum of space. "We should send through a probe first."

That sounded gas. Stanco pulled a small metal oval about the size of a discus off his back and clipped it to the wall. It glowed faintly as it began to cut into the door.

The minutes ticked away.

"How long could someone survive in there?" I asked. "There's air, so presumably they didn't just die."

Angel's suit's head appeared over Stanco's metal shoulder. I could see her portrait on the side of my vision, but I looked her in her optics, too. Some human habits died hard. "With food and water, a long time. The ship was well stocked, and no matter how strong that acid is, they must have had some time to prepare. There were armed guards at the first door to be breached, after all. As each door went down . . . they probably stockpiled as much as they could inside and waited it out. Fortunately, these doors won't open if there's no air on our side, so if they're in there thinking they're saved, they'll have to wait a bit longer."

Made sense.

"What do you think they did to pass the time?" asked Stanco. "Played cards? Drank?"

"Sex is an excellent recreational activity," said Angel, matter-of-factly. "Although I imagine that privacy would be at a premium."

"A substantial part of the crew would be Osmeons," said Stanco. "They wouldn't care."

"And some would be Erisians," I said. Just thinking about having sex while someone else watched was super weird.

Finally, the probe flashed a bright green, and Sandy connected the link.

Darkness. The probe's light turned on; the camera was looking at the back of a metal crate. It snaked out around it, thin optic fibre slipping between tiny cracks, weaving its way through a tightly packed maze.

"They barricaded the door," said Angel, the first hints of . . . something filtering into her voice. Stress, maybe? Relief? Fear? Did crazies from her world even feel fear?

The optic fibre tried to push a box. It didn't move. Its laser worked again, drilling a tiny hole. This, unlike the reinforced bulkhead, fell away quickly. Harsh, white light flooded in from the other side. The lens adjusted.

The secure storage room was a low-ceilinged metal box fifty metres squared. The far side of it was stacked with boxes, most neatly arranged, although some had been hastily opened. Deep scratches lined the floor where they had been dragged over and welded together to form a crude, additional barrier.

In the centre of the room, a pile of people, over thirty of them, lay huddled together on the metal, dressed in thick clothes. Weapons lay scattered all around, close at hand, ready to pull up at a moment's notice. Empty bottles and food wrappers lay scattered all around.

"O2 is solid," said Stanco. "It's pretty cold, though. -10 C. Miserable but survivable." He sighed. "No loot for us. Wakey wakey, sleepy heads."

Our view floated toward the huddle. It slid close to one of the people, a woman with long, dark hair who lay on her back. The camera manouvered around to look at her face.

Her eyes were rolled back in her head, skin pale and desiccated. A rusty stain spread out from underneath her chin, and the pistol she clutched in her hand was held by thin, shrivelled fingers. The camera moved to another one—a young boy. He, too, had blown his brains out on the deck. The camera panned over a half-dozen faces, all dead.

"This is why I don't fly coach," said Stanco.

The camera rose and swung out. "They had plenty of food," said Angel. "Water. Air. Warm clothes. The bulkhead was holding . . ."

"They probably heard the acid melting down the door," I said. "Decided they didn't want to be prey for the Earthborn."

Angel shook her head, her tone turning venomous. "This isn't their style. Earthborn desecrate the bodies of their enemies; they would never give up just because they were already dead. They couldn't let an opportunity like this go to waste." The only time she seemed to feel anything was discussing our long-lost cousins.

"You okay?" I asked her, using my implants to send the signal just to her.

For a moment, she said nothing, then her suit looked back at me. "We're all animals," she said. "Some just wear clothes."

"They're still people," I said. "Them and us. These dead civvies, the Earthborn, everyone they killed on Polema. All humans."

"What makes a human life inherently so valuable that ending one is so terrible?"

"Life is preferable to death," I said. "For most people."

"Not on Uynov."

I tried to grimace with muscles I didn't have control of any more. "Going to be honest Angel, and don't take it the wrong way, but why didn't you just kill yourself if life on Uynov was so bad? How'd you get to be here?"

"Suicide doesn't end pain," she said. "It just gives it to everyone else. When we die, the only thing we leave behind is the joy we give to others. I don't want my legacy to be distilled suffering."

I digested that. "Erisians believe all life is sacred, and only death is owed to those who cannot abide this simple tenant."

"People only say all human life is valuable because that means the speaker's life is valuable. It's an ultimately selfish action."

It was hard to argue with that.

"So," said Stanco, "if you two are done staring creepily at each other, are we going to head in or what?"

We sealed each end of the corridor with emergency bulkheads, then retrieved the probe. Air hissed through the tiny hole it had drilled, white and visible as it rushed to flood its new home, and slowly the pressure equalised. The *open* button turned from red to green.

Time to disembark. The world went dark again, and then Sandy's suit opened up and rotten, frigid air blew against my face.

I'd almost forgotten that smell. Dead things left to rot in a too-small place. I stepped out of the suit. The ship's corridors were so much bigger when I wasn't crawling through them.

I unclipped a light carbine from the outside of the suit and watched as Angel stepped out of hers, taking a weapon and shouldering it with the detached air of someone who had done so a million times before. I was nervous, and the smell was getting to me, but Angel might well have been taking a stroll down to the mess hall.

"Ready?" I asked, hand hovering over the button.

"Breach it," she said, and so I pushed.

The doors groaned, strained, the metal underfoot vibrating. The motors whined loudly. The reverberation travelled through the metal of the ship, shaking its deckplates, and then with a horrible grinding noise the bent, battered door retreated into the floor.

"Make *more* noise why don't you?" Stanco reached around with his giant metal fist and pushed the box-barrier away, breaking the welds and collapsing it easily. How strong the Immortal Armour seemed as a mere mortal . . .

Angel and I stepped inside, weapons shouldered. The smell of the dead got stronger as we drew close. I put one hand over my nose, holding my rifle with my prosthetic. It was strong enough to comfortably hold it up.

"We should check them," she said, her nose wrinkled but otherwise seemingly unbothered by the stench. "Whoever attacked this ship was looking for something. I intend to find out what."

I gave one of the corpses a nudge with my boot. "Where are all the bodies aside from these arseholes?"

She didn't answer. I looked her way, then followed her eyes.

One of the dead was wearing combat armour. Where she had found that I had no idea. Maybe she was a soldier, maybe she was a merc'. That didn't matter.

What did matter was the large claw protruding from the ceramic plate covering her gut. It was curved, nearly half a metre long and was wickedly serrated. It was dug in deep, bone yellow, and attached to a green, leathery limb which had been severed with a laser cutter.

"What the fuck is *that*?" I asked, crouching over it for a better view. She'd killed herself, just like the others, although instead of using a pistol she'd injected a dozen morphia needles into her leg.

"Caddy," said Golovanov in my ear, "retrieve that corpse when you go."

"Aye aye," I said, staring at the claw, transfixed. Despite all the medication its victim had injected, she still seemed so terrified . . .

"Sometimes," I said, "I think that if I ever decide to just kill myself . . . I wonder how it should go. Should I go the painless way, or the painful one? After all, once I'm dead none of it matters anymore. Maybe I can snatch a glimpse of the other side before I go."

"I have had my fill of pain," said Angel. "It is nothing to be romanticised."

I let go of my weapon, switched my rifle into my flesh-hand, then touched the bone; it was smooth, and covered in a thin layer of slime.

The slime began dissolving my prosthetic finger.

"Shit!"

Even though I'd had a metal and polymer arm ever since the war, human instinct was a powerful thing, and hard to override. I flicked my fingers, trying to get rid of the stuff; the array of sensors in my prosthetic fed me information. It felt cold, wet, tasted of brine and salt . . . and plenty of pain, too.

My finger dissolved up to the third knuckle before the acid became too diluted to do any more damage. I stared at the withered remains of my index finger. It hurt; the prosthetic was wired directly into my nervous system. I used a mental push to lower the implant's sensitivity, turning down the pain on that finger completely. It slowly went numb.

"You okay?" asked Angel.

"Yeah," I said, "but getting the body out is a no-go. That acid is wicked stuff."

Angel inspected the wound on the corpse. "It doesn't seem to be dissolving the victim," she said. "Maybe it reacts only to non-organic material . . ."

Before I could stop her, she slipped her glove off, and poked the bone with her finger.

Nothing.

"What kind of creature is coated with an acid that only reacts to metal?" I asked. "Some kind of bioweapon?" I felt a vague sinking in my gut. "Is the *Anchorage* . . . a weapons test?"

A faint sound reached my ears. The sound of rain on a metal roof, from above.

"Contact," said Stanco. "I got movement out here. Vibrations from the deck above. They're moving."

"They?"

Angel and I exchanged a worried look. The sound travelled directly above us, distant but audible, and then toward the stern of the ship. Toward the way we'd come. Drawn by the vibrations of the opening door.

Hundreds of those claws were making pitter-patter rain on the deck.

They were coming for us.

I ran toward my suit.

"Operations, we are egressing *now*. Right now!" My rifle bounced against my side as I ran. If whatever was coming for us reached the emergency bulkheads we'd set up, and breached them . . . I didn't want to think about it, but through those thin sheets of metal was the logical way to get to the meat the creatures had too long been denied. Sandy moved towards me, the suit opening up. Angel's AI did the same thing, presenting its open chest for boarding. We passed by the ruined boxes.

Something heavy slammed into the emergency bulkhead. A massive bone claw, just like in the gut of the dead woman, broke through the steel, smoke hissing as it dissolved the barrier.

Air rushed out. Alarms screamed. The button flashed red—the door, hopelessly jammed, strained as it tried in vain to seal off the breach.

Stanco opened up with his assault gun. It fired like a titan ripping cloth, shaking the walls and floor, impossibly loud in the cramped quarters, drowning out the howl of escaping air. Brass shell casings the size of a fist slammed into the bulkheads.

I practically fell into my suit. Darkness enveloped me as the armoured plates closed, and the gunfire became muted and distant. The only thing I could hear was profound ringing in my ears.

"C'mon," I shouted to the darkness. "Boot. Boot, damn you!"

Plugs attached themselves to my implants, then the ringing went away. For a second, there was nothing, and then I was a metal giant once more.

Bugs. A wall of eight legged bugs, each roughly the size of a horse, some smaller, some larger, all tearing down the shredded remains of the emergency bulkhead. Their eyes glowed red in the dimly lit corridor and the deck was soaked in the same black fluid I'd seen before. The blood.

They were all different; some had massive pincers, some huge claws, others were bigger or smaller or weird colours. A myriad of forms, all trying to tear us to pieces.

Stanco fired again. Rushing air blew the spider-like creatures back, and debris—including the bodies of the crew—thumped against them, but still they came, crawling, hissing, reaching for us with a host of teeth and talons.

I ignited the pilot light on my flamethrower and turned that corridor into a tiny piece of hell.

Orange and red consumed everything, the rushing, escaping air twisting the jet of flame and pulling it off in random directions. I saw dozens of the creatures be consumed by the flames, the sticky, high energy fluid seeping between cracks in their carapace. I brought my right arm around too and added autocannon fire to the mix, heavy shells wailing in the rapidly depleting air.

The deck plate underneath me gave way. I nearly slipped and fell, the escaping air buffeting me from behind.

"I got you!" Stanco grabbed hold of my suit's leg. "Hang on!"

I scrambled around, digging my fingers into the skeleton of the ship, trying to hold on. I felt Stanco's metal fingers weaken and a crate slammed into my back.

Then I lost my grip and, torn away from the metal by the rushing air, tumbled down the corridor.

Sandy fired the EVA pack, trying to stabilise us, but we were a big thing in a narrow box. The suit clanged off metal bulkheads, screamed as it was dragged along the floor, then tumbled head over heels as we were pushed towards the ship's stern.

I hit an exposed beam and bounced off. Then another. My vision went static-y as the suit's cameras took a hit. We spun and spun, puffs of nitrogen trying to stabilise us.

Finally, we got stuck arse-first in a door. This one had been melted through like the others.

My head hurt from the close proximity to gunfire and taking a spin through the insides of a too-small ship. A strange sensation, coming from my real body; fake parts of me hurt. Sandy was trying to tell me I was injured.

"Hey," I said, groaning as I eased myself out of the ruined door. "How about dialling down the pain some?"

"You're already heavily medicated," said Sandy. "Are you sure?"

Uh oh. "Did I break something?"

"A few somethings," said Sandy. "The human body is just not designed to survive these kinds of forces. Fortunately you have lots of implants."

We'd have to do something about that. There were ways to play with gravity, create it and negate it. The suit would have to be modified for future operations.

I couldn't think about that now. Not my job. I'd include it in my after action report, though.

Assuming I survived to write it.

"Let's get going then," I said. "If I need medical treatment . . ."

"You do," said Sandy, her tone sincere.

Then it was time to go. I magnetised my hands and went to crawl once again, back up the way I'd come, but my limbs didn't stick to the metal.

"Magnetism is damaged," said Sandy.

Dammit. I knew when I was beat. "Send out a distress signal. Have our escorts cut me out of the hull."

"You're not going to like this," said Sandy, "but that's a no-go. The antenna is damaged too, and by now we're deep inside the *Anchorage*. Metal of this size is going to function as a giant Faraday cage. Range is severely reduced. We can maybe talk to Angel or Stanco if they get close enough, but apart from that, we're on our own."

"Fine. We'll get closer to the hull so they can hear us." I started to move back the way we'd been blown, pushing off the metal deck for leverage.

Sandy flashed a red warning. "Lots of movement that way," she said. "Should I warm up weapons?"

AI were forbidden from giving orders or advice. Yet, she always seemed to find a way to let me know what she was thinking.

"So you're saying that we need to go deeper."

"I'm not saying anything," said Sandy. "But we're down to half a tank of flamethrower fuel and only packing a thousand more rounds of autogun ammo. There's a lot of hostiles out there."

I hoped Stanco and Angel were okay.

"Further toward the bow then," I said, and kicked at the burned-through husk of the door until it broke, and we sailed through.

Sandy drew red lines and I followed them. The corridors widened as we got further in, a change I took as a blessing. I was still forced to crawl, though, but it wasn't as hard. On the way we passed more battle sites; blood splatters and scorch marks marred the walls, standing as mute testament to the struggle.

As always, no bodies.

I wanted to talk to Sandy. No, that wasn't true. I wanted to talk to *Sandhya*. The woman I'd loved on Polema. I wanted her to tell me everything was going to be okay, like she used to. I wanted to hold her again. I couldn't focus on the mission.

Maybe my brain was damaged. Sandy had been non-specific about what kind of injuries I had. Everything hurt but I kept going.

We turned a corridor. Frozen drops of ice filled the vacuum like little snowflakes.

"The water processing room," said Sandy. "It must be leaking."

Ice wasn't dangerous in small amounts. The armour on my suit could deflect autocannon fire. The main risk would be that I'd be trapped. "Will that be a problem?"

"Just be careful," she said. "Water expands as it freezes. Structural integrity of the *Anchorage* is going to be low here; those walls will be close to buckling. Float where you can, touch as little as possible."

Again, I tried to guess what she was thinking. "You want to drive?"

"It would be more efficient if I did."

"Go for it," I said, and the EVA pack kicked in again. I floated amongst the ice crystals, the EVA pack moving the suit in ways I could not, tilting perfectly, tiny puffs of nitrogen guiding me forward.

As we passed the water processing room, I looked inside.

I don't know why I did. Human nature, I guess. I wanted to see the leak. I wanted to see whatever thing was inside there, mundane or mysterious.

I saw the glint of green reflecting in the ice. Definitely more mysterious than mundane. I shouldn't have stopped; I should have kept going, pushed on until I could get free of the hull and send out a signal to get picked up.

"What the hell is that?" I asked. "Stop."

The suit braked. I spun, facing the doorway, then drifted inside.

The room was packed full of chrysalises, olive green and bulbous, ranging in size from a few centimetres to the size of a man. They were sacs of fluid held in place by thin membranes; the majority were clumped together against a broken bulkhead, the others layered the floors and ceiling. Each one extruded thin brown tentacles which burrowed into the ice. Devouring it. Others curled around light fixtures, power outlets, and the door switch. Feeding.

Within were creatures. The smaller ones looked indistinct, just a blob, but the bigger ones . . . they looked human. An identical person. Androgynous, even genderless, attractive but remarkably plain; olive skin, brown hair. Their skin was markless, fresh, like a child's even though they looked about thirty.

"This is creepy as shit," I said.

"Sometimes I'm glad I'm a robot," said Sandy. "Golovanov will want a sample."

Wordlessly I extended my finger toward one of the larger sacs, and used my implants to activate the sample probe. With a flash of sparks the device broke off. It was broken too. Damn.

The *thing* in the sac looked at me. Did nothing more than move its eyes. They glowed red, faintly, just like the bugs had done. I looked at another one. It, too, reacted to my gaze by staring at me. Soon they were all doing it.

So if my sensitive equipment wouldn't work, I decided to cut to the chase: I punched one. The sac burst like a watermelon and my metal fist slammed into the creature beyond. Its blood exploded, red and rich, all over my fingers. I used my other hand to splatter another one.

"Preliminary examination of the facial structure of these creatures indicates a striking similarity to each other," said Sandy. "Scraping the samples off your fingers. Analysing. The two bodies we sampled are identical on a genetic level." There was something in her synthetic voice. A mixture of wonder and apprehension. "The DNA strands appear to be a combination of . . . at least a hundred individuals."

"That's why there were no bodies," I said. "The bug-things took them and, somehow, blended their DNA all together to grow this . . . person. But why?"

"I can't answer that even if I were allowed to."

I couldn't—simply couldn't—begin to understand what I was seeing, but the cold, empty way their red eyes stared at me told me there was only one thing to do. I floated back to the corridor, ignited my pilot light, and I poured flame into that room until there was nothing left in the tank. The fluid sacs burst, the bodies burned, twitching as flame and vacuum ended them. I emptied a hundred or so high-explosive rounds into the room just to make sure.

"Excellent work," said Sandy. "I was *really* hoping you were going to do that."

"Let's get the fuck out of here," I said, and as Sandy began steering us down the corridor again, I tried to get as far away from that room as possible.

Left. Right. Right. Left. Right. Right. Right. Right. Left. Straight on.

Without Sandy I'd be hopelessly lost. On the *Lahore* my implants guided me; here, the AI did.

How did people even get around before computers? I remembered they had maps. Gas memories. Or they just got lost a lot. Or . . .

My mind was wandering when it should be focused. For a moment, I felt odd. Like I was going to throw up—something I couldn't do without a mouth or digestive system. "Hey Sandy?"

"Yes?"

"I don't feel gas."

Sandy said nothing for a moment as the EVA pack guided us around another too-small corner. "You're dying."

So simply stated. My nervous system was linked up to the suit's sensors and inputs, but my brain was within my biological body, and it was screaming.

"How far away are we from the outer hull?" I asked.

"Six minutes," said Sandy. "Maybe less. I'm avoiding unstable areas. We wouldn't want to get pinned in here."

"We would not want that," I said. "Although I'm sure you'd be fine."

"I'd miss you," said Sandy, and I think she actually meant it. The way she said it, though, with Sandhya's voice . . . that hurt more than all the broken ribs in the world.

"Hey," I said. "Just saying. If it makes you feel better . . . you suits cost over eight hundred million credits *each*. My death benefit is only about five hundred thousand. Much cheaper for every single one of us to get blown up than one of you guys."

"That actually makes me feel worse."

"It wasn't supposed to make you feel gas, ya' dumb robot."

A few seconds of silence. Then, a yellow bar lit up around Stanco's portrait.

"—uddy," came his voice, heavily obfuscated by static, "you out there?"

"Stanco! Sandy, give him our locat—"

"Already done," she said.

"Hey, Caddy!" Stanco became clearer by the second. "Buddy, mate, I knew you were too fucking cool to be dead."

"Thanks for the vote of confidence," I said, "but let's not get too far ahead of ourselves. I'm hurting pretty bad. Antenna's damaged. So's my magnetic grip. I'm lost, and running low on ammo and options."

"Right," said Stanco. "I have a fix on your location. Hold tight." Seconds later, Stanco's suit flew around the corner, nearly smashing into me. "Found 'ya."

"You're a sight for sore eyes," I said. "Thanks for coming back for me."

"Angel wanted to exfil," he said, "but Golovanov ordered us back. You got all the other Immortals out looking for you too. We can't have you ruining our good name on our very first mission now, can we?" He hooked his arm around my EVA pack. "Okay. I'm going to guide you out of here."

"Sounds gas," I said, and again, the world seemed a bit fuzzy.

"Hey buddy," said Stanco. We were moving. He was moving me. "What's Eris like this time of year?"

What a weird question. "It depends on where you are," I said. "Planets are big. Frozen areas, forested areas, deserts . . . what do you like?"

"I like forests," he said. "Always do. Every time I got married, I'd take the lucky girl or guy to a forest. I like verdant things. Verdancy. Is that a word? Verdancy?"

Osmeons were polygamists. Sandhya had lots of husbands. And wives, too. Girls marrying girls. There was nothing wrong with that.

So I had to keep telling myself.

"Why do you need so many?" I asked. "Why not . . . just find the one? The person who makes you feel like all the world's right when you're with them?"

"Because," said Stanco. "Sometimes that's more than one person. And it's easier to trust when your marriage is a family." He steered us around a big corridor. "The last guy I married, right? He tried the whole monogamy thing. You know what he told me?"

"What?"

"Something like . . . *I thought having a vasectomy would stop my wife getting pregnant again. Turns out it just changes the colour of the baby.* He was doing the whole monogamy thing but she wasn't. I don't need that shit in my life. If my partners want to fuck around, let them. They're going to anyway. Better we do it on our own terms."

"That's brutal." I felt tired, distant. Too many thoughts of Sandhya, and of what I'd done to my wife. With her. With the soldier I met on a distant world . . . "Why are you telling me this?"

"Trying to keep you focused."

"'Cuz I'm dying?"

"Pretty much." Stanco steered us up to a tiny gap I didn't think we'd be able to fit through, and then—somewhat roughly—stuffed us through, scraping the hell out of the suit. "It's the game of war, buddy. Play stupid games, win stupid prizes."

"That actually makes me feel worse," I said, stealing Sandy's line.

"Hey," said Stanco. "I can't make *everyone* happy. I'm not pizza."

"I hate pizza."

He laughed down the line. "You can't hate pizza. Nobody hates pizza. You're a fucking monster."

I didn't know what to say to that so said nothing. We flew past various rooms. Quarters. Observatories. A bar.

"Hey, Caddy," said Stanco. He just wouldn't leave me alone. "Want a drink?"

More than anything. If I was going to die, I might as well do it with less pain. "Nah. There are demons in there."

"You what?"

"I used to have a drinking problem," I said. It was tempting to mute him but I didn't. "I still do. But I used to have it, too."

"Alcoholic, hey?" Stanco blasted open a section of the wall. The bulkhead splintered into a million shards. I barely heard the explosion. "You know there's an injection for that now."

Was there an injection to take away the pain in my chest when I thought of Sandhya? Was there a jab in the arm that could make the dead come back to me? "I know," I said. "I could just shoot myself in the head. That'd be gas, too."

"Mmm," he said. "Doesn't sound like a fun way to go. How does someone get like that? All suicidal like Angel?"

Easy answer but hard to say. "For most people, it's when someone dies who you love more than life itself. Substance abuse is gentle suicide."

"You're right where you're supposed to be right now." I could practically hear the smile in his voice. "You couldn't not be, friend."

Where I was supposed to be . . . "For me, the only thing worse than death is the end of the whisky. And I've been sober for a while now."

He chuckled at that, another prerecorded noise that filtered through the radio. "There's a saying on Uynov," said Stanco. "Angel told me. You treat a wound on the skin with grain alcohol. You treat a wound in the heart with spirits."

"Sounds gas. Spirits keep my spirits up."

"Except you're sober now," said Stanco. "So you've found something else, right?"

Something else? What was there? "Naw. Just because you're sober doesn't mean you don't miss it. Biggest days for relapses are anniversaries: first week, first month, first year, first decade. The shitty truth is, you're never really clean. You're just trying to beat your record for biggest gap between relapses, and eventually you die."

"Not today," said Stanco. "We aren't dying today. I'm far, far too funny to die."

"You're a funny guy," I said, groggily.

"My humour's like a little kid with cancer. Never gets old."

"The Prophets Wept . . ." I went to banter more, but from around the corner came the sound: rain on a tin roof. A stampede of spider-creatures, howling as they ran toward us.

"Okay," said Stanco, "Yeah. Maybe we *are* dying today."

Then I passed out for a bit.

I almost didn't believe I'd actually wake up in a real hospital, but as the world crept back to me, I recognised the familiar ceiling of the *Lahore*. A tray of food, along with a plastic cup of water, sat on my bedside table.

"Good morning," said Golovanov.

"Every time I see you in a hospital, something bad happens to me," I said, taking a deep breath. My whole chest lit up in pain; I shouldn't do that any more. Just shallow breathing. Sandy was right. So many broken ribs . . . "Or has just happened. Do I have any more prosthetics? Losing the arm was bad enough."

"Nah," said Golovanov, smiling. "You actually pulled through okay. I mean, you're beat up pretty bad, and you have a wicked-sick concussion, but you'll pull through."

"That's what I like to hear." I closed my eyes a moment. "So . . . what the fuck?"

"Your AI saved your life. Angel and Stanco carried you in. They deserve a fair share of the credit for that, too."

Sandy was saving me, just like her namesake. "I meant with the ship. The *Anchorage*."

Golovanov folded his hands in his lap, sucking in air between his teeth. "Yeah. Not sure what to tell you: appears to be . . . some kind of spider things. They can survive in space, and they're tough, strong, and adaptable. We got plenty of samples of their blood, along with the recordings from you and your team . . . so I'm sure Fleet Intelligence is going to have a field day trying to classify them. There's a myriad of breeds we observed, I doubt two are identical."

"The Myriad," I said, shrugging. "Well, hell of a first contact for humanity. Went to shooting in minutes. Mission accomplished, I guess."

Golovanov nodded. "Something like that."

I picked up a piece of stale bread and bit it. "You don't think they're aliens? Some kind of Earthborn bioweapon?"

His expression told me he didn't know. "We'll see," he said, standing up and tugging the front of his uniform down. "I have all seven other suits out there right now, combing over the wreckage, making sure that our nukes got every single one of those bastards—although if we could find one alive for dissection, that'd be useful, too. I've also put out a fleetwide alert. It was tempting to classify this whole thing, but I don't see the point. Not for something this serious. In a few days, all the colonies will know about it. I'm calling them a highly infectious biohazard for now, until we have information that suggests otherwise."

"Hopefully that's the last we'll see of them," I said, sitting up and folding my pillow behind me, making it into a half-chair.

Golovanov tilted his head. "Lots of ships go missing every month," he said. "Most are never found. I'm sure almost all of them have entirely mundane explanations. But what might have happened aboard the *Anchorage* if we didn't show up?" He put on his hat. "Do you really think that this is the first ship these creatures have attacked, or merely the first one that's been discovered?"

A sobering thought. Speaking of . . .

"I need a drink," I said, cracking a smile.

Golovanov's face darkened. "You know that's not an option," he said, and then without elaboration, turned and left.

"Happy New Year," I said to his back, and then I settled back into my bed, picking up a glass of water and taking a sip.

Mission complete.

For decades the area once known as America's Breadbasket has been under quarantine, protected from intrusion of a genetically engineered plague that kills sentient life on contact. Now the land is ready for resettlement—but first the plague must be neutralized. The key: a miniature golden cow whose gut flora is the antidote to the plague. The person who holds that cow holds the fate of the continent—and several billion NUbucks—in his hand.

BACKUP MAN
★
by Paul Di Filippo

I WAS WAITING PATIENTLY in a bar for a woman, a moldie and a splice, playing the AR overlay of that ancient heist film *Rififi* on my memtax, which I'd just upgraded to the newest model of living contact lenses, all jellyfish proteins laced with silicene circuitry and an RGB chromatophore micromatrix.

I knew that when that trio walked in, all hell would shake loose.

The bar was a trendy spot named The Holobiont's Hideaway, in the AdMo neighborhood in DC. Particulate-filtering airfish drifting gently through the biolit dimness; imene tuki and Karelian rune singing on the sound system; sombai cocktails at twenty NUbucks a pop. And even though Washington was something of quiet, backwater burg these days, with all the political action and players of the Northamerican Union centralized in Vancouver, this place was still jammed.

This decorous clientele made the impudent trio stand out all the more when they finally showed.

The woman—pumped up with printed muscles—wore a form-hugging secondskin whose jade-colored smart defensive exoscales caused her to resemble some giant bipedal gila monster. Her bare human face and mane of russet hair consorted oddly with the rest of her reptilian appearance. But any erotic allure was instantly quashed by the large spinner gun she held in her hand. From within its capacious disc-shaped magazine came the gentle hum of a propulsive wheel revolving at many, many RPM that belied its deadliness. Capable of dealing out hundreds of high-velocity, centrifugally expelled rounds per minute, the spinner quelled any lustful thoughts.

The unclothed moldie looked like every other moldie: a bulbous-limbed, vaguely anthropomorphic, protean shape that quivered with internal tides. Its translucent mycosymbiont "flesh," mottled in the colors and textures of the decaying matter on a forest floor, was threaded with filaments and gently circulating organelles. Its facial features brought to mind a bas-relief human phiz done in Play-Doh.

The splice's hybrid components, apart from the obvious baseline human contributions, were fairly evident: mandrill, hyena, osprey and bat. Across his barrel chest, the troglodytic transgenic wore a bandolier of spore bombs and paired lysing pistols.

The advent of the trio had cemented the room with stillness and silence. Appearing to be the leader of the invaders, the woman grinned as if relishing our fear.

"All right, my pretty little zoons," she commanded in a forceful and confident yet not overloud voice, "show me Drew Prosnitz, this minute, and no one suffers so much as a splinter!"

Drew Prosnitz was the name I was currently using. But I did not immediately reveal myself, wanting to see how serious these reivers were.

A few thousand nigh-instantaneous rounds of B2-alloy marbles opened up a hole in the ceiling, resulting in a surprisingly tiny cascade of debris—that section of the building's roof having been more or less shredded and atomized and dispersed outward in a cloud of wood and plaster.

A lonely unstanchable female sobbing from the back of the room accompanied my standing up.

"I'm Drew Prosnitz."

"Sniff him, Rowley."

The splice came over to me and stuck his snout into my armpit.

"It's him," Rowley growled, and I was glad I had opted for the full suite of tailoring. And then the splice barked the question I had been waiting for. "Where's the Golden Cow?"

"I lost it."

The woman leveled the spinner gun at my midsection. "Are you shitting me, Prosnitz? You don't just lose the key to forty million acres of rewilded prairie as easy as misplacing your memtax."

"Maybe 'lost' was the wrong word. It was taken from me."

"Who's got it now?"

"One of those rogue Russian bots, a kibe. A full artilect named To Wound the Autumnal City. He's gone to ground in Meccanoville, after suckering me in and ripping me off."

The woman lowered the snout of the spinner gun a tad. She looked slightly less distrustful now, which meant she had bought my story. I figured her overweening hubris and ego, combined with the allure of the prize and my apparent fucking-up, had partially disarmed her defenses. "Okay. Not great, but okay. That's all we needed to know. Meccanoville's tough, but we're up to it. Everyone just stay put for five minutes after we've gone."

The trio started toward the door.

"Wait," I said. "The Golden Cow is keyed to my suite. Right now, out of my hands, it's gone dormant. That's all that's stopped the kibe from using it. I'm the only guy that can wake it up."

"Goddamn it! Okay, Prosnitz, you just bought yourself a ticket to Meccanoville."

Outside, the night air was fresh and cool, promising a freedom not immediately obtainable under my present circumstances.

With Rowley and the woman trotting, and the moldie shlupping pseudopodishly along, we hustled around a corner to a trim Terrafugia four-seater PAV. I was shuffled roughly into the vehicle, in back next to the moldie. Its truffle smell filled my nostrils. Its fibrous flexible lips blorted out, "Huggit." It took me a minute to realize the moldie was sharing its name.

"Huggit," I repeated. "And Rowley. And—?"

"Yola. Now shut up while I lift us out of here."

The car's rotors took us aloft, and then we switched over to the fan propulsion and autopilot. When we hit our cruising speed of roughly 300 MPH, Yola disengaged her seat and swung it around to face me, as did the splice.

They both looked damn serious. Which I guessed was appropriate, given the stakes.

For the past twenty years, the Northamerican Union had been remediating the Second Dustbowl that had hollowed out the center of the continent before the climate was engineered back to stability. Now, finally, the pristine prairie was ready for recolonization. The reopening would be a Land Run akin to those of one hundred and seventy years ago, like the first Oklahoma rush of 1889. The area had been effectively quarantined against interference during those two decades of rewilding by being seeded with a gnarly silicrobe plague, sentient-specific and restricted to the dimensions of the zone by GPS parms.

The kickoff to the Land Rush would be the disabling of the quarantine plague.

That's where the Golden Cow came in.

The Golden Cow was a unique KidBuddy™-sized pet, created by the NU authorities. The gut flora in the Golden Cow constituted the shut-off signal for the plague. Bring the Golden Cow to the border of the region, send it across the line to poop, and the guardian silicrobes would deactivate themselves in a rapidly propagating wave, opening up the territory for settlement.

Always with an eye toward bread and circuses ever since the spectacle days of President Trump, though with considerably less gaucherie and bloviation, the NU—now going through one of its more defiantly anarcho-libertarian administrations—had decided to pull a Willy Wonka: Set the Golden Cow loose somewhere on the continent, and let it be found by some lucky citizen, no matter what temporary, collateral-damage disturbances of the peace resulted.

And that citizen would be guaranteed one percent of the hundreds of millions in Land Rush application fees collected from the Sooners.

The lottery-cum-scavenger-hunt had been mandated by a plebiscite conducted under government contract by the Omnicom Group of MadMen, who had offered a variety of scenarios for the reopening of the Second Dustbowl. Believe it or not, the Golden Cow riff had been one of the less insane.

That had been the plan. But I—or rather, the real Drew Prosnitz—had seen fit to jump the gun.

I could see by the abstracted refocusing in Yola's dominant eye that she was scrolling through my CV on her memtax, learning, maybe, that I was a somewhat exceptional, but basically jumped-up, thief whose ambitions had exceeded his powers.

Yola finished reviewing my stats and media profile and regarded me with some real appreciation. "Yotta slick, Prosnitz, the way you got in and out of the Royal Canadian Mint with the Golden Cow. I've never seen anyone spoof NU-level security like that."

I tried to sound sincerely proud—and bummed out at the same time.

"Yeah, I thought I was pretty clever—until I made the mistake of trying to bring that goddamn kibe onboard."

Rowley the splice said, "You should've known meat and silicene never share the same lifestance, Prosnitz. Hell, even the moldie here is hard to parse sometimes, and he's totally organic."

The lungless Huggit blorped out an affirmatory via its modulated eructions. "Metabolists rule!"

Yola said, "The only smart thing you did was key the Golden Cow to your self-suite. To Wound the Autumnal City is stuck with a dead key now. But we won't be, once we reclaim it."

Rowley's chimeric phiz conveyed doubt. "Meccanoville's a scary labyrinth, Yola. A meatgrinder. Think we can get in and out okay?"

"We've got Prosnitz here to help us zero in on whatever structure holds the Golden Cow. We barrel in hard and fast from above, before the kibes even know what's happening. Prosnitz, can we count on you throwing in with us? Four-way split? We could use an extra guy in the assault. Otherwise we'll just have to put a synaptic boot on you and ream out your suite signatures. That's a lot of work, and some other crew might interfere before we can do it. What do you say?"

I pretended to ponder. "Sure, why not? A quarter of a fortune is better than one hundred percent of nothing."

The atmosphere in the PAV grew more relaxed, and we all began to act like best pals. But I knew that in reality I would be deader than the Constitution once I gave up my suite signatures.

Rather, that would have been my fate, had I been the real Drew Prosnitz, who was instead sitting safe but frustrated in an NU prison cell.

The trip to Meccanoville took under two hours at our rate of speed. We spent the time discussing strategy and tactics. We arrived at the kibe metropolis just when dawn was a rumor.

Meccanoville occupied the former site of Detroit and environs, a sprawling congeries of undecorated, black spun-carbon-fiber windowless buildings of all shapes and sizes that obeyed rules of an architecture foreign to organic lifeforms. The territory ceded to the kibes by the Metabolist-Silicene Treaty of 2042, the semi-independent polity generally kept to itself.

The Golden Cow was unrecoverable by the NU authorities within these precincts, since an armed intrusion from official NU forces would have been tantamount to an act of war against a foreign country. A civilian attack was a mere felony.

Yola issued me a spinner gun, Rowley strapped on some more bombs, and, through an extruded organic pipette, Huggit slurped up from shipboard reservoirs several kinds of catalysts and acids that plumped out his vacuoles. I pinged the dormant Golden Cow, we homed in on its response, and set down on the nearest flat roof.

Yola and I wore heavy backpacks full of B2-alloy marbles that fed directly into our spinners.

The twinned streams from our guns swiftly opened up our passage inside. We jumped down into the unknown.

Have you ever seen an ancient bit of anime featuring this oddball sailor character named Popeye, called "Lost and Foundry?" Popeye's kid, Swee'Pea, wanders into a factory which features one deadly senseless apparatus after another, a host of robotic tools performing crazy functions incidentally injurious to mere meat. Swee'Pea narrowly escapes each terror, while Popeye gets hammered.

That was the best analogy I know to convey what we encountered in Meccanoville. The pitch-black place was flooded with non-visible frequencies that the kibes used in place of light. Luckily, our memtax adjusted and gave us false-hued sight. Heat, noise, motion smote us from every side as we dashed through the maze.

Many of the kibes ignored us or fled. The ones that fought back with all the Asimovian-limited personal defenses at their command, we cut down mercilessly.

Huggit sprayed his corrosive fluids to fine effect. Once, like an autonomous blankie, he enwrapped a kibe that was all flailing appendages and stopped it even at the loss of a good portion of his amorphous mass, gobbets of mycosymbiont flesh flying hither and yon. Leaping like a catnip-crazed kitten, Rowley hurled bombs full of nano-particulates that caused kibe joints to freeze solid. Yola, her secondskin harmlessly absorbing the impact of many projectiles, exhibited the unnerving habit of screaming like a banshee with every kill.

And me, I had to be careful not to show everything I was really capable of, fighting at Prosnitz levels only.

Somehow, during an interval that probably took under five minutes but seemed like an eternity, we fought our way to the inner lair of To Wound the Autumnal City.

The kibe that Drew Prosnitz had stupidly trusted lay coiled around the Golden Cow. The artilect known as City etcetera wore the body of a cyber-snake, with a fringe of branching manipulators emerging from its "neck" just behind its head in a fractal corona.

I sensed City's high-level suite probing mine, getting past my false ID. The kibe started to speak in the anomalous baritone of a famous actor. "Wait, you're not—"

I atomized the kibe's head before it could blow my gaff.

Yola grabbed up the sleeping Golden Cow, and we yotta scrammed.

Safely back in the airborne PAV, we looked at our trophy.

The soft, warm, somnolent form of the miniature yellow bovine, about as big as a baseline Shih-Tzu, hardly seemed worth millions of NUbucks, but it was.

"Wake it up," said Yola.

I tried to sound unsuspicious. "No need yet. You don't want it pooping in the cockpit here. Wait till we get to the Dustbowl."

Rowley looked up from the controls. "Nearest point of the border is just outside Wichita. About three hours flight."

A diminished Huggit said, "Must regenerate."

"Me too," I said. I realized suddenly that I was bleeding from a dozen non-serious wounds.

Yola dug out the first-aid kit and we all got patched up. Water and some nutritional bars helped restore us. Then I reclined my seat, and went to sleep.

That is, I fell into such a state that when the others trespassed and pinged my suite, as they were sure to do, they would find me unconscious, my telltales indicating deep sleep rhythms in my brain.

But my second brain, a rudimentary intelligence distributed across my microbiome and gut, would still be using my ears to listen.

And so I heard their whispered plans to kill me in great detail.

A fine Kansas morning greeted our arrival at a broad meadow at the edge of the Second Dustbowl. I "woke up" and climbed outside where I could stretch.

Yola set the Golden Cow down on the grass. She let loose a swarm of bonded notary-public drones to record our claim. "Okay, Prosnitz, wake it up so it can poop and make us rich."

"I think not," I said. "I'm taking the Cow back to the Mint and leaving you three here. I would have taken you all down earlier, but I didn't want to risk crashing the PAV."

"Like hell you are! We can get your suite signatures off your dead body."

"Sure. But you have to kill me first."

My backup systems had come online when I left the PAV. Now, I moved faster than any transgenic or modded human, and crushed Rowley's windpipe before the splice could even draw his lysing pistols from their holsters.

I spun toward Yola.

Not wanting to vaporize my valuable body, she put one single marble through my heart.

One of my hearts.

Despite the trauma, I didn't go down, and this failure to collapse stunned Yola just long enough.

I grabbed one of Huggit's hands, tore it off like ripping a piece of fruit leather apart, and crammed the myco-flesh into the bloody gaping hole in my chest. Then I picked up Huggit and hurled the weighty moldie at Yola.

The moldie instinctively flattened out as I had anticipated, and wrapped around the woman. Then I was atop the pair. I drove a fist and arm straight through the squelchy moldie and punched Yola in the head hard enough to dent her skull.

Huggit disengaged from Yola and reformed into his manlike shape.

"Am I going to have any trouble with you?"

"Huggit no trouble. You moldie lymph-brother now."

I looked down at the moldie hand sticking awkwardly out of my chest. "Okay, I guess so." I hustled Huggit back into the PAV.

Then, on a hunch, and definitely exceeding my official mission remit, I woke up the Golden Cow.

The miniature bovine lifted its belly off the grass, came to its feet and trotted toward the invisible barrier delimiting the preserve. According to the advertised scheme, it should poop, the silicrobe plague should go dormant, and the whole wide range open up for settlement. I figured the NU honchos could hit the reset button after any premature triggering.

But no such outcome happened. Instead, the Golden Cow stopped just short of the perimeter, turned, regarded me and spoke in a happy anime voice.

"This competition has been a test of the marketing penetration of Omnicom Group and the efficacy of its social media algorithms. Actual administration of the Second Dustbowl resources will be handled by the Department of the Interior. No monies will be forthcoming to any individual, despite all advertising, as per liability clauses twelve and sixteen in the revised NU Constitution."

The KidBuddy™ powered down. I picked it up and carried it into the aircraft.

Aloft in the PAV with a somnolent Huggit, I contacted my bosses at the Security Intelligence Service and let them know their duplicitous Sweepstakes, derailed by Prosnitz's larcenous derailment, could be rebooted.

And I could return to my real identity, get repaired, and wait on the shelf until SIS needed a backup man again.

CONTRIBUTORS

Based on Canberra, Australia, **David Adams** is a 32-year-old writer who mainly focuses on military science fiction and fantasy. His hobbies include patting his pet cat, avoiding deadlines, and sleeping way too much. David's main series is the *Lacuna* series, and the *Ren of Atikala* series, but the *Symphony of War* series is his new baby, with its spin-off series, *The Immortals*.

Robert Dawson teaches mathematics at Saint Mary's University in Nova Scotia. When not teaching, doing research, or writing, he enjoys cycling, hiking, and fencing. He has had over fifty stories and poems published. He is an alumnus of the Sage Hill and Viable Paradise writing workshops, and a member of SF Canada and the SFWA.

Eric Del Carlo's short fiction has appeared in *Asimov's*, *Analog*, *Strange Horizons*, and many other places. He wrote the *Wartorn* novels with Robert Asprin, and coauthored the novel *The Golden Gate is Empty* with his father Victor Del Carlo. His latest book is *The Vampire Years*, coming in fall 2017 from Elder Signs Press.

★ ★ ★

Paul Di Filippo sold his first story in 1977, and since then has sold over two hundred more, most of which are collected among his thirty books, which also include several novels. He is also a critic and reviewer. He lives in Providence, Rhode Island, with his mate of some forty years, Deborah Newton.

★ ★ ★

The Army took **David Drake** from Duke Law School and sent him on a motorized tour of Viet Nam and Cambodia with the 11th Cav, the Blackhorse. He learned new skills, saw interesting sights, and met exotic people who hadn't run fast enough to get away.

Dave returned to become Chapel Hill's Assistant Town Attorney and to try to put his life back together through fiction making sense of his Army experiences.

Dave describes war from where he saw it: the loader's hatch of a tank in Cambodia. His military experience, combined with his formal education in history and Latin, has made him one of the foremost writers of realistic action SF and fantasy. His bestselling Hammer's Slammers series is credited with creating the genre of modern Military SF. He often wishes he had a less interesting background.

Dave lives with his family in rural North Carolina.

★ ★ ★

Kacey Ezell is an active duty USAF helicopter pilot. When not beating the air into submission, she writes military SF, SF, fantasy, and horror fiction. She lives with her husband, two daughters, and an ever-growing number of cats.

★ ★ ★

A former Marine Corps K9 handler, **Michael Ezell** is a project coordinator for an Emmy-winning makeup effects shop in Southern California. His fiction has also appeared in the anthology "Fantasy for Good," and *On Spec Magazine*. You can find him on Twitter @SinisterEZ, or at sinisterwriter.com, his sorely neglected blog.

★ ★ ★

William Ledbetter is a Nebula nominated writer with more than fifty speculative fiction stories and non-fiction articles published in markets such as *Fantasy & Science Fiction, Jim Baen's Universe, Writers of the*

Future, Escape Pod, Daily SF, the SFWA blog, and *Ad Astra*. He's been a space and technology geek since childhood and spent most of his non-writing career in the aerospace and defense industry. He administers the Jim Baen Memorial Short Story Award contest for Baen Books and the National Space Society, is a member of SFWA, the National Space Society of North Texas, a Launch Pad Astronomy workshop graduate, is the Science Track coordinator for the Fencon convention and is a consulting editor at *Heroic Fantasy Quarterly*. He lives near Dallas with his wife and three spoiled cats.

Maine-based writers **Sharon Lee and Steve Miller** teamed up in the late 1980s to bring the world the story of Kinzel, an inept wizard with a love of cats, a thirst for justice, and a staff of true power. Since then, the husband-and-wife have written dozens of short stories and twenty plus novels, most set in their star-spanning Liaden Universe®. Before settling down to the serene and stable life of a science fiction and fantasy writer, Steve was a traveling poet, a rock-band reviewer, reporter, and editor of a string of community newspapers. Sharon, less adventurous, has been an advertising copywriter, copy editor on night-side news at a small city newspaper, reporter, photographer, and book reviewer. Both credit their newspaper experiences with teaching them the finer points of collaboration. Sharon and Steve passionately believe that reading fiction ought to be fun, and that stories are entertainment. Steve and Sharon maintain a web presence at http://korval.com/

Adam Roberts is the BSFA Award-winning author of several score science fiction short stories and sixteen science fiction novels, most recently *The Thing Itself* (Gollancz 2015). He teaches literature and creative writing at Royal Holloway, University of London.

James Wesley Rogers has a diploma that says he is a mathematician and business cards that say he is a software developer. He says he's a science fiction writer. There's probably no way of knowing which is correct. He lives in Ohio, at least until he can find a place on Mars.

Jack Schouten was born in Kristiansand, Norway, and was brought up in Surrey. He read Journalism and Creative Writing at Middlesex University London, specializing in science fiction, and his work has appeared in *Jupiter Magazine, the North London Literary Gazette*, and, *Shoreline of Infinity*. He lives and works in London and can be reached on Twitter at @JackSchouten.

Allen Stroud is a writer and lecturer at Buckinghamshire New University in High Wycombe, England. He runs the BA (Hons) Creative Writing for Publication course and is studying for his Ph. D. in Creative Writing at the University of Winchester. Allen is also the editor of the *British Fantasy Society Journal* (www.britishfantasysociety.co.uk). He can be found online at: www.allenstroud.com

Jay Werkheiser teaches chemistry and physics to high school students, where he often finds inspiration for stories in classroom discussions. Not surprisingly, his stories often deal with alien biochemistry, weird physics, and their effects on the people who interact with them. Many of his stories have appeared in *Analog*, with others scattered among several other science fiction magazines and anthologies.

Michael Z. Williamson is retired military, having served twenty-five years in the U.S. Army and the U.S. Air Force. He was deployed for Operation Iraqi Freedom and Operation Desert Fox. Williamson is a state-ranked competitive shooter in combat rifle and combat pistol. He has consulted on military matters, weapons and disaster preparedness for Discovery Channel and Outdoor Channel productions and is Editor-at-Large for Survivalblog, with 300,000 weekly readers. In addition, Williamson tests and reviews firearms and gear for manufacturers. Williamson's books set in his Freehold Universe include *Freehold*, *The Weapon*, *The Rogue*, *Better to Beg Forgiveness . . .*, *Do Unto Others . . .*, and *When Diplomacy Fails . . .* . He is also the author of time travel novel *A Long Time Until Now*, as well as *The Hero*—the latter written in collaboration with *New York Times* best-selling author John Ringo. Williamson was born in England, raised in Liverpool and Toronto, Canada, and now resides in Indianapolis with his two children.